EVA LAURENSON
XX – The History of Mankind

EVA LAURENSON

XX
THE HISTORY
OF MANKIND

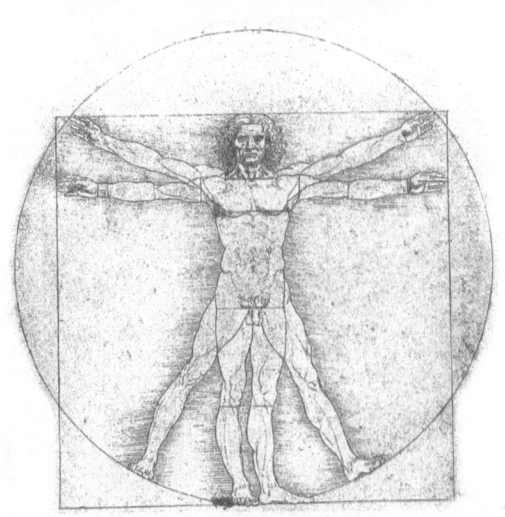

cub & calf

Content Warning: domestic abuse

1. Edition
Approved Paperback-Edition June 2022
Copyright © 2022 cub & calf publishing,
129 Kirkwood Street,
Armidale, NSW, Australia
All rights reserved.
Cover and Layout by Eva Laurenson
First Round Editing by Joe Pierson
Second Round Editing by Yan Laurenson
ISBN 978-0-6455135-0-9

For me

PROLOGUE

Like a silver ball, the pod rolled silently through the snowy solar forest. Hillary sat alone in her pod and watched the trees pass by. She had not bothered to turn on music or a projection; she loved the quiet presence in the solar forest before the sun stood high enough to activate the leaves.

Sometimes, in winter, the world looked like a clean slate on which history was written as time went on. Hillary thought about her biology assignment on the history of reproduction where they had touched upon the time of the greatest evolutionary leap that humankind had ever experienced, and the scribbled slate of the world's history had been wiped clean within a single year.

Two centuries ago, men and women existed on Earth. With sexual reproduction, genes from mother and father were mixed, and the resulting child was therefore a mashup of its parents. This maintained genetic diversity, which gave sexual reproduction an advantage over nonsexual reproduction. Although cheetahs apparently had very little genetic diversity for quite some time before they became extinct.

The forest was nearing its hundredth anniversary. Built to provide electricity to the Isle of Great Britain, it was not inviting to living beings. Rarely, animals found their way into the forest, and they made sure to leave quickly as there was nothing for them to live off or to hide under. Not that there were no animals around, quite the opposite, but they usually stayed in the woodlands of the high country. But in winter, footprints in the thick snow blanket gave away their presence in this uninhabitable forest.

Something that still exists is asexual reproduction. In some cases, the adult organism splits itself into two, like yeast or flower bulbs, or lots of ancient worms or fungi. Or a baby is formed from a cell that already has two sets of chromosomes. Some insects, reptiles or sharks can do that. I think it's called agamogenesis. It's basically like cloning yourself.

The bad thing about asexual reproduction is that both copies of a gene can be bad and there is no good copy to balance the bad gene. Then the child dies or is very sick. And even if there are no bad genes anymore, new genetic mutations can create a bad gene.

Hillary looked at her own reflection in the curved window. She looked like her mother, but there were subtle differences. Her jaw was wider and her eyes a little closer together. Her hair was also lighter, but that would probably change when she got older. She wondered whether she had mutations that her mother did not have that caused the differences. She also wondered whether she was attractive and whether she would meet someone at one point who would fall madly in love with her, just like in *Romeo and Juliet*. Shakespeare's story about the two star-crossed lovers sounded ridiculous and the actions of Romeo were so hurried and hasty that love must truly have made people blind. Or maybe this was just how men used to be. Yet, love seemed to be a concept that did not need to be rational.

The sun shone through the snow-covered leaves, and the undisturbed white blanket sparkled between the concrete trunks like a diamond cover. Then the leaves adjusted their position to embrace the full force of the morning sun, turning the rays into electricity. Hundreds of thousands of small avalanches broke loose, and for a few moments, Hillary's world was wiped out as the snow fell to the ground.

Eva Laurenson

CHAPTER 1

On March 13, 2054, the first manned Mars mission returned to Earth. Less than a hundred years after the moon landing, Houston's Johnson Space Centre prepared for the final act of their successful claim of another celestial body for humankind. The race had been on for decades, and other nations like China came close to achieving this historical feat. But in the end, the National Aeronautics and Space Administration had succeeded, albeit with a global collaborative effort. And right at this moment, every nation around this globe was watching, listening, or talking about the homecoming of the first five human beings who walked on the surface of Mars.

After half an hour of silence from the space capsule, during which the news presenters chatted with invited experts and peppered their questions with learned facts about space travel, the news broke that the command module had been located in the Atlantic Ocean, a thousand kilometres north of the Dominican Republic. All television broadcasts cut off the interviews and switched to a live feed from several drones filming the recovery.

The entire world was watching, just as they had followed the seven months that *Pilgrim* took to get to Mars and back. The crew had become celebrities, but it was Spacewalker Gabriel Stuart, the all-American boy, who had captured the hearts. "Mars was conquered, not by war, but by the ingenuity of men," he had said when his feet touched the red dust on the frozen planet, and just like that, he had immortalized himself.

"*Pilgrim* has returned. What we see right now are the recovery divers installing a floating collar and an anchor to stop the module from drifting away," said a news presenter on the TV in a café in Khartoum. The windows of the crammed café were wide open to allow the men, women, and children on the street to follow this historic event.

"One day, you will do something as great as this," said Rashaad Suliman to his three boys.

Rashaad had taken them to the streets of Khartoum so that they could soak in the atmosphere, instead of just sitting in their living room. This was a world event, and so it demanded sharing with the world.

"Two aircraft carriers were deployed for the recovery mission, but as we hear right now it will be the USS *Eagle* to take in the crew and the command module."

James Rice leaned closer to the little television inside the café, but a chorused *mahlaan* reminded him about the dozens of spectators behind him. Had they known who this Red Cross doctor was, their attention might have shifted. But James preferred to stay incognito and to wait on the edge of his seat for the first sight of his wife back on Earth. His heart was thumping, and tears of joy and relief welled up. Luckily, he was not the only one to be moved this way by the unfolding events, but he was probably the only one here who had a personal connection. He was proud of his wife and in awe that he was her husband.

"And here we go, the float and the raft are ready, and the divers are retrieved via helicopter. Next comes a crucial step in the recovery program, the decontamination of the module and the crew. Quarantine restrictions for moon missions had been relaxed after *Apollo 14* returned without any issues, but this is Mars, and who knows what aliens are aboard this spacecraft? With me now is Doctor Ian Marshal from NASA. Doctor Marshal, hello."

"Hello."

"Could you tell us what is happening right now?"

"Well, the decontamination diver is washing down the surface of the module with a solution of organic iodine before opening the hatch. Then he passes protective gear down to the crew before they're allowed to disembark. After that, the hatch is sealed from the outside and the module towed to the aircraft carrier."

"*Mahlaan!*" James had leaned forward again as the first astronaut climbed out of the hatch and into the raft on the side of the floating command module.

"There is the first crewmember. We can't tell who it is, but I've been told that the commander, Jeanette Rice, will leave the ship last."

James leaned back in his chair and took a deep breath.

"The astronauts will spend four weeks in quarantine before they are reunited with their families. The same will happen with the samples that were brought back from Mars before the scientists around Doctor Marshal can examine them. What will you be looking for?"

"We already have some ideas about the composition of the Mars surface from meteorites and the Chinese sample-return mission from 2032, which was able to sample from multiple locations over several days.

Besides the resampling of one location to give us an idea about decomposition on Mars over twenty years, our main focus lies on the physical effects that this flight had on the crew and how our equipment held up to allow a safe journey."

"Are there any reasons to belief that such a journey is dangerous for living beings?"

"Any space travel is dangerous. But aside from equipment failure, the effects on a human body include a loss of body fluid, astronauts can have up to twenty percent lower blood volume, which means the heart has less to pump and the heart muscle will shrink. This is something that happens to all muscles, but the heart muscle is, as you can imagine, of particular importance. So, we need to check on the crew, who probably have a low blood pressure now, and make sure that their vitals are okay and stable now that they are back on Earth."

"And what about diseases?"

"The crew will have full blood tests and swabs taken."

"I heard that bacteria grow particularly well in space."

"You are right. Bacteria and microorganisms have been found to survive and even grow in their virulence in space."

"So, do we need to be concerned about mutated bacteria or parasites?"

"No, all samples will be stored and analysed in a high-security lab. And the Earth's gravity should rein in the bacteria that enjoyed increased growth in space."

James relaxed in his chair and smiled at the screen. He had not listened to the interview but closely followed the images. The five astronauts had egressed the command module and been flown to the aircraft carrier. The commander, his wife, had just landed and waved shortly to the camera team before she entered the mobile quarantine facility on the ship. Four more weeks and he would be able to embrace her again.

* * *

Amy was excited. Five days ago, she had watched the recovery of the Mars mission with her friends Miranda and Ozzie at their Florida home. They had made it into a party. Little Toby had run around in a self-made spacesuit covered in aluminium foil, and Miranda had told her that they were expecting baby number two.

And now, Amy sat on a coach destined for Houston, Texas. She had expected the call, but when it came yesterday, she was barely able to breathe. They had told her that she was listed as a visitor for Gabriel Stuart and that she had been cleared by security. She was invited to visit the next day if she wanted. Of course, she wanted. It had been seven months since she had last seen Gabriel, and she had been counting the days to see him again. It wasn't that they had been together for years; in fact, they had been going out for only four months before the Mars mission took off, but they had clicked right from the start, and she had promised to wait for him.

They had met in a cocktail bar on Wall Street in Orlando. He had been visiting his parents on one of his few weekends off during the final stages of mission preparation and taken the chance to go out with friends and former colleagues from the air force.

They had looked strapping in their uniforms, laughing without a care in the world. Amy had envied them, and it had been far from her mind to ever enter their circle. She was a kindergarten teacher who could barely afford a cocktail, sipping on her strawberry daiquiri, trying to make it last for an entire evening. And then Gabriel had smiled at her as he leaned over the bar to order another beer.

"Is it good?" he had asked, nodding towards her glass.

She had gazed at him, chewing on her straw, and nodded like a little girl sucking a sweet lollypop.

"One more of these for the lady," he had ordered.

"A beer and a strawberry daiquiri coming right up," the bartender said.

And that was it. Amy, of course, had objected to him paying for her drinks, but her hesitation was swept away by his sparkling blue eyes that looked at her like no one had ever looked at her before. If Gabriel had worn a uniform that evening like his friends, she would have felt like the film *An Officer and a Gentleman* had become reality, and she would not have been surprised if Gabriel had introduced himself as Zack Mayo.

At first, Amy had felt alien in Gabriel's circle, and even the amount of attention that she received from him was alien to her. She had never been in a relationship where the other person paid attention to her needs, which was even more surprising to her as Gabriel was the first man she had dated who held down a well-paying job. And of course, the fact that he was an astronaut on the first crewed Mars mission gave a thrill to their courtship that could well have sprung from a Shake-spearean quill.

For the first few weeks after the mission had taken off, Amy had felt physically sick, as if suffering from withdrawal symptoms. After these feelings subsided, she wondered whether she had dreamt all of it, as it seemed too surreal to be part of her life. She followed the news of the mission, but after a while, she came to the realisation that Gabriel was probably too good to be true and that she should make herself comfortable again in her old life. And then, when she least expected anything anymore, a video message arrived with an of-ficial NASA logo in one corner. Gabriel smiled at her with his blue eyes from her computer screen. He had sent her a private message telling her that he loved her and asked her to wait for him.

So, she had waited, her life packed in a soft pink cloud of infatuation ever since, and she did not care whether it was all just a dream, so long as she would not wake up.

Right after the call from NASA, Amy had packed a small bag and jumped on the overnight coach that ar-rived at eight in the morning in Houston, Texas. In be-tween short naps against the window, she had watched the dark surface of the gulf, which had crept up over the land in the last thirty years and now separated New Orleans from the rest of the country like Atlantis before its fall.

Despite the sleepless night, she buzzed when she stepped outside the large arrival hall and steered to a taxi rank.

She held her phone to the outside screen of a waiting pod, and after she had proven that she had enough funds for a fare, the door slid open.

"The Lyndon B. Johnson Space Centre, please," said Amy, and an automated voice repeated her request to check that it was correct.

"The fare is 185 dollars. Do you wish to continue?" asked the autopilot.

"Yes," said Amy, as she imagined her bank account emptying painfully.

A bus would have been only a third of the price, but she had never been to Houston and would rather pay for a safe trip than try to figure out the public transport system.

The taxi quietly entered the stream of other vehicles coming and going from the terminal and navigated the city's traffic almost without stopping.

Amy sat in the back. She was too preoccupied to worry about the taxi fare for long and instead gazed out of the window as the houses and shops passed by. When they took a right turn, Amy caught a glimpse of the street sign announcing Saturn Lane, and her heart started racing. It still took a while before the taxi stopped in front of a building with an airplane stuck on the side.

"Thank you for travelling with Houston Taxi. We wish you a nice day," said the autopilot, and the door slid open.

Amy took her bag and made her way to the building where the pod had dropped her off. Something seemed off, and worries rose inside her. A family of four walked to the entrance of the space centre and entered without a check. Slowly, it dawned on her that this was a tourist centre and not the actual NASA base.

She asked at the reception desk and was pointed across the road, where she could see a guardhouse. She shouldered her bag and despite the cool spring air, she broke out in a light sweat.

The guard looked at her pleasantly. "The Space Centre is across the road."

"No, I don't want to go to the visitor centre. I want to go to the Lyndon B. Johnson Space Centre."

"My dear, this is an official NASA site. You need a pass to get in."

"But I've been invited to see Gabriel Stuart in the quarantine section," Amy explained.

"Ah, what is your name?"

"Amy Watson."

The guard checked a list and found her name. "What's your birthdate?"

"Twenty-seventh of May 2027."

"Do you have a cell phone?"

"Yes," said Amy and fished her phone out to lay it onto the ID reader that the guard held through the window.

"Wait here, I'll call someone to pick you up," said the guard when her identity was confirmed.

"Thank you." Amy beamed at the guard, relieved that he did not turn her away and that her name was truly on the list.

A small electric cart came, made a U-turn, and stopped by the guard house.

"Ms. Watson?" An attractive thirtysomething in chinos and a short-sleeved shirt craned his neck towards her.

"Yes."

Amy sat down on the passenger side and hugged her bag.

"Open up, Jim."

The boom lifted, and Jim, the guard, tipped his hat as they drove off.

"I'm Matt White."

"Hi, I'm Amy."

Amy was wondering who Matt White was. She had expected someone in a military uniform or at least in a lab coat, but Matt White could be anybody.

"In the back is a tablet with a form for you to fill in. You can either do it manually or just tap your phone."

Amy reached back and pushed her bag into Matt White's elbow, which made him swerve.

"Careful. No autopilot here."

"Sorry, I didn't mean to."

"It's all right," said Matt.

He was attractive, no question. But he was too late; she had already found the man she wanted to be with for the rest of her life. Then she saw the wedding ring on his hand and felt foolish for her idle thoughts.

She concentrated on the form that asked the typical security questions and personal identifiers. Whenever possible, she typed in her details, as she did not trust what other information any device was retrieving off her phone. The drive was perfectly timed, and when the cart stopped, Amy filled in the last number of her passport.

The Mars Receiving Laboratory had been built adjacent to the defunct Lunar Receiving Laboratory and was now home to the crew of the Mars mission for another twenty-three days. The building was plain white and two floors high with unassuming glass doors. On the left was a reception area where Matt handed Amy's tablet to a receptionist, and on the right was a waiting room with a vending machine selling fresh fruit, making smoothies, or grinding coffee beans for a fresh, hot brew.

"Someone will be with you shortly."

Matt smiled again at Amy and then disappeared.

Amy greeted the other two women in the waiting room with a nod; they looked at her, equally curious. Then she checked out the options for smoothies. If she had had the money, she would have picked the mango-banana smoothie.

Matt came back with a woman in her forties in tow.

"Ms. Watson, would you please follow Judy here," said Matt. "Mrs. Vargas, Ms. Hernández, Veronica is still being examined but should be ready soon," he noted to the other two visitors.

"Is everything okay with her?" asked the older of the two women.

"Yes, it's just the daily routine checks that all of the astronauts have to go through."

The two women sat back and chatted in Spanish.

Amy walked with Judy into the corridor and through another glass door, and Matt followed. At the end of the corridor was a potted plant in front of a ceiling-high glass window which let in the only natural light. To the left and right were offices. The doors stood open, and Amy could see men and women sitting behind desks working on computers.

"So, you are Amy Watson, twenty-seven years old and from Orlando, Florida?" asked the woman called Judy, checking a tablet.

"Yes." Amy smiled.

"And you are working as a kindergarten teacher?"

"Yes, I love children."

"Good for you."

Judy stopped halfway along the corridor in front of an elevator. She smiled too, but at the same time, her eyes were studying Amy. "Matthew will take care of your bag. You will get it back later. And I also need to ask you to provide fingerprints and a small blood sample before we enter the Q.C."

"Oh, okay, sure." Amy was anxious about what they would do with her blood sample. But she was not the type to object when prompted to give up any personal information. Certainly not when she was about to enter NASA's quarantine centre. They could have asked her to strip naked right here in the corridor, and she would have obliged.

Matt took her bag and disappeared into an office nearby, whilst Judy held out a little device like a card reader, only it scanned the fingertips placed on a small square on the bottom half. Then she turned the device on its side, where a small well the size of a fingertip was indented. Amy placed her index finger in the well, and a short, sharp pain passed through her hand when an invisible needle drew a drop of blood.

Judy looked at the device, and after a few seconds, a green light appeared. "Excellent."

She pushed the elevator button and held her own hand against another scanner. The humming from the elevator shaft indicated that the cabin was coming up from below.

Inside, Judy pressed a button for the third out of five underground levels. Amy felt like she was in a spy movie and smiled to herself.

"This is all so exciting," said Amy when she noticed that Judy was again studying her from the side.

"I'm sure it is. Follow me."

They stepped out of the elevator and walked along another corridor with doors on either side. Some had little glass windows with laboratories behind; others only had signs telling her the use of a room.

"You won't be able to touch Mr. Stuart. He is behind a glass window, but there will be an earpiece and microphone to talk to each other."

Amy smiled again; this time she felt like she was in a prison movie.

They entered a small room with a large glass window giving a free view of the quarantine facility that the five astronauts shared. It was like living in a large open-plan flat, but instead of a kitchen, there was a small gym, and the beds were hospital beds dividable by curtains. The only private space was the bathroom. This was probably still an improvement over the crammed spaceship the crew had shared on their months-long journey.

Amy saw Gabriel immediately. He was walking on a treadmill side by side with a tall woman whom Amy recognised as Jeanette Rice, the commander of the mission. The pilot, Adam Fjodorow, was lifting tiny weights, and the engineer, Philip Schuster, lay on his bed reading a book. The other spacewalker, Veronica Vargas, was still absent.

"Gabriel, you have a visitor." Judy had pressed a button to activate the intercom.

Gabriel turned around and beamed when he saw Amy through the glass. He stopped his treadmill and jumped off. He looked thinner than when he had left, and his usually strapping walk was swaying a little, but he was still the man she had fallen in love with.

As he sat down on his side of the window, he absent-mindedly smoothed stickers on his wrists that looked like circuit boards, and Amy noticed smaller stickers on his neck and temples.

Amy sat down on her side with dividers to either side of her, giving them some privacy. She put the ear-pieces in, and her heart jumped when she heard his voice.

"Hey, babe."

"Hi," she said. "You look like a robot."

"These?" Gabriel pointed to the stickers on his arms. "They are patch trackers to monitor our vitals at all times."

She nodded. "How are you?"

"Great. It's weird to be back, and I can't wait to get outta here."

"I missed you."

"I missed you more."

"So, tell me, how was it?"

"It was awesome. Surreal, but awesome. I was so nervous, but it was just like in training, except that I could see for miles. Red desert wherever you looked.

The worst was the trip there and back, you know. There is only so much a man can read."

Amy knew he was not an avid reader. Heck, he didn't even enjoy most movies. He needed to be active, so she could imagine how caged he must have felt for the last seven months. "And you are well?"

"Yes, everything came back normal so far, only need to get used to gravity again, take some supplements, and build up my muscles."

"I thought you looked thinner."

"Nothing to worry about. I rode a bicycle for two hours every day up there." Amy giggled at the thought. "I'm serious, and then another hour on a treadmill, so not all is lost."

"Oh, I missed you."

He paused and looked at her for a minute.

"What?" She started to feel uncomfortable.

"Amy. Did you wait for me?"

"Of course I did, that's why I'm here."

"Well then, Amy Watson …" He got up and walked to the wall-size window segment.

Amy followed, confused, on her side and then clapped her hands over her mouth when he kneeled and produced a small box from his pocket.

"Amy Watson, will you marry me?"

Amy could hear the other astronauts hooting in the background.

"Yes, I will!" She sat down on the floor and placed a hand on the window.

"This little box went with me to Mars and back. There is no other woman in the entire world who will have a ring like this."

"I love you so much." Tears of happiness ran down Amy's cheeks.

"You'll have to wait a little longer before I can put it on your finger, but as soon as I'm outta here, I want to get married and finally start our life together."

All her dreams, everything she could have wished for, had come true. They moved back to the table to talk in private.

"And I want to start making babies with you."

Amy flushed at his words. What would Miranda say? Where would they live? The rest of their conversation happened in a haze, and Amy listened to his stories from the mission, vaguely noticing that Veronica Vargas entered the quarantine facility and disappeared in the bathroom. Shortly after, the two women from the waiting room above followed Judy into the little room and were pointed to a stall next to Amy's.

When Veronica finally came out of the bathroom, Amy noted that her face looked puffy and her eyes were red, but she did not think anything of it.

Gabriel was still going on about the surface of Mars and how it felt walking on it when another voice sounded in Amy's earpiece, asking Gabriel to come in for a blood test.

"Okay, I gotta go. Can you come again tomorrow?"

"Sure, I'll try." Amy had not thought about staying in Houston. She had only been able to take two days off work and wanted to take the coach back in the morning. But Gabriel was gone before she could explain.

On her way out, she peeked around the divider to nod goodbye, but the two women and Veronica, who seemed to be crying, did not notice her.

Amy felt guilty when she overheard a private part of their conversation.

"How can you be pregnant?" asked the younger of the two visitors.

CHAPTER 2

Veronica's world had turned upside down since she had returned to Earth. At first, the doctors had believed that her unusual hormonal levels stemmed from the pill she took to supress her period in space. Only an hour ago, follow-up tests led to her diagnosis.

Instead of returning to the shared quarantine facility, Doctor Jackson had allowed her to stay in the examination room for a little while. She had sat on the examination table, unable to move, not believing what she had been told, for almost an hour. Judy had let her know twice that her mother and girlfriend were waiting, and she had just sat there staring at her feet dangling over the shiny white vinyl flooring.

And then, a voice in her head had told her to move. Nothing would be resolved if she stayed here, paralyzed by trying to keep the void around her thoughts intact. She let Judy know that she would be out in a minute; then she had counted to ten and let the motor cortex in her brain make her body move.

As soon as she saw her fellow crewmembers, though, her brain sent another signal, and she had turned into the bathroom to supress the panic attack that was rising from the depth of her stomach. When she came back out, she saw her mother and Cecilia waiting for her with beaming faces that turned to worries when they noticed her tear-stained face. It did not take long for them to wrench out the truth.

"I don't know." Veronica wiped her wet cheeks. "All I know is that my blood tests came back, and they just did an ultrasound, and I have a baby inside me."

"How can you not know?" Cecilia did not hide her distrust.

"You have to believe me, I did nothing. Nothing happened." Veronica was desperate. She knew how hurt Cecilia must feel, but there was nothing she could say or do to explain any of it.

"Did they rape you?"

"No, I don't know. I don't know." Veronica started crying again. This was all too much. She had felt awful for the past couple of months and thought she had a stomach bug. Not an ideal situation on a small space module with four other people.

"I thought you were taking the pill." Veronica's mother tried to move the conversation away from the speculations about how exactly her daughter had fallen pregnant in space with three potential fathers.

"I did."

"How far along are you?"

"About twenty-five weeks."

"I thought you looked a little rounder." Mrs. Vargas smiled encouragingly.

"If you don't know who the father is, will you do a paternity test?" interrupted Cecilia.

"They have taken a blood sample. Apparently, some of the baby's DNA is circulating in my bloodstream. But they don't know whether it'll work. If not, we'll have to wait until the baby is here."

"So, you'll have it?"

"Of course."

"I'm sorry, I need some fresh air." Cecilia got up and left.

Veronica wanted to cry out, but she didn't have the strength to face any more accusing rejection from the one person she just wanted to hold her.

"I'm so sorry, Mama. I don't know what happened."

"Sh-sh. It's all going to be okay. She'll understand."

"Understand what, Mama? That I betrayed her? That I'm having a baby she doesn't want?"

"Sh-sh. Do you know whether it's a boy or a girl?"

"What?"

"I'm sorry."

Veronica did not want to alienate her mother too. "They say it's a girl."

"*Bebita.*"

"You seem rather happy about all this."

"Whatever happened up there, I love you. And I didn't think I would ever become a grandma."

"I didn't think I would ever be pregnant either. Cecie is the one with the motherly instincts. I'm scared, Mama. She is right, how can I be pregnant?"

"For now, see it as a gift."

How could this be a gift? There was another human being growing inside her, something she never wanted to experience, something she could truly see as a punishment by a higher being. And how could her own mother be happy about her being pregnant, after she had almost bled to death giving birth to Veronica? Veronica pressed a hand against the glass, trying to find a grip in her turning world, and her mother mimicked holding it. "Only three more weeks and you can come home."

"Twenty-five days."

Veronica was hopeless, but she could not find the words to express herself. Of all the things that could have happened – the rocket exploding at launch, crash-landing and being stranded on Mars, dying in any way during their mission – falling pregnant and not knowing how it happened had never crossed her mind.

After her mother left, she took a shower because she felt dirty. Not that she *was* dirty, but she felt like she had to wash off a mark that had unknowingly grown and finally revealed itself. She checked twice that the door was locked, turning the handle, and testing that even a strong push could not open it before she undressed.

She looked at her naked body in the mirror, and her mother had been right: she was showing a bump. She had noticed it for the last month but thought it was fluids shifting due to the space travel or that she was simply bloated.

Carefully, she placed a hand on her swollen belly. The doctors had taped patch trackers on either side of her abdomen to monitor the baby in addition to the trackers that recorded her own heartbeat and blood pressure.

A slight grumble, as if bubbles popped just above her pelvis, made her fuzzy world suddenly razor sharp. She had felt that sensation before, but now she knew what it was. For a fleeting moment, Veronica was excited, the same heart-stopping excitement when you catch a glimpse of someone you love on the other side of a crowded room. But the feeling was tainted by the thought that one of the three men out there or maybe even all of them had violated her and she had no memory of it.

She stepped into the shower and sat down under the warm stream, her tears mixing with the chlorinated water. She apologized to the baby inside her for how it had come to be, for her rejection and inability to genuinely love it, for not knowing that it had already been there for months.

"Are you all right?" asked Jeanette when Veronica finally came out of the bathroom.

"Yes." She avoided eye contact, which probably gave away that she was not all right, but Jeanette did not ask any further questions.

Veronica pulled the curtains around her bed and pressed the button to solidify the fabric, transforming the space into a separate soundproof room. Jeanette must know what had happened on *Pilgrim*, and if she was not speaking up, she must be complicit in it. Panic rose in her. She stroked the solid fabric before climbing into her bed but left the light on. All she could hear was the automatic white noise that was played as soon as the curtains were closed to soothe the occupant. She felt something in her belly twitch, like a muscle spasm, and she wondered whether this was the little human moving inside her like an astronaut in space.

Veronica was surprised how well she slept, but she did not get out of bed until the disembodied voice of Doctor Jackson asked through loudspeakers whether she was all right. They could see from the patch trackers that she was alive and probably also that she was awake, but it was protocol to check on the astronauts if their routine changed unexpectedly.

Veronica quickly responded to avoid an escalation of the situation but took her time to get dressed. She tried to remember every single day of their journey, every time she zipped herself into her sleeping bag in her compartment, every time she woke up, and yet could not find a day when her memory seemed to have slipped. She could also not think of an area on the space module where any form of sexual intercourse could have taken place, unless very cramped and observed by others. Were men even able to have an erection in zero gravity? Her final thought was, and she was disgusted by it, that one of the men had jerked off and an image of free-floating ejaculate popped into her head. Based on everything she knew, this seemed highly unlikely. Maybe there was a mix-up with their disposable wash-cloths … She wondered how long sperm was viable outside the human body. Maybe sperm became even more potent in space like the salmonella bacteria NASA had studied. All in all, though, this possibility of an honest accident made her less anxious to face her fellow crewmembers, but she wanted to speak to a doctor about it.

"Sperm can survive for a couple of hours outside the human body." Doctor Jackson had paused a little too long before answering her question, and she knew that he thought it impossible that she could have fallen pregnant this way.

"There is no other way," Veronica insisted. After a moment of silence, she asked, "When will I know about the results from the paternity test?"

"We are trying to extract enough DNA for a full test. Unfortunately, we have not been able to get a good enough sample. The good news is that the baby does not have any chromosomal abnormalities, and it is definitely a girl."

Veronica was not sure how she felt about this news. She had barely accepted the fact that she was growing a baby inside her, but she was far from accepting becoming a mother and caring for this human being.

"Do you feel comfortable raising this issue with the rest of the crew?" asked Doctor Jackson, who had watched her closely.

"This issue?" Veronica thought as carefully and as quickly as she could. "I think it would be the right thing to do."

"I will elevate it with management, and we will arrange for a discussion group. If you could, don't talk about it to any of the others until then."

"Of course." Veronica studied the medic's face behind the oxygen mask of his BSL-4 hazmat suit.

Veronica hoped that Cecilia would come again and that she could explain her theory, or at least express her various and quite absurd ideas, but her mother told her the next day she had already returned to Orlando. That Cecilia had left without talking to her again was even more devastating than finding out that she was pregnant. At least before, someone was there to catch her, but now she realized that the person she had trusted was not there to stop her fall and that she had to learn to fly alone again.

She went to bed early again, but this time she turned the light off. She slipped into a dreamless sleep almost immediately. In fact, the following days she was able to sleep at any time of the day, whenever she had the chance to lie down. The doctors did not seem to be overly concerned and assured her that this was a common side effect of pregnancy but that she must continue with light exercises to prepare her body not only for gravity now but also for carrying this baby to full term. Unfortunately, the paternity test remained unsuccessful, and none of the medical team spoke about when the meeting with her teammates to reveal her condition would take place.

On the outside, Veronica carried on as usual. She sat down for meals and exercised with her fellow crewmembers, although she kept to herself and did not goof around as she usually did. She wondered how long it would take management to decide about telling the others of her mystery pregnancy. After a few days, she even grew impatient and almost angry about the lack of further communication, and Doctor Jackson seemed to avoid the topic altogether.

"Hey, look at this." Adam Fjodorow had taped one of his patch trackers to the half-drawn curtain around his bed. He intermittently solidified the fabric, which sent an electric current to the tracker, quite likely mimicking an arhythmic heartbeat on the monitors outside.

"Wonder how long it'll take them to raise an alarm." Adam's rhythm on the curtain consisted of dots and dashes, and for a while, they all watched the silvery fabric switching in and out of being a grey wall.

"Ask for some bananas foster for dessert," said Jeanette after Adam had finished his lunch order in Morse code.

It did not take long, and Doctor Jackson and Matthew White appeared on the other side of the glass.

Even Veronica laughed at their frantic faces that seemed to do a double take before realizing that they had been pranked.

Adam would be a great dad, Veronica thought.

"Very funny, Fjodorow." Doctor Jackson sounded more amused than he let on, but then his eyes rested for a moment on Veronica. She was surprised to see him turning to leave without another note.

"Sir, I thought we were going to have a meeting to discuss my, our conditions?" called Veronica.

Doctor Jackson turned back and considered her words.

"We could also just discuss amongst ourselves if not," Veronica added.

"No." Doctor Jackson looked at each of them. "I will arrange for a general meeting as soon as possible. And put those patch trackers back on, Fjodorow."

After Doctor Jackson and Matt had left, Jeanette turned to Veronica. "What is going on?"

"I think we should wait until the meeting."

To Veronica's surprise, Judy let them know with their lunch order to make themselves available this afternoon for a quick update.

"Dang, I already have a date," joked Gabriel and winked at Judy.

Veronica found his humour less appealing, and she hoped that Gabriel was not the dad.

"We'll be ready. What time?" asked Jeanette.

"Fifteen hundred."

Veronica was so nervous that she could not eat anything for lunch, even though Adam's order of beef stroganoff had apparently been received and the smell was mouth-watering. The vanilla ice cream on the bananas foster melted where it touched the warm butter sauce, gently reminding everyone not to waste a moment before eating the sweet dessert.

"They forgot the rum and banana liqueur," complained Jeanette when she took her first bite of a dripping banana sliver.

"Still tastes good to me," said Gabriel. "You sure you're not hungry?"

Veronica shook her head and wondered whether they had left out the alcohol because of her.

After the others had eaten and the trays had been collected, Veronica took a gentle walk on the treadmill, but the missed lunch and the growing foetus inside her made her so weak that she had to lie down after five minutes.

She stayed in bed, sipping water and nibbling on dry crackers, until a voice on the loudspeaker called in for the meeting.

The others had already taken their seats in front of the glass wall. On the other side sat Doctor Jackson, Doctor Allingham, the administrator for health and safety James Cohen, and to their surprise, NASA's deputy administrator, Riley Holmes, with a young lawyer named David Smythe.

"This is an extraordinary meeting, and to relieve you, there is nothing wrong with your test results. You are all fit and healthy," opened Doctor Jackson. "I will hand over this meeting to Ms. Holmes now."

"Thanks, Dick. Before we start, I would like to ask you to sign a confidentiality agreement regarding this meeting, the information you will be provided with during this meeting, and any information you receive concerning the content of this meeting from any source now or in the future, be it directly or indirectly."

The crew looked surprised, but one by one they placed their thumbprint on a display that showed the contract details.

Riley Holmes continued when Veronica placed her thumbprint last. She was not sure whether she should do it, as she had already told her mother and Cecilia about her pregnancy.

"I have spent the last few days in meetings discussing how to approach the issue, and I want to say in advance that NASA sees this as a private matter but is prepared to provide legal aid to Ms. Vargas, depending on the outcome of this and future investigations," the deputy administrator said.

"What is going on?" demanded Jeanette.

They all looked at each other.

"Ms. Vargas has returned from the mission pregnant." Doctor Jackson had dropped the bomb, and it had the expected reaction.

All eyes turned to Veronica. She stared at the white vinyl flooring again and wished for an invisible curtain to be drawn around her. At the push of a button, the curtain would become solid, deflecting the stares.

"Impossible." Jeanette broke the silence.

"It would appear so, yet all tests confirm that Ms. Vargas is already in her second trimester with a healthy foetus."

Jeanette eyed her crew one by one. The men shrugged and shook their heads in innocence, and Veronica pulled her sleeves over her hands before burrowing them between her legs. She wished she could just dissolve into non-existence, as there was no invisible curtain, and she felt the stares from her teammates.

"Not that it is against any rules. I just want to clarify that I did not, that I was not aware of any intimate relationships happening," Jeanette continued.

"Unfortunately, it appears that even Ms. Vargas has no recollection of intimate relationships and denies that any sexual acts were performed," responded Doctor Jackson.

The three men nodded in agreement.

"We have already tried to extract enough informative DNA from Ms. Vargas's blood to perform a paternity test ..."

"I don't recall agreeing to this," interrupted Philip Schuster.

"You signed an agreement that your blood samples taken within the mission plan can be used for genome analyses and tests," corrected the lawyer, David Smythe.

"Yes, but there are limits to DNA tests that are relevant to the mission."

"Subsection 27b of the Post Mission Testing includes the alignment of genomes between mission members, as well as any found organic molecules that can be regarded as or similar to deoxyribonucleic acid, which would include paternity testing," proceeded Mr. Smythe.

Even Philip Schuster was quiet now.

"In any case, we were not able to perform a paternity test at the current stage and therefore will be required to take further blood samples in the future, which falls under the civil law. As Mr. Schuster has correctly stated, under civil law, you can refuse the blood test, in which case a lawsuit must be filed, and a judge must decide. Since none of you are willing or able to shed light on Ms. Vargas's pregnancy and we would like to avoid a civil lawsuit in the future, we ask you to sign a consent form for a paternity test once the baby is born," said the lawyer.

"And what if one of us is the father?" asked Gabriel.

"Then it is up to Ms. Vargas to press charges."

"Charges for what?"

"Non-consensual sexual intercourse."

"Rape?"

"Not necessarily."

They were all dumbfounded, and Veronica would have liked to go back to bed and stay there until the end of quarantine.

Nonetheless, all three men eventually set their thumbprints on the display, agreeing to a paternity test.

After the meeting, Veronica stayed on her seat. She did not know what to do; every movement seemed impossible, as it would mean that time also moved on. Eventually she got to her feet and turned to her bed, but the other four were watching her, obviously wanting to talk.

"I'm sorry," Veronica sobbed.

She stared at Jeanette, who walked towards her and was surprised when she was embraced and held. Veronica buried her face into her commander's shoulder and began to cry uncontrollably.

"I'm sorry," whispered Jeanette in her ear. "All right. I know you all want to get your emotions off your chest, but I think we should all sleep on it."

Jeanette looked the men over and nodded to Veronica to retreat. Veronica was grateful. She had admired Jeanette throughout training and their mission, even had a little crush on her, but the last few days had made her question her commander's integrity. Now, as she drew the curtain and removed herself again from the world, she was embarrassed for having ever harboured doubts about Jeanette.

CHAPTER 3

The weeks had flown by, and as soon as Gabriel had been released from quarantine, Amy had introduced him to her parents. They had celebrated their engagement at a lovely Indian restaurant, and Gabriel had swept her parents off their feet just as he had done with Amy. Her mother was chuffed to have such a presentable son-in-law, and in a moment of confusion, which had been aided by the bottle of champagne they had with their dinner, Amy's mother had accidentally kissed Gabriel steadfastly on the mouth rather than the cheek when saying goodbye.

Now, Amy was trying on her third wedding dress at a bridal shop and thought she had found the one. When she stepped out in the t-long dress, covered in white daisies, her best friend, Miranda, did not seem to be impressed, though.

"What?" Amy asked.

"Do you like it?" responded Miranda.

"Yes, I do."

"Then this is the dress."

"But you don't like it."

"It's not something I would have chosen for myself. But this is your show."

"You'd have picked something with a see-through corset," teased Amy.

"Not at the moment," said Miranda, cradling her tiny baby bump. "But yeah, I would have gone for some more va-va-voom. It's just, I thought you'd wanted a princess dress with train and tiara and the whole she-bang."

"Mm-hmm. But they are so expensive … and impractical. I mean, we're having a tea-party theme on a lawn. A long dress would only get dirty."

"Get two! A long one for your inner princess, and a short one to fit reality, not that you're not a princess."

"That's even more expensive," laughed Amy.

"So what? You're only getting married once."

"I can't afford that."

"So, you like this dress?"

"I do."

"You look like a princess hosting a tea party." Miranda gave in and hugged her friend but added in a whisper, "While we're here, you should still try on the tiaras."

Amy was happy. She hadn't picked a tiara, but a beaded floral wreath that matched the dress with all its daisies and gave some sparkle with glass pearls. The whole outfit had still ended up slightly pricier than the budget that Gabriel had set her, but she was sure he would not mind. You only get married once.

The sparkling wine that she had had at the bridal store was making her woozy, and she had already tried twice to unlock her door before she realized that her thumb was too low for the print reader to recognize it. Miranda had insisted on getting a glass for herself, just to give it to Amy, so they were making the most of their dress shopping. Amy finally unlocked her front door and entered.

She had lived in this apartment for the last six years and dreamed many a time about living somewhere

where she had a separate bed and living room and maybe a balcony to grow some vegetables, or even a shared backyard for some chickens. It was still a nice apartment, fit for a bachelorette. The single room had a self-made little seating area with a lamp carved into the brick wall. In the other corner stood her bed with the rose quilt her grandma had passed on to her. The little kitchen was painted bright green and had philodendron climbing along bamboo sticks crisscrossing the ceiling. The even smaller bathroom was kept in a warm red, a colour she had picked to symbolically attract love and romance. And after all these years, this energy must have finally supercharged her life.

She dropped the bags with her new shoes and the box with the floral wreath and veil on her bed and then lay down herself. The afternoon sun shone warm through the window, and even though she was tired from the alcohol, she was too excited to nap.

Amy rolled over and pulled her cell phone out of her bag to call Gabriel.

"Hey, it's me," Amy said when he picked up. "I just wanted to tell you that I found the most perfect dress."

"How much?" asked Gabriel.

"I did go over our budget, but …"

"Oh, Ames. Why would you do that? Now I have to rearrange the catering," Gabriel interrupted her.

"You already arranged for a caterer?"

"Yes, it's a package deal that the venue offered. Catering, invites, photographer, all sorted out."

"And you didn't ask me?"

"Well, I'm the one paying for it."

Amy didn't know what to say to this. She had offered to pay half of the costs, even though this would have meant that she had to use up all her savings and ask her parents or Miranda for a loan. But Gabriel had insisted that he would pay for the wedding and even included her dress.

"I'm sorry. Of course, I will pay the difference," she answered instead.

"Thank you."

"So, is there anything I can do?"

"No, I think I've got it all. We just need to get the invites out as soon as the cards arrive."

This was not how Amy thought the wedding planning was supposed to go. She had expected Gabriel to stay passive, as most men she knew had done, and leave all the preparations to the bride, or at least she thought that they would have done the planning together.

But then, there wasn't much time either. As soon as Gabriel had been released from quarantine, they had gotten their marriage licence. Gabriel was so passionate about it, it almost felt like eloping. At the clerk's office, Amy had seen a brochure for a wedding venue with a Chinese pavilion by a small lake, which she immediately liked. Gabriel had interpreted her gaze correctly and suggested to have their wedding there. The only date that the venue was available within the sixty days that their wedding licence was valid was in only four weeks. So, maybe it was good that Gabriel was on top of everything, as otherwise most options could be booked out before she had even thought about them.

"Thank you so much for organizing everything," Amy said finally.

"Only the best for you, babe," responded Gabriel. "What are you doing tonight?"

"Nothing."

"Wanna go out for some drinks?"

"Sounds good."

"I'll pick you up at six."

Amy did fall asleep eventually, and when she woke up just in time to refresh her face, the unsettled feeling about Gabriel's hands-on wedding preparation had vanished. Miranda had also reminded her earlier that too many people worried about their wedding day not being perfect. But then it often is the imperfect things that make a day memorable, like her own father losing his dentures the day before, which did not stop him from giving the best gummy smiles in all their photos, or her nephew clearing out all the wine glasses whilst they had their first dance, only to spew over the dance floor when they had their second dance. Even flowers not getting delivered, a lost ring, or a former lover gate crashing only added to the excitement, in Miranda's opinion, but when you have found your soul mate the only thing that counts is your life together from there on out.

Gabriel picked her up at six p.m. sharp. They ordered a pod and went to Wall Street, where they sat outside at the Tiki Bar.

"What can I get you?" asked the waiter.

"A strawberry daquiri for my fiancée and an old fashioned for me," answered Gabriel.

"Too easy." The waiter bustled off.

"If I remember correctly, that was your favourite cocktail," asked Gabriel.

"It is, I'm impressed." Amy smiled.

"Are you warm enough?"

"Oh yes, I'm good." That was not exactly true. Amy was already feeling the evening chill, and in another fifteen minutes, she would be too cold, but she did not want to admit it. It was weird. They were about to get married, yet Amy felt that she had to keep up appearances and not fuss about too much.

Gabriel grabbed her hand over the table. "I've got some exciting news. I've been offered employment at Praides to train the fighter pilots."

"Oh, wow, that's great news! But I thought you wanted to go back to space."

"Well, it will be more of an advisory role, which allows me to get my fitness back up and apply for the next mission at NASA. And we would stay in the area, as they're using the facilities at the Kennedy Space Centre."

"That is wonderful!" Amy was relieved. She hated change, and she had already wondered if they could stay in Orlando after the wedding. But the Kennedy Space Centre was still too far away for her to keep her job at the day-care centre.

"Here you go. The daquiri for the lady, and the old fashioned for the gentleman." The waiter placed the glasses on the table and then hesitated. "Do you mind, we were talking, me and my colleagues, are you Gabriel Stuart, the astronaut?"

"The very same." Gabriel gave him a dazzling smile.

"Oh wow, would you, do you mind signing, um, signing this napkin for me?" The waiter was clearly star-struck, and Gabriel relished the attention.

Gabriel and Jeanette Rice had spent the weeks since quarantine touring from breakfast show to interviews and even a dinner with the president. And now, Gabriel got recognized wherever he went. Usually, Amy stepped aside, whilst Gabriel bathed in the attention he got from complete strangers. The only issue right now was that Amy wanted to talk about his new job and what it meant for her job. But one after the other, the waiters, bar staff, and eventually even other customers came over to take a selfie with Gabriel, get autographs on more napkins or even body parts. They barely managed to sip their cocktails, let alone talk about their future in private.

They walked home, which Amy usually enjoyed, as it gave them almost an hour to just chat. But tonight, Gabriel was so pumped that he could not talk about anything else but his fans.

"How embarrassing that is to get your cleavage signed with a lipstick," he laughed. "I mean would you do that?"

"No," said Amy, smiling. She was proud of him, there was no denying, and she felt lucky that she was his sweetheart, soon to be his wife.

"And boy, was that waiter giddy. Bet he can't wait to show my autograph to his gay friends."

"You think he was gay?"

"As gay as a lark."

"Huh. Maybe you'll become like a gay idol," said Amy innocently.

"I hope not. Lucky I'll soon have a wife to show off," Gabriel said with a laugh.

"You could already show off your girlfriend," Amy suggested.

"I just don't want you to get in any inconvenient situations until I can properly protect you when we are living together as husband and wife."

They had arrived at Amy's building block.

"Not long," he said and pulled her in for a kiss. "Are you going to ask me up for a coffee?" he added in a raspy voice.

"Maybe another night. It was a long day, and I'm really tired."

"All right. I'll pick you up tomorrow."

"Oh, I already have plans."

"Change them."

"It's movie night at Harry P's. Miranda and I have planned this for weeks."

"So, you'd choose Miranda over me?" sulked Gabriel.

"No, you could come with us. I'm sure we can get another ticket."

"What are they showing?"

"*Casablanca*."

"Never heard of it."

Amy smiled. She was not surprised that he had not heard of it. "It's an iconic movie that won like three Oscars 111 years ago," she explained.

She and Miranda must have seen it about just as many times and never missed a screening in a public space.

"Nah, I'll pass," responded Gabriel. "I'll call you the day after."

"All right. I love you." Amy nestled against him and kissed him lightly on the lips.

"I sure hope so."

"I do."

"Love you too. Good night then."

"Good night."

Amy opened the main door, and once in her flat, waved down to signal Gabriel that she had safely locked her door.

Amy and Miranda arrived early at the public Harry P Leu Garden for their open-air screening of *Casablanca*. They secured the perfect spot, right in the centre of the screen, not too far to the front and not too far back. They unfolded their camping chairs and wrapped themselves into blankets, as the nights were still chilly. Almost on cue, they both unpacked their popcorn, chocolates, and drinks for a proper film night. Amy had brought a thermos flask and was about to pass Miranda a camping mug, when Miranda unpacked two bottles of beer, passing one to Amy.

"What's that?" asked Miranda.

"Rooibos tea. I thought I'd be a comrade in arms. You're drinking beer?" responded Amy.

"No, I've got myself a zero-ginger beer, but I didn't want you to miss out because of me."

Amy looked at their options. "Beer first?"

"Yeah."

The movie started, and they quietly clinked their bottles. And when Rick said at the end, "I think this is the beginning of a beautiful friendship," they both were warming their hands on the camping mugs filled with steaming Rooibos tea.

They had met seven years ago at a party where Miranda's now-husband Ozzie had tried to woo Miranda by engaging her in small talk about the latest movie releases. Little did he know that Miranda was a movie buff, and their small talk quickly changed direction when Amy overheard Miranda proclaiming that Steven Spielberg's *Indiana Jones and the Temple of Doom* was racist. Amy, herself quite a movie aficionado, chipped in, and the two of them were soon deep in conversation about the most controversial Oscar wins, whether Johnny Depp deserved a comeback, and their love for movie nights at Harry P Leu Gardens. Ozzie served as their waiter for the rest of the night, and his efforts did not go completely unnoticed. They got married two years later, and Amy was Miranda's bridesmaid, complete with a fluorescent pink dress inspired by the movie *Bridesmaids*.

And now it would be Miranda soon returning the favour. They were walking along the garden paths to the exit, with the spring flowers illuminated by esoteric fairy lights.

"I thought about *My Best Friend's Wedding*," said Miranda, in reference to the bridesmaid's dresses.

"Those yellow-and-pink balloony thingies?" asked Amy.

"Yes! I could get one made with lacing in the back just in case I need some more spiel around my mid-section."

"That sounds amazing."

"And from the front, it works for a tea party, and from the back, it could be a ballgown to meet a princess."

"You really thought of everything," laughed Amy.

"I know, it's one of my specialties. Is there anything else your bridesmaid can do? You see, I'm on fire right now. Flowers, live swans, a flock of turtle doves?"

"I think it's all done."

"What do you mean?"

"Well, we're not getting live animals, but Gabriel has already organized everything. We only need to send out the invites," said Amy, blushing slightly.

"What sorcery is this?"

"I know. He is on top of everything."

"Obviously ... So, there really is nothing I can help you with?"

"I had the same reaction yesterday when he told me. But it is also a great relief. I mean, it's only four weeks."

"I see ... Oh, I bet he hasn't thought about giving every guest a dalmatian puppy."

"Miranda, please don't." Amy was not sure anymore whether her friend was joking.

"Too much? All right, all right. I shall find something that your lord and master hasn't thought of."

It was a small ceremony. Amy and Gabriel did not have any siblings or an extensive family, so the guests only included their closest friends and Gabriel's mission colleagues Jeanette Rice and Veronica Vargas, who both came without partners. Adam Fjodorow and Philip Schuster had already returned to their home countries but sent their well wishes with an e-card.

The Chinese pavilion was covered in climbing roses, and the first shy buds had opened, diffusing the green foliage with white and pink spots. On the lake behind it glided two swans in unity, and the afternoon sun started to dip the sky into a warm orange.

It was perfect, and when Amy walked down the short aisle between the white fold-up chairs her heart was pounding so hard that she feared her jugular vein could pop. She clasped her father's hand so tightly that it hurt, but she was distracted by Gabriel standing like a knight in shining armour at the steps to the pavilion that she didn't notice the pain. He had chosen a white wedding suit with a pink tie, and Amy loved how this colour combination softened his masculinity. He truly was the man of her dreams and the ideal father to their future children. He would be strong yet playful, attentive yet relaxed, all while loving her until eternity.

Amy's thoughts were interrupted as the quiet Ave Maria paused. Amy stopped in her tracks, but then Miranda, in her pink-and-yellow high-low dress, stepped forward and started to sing. After the first lines of Dionne Warwick's 'That's What Friends Are For,' more and more of Amy's friends joined in until they all bellowed out "That's what friends are for."

Amy had joined Gabriel by the pavilion, laughing and crying at the same time. Miranda had pulled off the most romantic and cliched surprise to contribute to the wedding. When the song ended, Miranda shouted a final "I love you" before Amy and Gabriel entered the pavilion to seal their future life together as husband and wife.

Night had fallen, and lampions now illuminated the trees around the pavilion. The party was in full swing; guests had left their allocated seats and mingled freely or got seconds at the buffet. Amy and Gabriel sat giggling at their table and enjoyed their day. Gabriel had thought of everything, picked Amy's favourite flowers, and requested her kind of music. It was the perfect start to their life together.

"Are you happy?" asked Gabriel.

"Very," said Amy. "I couldn't have asked for more."

"What about a honeymoon?"

"Maybe we can do something next year."

"You sure?"

"Yeah. I'm simply looking forward to waking up next to you every morning from now on." Amy laid her head on his shoulder.

"How about doing that, but in Casablanca for the next ten days?" And with these words, Gabriel pushed two flight tickets to the Moroccan city over the table.

"You didn't!" Amy picked up the tickets. "That's the day after tomorrow?"

"Yes. Enough time, I hope, for you to pack."

"But what about my work?"

"I handled it."

"What? How? When?"

"Two weeks ago. Called them and explained the situation. They've already found a replacement."

Amy was in shock, yet the excitement about a first proper holiday in years diluted her doubts.

Miranda came over and interrupted their conversation.

"Are you all right? You look like you've seen Patrick Swayze," Miranda said at seeing Amy's dumbfounded face.

"Yes, guess where we're going for our honeymoon?"

"Mars?"

"No. Casablanca!"

"What? No way. When did that happen?"

"My wonderful husband of four hours surprised me with these." Amy waved the flight tickets around.

"Casablanca, I'll be a squirrel in a skirt." Miranda grabbed the tickets. "Wow, Gabriel! I think I'm starting to like you."

"Thanks, Miranda," said Gabriel.

"Do you mind if I hijack your beautiful bride for a dance?" asked Miranda.

"Knock yourself out. But I'll be watching you."

Amy and Miranda stormed the dance floor, and after some upbeat pop-rock they slow-danced to Eric Clapton's 'Wonderful Tonight'.

"You know what?" asked Miranda. "I think that astronaut friend of Gabriel's is pregnant."

"What? Which one?" Amy craned her neck to Jeanette and Veronica, who were sitting at a table near the pavilion.

"Don't look. The younger one."

"Oh, I didn't notice. But now that you mentioned it … I thought I overheard them say something when I visited Gabriel in Houston. Just didn't think it was her."

"Yeah, the loose dress covers it pretty well, but she looks like she's further along than I am."

"Gabriel didn't mention anything."

"Well, think about it. If she's further along, she must have conceived the baby up there." Miranda looked up to the stars above them.

"Oh, I see." Amy finally twigged and slowly spun Miranda around so she could have a secret look over her shoulder.

* * *

Jeanette and Veronica watched the wedding guests on the dance floor.

"She looks happy," said Veronica, watching Amy dancing with Miranda.

"Yeah," said Jeanette, and after a while she added, "How are you and your partner?"

"Radio silence."

Veronica thought about Cecilia every day and imagined her sitting alone in their old flat, or even worse, not alone at all. She had moved in with her mother, and every time the phone rang, her ears perked up, but it never was Cecilia. By now, she feared that too much time had passed to reconnect without a world-moving reason.

"Do you want me to talk to her?"

Veronica thought for a moment. "Maybe. But I don't know what else you could tell her."

"Sometimes it doesn't have to be something else, just from *someone* else."

"And you would do that?"

"Sure. I kind of feel responsible for it too, you know?" Jeanette searched Veronica's eyes. "How's the baby?"

"Good. Growing well, making me pee every couple of hours; the usual, I guess."

"And how are you dealing with it? Are you getting used to the thought of becoming a mother?"

"I think so. I'm worried, but mostly about the truth that will come out once the baby is here. And whether I'm able to love her." Veronica thought about opening up more to her former mission commander, telling her about her choice not to puncture the baby's umbilical cord to have a paternity test done before the birth, but she didn't want their conversation turning to that point.

Jeanette grabbed Veronica's hand. "I'm sure everything will fall into place. One way or another."

"Thank you," whispered Veronica. "Have you, has your husband returned yet?"

"Two more days, and he'll return from his work in Africa for a couple of weeks."

"Any plans yet?"

"Just relaxing," said Jeanette with a smile.

CHAPTER 4

Jeanette had arrived back home last night after spending a couple of days in Orlando to attend Gabriel's wedding and enjoying a short city break. But to be honest, she had been city-hopping so much since they had left quarantine that a staycation of at least a month seemed to be a dream. Luckily, James was supposed to arrive tomorrow, and they could relax together, staying in bed all day long. But for today, she had one more task she wanted to finish.

Jeanette had just stepped out of the shower, thrown a bathrobe on, and was brushing her hair as she walked around the house. During their mission, she had shaved it off, but since they had arrived back on Earth, it had grown back so much that she had to look after it again. Maybe she would go to the hairdresser and get cornrows next week.

She poured herself an iced tea and sat down on her terrace in the shade of their grapevines, which were growing on trellises over the seating area. It looked like they could expect a nice harvest this year; maybe she would keep the gardener on, even though she was back now to look after her garden herself. He seemed to have done an excellent job, and she loved that she was back in time to enjoy the full bloom of spring.

She watched some bees flying around the hibiscus flowers, brushing their yellow legs against the hairy stamens of the blossoms, ready to receive the fertile pollen. She thought about the miracle that was conception, as well as the responsibilities that came with parenthood, for she was about to dictate a personal letter to Veronica's partner. She wanted to help her spacewalker in any way she could. NASA seemed to be busier keeping this pregnancy under wraps than investigating how it happened and helping the only person who was affected by it.

Jeanette picked up her tablet computer and started to dictate:

Dear Cecilia,

My name is Jeanette Rice, and I was the mission commander for *Pilgrim*. As such, I feel responsible for my crew, not only during the mission but also about their well-being before and after. My crew and I have trained together for many months, spent months on end in tight quarters, and I'd like to think that we got to know each other well, not just on a professional level.

I am very troubled about what happened to Veronica, as it is a mystery to all of us, and she deserves all the support she can get. I can only reiterate what Veronica must have told you already, that there was no chance for any intimate relations between crewmembers, and I have never even observed Veronica engaging in closer contact than the occasional punching of someone's shoulder.

I've gotten to know her as a woman with integrity and dignity. Although she did not speak much about her private matters, I did observe that she had a photograph of you with her and that she found comfort in looking at it during the long hours in space.

I cannot offer any explanation about how this pregnancy came to be, but I can wholeheartedly assure you that she loves and cherishes you and never said or did anything that would dishonour her feelings for you.

I can only imagine how you or she must be feeling, but I am sure that she is terrified about what has happened and what might happen. She has decided to give this innocent life that is growing within her a chance. This incredible act of selflessness should not go unnoticed and unsupported, and the greatest support she could get would be from you, the one person she longed most for during our mission.

I beg you to not give up on her and to look beyond the non-existent betrayal and see the woman who is facing a colossal task in raising a child she is afraid that she will not be able to love. And it is love we all need to survive, to live and strive. Without love, we are nothing.

I would like to meet you both and answer any questions you might have. I am happy to come to Orlando, but you are also welcome to come to Louisiana and have a vacation here in Baton Rouge. We have a lovely little guest room looking into our garden, which is currently in full bloom, and the beach is only a ten-minute drive away.

Warm regards,
Jeanette

Jeanette read through the words that had appeared on her tablet as she spoke. Only a few touch-ups where she had stumbled over her own words, but otherwise she was happy with what had poured out of her. She had thought about including some more personal touches but felt that this would have been inappropriate to send to someone who she had effectively never met.

Moreover, her own relationship was not the best example for someone who was asked to take on a child they did not want. She had told James early on in their relationship that she did not want children, and he was the first man who not only accepted it but understood where she was coming from and never changed his mind about it.

All throughout her dating history, she was surprised to find that so many men eventually, mostly when the physical attraction of the early loved-up months waned, searched their souls, only to find that they needed a child of their own for their happiness.

She had never felt this way. She loved children and enjoyed taking her niece and nephew out hiking and camping, teaching them survival skills and how to deflect a knife attack. But she would not be happy to have the responsibility for another human being day in and day out for a couple of decades if you were lucky.

She was happy by herself, making plans on her own terms, only having to look after herself and making the most of this single greatest gift that her mother gave her, her own life.

In James, she had found a kindred soul at a point in her life when she had already settled on living alone. He had not given her life a new meaning but was simply someone to share it with. What do they say? 'A joy shared is a joy doubled; a sorrow shared is a sorrow halved?'

The sound of a pod door pulled Jeanette out of her thoughts. She switched the tablet off and placed it on the side table.

She walked inside to see who was at the front when she heard a key turn and the door opened. For a few seconds she did not believe her own eyes. James stood in the door, smiling.

Jeanette screamed and jumped into his arms. "What are you doing here?"

"I took an earlier flight," James responded under her kisses.

"And you didn't tell me?"

He carried her in, dropped his bags, and closed the door behind them without putting her down.

"I wanted to surprise you."

"But I prepared this for tomorrow!" She climbed off him and picked up a large sign reading 'Smoking Hot Red Cross Doctor'.

He smiled again. Oh, that little crooked smile still made her weak. He pulled her in and teased her lips with his own. She pressed her body against his and let her hands wander along his arms, then his chest and hips, until the teasing developed into an intense caress, and she slung her naked legs around him again. On their way to the bedroom, they got rid of most of their clothes. No one who saw James out and about would have thought of him as a passionate lover. But that could not be further from the truth, and Jeanette had to admit that it was not just the sharing of their lives and life choices, but also the incredible sex that bonded them.

"I'm still mad at you for not telling me that you'd come earlier," she said when they lay side by side, their hearts still racing.

"I told you, I wanted to surprise you."

"How would you have felt if I, if I …"

"If you had returned from Mars without telling me? Quite disappointed, mainly because I would have known that you had returned, because you were on all channels."

Jeanette smiled. "Did you see me meeting the president?"

"And on *Gerry Colden, Good Morning America, Pancakes with Tracy* …"

"I only did that because of the pancakes."

"You were everywhere."

Jeanette was embarrassed, and although she did her fair share attending the press circuit, she only did the appearances that NASA had contracted her for and was glad that it was over.

"Oh, I tried not to read any news. It's so weird, don't you think?" she said, and it was true, but she was curious too. "What do they say? Did they report on any of us, how we were?"

"They say that the mission was a success and that you were all doing well, adjusting to the gravity of Earth again," James responded.

"Did they not discuss any of us in more detail?" Jeanette asked, trying to avoid raising any suspicion that something or someone might not have returned from the mission as planned.

"Becoming a little vain, are we? The only one they reported more on was Gabriel Stuart. I mean when I said you were everywhere, I meant *he* was everywhere. Up and down on all channels, to the point where people thought that he was the commander of the mission."

"Oh. Do you think I should have done more?"

"History will remember the facts, not the tenth breakfast show that your spacewalker was on."

Jeanette smiled, but a pang of conscience plagued her now. She was the first African American woman to have commanded a space mission, and above that the first crewed Mars mission. She was a role model for future generations. Maybe she should have made more of the media attention, but she also hated being asked the same questions over and over again. A questionnaire placed on NASA's website for everyone to peruse would have been her ideal scenario.

"Nothing about the other spacewalker?" Jeanette finally asked and feared she might have indicated that there was something worth knowing about Veronica. "Or Philip Schuster, our engineer, or Adam Fjodorow, the pilot?" she added to dilute the attention.

"Not outside your group interviews. Jealous?"

"Me? No."

"I think I saw Gabriel Stuart at the airport this morning. He arrived in a taxi, and boy, people freaked out. He waved like the president to all the fans, even stopped for some autographs."

"Sounds like him. He must be off to his honeymoon."

"Oh, so that was his wife. She almost got separated from him in the crowd."

"Yeah, I went to their wedding a couple of days ago."

"How was it?"

"Lovely. A friend of hers pulled one of those singing surprises."

"Where they start singing one after another?"

"Yeah. It was rather nice, but Gabriel didn't seem to be happy about it."

"Maybe he doesn't like surprises?"

"Maybe."

"I know someone else who doesn't like surprises," said James and disappeared under the covers.

"Well, at least … you know how to make … up for it," said Jeanette, relaxing into his seduction.

He knew that she had not come the first time around, as she was not one to fake it. Most of the time, he was able to hold himself back until she was satisfied, but after a longer separation, he would climax after only a few thrusts. She loved to feel his arousal, but she thanked the Lord when it was her turn and he offered it freely.

* * *

Gayle Hamilton was glad that the astronaut took a different flight at a different terminal, so his entourage of crazy fans would not disturb her any longer. He had stood in the drop-off queue next to her and proclaimed for everyone to hear that he was on his way to his honeymoon in Casablanca. And even though he asked his fans to give them some breathing space, he did not seem to get tired of posing for photographs. His poor wife stood offside, with a pinned-in-place smile that was still untarnished from this intrusion into their private life.

Somehow, this young woman reminded Gayle of herself. She also was once a young wife, heavily struck by love and blinded by a man who seemed to offer a life full of excitement and security on a golden platter. Alas, ten years later, she was a single parent of two young daughters, whilst her betrothed jet-setted around the world, sweet-talking financial bigshots, making obscene deals for his corporation, and no doubt also enjoying the 'team bonding' excursions to more or less private establishments.

At last, it was her turn now. The girls were old enough that their father could look after them, which did not necessarily involve him being physically present, and Gayle had jumpstarted her political career. She had been appointed minister for family and health of the United Nations of Europe two years ago and just finished a week-long meeting with her American counterpart in Washington, DC.

During the meeting, she had introduced her contraception bill, which had taken effect in Europe last month to curb rampant teenage pregnancies. Even though the United States of America was facing a similar issue, the bill was cause for a lot of controversy at the meeting. The secretary of health and human services saw such a bill as an intrusion into the personal decisions of underaged citizens as well as the prevention of God's creative will to see Adam and Eve's descendants to be fruitful and multiply. It was still astonishing to Gayle that a country that was at the frontline of globalisation and technology was still so entrenched in a belief system that saw half of humankind as inferior.

Across the ocean, in Europe, they had seen an unmanaged increase in young girls getting pregnant, even though the age at which most women conceived for the first time had been pushed back to 31.4 years. These young girls often dropped out of school and fell off the track, increasing the countries' unemployment rate by twenty percent for women under the age of twenty-five. After a decade of debating the causes and solutions to teenage pregnancies nationwide, the contraception bill was passed by a slim majority. From the age of twelve, girls were now required to get a hormonal implant in a one-off procedure that was modulated to act exactly for the number of years until the recipient turned eighteen. In this first month, about three percent of girls had been registered to have received an implant, and the numbers had kept on increasing over the last few days. Gayle monitored the stats every morning, even when she was away from home and off duty.

After this exhausting week in Washington, Gayle had taken a few days off to do some city hopping, first up to New York and then down the East Coast to Florida. The public transport was excellent, and the magnetic monorails provided all the comfort and speed someone on a tight schedule could ask for. Instead of flying home to take over her parenting duties, she decided to fly to the West Coast for some more city hopping and then to Australia to visit her nephew Mack in Brisbane. Mack was the only son of her late sister, who died more than ten years ago. Shortly after, her husband, Mack's father, had died during a shark attack. Since then, Mack had thrown himself into his work, barely finding time to catch up with the few family members he had left.

Gayle checked the time. Only half an hour before boarding. If she called home now, she might catch her girls before dinner.

"Hi, Mum! Inga, it's mum!" Hazel, her younger daughter who had turned thirteen just before she left, smiled from Gayle's screen, shouting for her sixteen-year-old sister.

"Hey, where are you?" Gayle asked, as she did not recognize the surroundings that her daughter was in.

"Dad took us to Greece as a birthday gift. Tomorrow we'll go on a three-day sailing trip," explained Hazel excitedly.

"Hi, Mum. Where are you?" asked Inga, who had joined them, dressed in what was likely the shortest white summer dress that she owned.

"I'm at the airport in Orlando. I'm about to fly over to LA in thirty minutes in one of those zeppelin helicopters," she explained, also smiling, even though she was furious that her husband had taken their daughters on a holiday that they had not agreed on and didn't even see it necessary to inform her about it.

"Cool. And when are you going to 'Stralia?" asked Hazel with a terrible Australian accent.

"On Monday. I will first visit San Francisco, though."

"Hey girls, the pod is here." The voice of Gayle's ex-husband sounded from another room.

"Just a minute! Talking to Mum!" shouted Hazel.

"Okay, but don't take too long," answered the dis-embodied voice of their father.

"Go, I'll call you in three days when you're back from your sailing trip," said Gayle, trying to stay calm in the face of the indirect confrontation with her ex.

"Okay. Say hi to Cousin Mack from us," said Inga.

"I will. And make sure to wear your lifejackets on the boat. Your father is as bad a sailor as he was a driver. Is the boat self-driving by any chance?"

"No," laughed Inga. "But Dad got us these crazy jackets that inflate as soon as they are submerged in water." Inga held up an elegant looking jacket made of some grey-bluish shimmering fabric. "Aren't they totally sick? Dad says that they also have GPS trackers and temperature control that functions with the salt from the sea so your body temperature ..."

"Come on, or we'll miss the dinner reservation."

"Okay, gotta go," said Inga.

"Love you," Gayle squeezed in before her girls disappeared to an apparently 'totally sick' holiday.

She was hurt that they had so much fun when she had hoped that her ex-husband would treat them as he had treated her, and that they would return being glad to be back with their mother. Apparently, this was not going to be the case.

Gayle tried to distract herself from this nagging feeling by focussing on her own upcoming adventures. She was wondering how Mack had been, how he looked now. For more than a year, they had only exchanged voice messages, due to their conflicting schedules and time zones.

CHAPTER 5

It was Saturday morning in Australia, and Mackenzie Murdoch tightened his wetsuit. With a tap on his chest, the neoprene fabric trimmed down to his body size, and then he picked up his surfboard from his little red convertible. He shut down the car with a closing motion of his hand on the bonnet and walked to the small path that led over the dune to the beach of Bribie Island. He had gotten up at five in the morning to drive an hour up from Brisbane to relax from the week.

As the beach opened in front of him and the waves washed over the sand, he stopped for a moment and watched into the distance over the calm and sparkling coral sea. Every time, this view opened a bottomless hole inside him, letting his legs come to a halt and stopping his breath for a few heartbeats. And yet he always came back to this beach. There were better surfs further up north, but it was here where he and his father had begun their surfing lessons almost six years ago. They had decided to take up a hobby together after Eleanor, his mother, had died of cancer. And about a kilometre further up the beach was the spot where his father had bled to death, after a shark had ripped off his leg.

Mack took a deep breath and forced his legs to move forward. He knew it was madness, and he should have sought out a grief counsellor long ago, but he was not ready yet to let go of the pain. If he had told someone about the significance of this beach, they probably would have thought him morbid or outright creepy.

The beach was still deserted and the water fresh when he entered. He knew that it was an unlikely time of year for shark attacks so far south, and yet he pushed his board out in front of him, thinking that death could be lurking for him under the water's surface today. He paddled out beyond the break zone and then sat on his board with his legs dangling to either side. For a while, he watched his feet in the water, taking hold of the tingling nervousness inside him. And when he felt in control again, he lay down on his board and took a wave towards the shore, stopping the torment for today.

Mack spent almost two hours in the water, and when he came back out, the beach had filled with sun addicts and a couple of surf school lessons for kids. As terrible as his thoughts were when he arrived, as relaxed was he now that he had overcome his fears once more. It was this conquering of fear that drew him back almost every weekend to Bribie Island.

He tapped his chest, and his wetsuit loosened so that he could pull down the upper half and let the early Australian autumn sun warm his skin.

"Hey, handsome, any chance to come down to Brisbane for a party tonight?" said a female voice behind him as he stowed his surfboard in his car.

Mack turned around and saw a twenty-something on hover-skates drawing circles on the car park next to him. Since most people did not own cars anymore but simply ordered a pod whenever they needed transport, most car parks were empty and had been adopted by hoverboarders. Mack still liked to have his own car at his disposal for certain activities off the beaten track such as rock climbing, camping, gorge walks, or getting to Bribie Island for a surf. Most of the more remote roads were not mapped for pods yet and owning a car to have full control over the routes became necessary.

"Isn't it a little far off to be advertising for Brisbane up here?" asked Mack.

"Maybe, but I was in the area anyway. So, you're interested?"

"You're in luck, I actually am."

"Cool." She smiled and did another circle around him. "It's our opening night at The Hive. If you come before ten, you'll get a thirty-dollar drinks voucher." She passed him a leaflet and smiled at him, twisting her head with every circle she drove to keep eye contact.

"Sounds good," said Mack with a smirk.

"And if you bring a female friend, she'll get in for free."

"Will you be there?"

"Definitely."

"Guess my female friends will have to pay for themselves then."

She smiled at him.

"What's your name?"

"Amanda."

"I'll see you tonight, Amanda."

"See ya then." She lifted her chin and then drove off to distribute more flyers along the beach.

This was another one of his adopted coping mechanisms. Flirting and sleeping around as if there was no tomorrow. He had his one and only girlfriend in high school, after that no more than a fling for a few weeks. It was not that he did not want an intimate and long-term relationship; after all, his parents had been a prime example for a blissful marriage until disaster struck. It was more that he always found something dismissible about the other person, often sooner rather than later.

The Hive did not disappoint. The bartenders mixed cocktails and added forced carbonation to it, making the drinks bubbly without diluting them with soda. A whole wall was dedicated to the new in-house fermented spirits, which had such tempting names as 'Ambrosia', 'Sunset Honey', or 'Honey Dew'. To Mack's surprise, Amanda was one of the bartenders swirling cocktail mixers around. He had thought she was just a pretty promo-girl hired to lure customers to the club.

"Hey, handsome." She smiled at him when he sat down at the bar. "What can I get you?"

"A whisky," answered Mack.

"Can I tempt you to a flavour experiment?"

"Sure."

She poured a couple of fingers of whisky and added another finger of rum before pouring it over some ice cubes.

"There you go."

A small chip in the bottom of the glass registered the drink and showed the price of twenty-five dollars on the top of the neon-lit bar. Mack added a generous tip, placed his phone down, and confirmed the payment with his fingerprint.

"Thanks very muchly," said Amanda.

Mack winked at her before taking a sip and swirling the mixture around his mouth. He was surprised that the flavours actually played well together. The sweetness of the rum smoothed the harsher spice notes from the whisky, but his Scottish heritage disliked the additional use of the ice cubes.

"Not bad," he said anyway.

"What's your name?" Amanda asked.

"Mack."

Another customer interrupted their introduction, but they had plenty of time to get to know each other on a superficial level, as Mack stayed at the bar for the rest of the evening. It was not that he did not like to dance; on the contrary, but with his thirty-two years, he was probably a decade older than most other customers here, and he felt slightly out of place. But then, dancing had not been the reason for him to come.

After Amanda's shift ended at midnight, they stayed another hour taking shots of all the different in-house fermented spirits, and Mack got a private introduction to the different flavours. As it turned out, Amanda was a shareholder of the club and involved in the creation of new and exciting drinks.

Another hour later, and Mack and Amanda lay heavily breathing in Amanda's bed. Mack rolled off the condom and put a knot in it.

"There's a bin in the corner," Amanda said and pointed with a heavy arm.

Mack flung the condom and was happy that he did not miss, as his head was spinning from the heavy drinking. When he turned to Amanda, she was already asleep, and the moon shone softly over her naked body. Mack watched her. She had an almost symmetrical face, although the fake eyelashes were a little over the top and the smudged lipstick uncovered thinner lips than they had made out to be. A strand of her honey brown hair curled over her chest, where her nipples had smoothed out in the relaxation of sleep. A hand rested on her flat stomach.

A sudden snort pulled Mack out of his gaze. He smiled about this very human sound that she would probably be embarrassed about if she knew that he had heard it. He finally took a deep breath to clear his head and got up to get dressed. He ordered a pod on his phone and then produced a small pair of scissors and a small freezer bag from his pocket. Mack sat back on the bed, studied Amanda's face again for a few seconds, and then cut some hair from behind her ear. He placed the hair in the bag and pocketed everything. She would probably not even notice the involuntary haircut.

The fresh air outside cleared his head, and the pod was already waiting to drive him to his apartment in St. Lucia.

Since he hit his thirties, Mack noticed that he started to have hangovers. It was already after ten on Sunday when he finally forced himself to get up to have a glass of water and an aspirin. He stayed under the shower until the sedative kicked in and he thought that he could start the day. He quickly pulled on a white T-shirt and shorts and slipped into a pair of beach sandals to do his usual Sunday morning run for coffee and a chocolate croissant, albeit a little later than usual.

"You are late," pouted the barista when he stepped to the counter at the corner café. He had been visiting this coffee shop after meeting the barista Claire during an early-morning run along the Esplanade. She was on a working holiday, and at first, he thought he didn't have much time if he wanted to hook up with her, but now she had been here for more than two months, and they were still just flirting.

"Sorry, won't happen again." He looked at her like a scolded child.

"All right, all right. But your 9 a.m. coffee got cold, so you need to wait a minute."

"I'll pay for both," Mack offered.

"No worries. Here, I saved you the last chocolate croissant." She pushed a brown paper bag over the counter.

"You're the best."

Mack placed his phone on the counter to pay and then stepped aside to wait for his coffee. He caught a glimpse of a strawberry-blonde woman waiting in line and retreated into a corner, but it was too late. She had seen him and did not hesitate to leave her spot to come and talk to him.

"Hey."

"Hey, fancy bumping into you here," she said, searching for his eyes. "You don't come to the diner anymore?"

"Nah, got sick of their menu," he responded, only looking at her briefly to gauge her emotions, but not long enough to show interest.

"Yeah, I know what you mean. Hey, um, fancy having our coffee together and then go for a walk on the Esplanade, to catch up or something?"

"There you go, Mack," the barista interrupted as she pushed his coffee-to-go toward him.

"I would love to, but I'm meeting my mum for lunch, and she's living on the other side of town," said Mack, as the eyes of both women rested on him. "Thanks, Claire," he said to the barista. "See you around," he said to no one in particular, leaving the coffee shop as low-key as possible.

This was the most awkward situation in a long time. For weeks, he had been flirting with Claire, and about two months ago, he had hooked up with the strawberry blonde, whose name he had forgotten already, and whose calls he consistently ignored. They had met in the little twentieth-century diner in Morningside, and he had made the mistake of giving her his phone number when she did not want to give him hers. But she did not seem to understand the concept of a one-night stand. At first, he had politely answered and chatted with her, but after he had run out of excuses not to meet up again, he simply did not pick up, too bashful to block her number. Why did she have to come into this coffee shop today, just when he was making progress with Claire?

Mack went back home and had his breakfast at the kitchen counter, reading the news on his phone projection. One of the astronauts from the Mars mission had gotten married and was now honeymooning in Casablanca. His wife looked cute, Mack thought in passing, as he flipped the page on the hologram to the science section.

An article of a Nature magazine paper about cryo-conservation of entire mammals caught his eye. Some scientists in India had managed to successfully revive a mouse, which had been vitrified for three months.

Mack was disappointed to read that the mouse only lived for a few hours before it died of organ failure. Nonetheless, thirty years ago, the only whole organisms that could be successfully cryo-preserved were embryos at blastocyst stage, if you could call an organism consisting of only three hundred odd cells 'whole'. Besides this, there was an article about breast cancer genes in dairy cows, a summary of the global summit on genome editing, including a discussion about the still-illegal applications in humans, and a scathing opinion piece on the contraception bill passed in Europe. He was offended by the last article, as it named his aunt in rather ugly terms.

Mack drank the last sip of his coffee and noticed that Claire had left a phone number on the cup. He smiled about this sweet gesture. He appreciated if the woman made a direct advance, even as subtle as leaving a number on a paper cup. She was probably still at work, and he decided to call her another day. Whilst she had made a favourable impression on him, there were still a few things he needed to test.

He connected his phone to his printer, opened a folder, and flicked through some headshots of women. At a photo of a brunette woman, he stopped and opened a linked file, which showed the woman's details (Jessie, 28, ~5.4 feet, ~8.3 stones, paediatric receptionist). He selected another one (Michelle, 25, 5.3 feet, 8.2 stones, personal trainer), and lastly, he selected Amanda's details (Amanda, 25, ~5.6 feet, ~9.3 stones, bartender). He printed the details on adhesive labels, placed the printouts on his kitchen counter, and then fetched three freezer bags with hair samples from his fridge.

When he started his collection, he had thought about the women, about their qualities both physically and intellectually, and the time they had spent together. But by now, this secret endeavour had become routine. It was like a habit that once served a purpose but now had become a compulsion. Accurately, he taped the details of each woman to the bag with their respective hair samples and then moved to his spare room.

Over the last couple of years, he had transformed his spare room into a small laboratory. He had bought the machines used over the space of several months, hoping to cover up suspicions with any authority. He did not know whether purchases of lab equipment were monitored; certainly, buying copious amounts of some chemicals was. Luckily, he was able to legally buy the DNA extraction kits through his research grant, where he had budgeted for surplus kits, in case any of his experiments required a repeat. By now, his home lab was fully equipped with a computer, centrifuge, water bath, pipettes, and large jars of Proteinase K, T1 buffer, sodium chloride, 100 percent and 70 percent ethanol.

Mack put on gloves, labelled some test tubes with the same details as the freezer bags, and carefully placed half of each hair sample into each tube. Then, he pipetted Proteinase K into the tubes for enzymatic digestion of the hairs and release of the nucleic acid. At work, he would be using the Pip1000 to prepare several hundred samples in one go, but for the few samples he processed privately, he resorted to the good old handheld pipette. He could have easily processed his samples at work, but there, he used blood samples, and he found it too risky should someone question where the hair samples were coming from. Once the DNA was extracted though, he did use the expensive sequencer at work, even for his private samples.

Monday morning started almost as bad as the day before. Mack was locking his bicycle when he heard, "Hi, Mack!" behind him.

Tom, the new post-grad, waited for him, beaming with the imperturbable smile of someone who had nothing else going for him. He dressed like his grandfather, including metal-framed glasses, had thinning hair already in his mid-twenties, and was one of the unfortunate ones who did not know that it was high time to pick up a razor and get rid of this tragedy altogether.

"How was your weekend?" asked Tom as he joined Mack to enter the Institute for Mental Health and Genome Research.

"Good. Had a quiet one. Yourself?"

"I did some cosplay with some friends."

They waited for the elevator, and Mack considered taking the stairs. Cosplaying was too far off his radar. But again, he did not want to reject someone so obviously.

"Don't you think it might be nice to meet people in real life?" he asked instead.

"What do you mean?"

"I mean instead of hanging out in some virtual reality?"

Finally, the elevator arrived, and Tom trotted after Mack like a devoted dog.

"Oh, no, we went out to Mount Coot-Tha and re-enacted life as nineteenth-century settlers," Tom answered.

"Ah, I see, not virtual at all then. That's much better."

"If you want, I can take you with me next time."

"Um, yeah, I don't think that's my thing. You know, I like solitary stuff, like surfing."

"Sure, sure. That sounds cool. I thought about learning to surf."

"Well, it's not for everyone."

They arrived at the third level, and Mack took the chance to quickly walk down the corridor to his office, knowing that Tom's shared office was in the other direction.

"See ya!" called Tom.

Mack smiled at him over his shoulder and walked on. Maybe Tom was more interesting than he looked. Maybe he was a really cool guy with a vibrant social life that was worth getting to know. But boy, did his first and any subsequent impressions hinder any kind of friendship closer than collegial politeness. Nonetheless, Professor Lamarck must have seen something in this computer-programming student to give him a chance to apply his skills to genomic analyses and earn a higher degree in research.

After Mack checked his correspondences, he went to the lab to process the DNA samples he prepared last week for his deep-sequencing study to identify genomic regions involved in the network of post-traumatic stress disorder. He included the DNA samples from his private endeavours that he had extracted yesterday and spent the morning in the lab. He found the repetitive work relaxing and preferred doing it himself instead of hiring a technician. Too often, he had found others being slightly less diligent in keeping their workspace clean or, even more aggravating, thoroughly cleaning shared machines such as the thermocyclers or the fourth-generation sequencer. During pursuit of his PhD, he had to discard an entire month's worth of brain samples, because another student had contaminated the lab with salmonella.

Besides these specific projects on deciphering the human genome for genetic causes of mental illnesses, he and Professor Lamarck were part of an international team to update the human genome database with sequence data of RNA from all major organs, as well as from participants of different ages. Ribonucleic acids gave specific insights into the activity of genes in different tissues or at different time points, whilst DNA only ever gave static information of all encoded genes in a cell. His particular efforts were focussed on the gene activity of patients before, during, and after psychotic episodes, as well as how drugs manipulated that activity. Unfortunately, obtaining brain samples, the organ that was most obviously involved in mental disorders, was the complicated part, as, for apparent reasons, he could not simply take biopsies from living probands. Even so, he had made some interesting discoveries from analysing blood, hair, or colon samples.

After lunch, Mack got a head start on his conference contribution for the World Congress for Human Genetics in Mental Diseases, held in two months time in Shanghai. He had been invited for the first time to give an hour-long plenary talk, and he was reasonably excited about this honour. He had just come up with a pun on *Witzelsucht* disorder when his phone rang.

"Doctor Murdoch, hello?" he answered the call.

"Oh, so official. This is your favourite aunt."

"Aunty Gayle! Have you arrived?"

"Yes, I have. Just checked in," said Gayle.

"How was your flight?"

"Too quick. I only managed one movie."

"Oh, so you took the Dynamo21?"

"Yes, thought I'd rather have some more time to meet up with you."

"I'm glad to hear that I'm more important than binge-watching blockbusters."

"When are you free so I can give you a long-overdue hug?"

"I can finish now. Which hotel are you in?"

"I'm staying at the Treasury, but give me an hour to have a shower."

"I'll wait for you in the lobby."

Mack dropped his bicycle off at home and freshened up before ordering a pod to take him to the Treasury in downtown Brisbane. He was excited to see her after all these years but also worried about the memories that this meeting might trigger. So, he braced himself, locked away his emotions, and picked up his aunt in the brightest of moods he had mustered in a long time.

CHAPTER 6

Gayle stepped out the elevator when Mack climbed the stairs to the entrance hall. It felt like yesterday that they had last seen each other, but their embrace held all the love of a long-awaited reunion.

"You look great," Gayle said, stroking his cheek.

"So do you. Divorce is doing you good," joked Mack.

"It's the parenting that has gotten so much easier."

"How are they? Inga is now sixteen, seventeen, and Hazel like twelve?"

"She turned thirteen almost two weeks ago."

"Two teenagers; can't believe that's easy."

"Easy when their father takes care of them," said Gayle with slight but not unnoticeable discontent.

"I see," said Mack.

"He's taken them sailing in Greece, and of course, they love it."

It felt good to talk to someone who was family but distant enough to hear her frustration for the first time. She was surprised herself how much anger she still harboured after almost seven years. When she had gotten married, she had thought, probably like every bride, that she had found the love of her life. And to top it all off came the lifestyle that he was able to provide. Summers at the French Riviera, winters in the Swiss Alps, and a large house in Paris. What more could a girl from a middle-class family from Glasgow want?

Yes, she had studied politics and international relations at Edinburgh University with the dream to one day work in the Scottish Parliament, but when she met Olivier during a summer internship in Madrid, he quickly swept her off her feet. At first, her parents were dismayed that Gayle was seemingly throwing away a career she had worked for since she was sixteen, but Olivier knew how to charm them as well. She finished her Master of Arts degree, and soon after, they got married and she moved with him to Paris. She took up work at a large import-export company for health equipment, but after several years with little upward movement in the ranks, she felt frustrated, and children seemed to be a welcome and socially acceptable distraction.

Unfortunately, after Hazel was born, Gayle did not find motherhood to be a life-fulfilling and satisfactory role and longed for a purpose outside of being a mother. She began volunteering for various social projects, eventually joining the European Social Party.

Olivier had nothing against her ambitions, as long as his own career advancements were not hindered by family matters. They hired a full-time babysitter, shortly after a cook, and finally took in au-pairs. His infidelity was the final trigger, but the main reason for their divorce was Olivier's unwillingness to take on any of the mental load that came with having young children.

The divorce was settled surprisingly quickly, and it hit Gayle even harder when she realized how happy Olivier was to buy his freedom by setting her and the children up in a nice house with enough money to keep the babysitter. After that, their only contact for years were phone calls for the girls' birthdays. Even Christmas he spent out of town and only sent presents from wherever he holidayed during that time of year.

At least this financially secure setup allowed Gayle to pursue her dream of a political career once more, but instead of the Scottish Parliament, her appetite had grown to become a player on the European floor.

Until her death, Gayle's closest confidante was her sister Eleonor. But she had moved to Australia when she met her husband during a gap year, and so their contacts were rarely in the flesh.

As Gayle recapped the last ten years of her life, Mack listened intently, even though he must have heard at least some of the details from his mother.

Mack and Gayle went out for dinner to a cosy Korean restaurant at South Bank, and when they wandered along the promenade back to Gayle's hotel, she felt guilty for having hijacked their evening with her sob story that happened to thousands of women every year.

For the last ten minutes, Mack had tried to explain to her what he was researching, and it sounded like he enjoyed his work immensely.

"I'm so glad to see that you're doing well," said Gayle finally, and she meant it.

She had wondered whether his research field of mental disorders reflected his own state of mind, as she had always found that many people who tried to help others often suffered from the exact same symptoms. "There is one thing though, we haven't talked about yet."

"That is?" asked Mack.

"Is there a special someone in your life?"

Mack laughed, and the little squeal he gave before letting out a joyful sound reminded Gayle of her sister. It tugged at her heartstrings more than she expected.

"No," he finally said.

"Not even someone that you have a crush on?"

"Not even that, unfortunately."

"Don't wait too long, you know, increasing age of the father also increases the risk of some mental issues in the child. I read that somewhere; don't actually know whether this is true."

"I know."

"Of course, you do. It's just, I'll have to wait until my girls are old enough for grandkids, and I hope that's still a long time away, so you are my next-best chance."

"I'd love kids one day, but only with the right woman by my side."

Gayle was pleased to hear this. If he had inherited any of his mother's parental instincts, he would be a wonderful father. Eleanor had always wanted children and had gotten Mack sixteen years before Gayle had Inga. Unfortunately for her, Mack stayed her only child, and for this she had doted on him with all her heart.

They had reached the Treasury and stopped at the grand stairs to the hotel.

"Your mother loved you very much," Gayle said and looked at her nephew wistfully.

Mack only nodded.

"Do you have time to meet again tomorrow?" asked Gayle.

"Of course, I do. What would you like to do?"

"I'd like to see the ocean, but if this is too much, I'll settle for dinner again."

"I'll pick you up at ten in the morning."

They hugged goodnight and were interrupted by a group of chattering businesspeople who walked up the steps.

Gayle noticed Mack throwing a glance at the only woman in their midst, as she swished her shiny black hair over her shoulder and smiled at her companions. They would make a nice couple, she thought.

In the middle of the night, Gayle had another encounter with the businesswoman, though not as she had imagined earlier. She got woken up by loud knocking on the neighbouring door and a drunken male voice demanding entry.

"Marsha. Marsha, are y'awake?" Gayle heard a loud whisper from outside. "C'mon, open up. I know you're awake."

Gayle heard a door open.

"Go to bed, Peter," a female voice answered.

"Oh, c'mon. We're having so much fun, let's have summore."

"Go to bed, Peter."

"A'right."

"Your own bed."

Gayle heard a dull bang, as if Peter had headbutted the door, and decided that her neighbour might need some support. She opened her door and stuck her head out.

"Everything all right?" she asked and recognised the pretty businesswoman with the black hair. "Do you want me to call security?"

Marsha looked at Peter.

"A'right, a'right. We're all goin' to, to 'r own beds," said Peter and staggered down the corridor.

"Thank you," said Marsha, and Gayle noticed how her composed attitude faltered.

"No worries. Don't open up again," said Gayle.

"I won't." Marsha smiled, tired. "Sorry for the disturbance."

* * *

In a different hotel, thousands of kilometres away, Amy and Gabriel were making out in the elevator on the way up to their suite in Casablanca. It was their first proper night after they had arrived and rested from their jetlag. They had just had a romantic candlelight dinner in the warm breeze on the terrace and were in the right mood for some honeymooning. Gabriel's hand glided under Amy's blouse, and she giggled. The elevator doors opened, and she stepped away from him, teasing him with her eyes to follow. Gabriel did not have to be asked twice. They continued kissing all along the corridor, and Gabriel pinned her against their door while fumbling to open it with his fingerprint.

Suddenly, the door opened, and Amy fell backwards into the arms of another guest.

"What on earth?" said the man who managed to catch Amy before she hit the ground.

"Oh my God, I'm so sorry." Amy jumped back up, and they realized that they had been leaning against the neighbouring door.

"So sorry, sir. Won't happen again," said Gabriel.

The neighbour nodded, still slightly irritated, and then recognized Gabriel. "Hey, aren't you the Mars astronaut?"

"Yeah, but don't tell anyone. My wife's already getting annoyed." Gabriel winked.

"Sure, sure. Hey would you mind. Just one sec."

The neighbour disappeared and came back with his wife in tow and a phone in his hand. After Gabriel had taken multiple pictures with the man and his wife in various poses, Amy had enough of waiting and entered their suite alone.

She opened the terrace doors and stepped outside. The wind billowed the silk curtains, and the full moon shone across the sea, a view she had already admired last night when she couldn't sleep. The peaceful atmosphere calmed her, yet there were still misgivings that all this attention that Gabriel got from total strangers always had to happen at the most inconvenient times. She had indicated her annoyance about it over dinner, and it frustrated her that he had to mention it to their neighbour in exactly the situation that she had tried to explain to him.

Gabriel stepped behind her and nuzzled her neck.

"Are you all right?" he asked.

"Yes."

It was not worth her while bringing her disappointment up again. How could she be mad at him, when he gave her all this? Eventually, his fame would fade, and they would look back and laugh about how crazy people reacted in the face of someone famous.

Amy leaned into Gabriel and reciprocated his caressing. They gasped in desire, their hearts beating loud, when Gabriel took her hand and led her to their fourposter bed, where the hotel staff had folded two swans out of white towels and spread a heart of rose petals around them.

They made love for a long time, and Amy watched Gabriel's face in the moonlight when he climaxed. Even though she did not come, it was arousing and satisfying to simply feel so desirable and close to someone else who took such intense pleasure in being with her.

Gabriel rolled onto his back and took Amy into his arms.

"Maybe we just made a baby," Amy said, and the thought filled her with happiness.

"Maybe." Gabriel pulled her in tighter.

She knew he wanted children just as much as she did, and falling pregnant during their honeymoon seemed like the most romantic thing that could happen.

"What name would you pick if it's a boy?" she asked.

"Michael, like my father and the archangel who weighs people's souls and defends God," he said without hesitation.

"And what if it's a girl?"

"Priscilla, after my grandmother."

Amy lifted her head to look up at Gabriel. "What about my mother's name?"

"Are you serious? A strong Christian name with a meaning, or Kelly-May?"

Amy thought about her response carefully, as she did not want to spoil the mood, but she could not help but feel hurt. "What does it mean then?" she finally asked.

"It means 'ancient'. Priscilla was an important woman who spread the word of Jesus Christ, so much so that she is often named even before her husband, Aquila."

"I like that."

"What?"

"More important than her husband," teased Amy.

"Well, we're gonna have a boy anyways."

"As if that's your decision."

"A boy to carry on my family name."

"I don't mind, as long as it is healthy."

Amy was happy, at least a lot happier than in her previous relationships. She had always attracted men who sooner or later turned out to be utterly useless and sponged off her. Even if they had a job at first, which usually was some temp work, entrepreneurial or artistic, they quickly ended up with no income, moved in with Amy, and paid for neither rent nor food. Every time, she ended up moving, as she could not bring up the courage to draw a line and throw them out. Except for the last time that Miranda was there, when Billy shuffled through the kitchen in boxer shorts in the afternoon, scratched his butt crack, and then drank milk straight from the bottle. Amy had just told Miranda that she hated their relationship, and Miranda took the chance to start an argument, which led to Billy standing, still in his boxers, on the street, collecting his dirty laundry from the sidewalk as Miranda chucked them out the window.

Even now, Amy felt sorry for Billy, and she had had anxiety attacks for weeks, fearing that he would come back to take revenge. But Billy turned out to be even more timid than Amy, and she later heard that he had crashed with a friend and eventually moved to California.

Gabriel was the first man who had a decent job and treated her to things. He was organized and planned for the future, instead of letting it just happen to him. Amy felt secure and finally settled, even though she would have to move again when they returned from their honeymoon. But this time, it was not to leave a part of her life behind, but to take control of her life and amalgamate it with his.

Amy listened to her body and imagined how Gabriel's sperm was now on a life-changing, even life-making journey through her cervix and up her fallopian tubes to find the holy grail that was her ovum.

The next day, Gabriel had booked an excursion into the desert. They would be dune cruising on quad bikes, but Amy had never driven a car in her life, much like most urban dwellers. She would have much rather ridden a camel than straddling this engine between her legs. She was also sure to remember stories about accidents where quads flipped over and squashed their riders, back when these vehicles were still modern. Their safety had not much improved over the last decades and Amy feared that this 'exciting' honeymoon adventure might well turn out to be a death trap. The headline of 'Newlywed bride killed by antiquated quad bike' looped in her head as she crept up a shallow dune.

"Come on, Ames! You have to give it more speed! You look like a granny on her mobility scooter!" shouted Gabriel from the top of the dune where he and their guide waited for her.

Unlike Amy and most other people in this day and age, he had learned to drive a car during his training in the army and enjoyed the thrill of speed and the unrestrained vastness of the desert to live out this excitement.

"But I don't want to. I am happy with my speed!" shouted Amy.

Gabriel rolled his eyes and then scanned the dunes on the other side.

"Look at this. If you'd imagine only a third of the gravity, it almost looks like Mars. But then, there is nothing that could get close to the real thing," said Gabriel when Amy finally arrived next to him.

"I know the real thing, and you don't know nothing," muttered Amy, having forgotten her reservation in the face of, to her, imminent death.

"Why are you doing that?" asked Gabriel.

"Oh, I'm sorry. I didn't know it was the 'Mock-Amy-Day' today." She immediately wished she had held her tongue.

"If you want to have a temper tantrum, then don't have it in front of other people," reprimanded Gabriel. "You are embarrassing."

Amy stared stiffly at the ground like a petulant child. Gabriel pulled the keffiyeh over his nose and drove off, sand flying up high behind him.

For lunch, Gabriel had booked a table back at the hotel, though Amy would have liked to go to the harbour or try the food market for some local dishes.

"I think we'll have the steak," said Gabriel. "And a bottle of the Merlot."

"Actually, I would like to try the tagine." Amy noticed Gabriel's surprised look but chose to ignore him. "What wine do you recommend with it?"

"I can highly recommend the Rioja," answered the waiter.

"I'll have a glass of that," said Amy happily.

"Is it still a bottle of Merlot for the gentleman?" enquired the waiter.

"No. Just a glass as well," answered Gabriel after another measuring look at Amy.

This was the beginning of the end of their happy honeymoon. Gabriel had planned their schedule and meals like a military operation, including daily sessions at the hotel gym, and Amy torpedoed most of them by simply suggesting alternatives. When they departed at the end of the week, Gabriel was livid.

"I'm sorry. I didn't mean to upset you," begged Amy.

"Really? It seemed you set out to ruin our whole honeymoon."

Gabriel thumbed a receipt for their in-house expenses and pushed the device back to the receptionist.

Amy mouthed a silent 'I'm sorry' to her, before following Gabriel through the lobby.

"You didn't like the food I ordered, you didn't like the excursions I planned. I'm surprised that you didn't complain about the destination I picked."

"I liked the food and the excursions, it's just … I would have liked some … other things every now and then." Amy tried to find the right words to soothe Gabriel.

Gabriel watched the porter loading their bags into a pod, ignoring Amy, who tried to catch his eye and hoped for a glimmer of settlement.

"Look, I loved everything that you did for me, but a marriage is about giving and taking. We need to …"

Gabriel got into the front seat of the pod without waiting for her to finish. "Exactly, and I'm always giving, whereas you're just taking, taking, taking." Gabriel slammed the door of the pod closed, leaving Amy close to tears.

"That's not fair," she whispered.

CHAPTER 7

James had returned to Khartoum after two blissful weeks at home that went by far too quickly. He and Jeanette had soaked in each other's company and simply enjoyed sitting next to each other, reading to their hearts' delight, or going for hikes and mountain bike rides around the many maintained preservation areas in Louisiana. For a few days, the thought started to manifest to look for work closer to home, but there were regions in the world that needed his support much more urgently.

At least his work at the hospital of the capital of North Sudan was quiet and not such a stark contrast to his own family life, as the war zone of Somalia had been. Only last year, he was setting bones, stitching deep lacerations where possible, and if that were impossible, taking off whole limbs. Here, his work was very much that of a general practitioner, looking after minor injuries, prescribing medicine for ear infections or birth control to women who most often already had a bunch of children at home, though increasingly often, also young women who were at the forefront of female liberation requested contraceptives.

So, it was not surprising to him to have Rashaad and Subin Suliman enter his little treatment room on his first day back at work. The couple were in their mid-thirties and Mrs. Suliman was already on record for having received iron supplements during a pregnancy four years ago. She wore a modest skirt and long-sleeved shirt, which covered her legs and arms, but their patterns of brown and yellow spirals in combination with a short, flaming-orange thobe wrapped loosely around her head and shoulders showed that she was a modern woman acknowledging the traditions of this country.

Mr. Suliman wore some, in comparison, very boring beige chinos and a blue shirt and was probably working in an office job.

Why was it that men's fashion all around the world was always so boring and forgettable?

"Have a seat. What can I do for you?" James asked pleasantly, as he glanced at his records.

"We have come to you to enquire about contraception. Allah has already blessed us with three sons, and we are eternally grateful for it, but we want to be able to pay justice to his gifts," answered Rashaad.

James did not need an explanation why people decided against having more children, or children in general. Since his first international mission as a young military doctor, he was so shocked by the suffering of the children in war zones, that he was convinced that he would break if ever something happened to a child of his own. These children lived through the trauma of losing their parents, being raped, or kidnapped by marauding criminals, or mutilated by treacherous weapons. And even if they did not suffer physically, the hell that is the sound of guns, the howling of hurting people, or simply the deathly silence of night after an attack was more than enough to drive most people crazy. Instead of having children of his own, he vowed to try to help others, thinking that it would be easier to detach from their horrible fates if it wasn't his own family.

"Of course. There are several options," James explained. "Condoms not only prevent pregnancies in ninety-eight percent of the cases but also provide a good protection against STDs."

"What are STDs?" asked Subin.

"Sexually transmitted diseases like chlamydia, gonorrhoea or HIV," clarified James, and the faces of his visitors showed that they did not need to hear any more.

So, he continued, as was his duty, to list all the available contraceptives with their benefits and side effects.

"I think we would like to take the implant," said Subin in the end.

"Of course. For the records, have you taken any hormonal birth control at some point in the past?"

"No."

"Do you have any abdominal pain, unusual vaginal discharge or bleeding, or do you suspect that you have a sexually transmitted disease?"

"No," said Subin, and James was happy to see that she answered his questions with confidence.

"Do you wish an examination?" he asked lastly.

Here, Subin cast a glance at her husband, who indicated that it was her decision.

"No," Subin said firmly.

James filled in a form. "Take this to the nurse. She will insert the implant here under your arm." James pointed to the underside of his upper arm. "You will get a local anaesthetic and then you'll be good to go. Some women report that their periods stop completely, but mostly everything should continue as normal, only with a weaker period flow. If you experience anything like constant headaches or migraines, itching skin, or nausea, please come again and we will see whether a different product is more agreeable with you."

* * *

Rashaad and Subin left the doctor's office happy that everything went without complications. They had heard that some doctors asked highly personal questions or even tried to change their patients' decision, especially if a woman showed up without a husband. That was also why Rashaad had taken an hour off work to accompany Subin, even though they had made the decision together and he believed no woman should be asked for her reasons to request birth control.

Subin looked at him with her large brown eyes when the nurse set the implant. He knew she hated needles, and he smiled at her, showing a distance between his hands indicating that the needle was almost twenty centimetres long.

Subin shut her eyes, and he smirked.

"All done," said the nurse, and Subin looked at her in surprise.

The implant looked like a thin ridge under the skin, only visible when the arm was lifted. Subin got up and slapped Rashaad across the arm for his prank.

"You know I hate needles," she said.

"I do, I'm sorry," said Rashaad and grinned even wider.

He offered his arm, and after a scornful look, she hooked her arm in, and they left the hospital.

They walked to a bus stop and waited on the side of the bustling road. Some rock pigeons were performing their mating dance on the sidewalk. The males billowed their iridescent necks, bobbing back and forth to impress more slender females. Street kids were selling water bottles and fruits to people stuck in the traffic jam, and a group of women in hijabs slalomed through the waiting cars towards an air-conditioned mall. Electric cars were still rare in Khartoum, and most people had not even heard of driverless vehicles, so the streets were clogged day and night, and the car fumes polluted the air.

"Are we doing the right thing?" whispered Subin, though no one would have heard their conversation over the street noise anyway.

"We have three healthy boys, it would be foolhardy to ask for more," answered Rashaad. "But I only want you to be happy."

"I am," said Subin.

He had answered what was in his heart but left out the corner where his own doubts were living. He truly only wanted her to be happy.

The bus finally stuttered to a halt, and Subin got on.

"I'll see you tonight," called Rashaad and waved at her as she walked to a seat in the back.

Several soldiers with duffel bags got on the bus as well, and Rashaad was uncertain whether this reassured him of his wife's safety or whether it made it more likely that a conflict would break out.

Sudan had now enjoyed almost a decade without fights, and the presence of soldiers had become rarer. But he had not forgotten the never-ending snapping of automatic guns or the whistle of flying bombs that had destroyed his hometown and killed several of his family members. And even after the war had officially stopped, the destruction and poor living conditions had claimed many more lives.

As he walked along the street back to work, he thought that his sons had never experienced any of it, yet they had a predilection for pretending to wield weapons and killing each other. He wondered whether this was just a boy thing or whether the aftermath of the war was still so present in people's heads that it penetrated to the next generation without them even realizing it. He hoped, he wished with all his heart, that he was able to raise these three boys to become peaceful men who respected life and treated everyone as equal.

* * *

Some seven thousand kilometres north of Khartoum in Brussels, Gayle Hamilton's children had other topics on their minds. Hazel chatted to her friends during the break between classes. The teenagers were showing off their budding figures in clothes that were way too short for the late-spring temperatures in Belgium, but to them they were the height of fashion. Plus, to their logic, freezing a little bit only meant that you burnt more calories to keep warm and stayed thin as a side effect.

"I wish my dad would take me to Greece. We only ever go to the Bretagne, every freakin' year," said Arina, as they compared their tans and Hazel won the contest by a long shot. "All I got was a birth-control implant."

"You already got it?" asked Hazel.

"Yeah, dummy, it was your mum who made the law."

"Don't you have one yet?" asked Tamara.

"Not yet ... My mum has so much to do that we haven't had time to go to the doctor's," answered Hazel, uncomfortably.

It was true that her mother was busy, even more so since she came back from her trip around the world a couple of weeks ago. Still, she usually found time to bring them to the dentist or attend sports competitions, and if not, then she arranged for Guillaume, her private assistant, to accompany them to any appointments. But for whatever reason, her mother had not yet bothered to get implants for Hazel or her sister.

"Can't your mum get the doctor to come to your house?" asked Arina.

"I don't know," answered Hazel.

She found it over the top; after all, they were not some super-famous family that could not walk around without people trailing them.

"My mum was, like, so upset when we had to go to the doctor's that she wouldn't stop cursing the poor man to hell. It was, like, so embarrassing," continued Arina.

"I'm sorry," said Hazel, as she felt responsible by proxy for Arina's hassle.

"It's okay, I mean, as long as those hoboes do the same. I mean, it's them your mum wants to stop from, like, reproducing and such. At least that's what my dad always says."

Hazel was confused, as she did not think that this was her mum's intention, although she was not exactly sure what they were and whether she agreed with them. "Did it hurt?" she asked instead.

"So much. The needle was like ... like as thick as a straw," exaggerated Arina.

"I thought it wasn't that bad. I mean, they numbed it before and all," said Tamara.

"Maybe I'm just more sensitive than you," Arina shot back, but Tamara just shrugged off the little jab.

"Can you feel it under your skin?" asked Hazel.

She was curious about these things. Needles, blood, and the inside of the human body were fascinating to her, and she had started to form an idea of becoming a plastic surgeon. Not because of the money and to give women bigger boobs, but because she wanted to help people who got burned or attacked by a dog. In riding camp, there was once a girl who had lost an eye from a firework that some dumbass had shot from their hand and then ricocheted from the house walls. She had been fascinated by that girl and her glass eye all summer.

Arina felt her arm for the implant. "Yes, there it is. Ouch."

In another corner of the schoolyard, behind some shrubs not far away from Hazel and her friends, hid Inga with her boyfriend Mark. They were snogging as if there was no tomorrow, or at least as much as they could before a teacher found them.

"D'you wanna come around tonight?" asked Inga, as Mark released her mouth and continued with her neck.

"What about your mum?" asked Mark between kisses. "I thought she's back from her trip."

"She is, but I could really need some help with homework," teased Inga.

Mark stopped his caressing. "For real?"

"Yes, and I think you've got the right equipment for it," said Inga as her hand wandered between his legs.

"Oh."

Hazel lounged on their big white sofa at home and watched a history documentary about the COVID-19 pandemic that crashed the world economy some thirty years ago. She was odd in this way for a thirteen-year-old. Her friends and sister watched series or movies about characters their own age, only in ridiculously kitsch scenarios, and the worst part of it was that they swooned over them and truly wished for their lives to be like that too. Hazel preferred the daily news, history documentaries, or at least fantasy movies, so she could dream about riding a dragon. And if she was not going to become a plastic surgeon, she thought about a career in politics like her mother.

"I'm home! Who wants some ice cream?" Hazel heard her mother shout from the hall.

"Me!" Hazel jumped up from her cosy spot and danced to the kitchen.

Gayle was unpacking shopping bags. As was their tradition, she bought treats every Friday, and they had a family splurge sitting on the living room floor, talking about their week and plans for the weekend.

"Ah, luring the sweet tooth," said Gayle when Hazel came in.

"What did you buy?" asked Hazel.

"Belgian vanilla."

Gayle placed a large bucket of ice cream on the counter, and Hazel fetched some bowls and spoons.

"Where is Inga?" asked Gayle.

"Upstairs, with Mark," said Hazel.

"Mark is here? Since when?" asked Gayle, trying to sound aloof.

"Don't know," said Hazel, scooping ice cream into the bowls.

Gayle finished unpacking, but her ears were sharpened, trying to hear any suspicious noise from upstairs. She had expected a situation like this for a while and wanted to be a cool mum who would not make a scene. She had 'the talk' with both her daughters, informed them about birth control and their right to say no, and she trusted her daughters to make the right decisions. Still, she took a couple of deep breaths as she climbed the stairs.

She hesitated in front of Inga's closed door and then reminded herself that eavesdropping was a sign of distrust.

"Inga? Would you like some ice cream?" Gayle knocked on the door but did not open it.

"Yes, what did you buy?" said Inga from inside. Gayle could also hear the rustling of some bedsheets.

"Belgian vanilla."

"Coming."

"And Mark, should you want some ice cream too, you are welcome to come down," she added, and smiled as she imagined their embarrassed faces behind the door.

Inga opened the door, and an uncomfortable but clothed Mark stood behind her. "Hi, Ms. Hamilton."

"Hello, Mark. Are you going to stay for dinner?" asked Gayle. At least they are both still dressed, thought Gayle, relieved.

Mark looked at Inga quizzically. "I think I should go," he finally said.

"Do you want me to call you a pod or drive you home?" asked Gayle.

"Mum! don't be so embarrassing," interrupted Inga.

"I just want your boyfriend to be safe," responded Gayle with playful indignation.

"Thanks Ms. Hamilton, but I'm here with my bike," answered Mark as he followed Inga down the stairs.

From the top of the stairs, Gayle saw for the first time her oldest daughter kissing her boyfriend goodbye.

"See you at school?" asked Mark.

"Yep."

"Good night, Ms. Hamilton." Mark waved as Gayle walked down the steps.

"Good night, Mark."

He was a good kid and Gayle was glad that Inga had not brought home a tattooed bodybuilder who was several years her senior. She would have had a tough time keeping her cool. Yet even with Mark, she could not shake her worries that came with knowing what teenagers in full puberty were most likely getting up to, given the chance.

"What have I told you about having boys over?" she asked when Mark was gone.

"We weren't alone," sulked Inga.

"Hazel on the sofa downstairs doesn't count." Gayle followed Inga into the living room, where Hazel was watching the evening news with a big bowl of ice cream.

"Not a step further, young lady. I want you to stay downstairs if Mark comes over, do you hear me? Especially when I'm not here." There it was. Gayle had come out with her first 'young lady' speech, and it was not well received.

"Mum!"

"Don't *Mum* me." There was no backing down now. "I am the minister for family and health in Europe, and that does not mean that I promote becoming a grand-mother by my teenage daughter!"

"We weren't doing anything."

"Maybe not today, but I know how one thing can lead to another, and I do not say that I don't believe you, just that I know what can happen."

Inga slumped onto the sofa and grabbed the bowl of ice cream that Hazel handed her.

"Then why don't you enforce your contraception bill onto your teenage daughters?" asked Inga.

"Because I trust you to not be as stupid as so many other teenagers," responded Gayle.

"What about all the other mothers who trust their daughters?" asked Hazel.

Gayle stared from her elder to her younger daughter. This was not going as she had anticipated. She knew that she should have been one of the first to get her daughters protected, as per her bill, and to be a role model. But she had been terribly busy in the last few months, and this type of doctor's visit was something she did not want to ask Guillaume to handle.

Deep down, though, she knew that her own struggle with side effects from the pill when she was a teenager contributed to her delay. Even back then, the dosage of hormonal birth control was much lower than when the pill first came to the market in the 1960s. And yet there still had been plenty of women complaining about headaches or mood swings, itching legs, or weight gain, not to mention the possible long-term effects like high blood pressure or deadly blood clots. And it was these long-term or deadly side effects that Gayle was particularly worried about for her daughters.

Hormonal contraceptives had come a long way, Gayle knew. She also knew that it was wrong and self-ish to force everyone else to subordinate to the new law and request an exception for her own family based on her own judgement. The law did circumvent the people's free will, and she had already felt the pushback including death threats. But it was for the greater good of the populace, who in this case needed to be reined in.

Gayle went to the kitchen to make herself an iced coffee. Eventually, her girls would need to get contraceptive implants, and even though she preferred later, sooner was probably better, as it could only be a matter of time until someone found out that she had not followed her own law.

CHAPTER 8

Veronica waited anxiously in a small café for Cecilia to arrive. She had dressed up nicely, put her hair back, just as Cecilia liked it, and put on her leather jacket she had worn when they first met. The jacket was too tight to close now, but that was all right, as it concealed her eight-month baby belly as long as she remained seated. She was nervous about seeing her after almost three months of no contact. Jeanette had told her that she had sent an email to Cecilia and received an answer that gave reason for hope, but it had still taken another week until Veronica received a message asking to meet up.

It was a café she had never frequented before, so she arrived fifteen minutes early to get comfortable. She wondered what it meant that Cecilia had suggested an unknown location and worried that it might fore-shadow that she wanted to leave their old life and their relationship behind.

The moment Cecilia entered the café, Veronica's world halted. Life had been dragging without her in it, despite the flurry of doctor appointments and moving back in with her mother. And now it had come to a full stop to acknowledge the bright light that had returned.

Veronica gave a small wave to attract Cecilia's atten-tion, which caused her jacket to open. She noticed that Cecilia looked at her bump and tried to cover it back up. If she turned away, she might well die.

"Hi," Veronica said, relieved as Cecilia sat down.

Cecilia studied her face. "How have you been?"

"Good. Well, that's not true. Let me start again," Veronica struggled. "Not so good, actually."

"You look good," said Cecilia, and Veronica noticed a mild smile.

They ordered a peppermint tea and a black coffee.

"Peppermint tea, huh?" asked Cecilia.

"I'm not supposed to drink coffee at the moment."

"Sounds like torture," laughed Cecilia.

"It is. Wait until you've tried raspberry-leaf tea," chuckled Veronica nervously, only to turn serious again. "I'm so sorry."

"Me too," said Cecilia after their short happy interlude. "I phoned your commander, Jeanette. And … and I wanted to say that I believe you."

This was too much for Veronica's hormone-riddled self, and she broke down crying uncontrollably. She wished this breaking of the dams had happened at home and not so publicly. But this single sentence from the love of her life had torn down any and all walls she had built over the last few months to survive this terrifying situation.

Cecilia switched seats to take her into her arms, and Veronica finally felt safe again.

"Is everything all right?" asked the server who had brought their drinks.

"Yes, yes. Hormones, first time expecting," Cecilia explained, trying to lighten the mood by hand-signalling that Veronica's pregnancy had made her a little cuckoo.

"Ah, I understand. Let me know if you need anything. The toilets are over there, if it gives you a low kick."

"This is so embarrassing. What now?" asked Veronica, when they were alone again, and she dared to show her face.

"I think we should look for a larger flat. You don't look like we have much time," answered Cecilia.

"Really?" Veronica was overwhelmed.

"I had some time to think things through, and I'm sorry for how I reacted. It's just, I don't think anyone has ever been in a situation like this before."

"Probably not."

"I didn't know what to think. I always believed you, and yet the whole thing is unbelievable."

"I know."

"And I realized how much I love you. And, and that I don't want to be apart, ever, and that I was a complete moron ..."

Veronica stopped Cecilia's self-punishment by closing her lips with a kiss. The world around them started to spin, and time finally moved forward again.

"Ow!" Cecilia exclaimed. "It kicked me."

They had been so close that Cecilia had felt the baby kicking in Veronica's tummy.

"I think she just said, welcome back," said Veronica.

She took Cecilia's hands and placed them on her belly. She loved watching Cecilia's face as she experienced for the first time the freakishness of a living baby moving around inside the uterus.

"This is so weird. Amazing, but weird. You know, I always thought that, if we had children, I would be the one who ..."

"I know. And believe me I would give it to you in a heartbeat, but I guess transplanting babies at this stage is not a thing yet."

"That bad, huh?" frowned Cecilia.

"I don't want to put you off, it's actually quite all right, but nothing I needed to experience."

"Have you decided on a name yet?" Cecilia asked.

"No. It's still too unreal to me," said Veronica.

"Well, I'd say that's pretty real. She's got a kick like her mother. We can take her to twilight soccer."

"I think it's actually her butt that she's stretching out right now."

"Oh. Well." Veronica laughed about Cecilia's perplexed face.

They had their drinks and chatted about the last three months as well as about Veronica's trip to Mars, which they had not had the chance to talk about so far. Cecilia listened fascinated when Veronica told her about her space walk on Mars, how she and Gabriel took soil samples, and how the equipment was so light with only a third of Earth's gravity that Gabriel had singlehandedly thrown a hundred-kilo freezer box into the storage compartment of their space capsule. Unfortunately, that had loosened a connection of the temperature regulator, and Phillip Schuster had to squeeze into the compartment on their way back to fix it, as the alarm kept on coming on whenever Fjodorow activated the thrusters to adjust their direction.

"Are you going to find out who the father is?" asked Cecilia.

"Yes, I think so," answered Veronica.

"And then?"

"I don't know. Probably nothing. I don't think whatever happened up there can be considered a crime, and the father will be just as shocked as we were."

Cecilia nodded. "I hope it's that Russian."

"Fjodorow?"

"Yes. He sounds like fun. Like someone who'd be okay to have around, if he wanted to get involved. Not so stuck up like the German or like this Gabriel. God, have you seen his interviews?"

"Yes. It'd be a shock to his wife too if he's the father. They recently got married."

"Bet she's just like him."

"I don't know; she seemed pretty normal."

"You met her?"

"I was at their wedding."

"Oh."

"But enough of that. I don't want to think about it," said Veronica. "Where do you think we should live?"

Right there and then, they started to look for suitable properties and quickly narrowed it down to an area near Veronica's mother. Her mother had already started to look forward to her daughter and granddaughter living with her and would most likely be disappointed that her plans were thrown out at such short notice. Veronica also wanted outdoor space to grow some vegetables, and they would need two bedrooms so that when the baby was old enough, she could move into her own nursery. This did not leave them with many options, even though most apartment buildings had now been fitted with small balconies to allow people to be more self-sufficient and reduce the environmental footprint of large-scale food production. They contacted the agents of five flats with balconies or communal gardens and got a response from two of them while they were on their second peppermint tea and coffee, respectively.

They arranged viewings for the weekend, and Cecilia walked Veronica home.

"I'd ask you up for a coffee, but I can think of several reasons why this might be awkward right now," joked Veronica.

"I shall see you tomorrow," said Cecilia. "We have lots to do. And I shall see you in a few weeks." Cecilia stroked Veronica's belly.

"Oh, just a sec." Veronica searched through her phone and sent Cecilia some ultrasound photos. "I know it looks like an alien, but I thought you'd like them."

"She's beautiful. Just like her mother."

They kissed goodbye, and Veronica walked up to the third floor, where her mother lived.

It took longer for her to climb the steps since she had hit the last month of her pregnancy, and when she arrived out of breath, her mother was already waiting for her in the door.

"How was it?" asked Mrs. Hernandez.

Veronica stopped a few steps short and smiled at her. "All good."

"Come in, tell me. I made you a raspberry-leaf tea," her mother waved.

It was a whole pot of tea, and Veronica told her mother everything about her reunion, between sipping the tea and visiting the bathroom to relieve her strained bladder.

Mrs. Hernandez could not help but shed some tears when she heard that they would move back in together, just as Veronica had expected. But then she came out with some news that was the perfect solution.

"Do you remember Mr. Summer from below? He died two weeks ago," she started.

"Yes, the police were here," Veronica said.

"I got in touch with the landlord, and apparently the flat is currently being renovated, and he's looking for new tenants as soon as possible. I know it's a little bit spooky to live where someone has died, but it would be so convenient and, well, you'd still be close."

"That's, that ..." Veronica was not sure what to say. She agreed that it would be very convenient, and she knew that the flat had a balcony, access to the communal garden in the yard, and maybe they could keep the beehive that Mr. Summer had established on the rooftop. But she was not sure what Cecilia would say to it. "Let me quickly call Ceci."

She left the room to phone Cecilia from her old bedroom whilst Mrs. Hernandez took the dishes to the kitchen.

"We think it is a great idea," said Veronica when she came back.

"*Que Dios te bendiga!*" exclaimed Mrs. Hernandez and shed tears for the second time. "I will call the landlord right away."

Now it was Mrs. Hernandez who scuttled out with her phone.

Veronica looked into the backyard and the vegetable garden, where each inhabitant of the block had a few square metres to grow crops. She wondered which patch Mr. Summer's was and thought that she would plant some carrots and potatoes first.

Everything fell wonderfully into place. The next day, they inspected the flat, it was the same size as her mother's, only mirrored, as it lay on the opposite side. Two bedrooms, a small living room, kitchen, and bath. One of the bedrooms was freshly painted and a new carpet put in, and although they signed the lease in the afternoon, they decided to wait with the move for at least a week, to allow the potentially toxic fumes of the paint and glue to dissipate. Mrs. Hernandez also wanted to sprinkle some holy water around, to make sure that Mr. Summer's spirit was well and truly sent off to the Promised Land.

In the meantime, they went shopping, and Veronica finally allowed herself to get all the cute onesies, frilly headbands, tiny shoes, and soft toys that the shops had to offer. They inspected baby furniture, bought a cot that could transition to a toddler bed, a pram that was easy to manoeuvre with one hand and that most importantly had a cupholder for when Veronica could drink coffee again.

Indeed, everything was perfect, albeit at the last minute.

* * *

On the other side of Orlando, Amy was also moving. They had found a small townhouse in a gated community outside Titusville. The community had been established less than ten years ago, and building sites were still for sale, but houses went up slowly. A lot of people were discouraged by the proximity to the ocean and the landslide that had recently happened in Cocoa West, where the dikes had disintegrated. The coast was still a ten-minute drive away, but too many properties had been abandoned due to the rising sea level and the slow but steady erosion of land, despite large efforts of building embankments.

It was a quiet neighbourhood, and Amy was unsure whether she would feel comfortable there, but Gabriel had ensured her that they could move, should they not like it. For now, though it was a good distance to his work, and Amy could finally have the chickens she always wanted, once they had built a chicken coop. Moreover, it was child friendly, with a large adventure playground and swimming pool at the centre of the compound. It also looked like Amy could start a part-time job at the community day-care centre, though Gabriel had told her multiple times that she needn't work at all, as he was making more than enough money. They had even merged their bank accounts so that Amy could access more money to run their household. At first, Amy had found it funny when Gabriel spoke about 'their household'. She was not a Victorian housewife, but when she realized how much Gabriel ate due to his rigorous workouts and how much laundry she now had to do, she was glad that it was coming mainly out of his pocket.

Her departure from her old childcare facility was heart wrenching. It had been a perfect fit; she got along with her co-workers, the director was very understanding and had insured that any pregnant carer could take paid parental leave of three months or six months on part time pay, and Amy had already counted on that for when she had a baby. The children had each drawn her pictures, and several cried when they understood that Amy was not coming back the next week.

The day-care centre at the compound looked bright and modern but seemed to lack space for children to get dirty or experience the world with all their senses. Amy always thought that a child learned best through trial and error, and for this they needed a variety of stimulation, which nature provided free of charge. In fact, the cleanliness had reminded Amy on the NASA quarantine facility, where walls could be hosed down and harsh chemicals used from top to bottom.

Now, Amy stood in the doorframe of the little room next to their new bedroom and gazed into the distance.

"What are you thinking about?" asked Gabriel as he wrapped his arms around her belly.

"I think this would be the best spot for a cot." She pointed at the centre of the opposite wall. "Not right under the window, in case there is a draft, but also not in the corner, so that it gets plenty of natural light."

"Maybe we can paint it some colour or even a mural with animals or a jungle," suggested Gabriel.

"Are you gonna do that?" asked Amy with a smile.

"God, the kid would be scarred for life if I did it."

"A soft peach would be nice for a start," said Amy.

"What if it's a boy?"

"It's not blue or pink. Peach would resemble the colour that a baby can see in the womb through the layers of blood and fat. I think it might be soothing for a newborn."

Gabriel contemplated this silently.

"I got my period this morning," continued Amy.

Gabriel held her for a couple of heartbeats but then left her without another word. He always had trouble expressing any vulnerable feelings.

A tear rolled down Amy's cheek. It would have been perfect if she had fallen pregnant on their honeymoon, but she knew it could take months to conceive, even for young and healthy couples like them. Still, she was gutted when she saw the pink colour on the toilet paper in the morning. Experiencing Gabriel's quiet disappointment now made her sad and doubting whether everything was all right with her body.

She walked to the window overlooking the small garden, thinking that they should buy some curtains and a fly net.

The next day, Miranda came around to have her own little inspection of Amy's new abode.

"So, it took thirty-five minutes with a pod, off-peak, on a weekday. Not bad. Let's see the rest," she demanded.

Miranda had been able to come by on a Friday, as she had stopped working in her hair salon. The potentially toxic fumes from those new everlasting hair dyes and her swelling ankles had put a stop to it. But it was her salon, and she was the boss, so she could do whatever she wanted. She had hired in a new hairdresser as soon as she found out she was pregnant again, and his talent for textured razor cuts eased Miranda's decision to leave work earlier this time around.

Amy showed her around the kitchen, toilet, and living room downstairs and the two bedrooms and the bathroom upstairs.

"Is this one of those loos that tell you whether your poo is too mushy or if you'll die soon from a heart attack?" she asked, as she test-sat on the toilet seat.

"I don't think any toilet does that," laughed Amy.

"In Japan they do."

"They might tell you whether you have a deficiency or too much sugar in your urine."

"See, and that's a sign for diabetes."

"All right, all right, but I don't think we have those," surrendered Amy.

"I better test it," said Miranda.

"I'm sure these are just normal …"

"Shh, out, I just really need to pee. This baby is gonna be a drummer, I tell ya."

Amy understood as Miranda pulled down her undies and she left the bathroom.

She wandered around the living room, but until their furniture got delivered, there was no point unpacking any of the boxes.

"Hey, wouldn't it be cool if your loo could tell you whether you are pregnant?" said Miranda when she finally came back downstairs. "I mean, instead of doing this," here she squatted and pretended to hold a pregnancy test between her legs, "you could just elegantly take a piss, and then a nice voice would tell you, 'Milady, you are knocked up'. Speaking of which?"

"Nope, unfortunately not," answered Amy.

"Ow. You better hurry, I want to push prams together."

"It was our first cycle, a miracle if it had worked right away."

"I know, I know. No pressure. Stress is the mother of all … whatever. But let me tell you this: once you have a bun in the oven, alcohol is off limits, but until then, a nice glass of red wine to relax and then some foreplay to make it all …"

"Miranda!"

"Too much?"

"Little bit."

"Sorry. Okay, let's see the garden, make sure there are no hazards lurking in those well-trimmed bushes outside."

It didn't take long to show Miranda around the garden, as there were only a few newly planted hedges and soft green grass. Amy grabbed a blanket out of a box, and they sat down in the sunshine to talk about movie night at Harry P's in a couple of weeks, where they would be showing the Korean film *Parasite*. Miranda was a huge fan of Korean and Japanese film culture, and they were quickly wrapped up in a discussion about the differences between films from different countries. A fun thing they sometimes did was to pick a surprise movie that neither of them knew and watch the first ten minutes without sound. Whoever could pick the country of origin got to pick the next movie.

They were still in the garden chatting when Gabriel came home.

"Hi, Miranda," greeted Gabriel.

"Oh gosh, is it really that late?" said Miranda, and rolled sideways to get up.

"You look like a stranded whale," laughed Amy.

"You laugh now. This one's popped out much quicker. It's like having a second spine that bends in the other direction than yours. I know a lady who couldn't get out of her bathtub and was stuck for hours before her husband came home," Miranda said.

"Can I call you a pod?" asked Gabriel.

"That would be lovely, muffin," answered Miranda.

Gabriel looked confused at the endearment and left without another word.

"He seems grumpy," said Miranda.

"He didn't take it too well that I'm not pregnant," explained Amy.

"Sheesh, good things take time."

The pod arrived within five minutes, and when Amy turned back to the house after Miranda had left, she found that they definitely needed curtains, as she could see Gabriel moving around in their bedroom.

"Was she here all day?" asked Gabriel when Amy came back in, finding him pumping up an inflatable mattress.

"For about five hours."

"I expected that you would have unpacked some things, made the house liveable, but not even the mattress is inflated. Were you thinking of sleeping on the floor?"

"I'm sorry."

"I don't want her to be over all the time."

"She wanted to see our new house," said Amy.

"I don't care. She's not part of our family."

"Why don't you like her?" asked Amy.

"I never said I don't like her. I just don't like her interfering so much. First that song at our wedding without telling us ..."

"It was a surprise."

"And then you constantly hanging out with her, even ditching me for her."

"I never ditched you."

"And it only got worse since she doesn't work anymore."

"What do you want me to do?" Amy decided that Gabriel must have had a difficult day, and there was no point arguing about his unreasonable behaviour.

"I want you to take our relationship, our marriage, seriously."

"I am."

"I want you to keep your end of the bargain, and when I'm bringing in the money to pay for our life, I want you to at least spend your time making our life comfortable and not hang out with friends all the time."

"All right," agreed Amy, dismayed. She really could have prepared the mattress, and she was sure Gabriel would have appreciated some dinner.

"And what's this 'muffin'?"

Now, Amy had to smile. Gabriel hated it when people who were not in a relationship used pet names for others.

"I'll tell her not to call you 'muffin'."

Gabriel grunted and then tested the pressure of the mattress. Together they put bed linen and blankets on.

"How was your day?" asked Amy when Gabriel seemed to have calmed down.

"Good, I worked those new recruits hard. And NASA has announced another manned space mission next year."

"To Mars again?"

"No, that won't happen until the recent samples have been thoroughly researched. It's just some new engine testing for the space station."

"Are you going to apply?" asked Amy.

She knew how much Gabriel wanted to prove himself with another mission, show that he was not a one-hit wonder.

"Yep. I'll have to increase my training."

"When is the deadline?"

"In three months."

CHAPTER 9

Amy had just interviewed for the job at the day-care centre of the compound and was told that she could start the next week on a part-time basis. She was shown around the place and found everything clean and modern, but at the same time thought that she would try to send her own child somewhere else. Nonetheless, the children seemed happy, interacted with her pleasantly, and were interested, showing off their paintings and how they could shoot a ball from a toy cannon. Upon demonstrating this, the ball was promptly removed, but not before some joyful screams from the tiny crowd.

One child, little Poppy, immediately connected with Amy, and she felt her tiny hand in hers when she investigated the rubbered outdoor play area.

"Do you like it here?" Amy asked the slight girl.

Poppy nodded with big, happy eyes.

"Do you want to show me your favourite toy?"

Poppy nodded again, and Amy followed her to a dollhouse, where she picked up the mummy and daddy doll that had been left on the floor by the previous player.

For a while, Amy just watched Poppy play in silence. She was very timid and careful with both dolls, almost like she didn't know what to do with the two characters, yet she was very tenacious and obviously engrossed in her game. Still, something seemed off to Amy, although she couldn't quite place it.

"I think I should go," said Amy, when the call for lunch came, and Poppy's big eyes turned sad. "But I will be back next week, and we can play a bit more. Is that okay?" Poppy looked like she was thinking about this offer and finally nodded ever so slightly.

After this, she met up with Miranda in Orlando to shop for some baby clothes. Even though Miranda was expecting another boy who would simply wear Toby's old clothes, they both agreed that shopping for baby clothes was an enjoyable pastime.

"Why can't they make cute and affordable things for boys?" said Miranda as she was fingering a tutu for a new-born.

"Would that be practical for a tiny baby?" asked Amy.

"No, but still. Gray joggers and a blue checked shirt? My pops dresses better."

"Don't look. I think you were right." Amy pulled Miranda around the next clothes rack. "There is Veronica Vargas, the other spacewalker."

"Where?" asked Miranda. "See, I told you she was pregnant."

Veronica was also shopping with a friend, and she looked like she was about to pop, literally. Miranda and Amy were still ogling the other two women, when Veronica suddenly stopped and stared at the floor.

"I think I just peed my pants," they heard Veronica whisper.

Amy and Miranda looked at each other. "Thundercats are go," they said simultaneously and burst into giggles.

"Miranda, no," said Amy when Miranda pulled her towards Veronica and her friend.

"Hey, hi. Can we help you?" asked Miranda.

"I think we're okay," replied Veronica's friend whilst Veronica wrapped her jacket around her waist to cover up the growing wet patch on her trousers.

"Hi Veronica, it's me, Amy, Gabriel's wife." Amy was uncomfortable at meeting Veronica in such an embarrassing situation, at least for her, but she also felt obliged to introduce herself again, since Veronica had attended her wedding.

"Yeah, hi," responded Veronica.

"Look, I've been in the same situation before; well, I was at home, but still, my waters broke unexpectedly. Here, take this." Miranda pulled out an extra-large period pad from her bag and handed it to Veronica. "Go to the bathroom and check whether it's pee; it should smell like it. If there's blood, go straight to the hospital, if not and you are not experiencing any heavy contractions yet, go home, call your doctor, and relax," said Miranda.

"Thank you," said Veronica, stunned by the unexpected advice.

"Take care." And with that, Miranda tucked her arm under Amy's and wandered off.

"You sounded like a doctor," said Amy, astounded.

"Well, lots of ER series, and it's pretty much what the nurses told me on the phone when Toby made his entrance. Somehow, my brain backed up everything that was said that day and went blank for three months the next day."

Amy buzzed inside. Her thoughts were racing, and she swore her ovaries popped knowing that Veronica was having a baby anytime now. She could not wait to fall pregnant and cradle a baby of her own. She hoped for a boy that looked like Gabriel. A little clone to love just as much.

* * *

Veronica looked down at her wet pants. "I don't think it's pee. I can't stop it."

"Are you having contractions?" asked Cecilia.

"No. Let's put this pad in and then go home," said Veronica, looking around for a bathroom sign and a way to it without passing by any other shoppers.

It took them a few minutes to find a bathroom, and Veronica tried to walk as normally as possible, to not draw any more attention to her soaked pants.

"It doesn't smell of anything," said Veronica as she sat on the toilet trying to stick the pad to her wet underpants.

Cecilia bent down and sniffed. "At least there is no blood. Let's go. I ordered a pod."

Veronica had just washed her hands and adjusted the jacket around her waist when her entire belly painfully cramped.

"Oh, shoot!" Veronica exclaimed and held on to the sinks. "I think I'm having a contraction. And it bloody hurts."

"What do we do?" asked a panicked Cecilia.

Veronica focussed on her breathing. "I think it's gone. Let's go home and pick up the hospital bag."

"You sure?"

"Yeah. They said at the prenatal class that this can go on for a few hours and to come in when the contractions are five minutes apart."

They left the shop and looked for their pod. It was a busy Saturday, and it took them several minutes to find it. Veronica wished they would install screens that showed the name of the person who ordered it, instead of holding their phone to an ID pad, only to get a red lamp telling you that this one was not yours. But apparently that went against privacy laws. Why can't people put in a made-up name like Rapunzel?

Finally, they found their pod. It smoothly lined up into the street traffic when Veronica had another contraction.

"That's rather close together."

"Fuck!" Veronica exclaimed. "I knew it would hurt, but this is a whole new level. Gimme your hand so I can squash it."

"Hey, I didn't put it in there," said Cecilia, still dutifully letting her hand be squashed.

"Wrong timing."

"Sorry."

"I think it stopped again."

"Okay, let me get the contraction tracker started, cause this is freaking me out," said Cecilia as she fumbled with her phone.

"I'll call my mother to let her know that it's started … Hi, Mama. Yes, well, I have contractions … We're on our way home. Can you get the … ouch."

"Is that another one?" asked Cecilia and started the timer when Veronica nodded.

"No, Mama ... we're five minutes away ... It'll be fine ..." said Veronica in between deep breaths, trying to calm her mother, who, she could imagine, was now running through her flat like a headless chicken. Shouldn't Cecilia and her mother be calming her and not the other way around? "Okay, see you soon."

"Has it stopped?" asked Cecilia.

"Yes."

"Okay, that was fifty-five seconds. Is that good?"

"I don't know, but if it stays like this, I want to go to the hospital. I'm not putting up with this much longer."

"Really?"

Veronica looked at Cecilia in disbelief. Any woman who said they enjoyed this experience must be mad. "Yes. I really cannot recommend this experience."

"Think about the baby you will hold at the end of it."

"That distraction might have worked if I had wanted this baby." Veronica's heart sank for having made this comment. It was not the baby's fault, and she was determined to love it no matter what, but she still had not overcome the void surrounding its conception and the speed at which this new reality had been thrust upon her. "You were the one who wanted to go through with this."

"I know. And I would take the suffering from you in a heartbeat."

Veronica kissed Cecilia passionately, for it was her love that would get her through this.

They arrived, and Veronica's mother was already waiting for them on the pavement, purse in hand, a suitcase and a bag by her foot, and a backpack slung over her shoulder.

"Hey, Mama," said Veronica.

"*Mi querida*," said her mother and gave her a hug.

"You look like you're going on a survival trip," joked Veronica, who clung to her mother's shoulders as a new contraction folded her over.

"You never know how a birth might work out," responded Mrs. Hernandez, and whilst her mother's preparedness gave her some comfort, the idea that a birth could require provisions that could last an entire household for three days made her slightly freak out.

"Is this another one?" asked Cecilia, fumbling with her phone to get the timer started.

Did she really have to ask? What did it look like?

"That's only six minutes apart," said Cecilia.

"We best get to the hospital," said Veronica, again taking charge.

"Right," said Cecilia, turning around to their pod. "Hey, wait!" shouted Cecilia when the pod switched to 'occupied' and drove off.

A booking must have come in, and they had not indicated their need for continued transport quick enough.

"Oh, fuck!" exclaimed Cecilia.

"Watch your language. You're about to become a mother," reprimanded Mrs. Hernandez.

"I'm sorry. What do we do now?" asked Cecilia.

This was getting ridiculous. Cecilia was otherwise a street-smart woman, thinking on her feet, able to hack computers all around the world. But now, her brain functions seemed to have just gone on holiday.

"Just order another one," said Veronica, who was now circling her hips because in the prenatal class, this was suggested to move the baby's head into the best position to pass through the birth canal, but more importantly, moving around helped her release some anxiety.

Veronica had just endured another contraction when the new pod arrived and all three of them clambered in, including their luggage.

"The last contraction lasted for fifty-five seconds again and was five minutes and thirty-three seconds apart," explained Cecilia, scrolling through her records.

"Here, you should drink something. Your lips are already cracked," said Mrs. Hernandez, and she shoved a straw into Veronica's mouth. It was diluted orange juice.

"Can you call the maternity ward?" asked Veronica, pushing away the juice.

"What?"

"The maternity ward, so that they know we're coming." Why did everyone need directions from the one person who should be the centre of everyone's attention? But maybe she shouldn't be too hard on them. It's not like they went through this every day either.

It took them more than double the time to walk from the car park to the maternity ward, as Veronica had to stop three times to let a contraction pass. At least the admission process went smoothly; NASA had arranged for outstanding care that they would have otherwise not been able to afford, and before the next contraction could hit, the nurse reassured Veronica that her cervix was almost fully dilated, and it should be no more than an hour before she could start pushing.

An hour still seemed to be a long time, but by now she knew how many breaths she needed to take before a contraction would stop.

"It should stop now," said Cecilia, who was glued to her phone, still tracking her contractions.

"Could you just put your phone away now? I think we have established that I'm having a baby and you're missing all the fun," snapped Veronica.

"Sorry," mumbled Cecilia. "It just gave me something to do."

"I know," said Veronica, feeling sorry and at the same time happy that the others were kind of suffering with her. "Could you get me some more water?"

"Here, I got a bottle with this sports cap, so you can drink in any position." Mrs. Hernandez hurriedly produced a water bottle and some biscuits that she handed around. Even the nurse who came in to check on Veronica was treated to some chocolate.

"Good news, you are fully dilated. If you have an urge to push now, go ahead and get that baby out," said the nurse with a smile.

"Really?" Veronica could hardly believe it; it had only been three hours since her waters broke. Maybe this wasn't going to be a three-day survival trip.

"Always in a rush, just like her mother," said Mrs. Hernandez.

She and Cecilia each held Veronica's hands on either side, smiling at each other, whilst Veronica closed her eyes to catch her breath before the next contraction.

"I'll go and get the doctor." And with that, the nurse disappeared.

Shortly after, Veronica did indeed feel the need to push, and for the first time, she let out an animalistic groan as she bore down.

She was happily surprised that the contraction stage was not going to last several days, as she had heard from other mothers, but now she felt like being ripped open by hundreds of little cuts that burned as if cleaned with disinfectant.

"Get it out, get it out, get it out!" she screamed when the baby's head crowned, and then, with her last strength, the baby glided out, and the pain was gone.

Veronica did not think it possible, but when she heard the baby scream and whimper, she wanted to protect it. "It's all right. Everything's all right now," she cooed as the doctor placed the baby girl on her chest.

"Do we have a name yet?" asked the nurse, who was filling in a form.

"I thought about Verity," Veronica said without taking her eyes off the baby.

"I love it," said Cecilia.

Veronica was tired. She had been up half the night, the adrenaline pumping through her body from the birth and thoughts circling in her head whilst she watched baby Verity sleep in a cot next to her hospital bed. She had the luxury of a single room and decided to stay for a few days to make sure that everything was all right with her and the baby, and also because she was anxious to start this new chapter in her life, which she still doubted that she was cut out for.

Verity wriggled slightly in her wrap, which tied her arms close to her body. She was beautiful, a full head of hair and long curved eyelashes, and yet Veronica still had problems embracing motherhood. Her first instinct had been to protect this innocent and defenceless human being, but now the tears welled up and she was homesick for her old life. It was as if this little person had been left on her doorstep and she was expected to care for it until it was old enough to fend for itself. She did not feel that Verity belonged to her, and she wasn't even sure how upset she would be if someone came to take her away again. Yet, she had made up her mind to accept this person, care for and protect her, and she would do the best she could.

Verity started a toothless wail, and Veronica shifted to the edge of the bed to pick her up. Her body hurt as if she had done an extreme session at the gym, and she was sure that she had pulled a muscle in her calf during labour.

She shuffled back into bed with the baby in her arm and tried to get Verity to latch on to her nipple as they had shown her in the prenatal class. But it was one thing practicing on a doll how to hold a baby and support the head with one arm whilst moulding your breast with the other hand and be told that instinct would do the rest. It was a whole different thing to have the actual weight of a new-born in your arms and being afraid to snap its neck with one improvident movement.

Finally, Verity latched on, and Veronica had the impression that she was properly drinking. The suction on her nipple was weirdly pleasant in a non-sexual way, and for the first time, Veronica thought that she could keep this baby alive. But when she put Verity back into her cot and hummed a lullaby to get her to sleep again, she was once more overwhelmed by doubts and regrets. Whilst still in quarantine, the doctors had suggested the possibility of an abortion which, at the time, she had decidedly rejected, and even though the baby pressed heavily on her bladder and spine towards the end of the pregnancy, she still lived her life as usual. She went to the shops by herself, played computer games for hours on end, and even made plans to return to work as an advisor for NASA's science and technology team. But now it dawned on her that she would be able to do only a fraction of these things, constantly having to care for an utterly helpless human. She started to cry, tormented that she was so selfish to mourn her independence instead of being fulfilled with motherly feelings.

A nurse came in to check on her.

"Is everything all right?" asked the nurse when she noticed Veronica's tears.

"Yes, yes. Just emotional," said Veronica as she dried her face.

"And how is the baby?" asked the nurse after an understanding nod. "Has she nursed?"

"Yes, I just fed her, and I think she actually drank properly this time."

"Excellent. You should try and sleep too. If you like, we can take her to the nursery and bring her back when she needs a feed."

Veronica gladly accepted this offer, but when she got herself comfortable, she weirdly missed Verity, and despite being exhausted, it still took her a while to fall asleep.

After a few hours of dreamless sleep, Veronica was woken up by the nurse bringing Verity back.

"I'm sorry to wake you up, but your little girl has been very patient," said the nurse.

"What time is it?" asked Veronica, noticing morning light coming in through the window.

"Almost seven. The day shift is taking over now and will come around in the next thirty minutes. I'll be back tonight," explained the nurse, as she handed Verity to Veronica.

Even though Veronica had only slept for about three hours, she awoke refreshed, and the dark thoughts from the night had been erased with the breaking morning. She nursed Verity and changed her diaper. Breakfast arrived as she was pulling faces and cooing to Verity, who stared aimlessly in the direction of her face.

After breakfast, the new shift introduced themselves, and then Cecilia and Mrs. Hernandez arrived, which gave Veronica a chance to catch up on some more sleep.

They gave Verity her first bath, which she seemed to enjoy immensely, probably because the warm weightlessness reminded her of the last nine months in the womb.

Veronica looked at Cecilia, who held Verity in her arms and inspected her little ears.

"She looks just like you," said Cecilia, enamoured.

"Yeah?" Veronica was happy.

"Yeah. I thought we'd be able to see some similarity to the father, but I can see only you."

Veronica knew that Cecilia didn't mean to upset her, but so far, she had avoided the thought about the paternity, which ultimately would shed light on what had happened in space nine months ago.

Unfortunately, Veronica could not escape these thoughts any longer, as shortly after, two doctors arrived to take saliva samples from her and the baby to carry out a paternity test.

Gabriel Stuart, Adam Fjodorow, and Philip Schuster had already given their samples back when they were still in quarantine, and it should only take a couple of days now before they had certainty.

* * *

"Hey, I'm home," Amy shouted from the hall.

She found Gabriel ironing in front of the television and ignoring her.

"Is everything all right?" she asked.

"I thought you'd be back some hours ago."

"Sorry, we lost track of time. Look what I got." Amy produced a tiny pair of space boots in a silver metallic material.

"So, you were shopping for six hours, and this is what you got? What else did you get up to?"

"Well, I wasn't shopping. Miranda needed to buy baby stuff, and since we're not pregnant yet, I thought it a little premature to buy things myself."

"Hm," Gabriel grunted.

"And guess who we saw in the shop?" Gabriel just stared at the TV and folded a pair of his underpants.

"Veronica Vargas. And she was pregnant, and her waters broke right there. We saw it all."

"What happened then?" Gabriel's interest was piqued.

"Miranda gave her a pad, and I guess she'll be giving birth soon. And you know what?"

"What?"

"If she was nine months' pregnant, she would have had to have, you know, nookie, up there, whilst you were on your mission." Amy was gleeful and happy that Gabriel also seemed to get out of his grump about her being late.

"I bet it was Fjodorow."

"Did you see anything?"

"Nope, but he's so scrawny that they could have fitted into one compartment whilst we were sleeping."

"That sounds kinda sexy, weightless sex." Amy stroked his arm and let her fingertips wander up to his ear. "Why are you ironing your underpants and socks?"

"Because I like it when they are neatly folded away."

"You know, I think I'm ovulating, and I find a man doing housework rather sexy."

Gabriel continued ironing his stack of underwear whilst Amy kept on caressing his neck. She slipped her hand under his shirt and explored his muscular torso. Then she opened his belt and unzipped his trousers.

When she went down on him, he briefly stopped her, but only to turn off the iron. Then he followed her willingly upstairs, where she climbed onto their bed like a cat and took off her own trousers. As usual, this part interrupted the seduction, as taking off clothes always required an awkward pause and distortion before slipping naked under the sheets.

The sex was less romantic and more pragmatic and was over before Amy could get really aroused. Maybe they had been doing it too much recently in an effort to get pregnant. She had become weary of it herself, but the thought of holding a positive pregnancy test in her hands kept her going.

"Next time, it would be great if you could iron all of my clothes before putting them away," said Gabriel and got up to take a shower.

For the first time, Amy honestly thought about whether she was selfish for wanting a baby so badly. Gabriel seemed to be under a lot of stress at work, judging from his mood, and maybe they should hold off with their family planning. Most people underestimated how hard it was to look after a baby day and night and it usually put couples under a lot of pressure.

CHAPTER 10

Mack had polished his joke on *Witzelsucht* for his plenary talk at the World Congress for Human Genetics in Shanghai and had earned benevolent laughter from the auditorium. The pressure he always put himself under before giving a talk had paid off. The subsequent discussion time was easily passed. In fact, he found that questions for plenary talks seemed simpler to answer than for focussed research talks, probably because plenary talks covered a large research area in more general terms that were easily defended. After five days filled with hundreds of scientific talks on the impact of genes on various human diseases and disorders, recent and historic changes in the human DNA in relation to environmental impact, and advances in data collection and statistical modelling, Mack was worn out.

He used to enjoy these conferences and eagerly listened to as many talks as he could, fuelled almost exclusively by litres of coffee, but after a dozen conferences all around the world, he felt that little progress had been made over the years. Now, he spent most of his time catching up with colleagues, and it was the exclusive lunch breaks and evening drinks where the real advances were made — at least for individual careers. But even these networking opportunities were losing their appeal. At Mack's stage and career plan, unless you got in with political or economic leaders, rubbing shoulders with yet another professor was rarely making any difference anymore.

The conference dinner was in full swing after the dreaded thank-you speeches of the organizing committee had been wrapped up. Almost three thousand scientists from all over the world, dressed up for the occasion, tucked into the four-course meal and emptied one wine bottle after another.

The World Congress organizers had once more surpassed themselves, and the hall resembled an outdoor garden with Chinese lanterns illuminating potted trees.

A band in traditional Chinese dress played some old rock 'n' roll music, which surely would draw a large crowd of nerds dancing their hearts out later, something no one would believe happened at every conference.

A hologram announced the next World Congress in four years' time in Calgary, and underneath, the first dancer jazzed across the parquet to pick up a colleague seated at a different table.

Mack sat with his colleagues from Brisbane at one of the fancy-styled round dinner tables. He had made sure to sit as far away as possible from Tom, who still tried at every chance to make small talk and befriend Mack.

A server in a traditional Chinese costume scuttled over. "Would you like more wine, sirs and madams?" she asked.

"Yes, please," answered one of Mack's senior work colleagues, Carole Higgins, who already slurred her words.

"For me too," said another.

Professor Lamarck stared at his phone, reading something, and did not notice that his glass was refilled.

"Is everything all right?" asked Mack.

"Hmm? Oh yes, just got an interesting email from NASA," responded the professor.

Mack raised his eyebrows. That sounded indeed interesting. "What do they want?"

"I'm not sure; seems rather secretive."

"Maybe they want you to fly to Mars," joked Mack.

"An old geezer like me? You look more like their stock," laughed his mentor and took a sip from his replenished wine glass.

Mack had been lucky in getting into Professor Lamarck's group as a young student. Not only was he a brilliant mind who looked after his students, but he had managed to make a name for himself in actual influential circles, and Mack made sure to stay in his good books. If nothing else, being regarded as Professor Lamarck's successor was a pretty good career path that he would not jeopardize.

"Any plans for tonight?" interrupted Carole from the other side.

"I might dip into Shanghai's nightlife later," Mack offered.

"Oh, and I thought I could get you to dance with me," grinned Carole.

"For you, I'll wait," said Mack with a wink.

"Oh, you charmer. Well, I don't want to make you wait too long, so come on now before the moment's gone."

"A woman who knows what she wants. Attractive."

Mack got up and offered Carole a hand, which she took to pull him to the dance floor.

"If only I were twenty years younger," said Carole.

The band had just started 'A Hard Day's Night' from the Beatles, and Mack swirled Carole around, catching her before she lost her balance, only to continue hopping along with her in a made-up swing dance. He had always planned to take dance lessons for exactly these situations but had never gotten around to do it. At least the dance floor filled up quickly, and soon they were surrounded by twitching legs and arms that were just as unprofessional as they were.

About an hour later, Mack had left the conference dinner and Carole in the arms of his former PhD co-supervisor and entered a bar. The street sign had announced *Karaoke Night*, and so Mack was not surprised to see a drunken businessman belting his lungs out to Frank Sinatra's 'My Way'.

He ordered a cocktail at the bar, which came steaming in liquid nitrogen, and then turned around to watch the bold singer.

But his attention was quickly drawn to a businesswoman also sitting at the bar, swishing her shiny black hair back as she turned to pick up her own glass.

Their eyes met, and Mack was surprised when she held his view and smiled. Even though he had a successful career and earned good money, he still felt intimidated by folks who dressed up in suits that needed to be dry-cleaned on a regular basis or who wore shoes twenty-four/seven that made every podiatrist cringe.

"Waiting for someone?" she asked.

"Nope," replied Mack, putting on his most laid-back baritone.

"Good, me neither."

Mack laughed, as he found that this was a simple but neat pick-up line. "I'm Mack."

"I'm Marsha."

"Marsha? That's an unusual Chinese name."

"Don't you know, we pick our names from last century's TV shows, cause nobody can pronounce the Chinese?" she said seriously.

It had started so good.

"No, honestly. My mother is Russian, and my father Taiwanese," she laughed at his expression.

"Dang, so I was even wrong with the Chinese?" Mack tried his best to recover and keep the conversation going. Why was he so intimidated? He normally had no problems sweet-talking women that he found attractive.

"No worries, I can hardly distinguish any Asians either."

"What're you drinking?" Mack tried to move the subject to something more innocuous.

"Whisky," Marsha said and swirled her tumbler with the amber liquid.

"On the rocks?"

"Never."

"A true scotch then."

"By association."

"Two Ardbeg whiskies and a dash of water," ordered Mack and left his cocktail untouched. "So, what do you do, where do you live?"

"Scotland, United Banks of Europe. Yourself?"

"Australia, human genetics."

"Interesting. Anything discovered lately?"

"A few minor genes here and there. Nothing as big as the breast cancer genes some sixty years ago."

"Aww." She mocked him, but not without giving him a playful pat on the wrist.

Several hours later, they were still sitting at the bar, now with a good collection of whisky glasses lined up. The Japanese whiskies she had introduced him to had been exceptional.

"I'm glad you sat down next to me," said Marsha, still well enunciated despite the large amount of alcohol they had enjoyed together.

"Me too." Mack started to have trouble moving his tongue at the required speed for speaking.

"I dreaded to go back and sit with my colleagues at the hotel bar."

"I left a drunk mid-fifties lady alone at a fully stocked conference dinner to come here. She's probably sitting at the hotel bar now too."

"Lucky me."

"Lucky me."

"Shall we leave and see if we can sneak by the poor lady?" suggested Marsha.

"My hotel?" Mack hesitated as he normally avoided bringing anyone home or even just to the hotel where he was staying. It was easier that way, as he would leave before the morning and could stay uncommitted.

"Yeah, if you don't mind that I'll have to leave before you're awake."

That took him by surprise. "Love it."

Mack was worried that he could not perform with all the alcohol circulating in his blood, but it also meant that all inhibitions were gone, and they baptized the entire hotel room. He wondered whether the cleaning staff regularly wiped the inside of the wardrobe or would recognize the smudge on the window as a butt-print.

They ended their tête-à-tête in bed, and Mack didn't even mind that Marsha went to sleep. He waited until she was breathing regularly, then took a photo of her with his phone and cut of some of her hair. He had made it a habit to always have a few freezer bags with him, the way other people carried condoms. You never knew what might happen or where you'd find the love of your life.

He slipped back under the blanket and went to sleep. When he woke up the next day, he was slightly disappointed that Marsha was indeed gone.

* * *

Whilst Mack had enjoyed a carefree evening at the end of the conference, his aunt Gayle was stuck up to her neck in work at her parliament office. She was skimming through the statistics of teenage pregnancies and the uptake of hormonal implants in Europe. She knew that she could not expect any statistically significant changes over the space of only a few months, but she had hoped to see at least a downward trend in pregnancies of underaged women. Last month, there was a slight dip in the numbers, but this month, it was back up and even a little higher than previously. Europe needed more children overall, but from educated and taxpaying women, not from teenagers who would likely drop out of school or at least were less likely to take up a job that fully supported them.

Another statistic that seemed to be going up was the number of abortions, not only for teenagers but all fertile age brackets across all social groups. Gayle hoped that this was a sign that abortions had well and truly lost the stigma of child murder and it simply meant that women were able to decide over their own bodies.

At least the number of hormonal implants was steadily going up as expected, and hopefully the other statistics would reflect this trend soon.

"What else have you got?" Gayle asked her private assistant, Guillaume Marais, who was standing ready with more files.

"This is a summary of the complaints we have gotten regarding the contraception bill. And here is our press statement addressing those criticisms." Guillaume handed her several sheets of paper.

A screeching voice sounded in from the marketplace in front of Gayle's office. "God has not intended for genes to be in our food! You, you! This is the devil's food you're stuffing in there, you pigs, you fallen Adams. Oh, you sons of God, come back to the right path. Find a wife who can cook you healthy food and bear your children."

Crazy Betty must have been standing on the fountain again, berating people coming out of the McDonald's across the street.

"Could you close the window, please? It's hard to concentrate when you've got a market crier in your ear," asked Gayle, and Guillaume did as he was bid.

Gayle started to go through the press release and scribbled on and crossed out sections of the file with a red pen, whilst Guillaume stood by the window, watching the two police officers who were approaching Crazy Betty now.

"Okay, I think this is good now. Type it up and send it to press relations with the note that I will be making a statement tomorrow morning."

Gayle passed the file back to Guillaume, and her view passed the stack of newspapers on the corner of her desk. An image on one of the tabloids caught her eye, and she pulled it out.

Her pulse shot up. Across a picture of Inga leaving a drugstore, the headline shouted: 'Is she pregnant? Teenage daughter of Gayle Hamilton, Minister for Family and Health, buys pregnancy test.'

"Have you seen this?" Gayle turned to Guillaume, who was also reading the headline over her shoulder.

"No."

This was exactly what she had been dreading. Surely, there was a simple explanation to it, but just the fact that a tabloid had taken aim at her daughter meant that she could get some seriously inconvenient journalistic attention.

"Get a pod. I need to go home," ordered Gayle and scrambled to pack her bag, whilst Guillaume tapped hastily on his phone.

After only fifteen minutes, the pod arrived at Gayle's gated property. She punched the door code into her phone and waited for the iron gates to swing open.

"Come on," she muttered impatiently.

Finally, the government pod drove up the driveway and stopped by the front door of the large white villa.

Gayle pressed her thumbprint on the door pad and stormed inside.

"Inga! Where are you?"

She swept by the living room, where Hazel was watching the news as usual, and straight upstairs.

Inga had just finished her maths homework when her door burst open, and Gayle walked in.

"What is this?" demanded Gayle, waving the tabloid around.

"What?" asked Inga innocently.

"Are you pregnant?"

"No!"

"Then why is there a cover story with a picture of you buying a pregnancy test?"

Gayle stared at her eldest daughter, eyes bulging, but this was no laughing matter.

"Because ... I ..." stammered Inga.

"Are you pregnant?"

"Yes."

"Yes?" Gayle could not believe her own ears. She had clung to the hope that Inga had bought the test for a friend.

"Yes." Inga reaffirmed Gayle's greatest fear.

Gayle stared at her daughter, her mind blank, apart from this one blurred but inconvenient truth.

"You have to have an abortion."

This was the only way forward that Gayle could come up with.

"But—"

"I *need* you to have an abortion. I have passed a law, and my own sixteen-year-old daughter, whom I trusted, goes and gets herself knocked up."

"I didn't get knocked up," protested Inga.

"So, you tell me you wanted to get pregnant?"

"No, I just didn't get knocked up. It was my decision to have sex too."

"Fair enough. I assume Mark is the father?"

Inga nodded, embarrassed.

"Does he know that you're pregnant?"

Inga shook her head.

Downstairs, Hazel leaned against the doorframe of the living room, listening to the conversation above.

The rest of the evening, Gayle made urgent phone calls to private doctors. Never in a million years did she think she would be doing this. If there was not so much at stake for her due to her job, she would have reacted differently, maybe listened to her daughter and given each other time to think and talk things through. But she had worked hard for so many years to be where she was now, to be able to provide her family with all the amenities that they enjoyed every day without having to rely on her ex-husband. And she was determined to make a much bigger impact in the world than she had achieved so far.

She pulled some strings to get an appointment the day after tomorrow with a small but highly recommended practice that specialized in women's health. When she hung up, she poured herself a large glass of wine and settled at the kitchen counter.

She heard Hazel knocking on Inga's door upstairs, but she did not open it. Why did this happen to her? Inga should have known better and at least used some protection. Gayle realized that she did not even know whether it was an accident and intended to be more understanding with Inga the next time they spoke. In two days, everything would be over again, and they could return to their lives.

The next morning, Gayle phoned in to Inga's school to let them know that she was down with the flu and would not come in for at least a week. She called her own office to postpone the press statement and let them know that she was working from home, and then swore in Hazel to not tell a word to anyone. Another day later, and she took both her daughters to the private practitioner with a small medical centre in an area where rich people did not look across their hedged and highly fenced properties.

After Gayle had filled in the paperwork at the reception, a nurse led Inga away; shortly after, Hazel was called in from a different treatment room. Gayle observed with a stern face the doctor preparing the needle with the hormonal implant. Despite the circumstances, she was relieved with her decision. She should have been a role model and gotten her daughters treated as one of the first in the nation. Maybe this could have made an impact, and more families with young daughters would have followed by now. At least she need not worry anymore that someone found out her own daughters had not received the implant yet.

"That was it. Now you are protected for the next five years," said the doctor pleasantly as he set the hormonal implant into Hazel's upper arm.

"Protected?" asked Hazel.

"Yes. From pregnancies," replied the doctor, slightly confused.

"That sounds like babies are a disease."

"Well, maybe *protected* is the wrong word."

"I'd be happier if I got protected from STDs."

"Hazel, that's enough," Gayle interjected. "Are we done here?"

"Yes," said the doctor.

"Thank you very much." Gayle opened the door and implied Hazel should get out.

"What has gotten into you?" asked Gayle as she pushed her daughter towards the empty waiting area.

Hazel slumped down on a chair, absent-mindedly touching her arm with the implant.

"Why can't people decide about their own bodies?" Hazel asked.

"They can, but we can't keep providing for teenagers who destroy their lives by having a baby before they even finish school and have a job," explained Gayle in the simplest terms she could come up with on the spot.

"Some of them finish school and become really successful."

"Vanishingly few."

"Did you know that federal judge Susana Rodriguez-Brown got her first child when she was fifteen? And she says it was only because of her baby that she made something out of her life."

Gayle wondered where that child of hers, who had barely entered puberty, had gotten all this information. "No, I didn't know that."

"So, why not continue with counselling teenagers and let them make their own decisions?"

"Because people like Judge Rodriguez-Brown are the exception to the rule," said Gayle, increasingly exhausted.

In a different situation, she would have been proud of Hazel for standing her ground, questioning the *status quo*, and forming her own opinions. But right now, she just wanted to get home and have a nice cup of tea.

A nurse wheeled Inga into the waiting area, clamping a tissue in her hand, her eyes red and puffy.

"Here we go. I hope you get better soon," said the nurse cheerfully.

Tired, Inga only nodded.

"Thank you very much," said Gayle. Another step done.

"No problem. I have endometriosis. I know how crippling it can be. But Doctor Charton is one of the best. You might feel a little weak, but nothing to worry about. Bedrest and plenty to drink. I had my husband carry me up and down the stairs," giggled the nurse.

Inga's treatment had been officially filed under endometriosis, to avoid any news about her abortion ending up in the press.

Gayle listened to the nurse's chitchat whilst offering Inga an arm to get up, but Inga pushed her aside and left shaky but determined on her own.

"Well, seems I won't have to carry her anywhere," said Gayle, smiling at the nurse. "Let's go," she ordered Hazel.

They left the practice. The sun shone through the green leaves of the old oak trees in the front garden, and for a fleeting moment, Gayle wondered how quiet it was. The birds were probably sheltering from the summer heat somewhere between the shady branches.

Inga had already sat down in the pod, staring blankly out the window. Surely, she didn't want to have a baby at her age, thought Gayle. Hazel, on the other side, also looked out the window, but her face showed the fight that was brewing in her head, and Gayle knew she would have to face some serious dis-cussions. But she had done the right thing, and Inga would eventually come around.

CHAPTER 11

It had now been four weeks since James went back to Sudan, and Jeanette had kept their routine of reading and outdoor activities going. She had taken her sister's children on a camping trip, and even though they stayed on a maintained campsite during the nights – on her sister's orders – she still took Nola and Louis out on hikes, where they cooked their meal over an open campfire. She showed them how to use Vaseline to make a cotton ball burn longer, how to build a shelter from sticks and leaves, and how to hunt with a bow and arrow, albeit using tree trunks as their targets.

For her fourteen years, Nola was so good with Jeanette's compound bow that it took Jeanette by surprise when she shot a small wild pig.

"I'm so sorry," gasped Nola, when the pig squealed in pain and ran confused right into Jeanette's arms.

Jeanette swiftly cut the wounded animal's throat, acutely aware that Nola and Louis were watching her.

After the pig showed no eye movement anymore, she finally let it go and made them sit down where they could still see the dead animal.

"I didn't mean to kill it. It was just there, and then …" Nola was crying.

"Anything can be a weapon. This rock, this stick, even your bare hands. That is why we need to be mindful about our actions, or the consequences can be deadly," explained Jeanette, putting an arm around Nola. "It was a good clean shot, Nola, and now you know to never raise any weapon against another living being unless you are sure about what you're doing and accept the consequences."

"I will never touch any weapon again," sobbed Nola.

"That is a good resolution. Do you know what the best survival tool is for yourself and others? Your brain."

"What do we do now?" asked Louis.

"This looks like a healthy hundred-pounder. I'm sure Stevy will be happy to get a good roast going when we're back."

They tied the legs of the pig to a sturdy branch, and Jeanette carried it over her shoulders back to their campground.

Growing up in the bayou, Jeanette had loved survival camps, and the way that it had taught her to think and problem-solve had secured her the spot as mission commander at NASA. She was thinking about that weekend with Nola and Louis when she returned to Houston for her second post-mission examination. Maybe she could start to volunteer at those survival camps to teach more kids how to think on their feet and make use of everyday items when they are in a pickle.

She entered the Mars Receiving Laboratory with Matt White and followed him to a changing room.

"How have you been?" asked Matt.

"Rather good. Relaxing as much as I can. I'm glad the media circus has calmed down," answered Jeanette.

"It can be overwhelming. But you did a fantastic job."

"Thank you."

Jeanette found it funny that Matt, who had only ever stood in the background at press conferences and did not even keep a social media account that could attract any public interest, pretended to know how it must have been to be invited to every major, medium, and minor talk show, breakfast club, or business conference, only to repeat the same stories from their mission and try to keep some sense of self and privacy.

Some crewmembers, like Gabriel, seemed to enjoy how people clung to his lips and listened to every word he said, as if he was giving out the secret to everlasting life. But for Jeanette, the official dinner with President Reed had been the last occasion she was obliged to do according to her contract, and that was it for her.

"Gabriel Stuart is already in the gym, so when you are ready, we can start your second post-mission checkup."

"What about Vargas?"

"She will be examined separately at her home."

"Has she given birth yet?"

"I'm not authorized to talk about it." Matt's smile was an impenetrable fortress.

Jeanette knew that Schuster and Fjodorow were examined in their home countries, and she wondered how long it would take to determine who the father was.

In the gym, Gabriel was already warming up. He looked fit. He must have been training rigorously, and Jeanette felt fazed, as she knew that she had slacked off here and there. Instead of a pulse-raising run, she often opted for a nice stroll around a national park. Her current day job was still to draft reports on their mission and provide feedback on training, equipment, and technologies, which was a rather sedentary activity. At least she could do this from home and was not required to attend the space centre.

"You look good, Stuart," said Jeanette.

"Thank you, Commander," said Gabriel, and Jeanette was reminded of his military background.

"At ease," laughed Jeanette. "I'm not your commander anymore."

"Of course," said Gabriel, and Jeanette had the impression that he was swallowing hard to not add 'Ma'am'.

"I heard you took up a job at Praides?" asked Jeanette.

"Yes. I'm training new fighter pilots and advise on training for high-speed flight."

"You look like you've been training quite a bit."

"Not overly, but I need to stay on top of the recruits."

Their conversation was interrupted by Doctor Jackson, who entered the gym with his assistant.

"Nice to see you both again. You look well and relaxed. So, let's change that. It's the same procedure as last time. I will check your vitals, and then you both run for thirty minutes. After that, you get a short break, and then some cognitive solving tasks before lunch. Tomorrow, we do some more physicals, take some blood samples, et cetera, and then a final questionnaire. Doctor Spencer will fit you with your patch trackers that must be worn for the next twenty-four hours," explained Doctor Jackson.

Jeanette and Gabriel knew the drill. Apart from changing tasks in the cognitive test, the examination was the same as when they had entered the Mars program three years ago.

Their oxygen levels were measured before and after each exercise, and Jeanette was pleased to hear that she was back up to eighty percent of her pre-mission condition. Gabriel passed the physical tests with flying colours and seemed pleased with himself, but he was disgruntled at lunch.

"So, how did you do on the cognition test?" asked Jeanette, tucking into her salmon filet.

"A little under my pre-mission performance, but better than at the last one," said Gabriel.

Jeanette had heard through the grapevine that Gabriel had bombed the last tests, and judging by his mood, he could not have improved much. These tests were not just judged on the speed and accuracy to solve a problem, but also included other tasks aimed at personality traits, and Jeanette suspected that this was the area that Gabriel was failing. A high-performing astronaut should take the feedback to improve oneself and not be so taken aback, as Gabriel seemed to be.

The next day, Jeanette made sure to keep the conversation light, especially because the examinations today included fertility testing, which she did not want to get into with Gabriel. Maybe this was something he would be proud to talk about, but this was a topic where Jeanette felt uncomfortable.

Ten years ago, she had chosen to undergo an elective hysterectomy and oophorectomy. She already knew at the time that she did not want to have children, and a genetic test that was carried out when she first applied to become an astronaut had indicated that she was a high-risk carrier of a mutation in the *BRCA* gene, causing breast and ovarian cancer. Removing her ovaries and the uterus supposedly halved her risk of getting breast cancer and lowered her risk for peritoneal cancer by more than eighty percent. That way, she also did not have to deal with having her period during a long space mission, something that Vargas had supressed by taking progesterone pills during their trip.

Oddly, Gabriel's mood did not improve after the final sets of tests, and Jeanette wondered whether he had received some more bad results. She knew that male fertility was decreased after space flight, due to the increased radiation in space, but since sperm was constantly produced and a full cycle took around two months, sperm count and motility should recover after the astronaut had returned to Earth again. Gabriel had always talked about starting a family after the mission, and by getting married, he had shown that he was serious about it. If he indeed had fertility issues, Jeanette could imagine how this disheartened him, and for the first time, she felt sorry for Gabriel.

Something touching the subject was nonetheless burning on her mind. "Did you hear anything about Vargas?"

"No, but I think she gave birth last week," responded Gabriel, uncommitted.

"How do you know? Did you get a result from the paternity test?" asked Jeanette.

She assumed that she would get notified as the commander of the mission, but then, this was now a private matter and out of her control, so it would not be unexpected if NASA was not keeping her in the loop.

"No results on my end. But my wife saw her in the shops the other day, and apparently, she went into labour that day."

So, NASA had indeed left her out. She could understand, but as the former commander, she wanted to keep supporting her crewmembers in things that were a direct result from their mission. She made a mental note to get in touch with Vargas and see how she was as soon as she got home.

* * *

Veronica had been home for a week now and slowly found a rhythm to her new life. Breastfeeding worked better and better, but her nipples had raw, open wounds, and every time Verity latched on, she counted the minutes until the pain eased. At least birth had been over after a while, and even if she had been in labour for much longer than she had been, breastfeeding was hands down more torturous because it was repeated every four hours of every day.

Veronica had tried all the ointments on the market, but whilst some of them provided relief, at least for a few minutes, a lot of them had to be washed off before the next feed, and none of them helped heal the cracks. Finally, she had given in to her mother's advice to always wash her breasts after a feed and then let them air-dry for as long as possible. As weird as it was for the first day to basically walk around in their flat with a boob hanging out, it did help, and so Veronica had gotten into the habit of showering several times a day.

She had also quickly realized that sleep deprivation was the death of all sanity and forbidden Cecilia to be up with her at night when the baby woke, as she needed Cecilia to be well rested and resilient throughout the day, so she could have meltdowns and know that someone had her back.

Luckily, Cecilia's job as a data cleaner meant that she was super flexible and could take on clients from anywhere at any time. She even managed to grow her business, as her clients never learned to keep private things private. Instead, they blasted photos of drunken nights out onto the internet, using dubious providers to send nudes, or not-so-secretly troll minorities. By now it had gone so far that Cecilia came into moral conflicts about taking on regular customers, as they seemed to treat her as their get-out-of-jail-free card for being able to erase any traceable offense that they committed online. Still, most of her customers were college students who feared that their party excesses during spring break and the records thereof might be found out by a potential future employer.

As Veronica took her third shower of the day, Cecilia carried baby Verity, who always perked up with a full tummy, around the living room. She was watching the bees collecting pollen from the flowers on their balcony when the doorbell rang.

Cecilia looked at the door screen and saw three men standing in front of the door, one of them having the NASA emblem on his jacket.

"Hello?" said Cecilia into the intercom.

"Hi, we're looking for Ms. Veronica Vargas. I am Doctor Jackson from NASA," answered the man with the jacket.

"Can you provide a thumbprint?" asked Cecilia.

She was cautious, as they did not want any press to get wind of Veronica's pregnancy and were worried that some nosy journalist might pull a stunt. But the man held his thumb against the reader, and his identity was confirmed as Doctor Richard Jackson.

Cecilia let them in and watched that no unauthorized person entered the building after them.

"Veronica will be with you in a moment," Cecilia explained after the men had climbed to their second floor flat and followed her into their living room. "Have a seat."

"No worries," responded Doctor Jackson. "May I?" He asked with a warm smile and nodded towards Verity.

Cecilia turned the baby around, who stared quizzically into the man's face.

"What a beautiful baby," Doctor Jackson said.

When Veronica came out of the shower and found three men in her living room, she almost jumped back into the corridor, as she was only wearing a towel. Luckily, she had not chosen to give her breasts some fresh air straight away.

"Doctor Jackson," stuttered Veronica, and then she remembered that it was time for her second check-up. "I completely forgot you were coming around."

The physician looked up from the baby and gallantly ignored Veronica's lack of clothing.

"No worries. If you haven't heard of it, baby-brain is real," said the physician.

"Baby-brain?" asked Veronica.

"The brains of mothers that are in tune with motherhood tend to focus on the important things in this special phase of their lives. That also means that everything that is unimportant for survival and well-being of mother and child is often unintentionally forgotten."

"Aha," replied Veronica. "Just give me a minute while I get dressed. I haven't forgotten that."

"I'll see if she's ready for a nap, if that's okay," said Cecilia and followed Veronica with Verity on her arm to the bedroom.

Veronica thought about Doctor Jackson's words as she got dressed. Her first reaction was surprise that the man was able to offer such an insight into a mother's life, but then he might have children of his own. Veronica did not know. As the words sank in, she started to feel elated. She had indeed been forgetting things like shaving her legs, ordering food, or even her own phone number, to the point where she planned to tell Doctor Jackson about it. And now she had even forgotten the appointment with Doctor Jackson for her second post-mission examination. But more importantly, Doctor Jackson had said that her forgetfulness was a sign that she was in tune with motherhood, something she was still doubting.

Refreshed and in good spirits, Veronica came back into the living room. "Do you want me to do some lunges this time?" she asked, knowing that the others had done a physical examination.

"No, I'm happy if you tell me that you are taking it slow. You shouldn't really be doing exercises until about six weeks after birth, and then you should slowly ease yourself back in. Have you considered attending a postpartum fitness class to strengthen your pelvic floor muscles?"

"My what?" asked Veronica.

"Do look into it. That's the one exercise I strongly recommend. There might even be some mom-and-bub classes where you can take the baby with you."

She started to like Doctor Jackson more and more as she discovered his softer sides. "I promise I'll look into it."

"Right, now to the examination. We'll be doing pretty much the same as last time if you are ready for it. I know you might not have been prepared for our visit."

"No, it's all right. We should have four hours before I'm required on the baby front again," replied Veronica.

"Excellent. Before we start, I have to talk to you about a different matter. The paternity test came back inconclusive."

"What do you mean?" The high that Veronica had been on for the last few minutes evaporated at the word *paternity*. "I thought you said that this test should give a result."

"It should have done. We had enough DNA available and tested more genetic markers than are normally used in a paternity test, but the highest match we found was twenty-one out of thirty-five markers."

"That sounds like a good match," said Veronica.

"It is not. Considering that all humans share ninety-nine percent of their DNA sequence, these tests are designed to look specifically at those regions that vary from one person to another. For a paternity not to be excluded, we only allow for one to two mismatches, which is within the chance of a mutation or more likely a genotyping error occurring," explained Doctor Jackson.

"What do you mean by 'not exclude paternity'? I thought you wanted to prove paternity."

"With only a limited number of genetic markers, a conventional test only ever confirms a paternity with a 99.9 percent probability, but never proves it. To prove paternity, we would have to compare the entire DNA sequences, which brings me to the extra purpose of our visit. We would like your consent to collect blood samples from you and your child to sequence your entire genomes. As there are no other possible fathers but your three colleagues, we assume that this is a never-heard-of case where the chosen markers were not able to yield a conclusive result."

"I see," said Veronica. "What if I don't wish to know who the father is anymore?"

"That would be your decision." Doctor Jackson studied Veronica's face as she thought about it. "How about we carry on with the examination first?"

Veronica's cognitive test results were lower than at her first post-mission examination, but Doctor Jackson was not worried about it, and Veronica did not care at the moment.

"Have you made up your mind about the paternity test?" asked Doctor Jackson at the end.

"Could I have a minute to talk to my partner?" asked Veronica.

"Certainly."

Veronica found Cecilia still in their bedroom, where she played with Verity on their bed.

"Done?" asked Cecilia.

"Almost."

"Good, cause the little guts here has been behaving very well for the last thirty minutes and would like a refill."

"The paternity test was inconclusive."

"What? How is that possible?"

"Apparently, it's never been heard of. They want to do a full genome scan, but ..." Veronica hesitated. "I don't know if I need to know who the father is."

Cecilia stayed quiet, and Veronica wished she had just blurted out her feelings instead of mulling them over.

"It is your decision; however, this is not just about who the father is but also about what happened up there. Don't you want to know that?" said Cecilia finally.

"I don't know." Veronica could not hold back her tears.

She did not want to know how it happened; that it happened was enough for her to deal with.

"If it wasn't just a one-in-a-million freak accident, then whoever ... whoever violated you must be held accountable for it." Cecilia took Veronica into her arms and let her sob until she fell quiet.

"All right," Veronica finally said.

Doctor Jackson quickly drew a few millilitres of blood from Veronica and Verity whilst she was breast-feeding. After a short outburst of protest from Verity, she quickly nuzzled back in, and Doctor Jackson and his assistants bid their farewell.

"She is a lovely baby. And she looks just like you, if I may say," said Doctor Jackson.

"When will the results be ready?" asked Veronica.

"We'll be in touch, but it shouldn't take longer than a few days."

Veronica felt like this was déjà vu and remembered what they had said after the saliva sample at the hospital. But what if even a full genome alignment did not reveal who the father was? This was highly unlikely, and she almost felt sad that this final test would now inevitably reveal the truth. Had Doctor Jackson still been there, she would have reversed her decision. She and Cecilia were the parents, no matter what, and the revelation of the father would not change anything about it, except maybe complicate matters.

CHAPTER 12

Amy and Gabriel had finally assembled all their furniture and unpacked every single box of their old lives that stood now joint and in harmony on the shelves. Amy had taken the chance to thin out her possessions, and Gabriel had her back when she considered keeping one or the other item. He had rightfully pointed out that if she hadn't used that macrame kit in five years or attempted to learn percussions, she probably won't do it now that they were planning to start a family.

Her life felt ordered and streamlined as it had never been, and to some extent, it was good to know exactly what was supposed to happen every day, to treat herself to little things when all the chores had been done. Yet, there was some restlessness in the undercurrent, and Amy could not shake the fear that Gabriel would turn his back on her if she did not do everything to his standards.

A relief for this fear was meeting up with Miranda, which was unfortunately also exactly the trigger that she wanted to avoid, so they met whenever Amy was in Orlando to run errands or when Gabriel was out for a foreseeable amount of time.

This Saturday, Amy had already done the groceries for the week and cleaned the bathroom and kitchen whilst Gabriel was out leading a weekend course for potential recruits.

So, Miranda had come by as Ozzy was also working this weekend and little Toby was visiting the zoo with his grandparents. They finished watching *Thelma and Louise*, another classic they had seen together many times.

"I think there hasn't been a movie since, when was it released again?" asked Miranda.

"It was 1991," Amy answered.

"That's fifty, sixty, sixty-three years, where women were put front and centre. I mean, men didn't really matter to the story."

"I think at the time some men felt it was degrading."

"But it is not; they just didn't matter to the story. If anything, it told the truth."

"I don't know, it's kinda degrading. I mean Thelma's husband was pretty bad, and that guy in the roadhouse was a rapist. Heck, even Brat Pitt's character is a petty thief," Amy thought out loud.

"Who cares? He looked hot. But if you want to argue it like this, Louise shoots that fucktwit in the car park, they blow up a tank, drunk driving, casual sex, armed robbery. They don't do nice things either. What I'm saying is it's the women driving the story, literally and figuratively."

"I think we can agree that it is one of the best movies of all time," said Amy.

"Amen."

"Would you like something to drink?"

"Whatcha having?"

"How about a nice fennel tea?" offered Amy.

"I won't say no to that," said Miranda. "But only one. I need to pick up Toby from the grandparents, and I don't want to get smashed."

Amy made two cups of tea.

"You don't have to drink this crappy fennel tea with me. Have a glass of wine while you still can," said Miranda.

"No, it's all right. And Gabriel would be upset if I drank during the day."

Amy covered the two of them with a blanket, and they had a toe fight on the sofa.

"Oh, that guy should get his act together and be a man," said Miranda.

Amy smiled ashamed and nipped on her hot tea almost burning her lips.

"Come on, if he can't make you happy, how does he think to get you pregnant?"

"You must be very happy then with Ozzy," teased Amy, looking at Miranda's burgeoning belly, which she currently used as a table for her mug.

"I am. I curse him every day for what he's done to me," Miranda gestured around her mid-section, "but between that, he makes me very happy."

"And who says I'm not happy?" Amy's eyes watered up unexpectedly.

She thought she had found a man to have a similarly happy partnership with, but she was now conflicted about whether she should just be happy with what they had or whether her longing for a baby was justified. She was not jealous, but she envied Miranda.

"Oh, honey, what's up? Tell it to Auntie Miranda and little Patrick." Miranda tried her best to crouch over her belly to give Amy a hug.

"I don't think it's the best time for us to have a baby," confessed Amy.

"There's never a good time for a baby."

"Maybe … but I think I also don't … want a baby anymore." Amy was surprised at her own words and tried to come up with a better way to express her feelings, but she always ended up at the same phrase.

"You're kidding. You've wanted to be a mum since, like, forever."

"And I still do. It's just … I think I don't want a baby with, with him." Amy was ashamed for speaking this truth out loud. "At least not right now."

Miranda looked quizzically at her friend and waited for more.

"Maybe we should've waited with the wedding until we knew each other better," Amy mused.

"So, it's not as romantic anymore, huh?"

"Ever since we went on our honeymoon, he's changed."

"Is he beating you?"

"What? No."

This was not where Amy had intended this conversation to go. Gabriel would never hurt her, and she was mortified that she had given the impression that her marriage was on such a rocky boat.

"Is he possessed by some alien thing, like Johnny Depp? Oh, that's so funny," Miranda couldn't stop laughing. "Do you get it? *The Astronaut's Wife*? You? I'm sorry, I'm sorry, oh no, I think I peed myself." Miranda finally held it together. "So sorry, hormones, they don't just make you mopey."

"He's just so stressed with, I guess, his job or getting another mission that no matter what I do, he gets upset with me. I don't know what else I can do."

"Oh, honey. Maybe a baby is all it takes."

"I've gone back on the pill yesterday," confessed Amy.

"And you tell me that now?" Miranda theatrically clapped a hand over her forehead.

She really knew how to lighten the mood, thought Amy.

"When else should I have told you that?"

"I don't know, maybe when you opened the door. 'Come in, Miranda. I'm back on the pill cause I don't want to carry Gabriel's alien spawn'."

"I've made my decision," concluded Amy.

"I know, and whatever your reasons, I'll be there to support you."

She also knew when jokes were not appropriate anymore.

Their conversation was interrupted by the front door opening and closing, and Amy's heart missed a beat. Was it this late already?

Gabriel stopped in the doorway to the living room, silently taking in the scene of his wife cosied up with her friend on the sofa.

"Hi, Gabriel!" waved Miranda over Amy's head.

"Hi, honey, is it that late already? We've been watching old classics," explained Amy, pretending utter innocence.

"With Brad Pitt," giggled Miranda, as Amy untangled herself from their blanket.

Gabriel just stared at them, obviously clueless who they were talking about.

"The hottest man there ever was?" clarified Miranda, looking just as stunned as Gabriel.

"Gabriel doesn't watch old movies. He had to look up *Casablanca* on Wikipedia," said Amy.

"What's with dinner?" interrupted Gabriel.

"I was going to make mac and cheese," said Amy.

"What stopped you?"

"It'll be ready in twenty minutes."

"If you start now."

"I should go then and let the man eat before he turns into the Hulk." Miranda squeezed into the hallway, raising eyebrows to Amy.

"Thanks for coming over, Miranda," said Gabriel, but the words did not reflect in his tone.

"Always a pleasure," said Miranda courteously.

Gabriel left them alone and went into the kitchen.

"I see what you mean. If he at least had Brad's chiselled jawline," whispered Miranda to Amy.

"Miranda!" exclaimed Amy, handing over her purse.

"What? Don't deny that you have the hots for Brad. That's what our friendship is based on."

"See you next week." Amy kissed Miranda on the cheek.

"Bye, Gabriel!" shouted Miranda along the hall.

Gabriel stood in the kitchen, overhearing the conversation in the hall but staying silent when Miranda shouted her farewell. He played absent-mindedly with a pear in a bowl of fruit and pressed his thumb into the soft tissue.

The front door closed, and Amy came into the kitchen.

"So, you had a nice day?" asked Gabriel.

"Yes, I did," said Amy and began her dinner preparations.

"You went twenty dollars over your grocery budget for this week. What did you buy?"

Amy was dumfounded. "Coffee was on deal, and I bought several packs to save money."

Gabriel batted his eyes. "And what about the coffees you always get when you're in Orlando? Don't pretend I don't know that you are meeting Miranda every time."

"It's just a small cappuccino for like half an hour," defended Amy.

"And why is it that you must see her all the time? Do you talk about me?"

"No, well, sometimes. Nothing personal." Amy felt uneasy and she couldn't steady her gaze. She did talk to Miranda about their relationship, but it was more about her own emotions, and not that Gabriel had done anything wrong. How could he know anyway?

Amy filled a kettle with water and put a pot on the stove.

"Don't lie to me," said Gabriel quietly.

"Just that you are stressed because the application for the next mission is coming up."

"So, you lied and you do talk about private matters. How do you think that makes me feel? Do you ever consider that I might feel ashamed when you tell others about my private issues? You are my wife, and you should know better. I don't like it when you meet her."

"She is my best friend. Or do you want to tell me who I can be friends with or not?"

That was bold, Amy thought. And she paid the price for it when Gabriel swept the fruit bowl off the table.

"Don't talk to me like that."

He cornered her like a dark tower of doom, and Amy backed off until she hit the kitchen aisle.

"I'm sorry," muttered Amy, confused and utterly intimidated. She realized that he was stressed, but that was no reason to react like this. Surely, there must be another reason than him disliking Miranda.

"And don't talk to other people about me. When I come home, I expect respect, especially from my wife," Gabriel continued.

"I do respect you." This was ridiculous. Where was this coming from?

Amy had no time to come up with a reason for Gabriel's behaviour when he hit her across the face.

"I know what respect looks like, and it doesn't have your face."

Amy held her cheek and found blood on her fingertips. Her world had turned upside down. Not even an hour ago, she had ensured Miranda that Gabriel was not hitting her and had found even the mention of it ridiculous. Did Miranda suspect that something like this could happen?

Gabriel looked at his watch. "You have thirteen minutes left for your macaroni and cheese," he said before leaving the kitchen and turning on the TV in the living room.

Amy was shaking in shock, and finally the tears were coming, but she stifled an audible sob in a kitchen towel. This was the man of her dreams; how could it have all turned into a nightmare? He was good looking, had a well-paying job, remembered her favourite foods and drinks. Yes, he did not share her interest in movies or liked to try out new things, but he took care of her.

She really should start paying more attention to him. After all, he did call in the morning, letting her know when he would be home, so she could have dinner ready. She made a promise to herself that she would do anything in her power to make this marriage work. He was still the best thing that had ever happened to her, and she was prepared to make a greater effort in providing a loving home.

* * *

Whether he realized it or not, Mack was not yet prepared to make a greater effort in finding the love of his life, outside of secretly collecting DNA samples.

He came home after his Sunday morning routine, although he had tried a new café this time, because he had gotten lucky with Claire last night. She was supposed to continue her trip around Australia next week before returning home to France, but he wanted to make sure that he did not run into her, as their chemistry was not right after all.

He had his chocolate croissant and coffee from a bakery at a shopping mall downtown. It tasted different, but he might get used to it, and if not, he could return to his old coffee shop next week. He read the news again on his phone projection over the kitchen counter, skipped over a headline proclaiming that the poultry industry in Australia was collapsing because hens laid no fertilized eggs anymore. Probably another bird flu making the rounds, Mack thought.

Apparently, abortions were increasing world-wide, which caused violent clashes between pro-lifers and pro-choicers to the point that the US government had sent police to abortion clinics to provide women with safe access. Mack understood both sides, but in the end, he believed it was a private matter and a private choice that everyone had to make and live with. All you could do was to educate and inform people at every stage. He thought about his aunt and her contraception bill in Europe and quickly checked whether her line of action had had any impact yet. Nope, it looked like Germany, Belgium, the Netherlands, almost every northern European country was also showing a considerable uptick in abortions. Poor Gayle, she probably had her hands full if European politicians were scrutinized by the media anywhere close to what happened in Australia. He should give her a ring soon and see how things are.

But for now, there was nothing more noteworthy in the daily news, so Mack proceeded with his Sunday routine. He fetched a freezer bag from the fridge with dyed red hair from Claire. He wondered how well the DNA extraction from dyed hair would work and whether the colouring would interfere with the chemical reactions. He printed labels and retreated to his lab. Tomorrow, he should have space on the sequencer to include the sample and get results.

As the water bath with the enzyme digestion softly shook in the background, Mack skimmed through his database of pictures of women. He reminisced about some of the encounters. There was Brianne, the strawberry blonde whose name he had forgotten. Although with some rustic charm, he had only hooked up with her to increase his sample size and because she had stood silently next to him for an hour whilst he was chatting up Elisabeth. Elisabeth later left with this dude from the band, so he had struck up a conversation with Brianne, which was more of a one-sided questioning and a lot of nodding.

He had genuinely been interested in some of these women, even imagined how it would be to get to know them better, wake up next to them every morning or what their children would look like. But his final screening, which made or broke any chances of a continuing relationship, had so far always thwarted any further advances from Mack's side.

He finally pulled his head out of the clouds and got on with his task. The last month, he had sequenced the genome of three more women, but due to his conference travels, he had not had time to screen the sequences for lethal or unfavourable mutations.

Mack opened the editor and ran a program he had written back when he was a PhD student, to create a risk score for all known functional mutations causing or at least increasing the risk for any known heritable illnesses, from cancer to schizophrenia. Even though he had purchased the best computer he could get for private use, the program took almost ten minutes to scan all three billion base pairs and crunch the numbers.

Finally, the results came in, and one by one, the DNA sequences of the new candidates appeared on the screen. Mack scrolled to the beginning of the sequences and noticed on the fly a blur of red and green regions indicating favourable or unfavourable genome variants.

The names of the women who had unknowingly participated in this experiment stood at the beginning of each sequence: Michelle, Amanda, Min-Ju, Marsha.

Mack clicked on the first name, and a list of genotypes for several hundred genes opened, right on top the breast cancer genes *BRCA1*, *BRCA2*, *TP53*, and *PTEN*. The list of genotypes was also coloured in red and green areas, and poor Michelle would probably develop cancer sooner or later. Sometimes, when Mack saw a result like this, he thought about whether it was his moral obligation to inform these women to take their cancer screening seriously. He could pretend that he was encouraging people to get screened in general, without revealing how much insight into their future he had gained, but then he was, like most people, not that invested in other people's well-being if they had not become part of his life. And to become part of his life, a woman had to achieve a risk score under five percent, something that none had managed so far.

Mack opened the next file. Overall risk score twenty percent, better than average, but some major indicators for diabetes and heart disease. This could be managed with diet and exercise, but he not only wanted a wife who was healthy but also lowered the chances of his children getting any heritable diseases. This was at the heart of his search, a woman to grow old with and a mother for their children who would not die a premature death due to some stupid genetic predisposition.

Mack opened the last file and stared at the screen almost in shock. The risk score was 4.5 percent. A quick scan of the list of genes verified that no major defects were detected, and the few red flags highlighted the potential for short-sightedness, colour-blindness, and male baldness. Certainly, all things that he could compromise on in exchange for a long and happy relationship. He checked the name and smiled at the memory of Marsha's long, black hair and their stormy night in Shanghai. This was certainly a woman he had imagined waking up to in the morning.

The phone rang in the living room, but Mack let it go to answer phone as he gazed at a photo of a sleeping Marsha.

At first, he did not pay much attention to the voice in the other room, but then it hit him right into the stomach.

"Hi Mack, it's Michelle. I don't know how else to put it, so, I'm pregnant, and you might be the father. Call me. In case you've lost it, my number is 0465116378," said a female voice.

Mack's face froze in horror, his fingers pressed down on the table. Eventually he stumbled to his phone and listened to the message again. And again, finally noting down the phone number she had so thoughtfully left. This could not be. He was always so careful. Besides checking that his hook-ups took the pill, he always used condoms.

Mack paced up and down in front of his phone on the kitchen counter. This was ridiculous. He picked up the phone and dialled but immediately hung up.

Instead, he grabbed his keys and left his flat. After walking aimlessly along the river, he stopped at a bottle shop and got himself a cheap bottle of whisky. When he arrived back home, he had already drunk half of it.

Mack slouched on his sofa, plonking the whisky bottle on the table, and dialled with drunken fingers.

"Hello?" Michelle answered.

"Michelle? This's Mack."

"Oh ... hi, Mack."

She sounded confused. Why was she confused? She had asked for a call back.

"Hullo. Hi," mumbled Mack, sorting his thoughts.

"I guess you're calling because of the, um, the baby?" asked Michelle.

Why else would he call? He hadn't called her once in the last two months since they hooked up.

"Yeah, yeah ... I thought you were taking the pill?"

"I was. I don't know how it happened."

"I have a petty, um, pretty good idea how."

"Well yeah, stupid, ... Listen, you were not the only one."

"What? ... How, how many are there?" Why was he upset about this? He should be happy about this little ray of light that had just burst back into his life after a torrent of rain.

"Doesn't matter now. I've decided to have an abortion."

"Abortion. Really?" The clouds in Mack's world opened.

"Please don't make this any more complicated."

"Complicated? I was worried I'd be a father with you ... sorry, I didn't mean ..." Oh, shut up, Mack.

"Well, you won't."

She sounded hurt, and she had every right to be. Mack agonized over an appropriate answer, but his brain was not very helpful. If only he had made this call before he downed a pint of sharp whisky that had an aftertaste of raw onion and burned his tonsils.

"I guess, then, it was nice talking to you. Not that I don't support your decision, I mean, also if you'd decided differently, I mean to keep it, but I think this is best. For everyone." What a cockup.

"Clearly for everyone," responded Michelle.

"Yeah, yeah. Oh hey, while you're there, get a checkup for breast cancer."

"What?"

"One can never be too cautious. I mean, never mind."

"Goodbye, Mack."

"Yeah, bye."

Mack fell face forward on his sofa and screamed into the cushions, which turned into hysterical laughter and finally into a comatose sleep.

Unfortunately, the tide had not turned yet in Mack's thunderstorm. He was rudely woken up a couple of hours later by his phone, but before he could answer, the ringing stopped. Mack's head pounded painfully, and he heaved himself up to get a glass of water and a painkiller.

The phone began ringing again, and Mack scrunched his eyes closed. The answer phone popped on, and another female voice left a message.

"Hey Mack, it's Brianne. I have some news, and I'd like to meet up. Could you come to the café where we met last month, say in an hour?"

"How do I know where we met last month?" muttered Mack, and slowly his brain caught up and reminded him that it was his usual Sunday morning café that he had planned to avoid for the next week or so.

Before Mack entered the café, he peered through the windows to see if Claire was still working there, but he did not see her. Instead, he spotted strawberry-blonde Brianne at a table, munching away on a huge stack of pancakes.

He entered and sat down opposite her. "Hey, Brianne, how's it going?"

"Oh hey," she squealed through a mouth full of food. "Not too bad. Do you wanna order anything?"

"Nah, I'm fine. You wanted to talk to me?"

He did not want to stay longer than necessary. He did not even know why he had come in the first place. After all, it was rather unusual to leave someone a message and expect that person to actually turn up. But this was Brianne. After her initial shy silence, she had turned out to be a real talker. Unfortunately, nothing she talked about was interesting to Mack.

"You sure? These pancakes are awesome," she insisted.

"No, I have to get something for my mum, so I don't have much time."

"Oh, all righty."

"What is it?" Mack grew increasingly frustrated.

"Um, so, you remember that night, um, when we met? I know we used a condom, but I checked, and they're just like ninety-eight percent effective when used correctly." Mack didn't like where this was going. "I think, we're like the last two percent."

"I'm sorry, are you trying to tell me …"

"I'm … pregnant and, and you're the father."

Brianne looked at him with flushed cheeks, and Mack simply blanked out.

This was utterly surreal. Was he in a time loop, where the same scenario happened over and over again only with different people in it?

"Are you okay?" asked Brianne, who must have noticed by now that Mack was not actually looking at her but at a far-away spot behind her head.

"Yeah, yeah. No. Are you sure? I mean, how far along are you?" Mack asked.

"The doctor said I'm in the seventh week, and you were kind of the only one, like, in a year."

Mack studied her face in horror. A scream was making its way up his throat, but before it could slip out, Mack jumped up and rushed out of the café.

"Mack? Mack!" he heard her crying after him before the door closed.

A pair of broody, scaly-breasted lorikeets got between Mack's legs as he stumbled onto the pavement.

"Seven weeks my ass," muttered Mack, fending off a flurry of red and green feathers. "Wait."

Mack turned around and walked back to the café. He found Brianne at the counter, paying her bill.

"We had sex once, and that was sometime mid-May. Looks like you forgot a poor beggar in between. Ha. Ha ha," Mack cackled as he left for the second time. He didn't care that he just made a scene, and everyone had looked at him. This is how it must feel to go mad, he thought.

"But you were the only one," croaked Brianne, but Mack was gone.

"Chin up. He'll come 'round," said the barista and passed her a napkin to wipe away her tears.

CHAPTER 13

James started his computer to check the patients who had asked for an appointment. Outside on the window-sill, a pair of rock doves switched their incubation duties for the second hatch of the year. The female had been out during the night and now inspected her two eggs, whilst the male stretched a wing, catching the morning sun on his iridescent neck feathers.

James liked the two birds who had now nested in his window for the second year in a row. He called them 'Lovey-Doveys' when he spoke to Jeanette about them. Rock doves mated for life, and by now, James thought he recognized the love that the two birds had for each other, as one would get restlessly worried when the other was late, and they greeted each other with some gentle feather pecking. Of course, this could also be a bird way of berating each other for staying out too long, but James preferred to think about them as a loving couple.

He wondered how long the incubation period was, as he thought that this time, they sat much longer on their eggs than previously. A quick computer search told him that incubation took, on average, nineteen days, and the hatchlings left the nest after another month or so. He was sure the pair had laid their eggs not long after he had returned from home, and he made a mental note to pay more attention to his feathered companions.

But now he had to get ready to see his first patient of the day. He walked into the waiting area and called out for Subin Sulliman. She had visited him with her husband last month to request birth control, as they already had three boys and did not want any more children. This time Subin came alone.

"Take a seat. What can I do for you?" James asked, as they entered his office together.

"Thank you, Doctor James," said Subin. "I have been feeling rather sick the last few days, but I don't know what it is."

"Are you in pain?" James asked.

"No, I just feel sick in my stomach, like throwing up."

"Have you eaten anything unusual?"

"No. And my family are all well too. I wash all fruits and boil our water."

"Does it get better or worse when you eat?"

"Better when I eat, but only small amounts."

"I see that you received a hormonal implant last month. Did you bleed since then?" James dug deeper.

"No bleeding, but you said that could be a side effect."

"It is, though it is more common that periods continue on an implant. Could you lie down here, and I will feel your stomach, see whether something hurts or is a little tender."

Subin lay down, and James pushed his fingers into her belly at various places. She was pain free, and he could not detect any unusual hardening.

"Are you feeling sick right now?" James asked when Subin had sat down again.

"A little," said Subin.

James had a quick look at Subin's eyes and then felt her thyroid glands. "I would like to run a quick blood test to check for any infections."

"Is there anything wrong with me?" asked Subin.

"I haven't found anything. My best guess is that you are a little low on red blood cells."

James prepared a needle to draw blood from Subin's arm. She turned her head away as he punctured her skin.

"All done," he said to release her from her misery. "You can go home, and we'll be in touch when the results are in, or you can wait half an hour if you have time."

"So quick? I'll wait," said Subin, surprised.

James accompanied Subin to the waiting area and passed her blood sample on to their little laboratory, which was able to carry out simple blood tests on the spot.

He attended to two more patients before Subin's test results came back. She sat down nervously, looking paler than thirty minutes ago.

"Are you feeling all right?" asked James.

"A little more queasy right now," Subin confessed.

"Well, I have your results, and you are not sick," said James, studying the report.

Subin exhaled, relieved.

"The reason you are feeling a little sick lately is because you are pregnant," James explained.

Subin stared at James, and he saw the blood draining from her face and her eyes roll back. He caught her just in time, as she slid from the chair, to gently place her on the floor.

"Sister!" called James. "Can you bring us a glass of water and some biscuits from the tearoom," he ordered as a nurse appeared in the doorframe.

Slowly but surely, Subin regained consciousness.

"What happened?" she whispered.

"You fainted," said James gently. "Here, you should drink a little, and if you can, take a bite. We have plain shortbread, raspberry drops, or salted caramel wafers."

James held her head as Subin sipped from a paper cup.

"Do you remember what I told you before you fainted?" asked James.

Subin nodded wearily.

After a few minutes, James helped her back into the chair. "Based on your reaction and that you requested birth control, I would like to advise you that there are options if you do not want another child. You don't need to decide now, and it is perfectly understandable if you wish to think about it or talk to your husband first. Here, this covers everything from adoption to abortion. Read them carefully, and please make an appointment with me or another service to discuss and get further help."

"Thank you," whispered Subin, staring at the leaflets that James just passed to her.

At the end of the day, James had given another two women those leaflets. One was only nineteen years old and in tears, swearing that she was a virgin. Of course, it was possible to conceive a child without penetrative sex, however, very unlikely. James had looked this up recently after a colleague from the University Hospital made fun of the increasing number of young pregnant women claiming to be virgins. On one side, James found it encouraging that more women had gained the confidence to request abortions. At the same time, he found it upsetting that they still felt the need to deny that they were sexually active. He wondered what would happen to the women. Were they in danger as they had been twenty or thirty years ago of being expelled from their families and community, or even worse, punished sometimes to death? He hadn't heard of any such punishments in Sudan since he arrived almost eighteen months ago.

Engrossed in thought, he resolved to pay more attention to the situation of these women. The comparable peace to other countries or war zones had made him complacent of keeping an eye out on how life for his patients, and society at large, could be improved. Something that should never be neglected, no matter how good things appeared to be.

James finished his last patient report and turned off his computer, ready to go home, when he noticed that the Lovey-Doveys had abandoned their nest.

* * *

Subin sat on the bus in a trance. She was pregnant again. They should have gone with the vasectomy, but then they were not one hundred percent convinced that they never wanted a child again. It was just that at the moment, they could not afford another child, and their three boys were quite a handful.

The bus crossed the Victory Bridge over the White Nile, and Subin saw heavy rainclouds gather on the horizon. At last, it seemed the rainy season was about to begin, giving the land and the dry and dusty streets a short refreshment. Where other parts of the world fell victim to rising water levels, Khartoum, like so many cities in Africa, watched their rivers flow sluggish and dry. She remembered when the bridge was rebuilt after a particularly heavy drought had exposed the old concrete foundations, which were eroded after a century in the mighty river. Even though building on the riverbanks was not allowed due to unpredictable flooding that still occurred, slums of small huts built from corrugated iron sprouted from the bog like sharp mushrooms. And when a flood came, the mushrooms and their poor inhabitants who had fled the expanding deserts were swept away by a gushing rapid of muddy water. Wasn't it ironic?

Subin wanted to lean her head against the window to cool her forehead, but even this small gesture could have been seen as a sign that something was not right with her, at the very least that she had a headache, and she did not want to draw any attention to herself. She got off a few stops after Fifteenth Street to pick up her four-year-old from her mother's.

She reassured her mother that everything was all right, as she did not want to reveal her pregnancy until she and Rashaad had decided on what they wanted to do. Even though abortion rights had been extended in the last twenty years, a married woman was still only allowed to terminate a pregnancy if her husband agreed to it. And whilst Subin had no doubt that she and Rashaad would come to an agreement, one way or another, she was unsure which way her heart was pulling. Maybe this was the little baby girl she had always longed for, or it was another boy to add to her rat pack. She loved her children, but deep inside, she did not want to have another boy who would run wild, pretending to be a soldier or some other warrior that inevitably made a lot of noise and brought chaos to the house.

She decided to walk the few blocks back home instead of paying for another bus trip. Her youngster was running ahead on the pavement, chasing birds, and Subin had trouble following him. The nearing rain front had pushed sultry air into the city. It felt like three years ago, when the riverbanks flooded, and bodies were found for days after, even outside the city boundaries. She wondered whether the authorities would bother to evacuate the banks this time or at least give out a warning, but she suspected even if they knew, a natural catastrophe would most likely play into their hand by cleaning out the unwelcomed slums.

"Aarif," she shouted as he approached the busy Mohammed Najebi Street. "Wait up!"

Aarif stopped and waited, but not without jumping here and there to stir up the birds, giving Subin heart attacks, as with every jump, she saw him landing on the street and under the wheels of one of the thousand cars.

She should have taken the bus, Subin thought when they finally arrived at their building block. She was drenched in sweat when they reached their sixth-floor apartment. Once inside, she did not have much time to relax, as Aarif was demanding something to drink and then for cartoons to be turned on.

With her last strength, Subin fetched a cold Vimto can from the fridge and made herself a tea before slumping down on the sofa. The sweet tea brought back some of her vigour just in time to start dinner when Mohamad and Malik returned from school.

"And what did you learn today?" asked Subin from the kitchen, putting on an atmosphere of normalcy.

"Nothing," shouted seven-year-old Malik from next door.

"That's mine! Mama, Malik took my Vimto!" screamed Aarif.

"Malik, give it back!" shouted Subin from the kitchen.

"It's mine," Malik answered.

"Come and get yourself another one from the fridge. And take one for Mohamad," called Subin.

A scuffle from the living room and a loud bang told her that the boys were still fighting over a half-empty can and that one of them had just hit the floor. Mohamad, her ten-year-old, came in as a wailing broke out in the next room.

"How are you?" asked Subin, ignoring the noises from her other two sons.

"I'm good. Can I help you?" asked Mohamad.

"No, thank you." She stroked his head. "Dinner will be ready when your father comes home. Just stop those two from hurting each other too much."

Mohamad nodded and trotted back out with two cold cans. The fighting stopped, and all Subin could hear was the cartoons on the TV for a while.

As she stirred a pot, she tried to sort her thoughts about having another baby and the impact it would have on their future life. Her world seemed suddenly so small, like nothing existed outside of that kitchen, even outside of her own body.

Rashaad arrived home thirty minutes later, and Subin served Kisra bread with red lentil stew. She stood in the door watching her hungry family devour the meal, squatted around the coffee table.

"Sit," said Rashaad.

"Later. I'll make us some Karkaday tea first," Subin replied.

Now that she knew what made her sick, she also knew how to remedy it. She should not drink too much black tea anymore, but the sweet hibiscus tea was a refreshing alternative to quench her thirst and relieve the sickness, which was often simply a result of her low blood sugar levels. She thought about her previous pregnancies, how her sense of smell had changed so much that she had trouble walking around the Souq market without throwing up. Brushing her teeth was also always a source for gagging. But all of this had also given her the assurance that she was carrying a child even before her belly started growing.

She was just dissolving a generous amount of honey in the tea when the first thunder rolled over Khartoum. Shortly after, the grey clouds dropped their heavy load.

"Karkaday, huh?" asked Rashaad when she finally sat down.

"Yummy," shouted Aarif and proceeded to jump on the sofa, before Subin could answer.

"Careful, sit down when you drink," Subin reprimanded him.

It was another two hours before Aarif went to bed and yet another couple of hours before her two eldest sons had finished their homework and disappeared quietly into their shared bedroom to not wake up Aarif.

And finally, Subin and Rashaad were alone. This was the time of day she enjoyed most. This hour of calm before she went to bed, as she had to get up early in the morning again to get through another day.

"So, Karkaday?" repeated Rashaad, after pouring the last glass and handing it to Subin.

"Refreshing," replied Subin and took a sip. She did not know how to break the news to him.

"So is the rain," said Rashaad.

"I'm sorry," sobbed Subin. Uncontrollable crying was another of her pregnancy symptoms.

"How far along?" asked Rashaad.

"Four or five weeks," said Subin.

"That's just after you got the implant."

"I know. It should have worked. I'm so sorry."

Rashaad took Subin into his arms. "Don't be. We should be happy. Allah wants us to have another child. We must be doing good."

They sat and embraced for a long while, listening to the rain drumming against their window. Subin thought about all the children in the slums who would probably wake up to a different world if they'd go to sleep tonight at all. Maybe they'd lose their broken toys, maybe even a parent or their own lives. Would she really want to set another child into this world?

* * *

Family life could not be more different in Orlando. Veronica and Cecilia were having breakfast in bed with baby Verity lying in their midst, wriggling around like a worm, and happily cooing as if she was partaking in their conversation. The rain pattered down on their balcony, giving them a good excuse to stay in bed.

"I don't think I ever wanna get out of bed again," said Veronica and snuggled into her pillows. "Why can't I get paid for sleeping? Maybe I should apply for a sleep study."

"As long as you come back to breastfeed," laughed Cecilia.

"When do we start giving her solids?" asked Veronica.

"Still a while to go. Sometime around six months."

"So long?"

"You should read a bit more," said Cecilia and passed her an infant-education book from her nightstand.

"It should have been you," said Veronica and put the book down on her nightstand.

This remark had caused an awkward silence, and Veronica knew that Cecilia did not know what to answer to it. She was always the one who wanted to carry a baby and breastfeed, but of course, suggesting that she should have gotten pregnant during a space mission without her consent was unfair.

"I wonder when the results of the paternity test will be ready," Cecilia finally said.

This now caused Veronica to stay silent, as she did not want to know the result. She had found a happy place of denial. Caring for a new-born had become easier now, as she had learned to recognize the cues and caught up on some sleep.

The doorbell absolved Veronica from continuing their conversation.

"I'll get it," said Cecilia.

"Who is it?" called Veronica when Cecilia talked to someone at the intercom.

Finally, Cecilia came back in. "You better get dressed. It's Doctor Jackson again."

"What? Why?"

"It's the paternity test."

"Speak of the devil and he does appear."

They both slipped into some presentable clothes just in time when Doctor Jackson knocked on the door.

"I thought you'd just send a letter with the results," said Veronica when Doctor Jackson had sat down in their living room.

"Normally, we would have done that, but the results are unfortunately not normal," replied Doctor Jackson.

"What do you mean?" Veronica started to panic.

"Ms. Vargas, I must ask you and your child to come with me to Houston. There have been some … irregularities which must be contained." Doctor Jackson threw a glance at Cecilia.

"What irregularities?" asked Cecilia.

"Unfortunately, I am not allowed to talk about the matter any further for now. But I can assure you that you are not sick or in any danger," Doctor Jackson tried to diffuse the situation.

"Can I come with her?" asked Cecilia.

"I don't think that's possible."

"What if I don't come?" asked Veronica.

"Then I have two officers waiting downstairs and this court order to take you with us." Doctor Jackson handed Veronica a letter.

"You can't do that. What are the reasons? Who is this judge who signed this without reasons? I've done nothing wrong!" Veronica had gotten up and walked to the door. She wanted to scream but her body was so tense that nothing erupted. She had done nothing wrong. Why was she going to get punished?

"How long will she have to stay in Houston?" asked Cecilia.

"A few weeks, maybe a month. But there is no definite end date," answered Doctor Jackson.

This was ridiculous! What was going on? Veronica opened the door decidedly silently, wishing that the doctor would go and disappear forever.

"And you cannot tell us anything else?" Cecilia looked outside the window and saw two grey umbrellas waiting by a black pod.

"Not right here, not right now."

"I'm coming with her, or you'll have to drag her out with me on her legs," Cecilia said.

Veronica was desperate but hearing how Cecilia stood up for them gave her strength, and she wondered whether she would get penalized or whether she was just overreacting. It must be something worse than a vitamin deficiency; maybe a genetic disorder that they had discovered, and going back to the headquarters with her daughter would be the best thing to do.

Doctor Jackson rubbed his eyes. "You will have to enter the facility under the same conditions and sign an NDA. I cannot promise that you will be allowed in once we are there, but if these are my options, I'll take both of you. Please pack only a few private items and what you need for the baby. You will be provided with all necessary items at our facility."

Cecilia nodded to Veronica, who slowly closed the door again.

Half an hour later, Veronica knocked on her mother's door to let her know that she was going to Houston for a post-mission examination and that Cecilia and the baby were accompanying her. She shouldn't worry, and they would give her a call when they knew when they were coming back.

Mrs. Hernandez was suspicious, but Cecilia called on cue from downstairs, giving Veronica a reason to leave and stop her mother from asking too many questions.

What on earth is happening, wondered Veronica as the two umbrellas guided them through the rain to a spacious pod. Clearly, something was wrong, no matter what Doctor Jackson tried to tell them. She was only glad that Cecilia was with her this time.

CHAPTER 14

Over the last couple of months, Amy had gotten into a good rhythm in her new life with Gabriel. She kept the house tidy, made sure to iron their clothes before putting them away, and the new bank account that Gabriel had opened for her covered their weekly grocery shops. Gabriel took care of their mortgage, insurances, and other expenses, so that Amy did not have to worry about these things. Sometimes, she wished that she still had her own bank account, but all her money went into their mortgage, and her income didn't even cover half of her share. Overall, her life was a lot more upscale than she could have ever dreamed of. And having left the mental stress behind of trying to have a baby right away had worked wonders in the bedroom. Amy had stopped charting her ovulation or instigating sexual intercourse at fixed times; but she had also not told Gabriel that she was taking the pill again.

The only thing that Amy hadn't changed was seeing Miranda, although she avoided going out for coffees now and instead invited her over when Gabriel was out, to leave no trace online.

Even Gabriel's mood seemed to be on an upswing, despite the fact that he had thrown the laundry out the window when he had found that his white shirts still had yellow sweat marks under the armpits, and he had punched a dent into their fridge when Amy had forgotten to buy eggs for his lunchbox. She hadn't forgotten the eggs; it was just that there seemed to be a shortage of eggs, and they were simply out at the supermarket.

Luckily, they would soon have their own egg supply, as Gabriel had built a chicken coop, and Amy had ordered four Easter Eggers, which laid blue eggs. She had seen beautiful hand-carved eggs in a home-maker magazine and thought that this might be a hobby she could pick up once her chickens started laying.

It was Friday, and Amy had spent most of her day at work with the children making autumn decorations from colourful red leaves.

She had started to feel a little woozy before lunch and wondered whether they should switch the glue. The fresh air during their afternoon playtime outside had made her feel better, but just the last hour or so, she became nauseated again.

Gabriel was working late, expecting a call from NASA to discuss his last examination results and what support he could give for upcoming missions. Miranda and she had made plans to make use of the free afternoon, but considering how Amy felt right now, she thought to call Miranda to postpone their meetup. However, when she finally found a chance to pick up her phone, she found a message that Miranda was already on her way.

Now, Miranda sat straddle-legged on a bench made for children in the hallway of Amy's childcare centre. The coat hangers and lockers around her were already empty, and only Poppy was still waiting to be picked up.

Heavy retching sounded from the staff toilet. Amy had just put out the bin with the soiled diapers from the baby room, and the smell had made her sick to her stomach; she had barely made it back to the toilet.

"So, how was your day?" Miranda asked little Poppy, who just stared at her enormous belly. "Yeah, I know, shouldn't have eaten a whole cow for lunch," Miranda joked, patting her belly, and Poppy's eyes grew even bigger. "What did you have for lunch? I heard they make some excellent elephant bottoms in these parts of the country. Have you ever tried one? No?"

Amy came out of the toilet.

"Thank goodness. This child wouldn't stop talking. Are you all right?" Miranda asked Amy.

"Yes, yes." Amy waved, exhausted.

"Didn't sound like it. Poppy here said it sounded like you called some dinosaurs."

"I'm fine." Amy grabbed her coat, and together they left the kindergarten with Poppy in tow.

Outside, the fresh air cleared Amy's head. She had been feeling funny on and off for several weeks now, but this was the first time she threw up.

If she had a stomach bug, she knew she should stay home and not work with children, but she had a hunch that it wasn't a stomach bug.

They walked along the manicured gardens of the new buildings of the compound to drop off Poppy. Ever since Amy had walked the child home once, her mother took increasing advantage of this exclusive but unagreed service.

"I need to ask a favour of you," Amy finally said.

"Sure."

"I think I'm pregnant," whispered Amy.

"What? I thought you were back on the pill," exclaimed Miranda.

"I am. But I haven't gotten my period for the last two months, and I have this slight motion sickness almost all the time."

"Have you gone to the doctor yet?"

"No, that's why I need you to get me a pregnancy test."

"Why?"

"Everyone knows everything here, and I haven't gotten around to go somewhere else to buy a test. I don't want Gabriel to find out from some nosy neighbour or question the grocery bill."

"Why would he question your grocery bill? Those tests aren't cheap but surely they don't break the bank?"

"Maybe, I just don't want him to get disappointed again," pleaded Amy.

"And I wouldn't look suspicious? I mean, if I didn't know that I am pregnant by now, there would be something seriously wrong with me, don't you think?" said Miranda, pointing at her full-term belly.

"Please?"

"Okay, okay. Point me to the shop, and I'll meet you at home. Maybe a little walk will make this baby come out too."

"It's two streets down and around the corner from where Poppy lives," explained Amy.

"Can't wait to see you with your own mini-me," said Miranda as she watched her friend walking hand in hand with the little girl.

"Someone as cute as you, Poppy, hm?" said Amy as she stopped at a curb to look out for pods and cars to teach Poppy how to safely cross the road, even though there were no vehicles around. "Or as handsome as your Toby, cause apparently Gabriel has decided that we're gonna have a boy."

"Boy or girl, he's gonna have to take what he gets. As long as it's healthy," countered Miranda.

"That's what I always tell him, but he seems to be convinced he has a say." Amy laughed.

"So, what's he gonna do if it's a girl? Dump it in the trash?"

"Miranda!"

Little Poppy looked at Miranda again with wide eyes.

"Yes, my little angel, men do strange things," she explained in a happy baby voice.

They stopped at the next street corner.

"The shop is right there; you can see the sign."

Amy pointed at a blue-and-white sign announcing Neville's Corner Store.

"Sure thing. When's her mother going to start picking up the child again? I didn't think this personal drop off service was a thing yet," asked Miranda, looking at Poppy, who had started to suck at her thumb.

"I don't know. She hasn't said anything."

"If you don't say something, that drunk of a mother won't tell you differently."

"Miranda!"

Poppy looked now with wide eyes from one to the other woman.

"Stop calling out my name like that. You'll give Poppy a wrong impression of me."

"A wrong impression? I think you do that yourself"

"No, no. Listen to me. At that age, it is more about *how* you say things, rather than what you say. The first two years, you have pretty much free rein, as long as you do it in a happy voice," refuted Miranda, falling back into her baby speech.

"Thanks for the lecture in mothering skills. And Poppy is four."

"Really? She looks so tiny. Must have been the drinking during pregnancy."

"Miranda!"

"What? Her mother wouldn't hear anything she doesn't know already."

"All right. Shouldn't take too long," said Amy, agitated.

Miranda was right, but as long as Poppy's mother didn't get any help for herself, she wanted to keep an eye on the little girl.

Poppy's mother half opened the door and squinted into the sunlight. She mumbled some words of gratitude and some more platitudes as excuses before shutting the door and shielding her life from the world again.

Amy walked down the trimmed front garden, which looked exactly like hers and wondered what other tragedies happened in the compound with its lined-up houses and immaculate little flowerbeds.

On her way home, she felt sorry for making her heavily pregnant friend walk around the block to get her a pregnancy test. But whilst at first, she had felt welcomed when the salesclerk at the corner shop, the trainer at the gym, or the neighbourhood patrol greeted her by name, she now felt stalked when the corner store had already half-packed groceries ready for her, and she only needed to fetch the odd item here and there.

She could have just bought a pregnancy test herself next time she visited Miranda. But she was also always so tired that she had only left the house in the last couple of weeks to do the laundry and water their new tomato plants and then fallen asleep on the sofa until Gabriel came home.

Amy had just made a tea when Miranda rang the doorbell.

"Here, bought you a multipack. They can be addictive," said Miranda.

Another minute later and Amy peed on the test stripe, whilst Miranda went through her cosmetics and tried her perfume.

"Urgh! Is this the one you always use?" asked Miranda after sniffing her wrist.

"Yes," replied Amy.

"No wonder Gabriel is so stressed. I need a painkiller after that."

Amy pulled her pants back up. "His mum gave it to me when we got married. Apparently it's the one she wears. How long do we have to wait?"

"It says five minutes, but mine always showed it almost straight away. There, two blue stripes. You are pregnant, girl!"

"What?" Amy checked the prescription pack.

The fluttery feeling of excitement only slowly spread as the certainty sank in.

"Have you been using the perfume lately?" asked Miranda.

"No," said Amy, checking the two blue stripes again. "It kind of made me nauseous."

"There you go! Before, his fighter pilots thought you were his mother and refused duty."

"Miranda!" Sometimes her jokes really made her uncomfortable.

They had a cup of tea together and pondered about how far along Amy was by dissecting her private life and how she should break the news to Gabriel. Miranda championed using the remaining pregnancy tests to lay out a trail to the nursery and then have some steamy hot sex whilst they still could. But Amy was too anxious to focus on their conversation or even to reprimand Miranda for her outrageousness, and Miranda left shortly after, because she felt a tugging in her lower back and wanted to lie down at home.

The news about her pregnancy had given Amy an energy spurt, but instead of a treasure hunt with an erotic end, she opted for a romantic dinner. Dressed up, she sat at the set table, fondling knitted baby socks she had made on a hunch already last week.

Finally, a key turned in the front door, and Amy jumped up to greet Gabriel.

"Hi, honey," said Amy and slung her arms around his neck to kiss him.

Gabriel eyeballed the setting. "What have you done?"

"What have *we* done?" said Amy.

Gabriel coldly removed himself from her loving hug.

"I made potato gratin," said Amy, confused.

"No lamb rolls this time?"

"No."

"What is it?"

Amy hesitated. This was not going like she expected. "I am pregnant."

Gabriel just stared at her boorishly. "What?"

"I am pregnant," said Amy, smiling, and held the pregnancy test towards him.

Gabriel slapped her so hard in the face that she had to catch herself on the table.

"Whose is it?" roared Gabriel.

"What do you mean?"

Amy held her cheek and tasted blood. This all happened so unexpectedly that she didn't even have time to well up.

"Who are you sleeping with?"

"No one!"

Amy panicked. Gabriel had a look in his eyes that changed her husband into a dangerous stranger. As she backed off, Gabriel followed her like a bloodhound and finally slapped her again.

"Stop lying to me! Who is it?" he shouted.

"Just you! Just you!"

For a split-second, Amy considered shouting for help, but it was too late. Gabriel punched her in her stomach, sending her to the floor, unable to speak. How could this romantic evening have turned so suddenly into a nightmare?

"Guess what I received just now from NASA?" asked Gabriel diabolically as Amy dragged herself away from him. "I was told that I am infertile. Infertile, do you hear me?" With every 'infertile', Gabriel kicked her in the stomach.

"No!" whispered Amy, shielding her head with her arms, and pulling her legs to her stomach to protect the baby.

"And you still don't have the decency to tell me the truth?"

Gabriel bent down to pull Amy's head back by her hair. "You know, I suspected long ago that you weren't just seeing Miranda on the side. Last chance. Whose is it?"

Amy's voice was gone; her eyes swam in tears, silently begging him to believe her. The next punch sent blood splatters over the floor. Something crunched inside her skull, but Amy had little time to worry about what just broke, as Gabriel proceeded kicking her in the stomach. All she could think about was to protect that little human being inside her that she had already grown to love.

"Thou shalt not bear false witness!"

Amy's face was barely recognizable anymore, but Gabriel did not stop in his delusion.

"Thou shalt not commit adultery! You whore! You dirty fucking whore!"

Amy's puffy eyes closed as she finally fainted.

When Amy woke up, she was still lying on the floor by the set dinner table. The house was quiet, and a cold morning light flooded in through the terrace doors. Her eyes were so swollen now that she could only see through a slit, and her vision was blurred. She could not tell whether this was due to her eyelashes being clumped together with blood or whether blood vessels had ruptured in her eyeballs. Carefully, she shifted her head to look across the floor to the door. The room seemed empty, and she tried to prop herself up, but a painful abdomen stopped this endeavour.

For now, she had to remain where she was. One by one she focussed on her body parts, determining where she felt pain, whether it was simply due to bruising, broken bones, or worse, external or internal bleeding. Deep breaths caused pain in her ribcage, and she was sure that she had broken ribs. Her abdomen felt like a hot lump, and a throbbing headache started between her eyes. Her legs and arms were fine, though they were tense and the skin painful to the touch.

She thought about what to do next and wondered if Gabriel was still in the house and whether he would agree to get her help or continue the abuse as soon as he realized that she was awake again. The terror of last night swept over her, and an instinct told her to get out of the house as quietly as possible.

Amy dragged herself to the terrace doors and pushed them open with her fingertips. Her head felt like it was bursting now, but the cool morning air kept her spirits alive. After a few minutes, she got up into a crouching position, and just as she wanted to slip outside, she saw her phone on the charger station within arm's reach. She grabbed it and limped into the garden, one hand on the house wall, the other clutching the phone.

She was dizzy, but if she collapsed here, no one would see her from the road. She turned on her phone, and a love song she had prepared to play yesterday blared out its romantic lyrics with acoustic guitar backing.

"Shit," she whispered and hysterically tried to find the button to turn off the music.

Amy held the phone close to her face to make out names and finally managed to dial Miranda's phone number.

"Come on, come on," pleaded Amy as no one picked up. "Hey, um, I need help," Amy wept on the voice mail. "I ... Gabriel, I'm hurt. I don't know where he is. Please. Help!"

Amy had made it to the gate and fumbled to open the latch. She stepped on to the pavement, but the few steps without any support drained her energy quickly, and she fainted again.

When she woke up again, she was lying in a bed, a cover tucked around her, and she felt oddly safe, like in a womb. The pain was gone, at least the physical hurting, but the bandages all over her body reassured her that she had not dreamt it all.

She did not want to open her eyes, as she was worried to find that she was at home and Gabriel would look at her.

Soft noises in the room told her that she was not alone. There was a quiet nuzzling sound and an odd scratching near the foot of her bed.

"Toby, stop it! Daddy will bring you some paper." Miranda's voice broke the quietness.

Amy's heart ached, and tears welled up as the relief that she was indeed safe overcame her.

A door opened, and someone entered accompanied by the smell of hot chocolate.

"Thank you, my honey bunny," said Miranda.

"No problem, buttercup," said Miranda's husband, Ozzy.

"Could you go and see if you can get some paper for Toby to draw on?"

"That's ma boy," said Ozzy after a short shuffle.

"Some paper?"

"D'you want to come with me, Toby, and see if the nurses have some paper and chocolate for us?" asked Ozzy.

"Oh yes," piped the voice of Toby, and Amy heard them leaving the room.

"How are you, honey?" asked Miranda finally. "I know you're awake. Your snoring stopped."

Amy blinked.

"I know it's hard, but the doctors said you're stable with no permanent damage."

"What about the baby?" Amy whispered.

"You'll be able to have another one."

Amy turned her head, and tears rolled out of her swollen eyes.

Miranda tucked away her breast and burped her new-born baby.

"You had your baby?" Amy said when she noticed the blurry shape of Miranda softly bouncing up and down, patting the baby's back.

"I'm sorry I didn't pick up when you called, but I was in the middle of something," Miranda explained.

Amy sniffled, a mixture of crying and smiling.

"As soon as we heard your message, Ozzy came out and found you on the pavement. They brought you to the same hospital, so we can be bunk buddies for a few days."

"I'm sorry," cried Amy.

"For what?"

"I don't know."

Miranda put the sleeping baby in a mobile cot and climbed into Amy's bed to hold her weeping friend. "Then stop being sorry. You are a wonderful person, inside and out."

"Outside?"

"Well, if you like blueberry crumble, definitely."

Amy smiled and winced at the same time.

"And I love blueberry crumble," reassured Miranda.

"Gabriel doesn't."

"He must have done, otherwise there is no excuse for making you look like one." Amy started crying again. "But the important thing is that you don't like that third-class knock-off of a Zack Mayo anymore."

"I hate Zack Mayo."

"Good!"

"And I hate *The Astronaut's Wife*."

"Good. You mean the movie, right?" Amy nodded. "And you hate the third-class knock-off of a Zack Mayo, who's delusional about blueberry crumble, right?" Amy nodded again. "Just checking, cause I have *An Officer and Gentleman* waiting at home for us."

"What home?" asked Amy.

"Our home," answered Miranda. "You'll stay with us for as long as you need to."

Amy smiled and wiped her face dry. "I want a divorce."

"Anything you want, honey, anything you want."

The door to Amy's hospital room opened, and Ozzy and Toby came back in.

"Look who's awake," said Ozzy.

"Shh, we're sleeping," mumbled Miranda. "Don't move," she whispered into Amy's ear. "I could really do with a nap."

"Hi Ozzy, hi Toby," said Amy, holding on to Miranda's arm and feeling the warmth of her body against her back.

"Amy, look what I drew for you," squealed Toby and pinched the patient's chart from the foot of the bed.

He came over and showed her the stick figures he had drawn in black ink, which were clearly playing football.

"That's very good, Toby," said Amy, but behind the picture, she could read the doctor's diagnosis: basal skull fracture, abortion due to forceful abdominal impact.

CHAPTER 15

Gayle had been working overtime for months now, and her trip around the world, including visiting her nephew in Australia, seemed a lifetime away. Every now and then, a desire to visit Mack again and to take her girls with her slipped into her mind. Surely surfing at the Gold Coast and scuba diving at the Great Barrier Reef, or what was left of it, would beat sailing in Greece with their father.

And the girls deserved some distraction. Since the abortion, Inga had begun to retreat from their Friday night family time early and thrown herself into her schoolwork. For the first time ever, she had aced a maths exam, and Gayle was proud of her eldest daughter. She knew that Inga was smart, if only those pesky hormones wouldn't stop teenagers from achieving their full potential in these formative years.

Now that Hazel had also entered her teenage years, she dreaded the day that her clever girl would switch from the news to the shopping channel and replace newspapers with fashion magazines. She was extraordinary in that respect, and Gayle's feminist heart swelled whenever Hazel questioned a *status quo* and was able to back her reasoning with scientific facts. Quite extraordinary for such a young person, indeed.

Maybe next year for Hazel's birthday, they could fit in a trip to Australia.

Gayle had already been at work since seven in the morning, as the latest European demographic statistics had come through late last night. She leaned over her desk and studied some graphs while Guillaume was standing ready with more paperwork.

"I don't get it. We should see some reductions in unwanted pregnancies, but it's just going up. The only silver lining is that teenage pregnancies seem to explode over there as well, and five months ago, America was so hostile against us for our family politics."

Gayle was at a loss. By now her conception bill should have shown some impact with fewer teenage pregnancies, but everything seemed to point in the opposite direction. What was worse was that journalists had dug up statistics about the increase in abortions as well and started to draw links to her conception bill in their reporting. Surely, a law to prevent pregnancies could not possibly be linked to an increase in abortions, but these hacks knew how to spin a story.

Ever since the conception bill had been announced, she had gotten even more angry letters accusing her of blasphemy, encroachment of privacy, and violation of the civil rights to autonomy over one's own body. But with these new stories, the amount of hate inundating her almost every day started to erode her sense of security. A nagging dread that something, even just a spiteful comment that impacted her daughters' lives, accompanied her from the point she dropped off her daughters at school until they were back home.

"Yet the Americans don't seem to present a reason for the unusual pattern or prepare any counteractive measures," offered Guillaume and pulled Gayle out of her gloom.

"Well, if this continues, we have nothing to show for it either. It's like for every implant, someone gets pregnant."

Guillaume stared beyond Gayle on the silenced TV screen showing the daily news.

"What?" asked Gayle.

"Isn't that Hazel?" said Guillaume, pointing to the screen.

"What?" Gayle's heart froze in dread that her fears had come true. The screen showed a live report from her daughter's school, with someone shoving a microphone in Hazel's face. "Volume up," ordered Gayle, and the television sound came on.

"Who is the father?" asked the TV reporter.

"I don't know," answered Hazel.

Gayle stopped breathing. Her daughter had just admitted on live television, albeit indirectly, that she was pregnant.

"How many men have you slept with?" continued the reporter.

"None of your business. The point is that I decide about my own body," snapped Hazel.

Gayle swung around on her chair, out of her mind. "I have to get to her. We have to stop this."

"I'll get a pod," said Guillaume and hastened out of the office.

Guillaume had been working for Gayle now for almost five years, and she had found him highly dependable and upright. She would have trusted him with almost anything, and if it weren't for their age gap and total lack of sexual chemistry, he could have been the man to persuade her to get married again.

Gayle picked up her bag, locked her office, and found Guillaume waiting by a grey pod in the underground garage of the ministry building.

"I thought it would be less suspicious if we take a non-official pod, considering that the press is already out there and waiting," said Guillaume.

"Good thinking," said Gayle and jumped in.

She disabled the autopilot, as she would have to cruise around to find Hazel. Fortunately, it did not take her long to spot her younger daughter. Hazel had taken a short-cut and was just coming out of a lane.

"Hazel!" shouted Gayle, quickly checking whether there were any paparazzi around.

Hazel ran over to her mother and got into the pod, but as soon as they started driving, they noticed that they were being trailed. There was no point in trying to shake them off, and the best option was to get home quickly. The only words that were spoken on the way were Guillaume's ordering security guards to the house ahead of their arrival.

When they arrived, crowds of journalists had already gathered on the street shouting questions, but the security guards paved a way to the gate of the property, and Gayle pushed Hazel quickly through the front door.

The noise was shut out by the heavy door, and Gayle guided Hazel with one arm further into the living room and onto the sofa. Guillaume walked silently around the room and closed the curtains.

"How do you know that you are pregnant?" asked Gayle finally.

"I got one of those pee-on-a-stick tests," said Hazel, pulling out the test from her school bag.

Gayle picked it up. Two blue stripes. It was too long ago for her to remember whether one or two or no stripes indicated a pregnancy, but she went by her daughter's word.

"But why? How?" Gayle was furious. She had anticipated dozens of worrisome scenarios, and in each she had protected her daughters like a lioness, but this was something she did not expect in a million years.

"I don't know. I didn't have sex or something," said Hazel, blushing.

"But … did you get intimate with a boy?"

"No, I didn't."

Hazel looked disgusted, and Gayle believed that her reaction was genuine, yet. "That's impossible. Who is it?"

"There's no one," reaffirmed Hazel.

"I'm only trying to help you."

"I didn't do anything."

"Then you are not pregnant."

"Well, I haven't had my period for more than three months, I gag when I brush my teeth, and my boobs got bigger."

Gayle threw a look over to Guillaume, who stared out of the window between a slit in the curtains, pretending not to hear a word.

"Guillaume, prepare for a visit to Doctor Charton … in confidence. Here is the address." Gayle scrolled through her phone until she found the address, and Guillaume's phone pinged when he received the message. "As soon as possible."

Guillaume left the room to make the call from the kitchen.

Gayle rubbed her temples in exhaustion whilst Hazel sat between the white cushions, her arms determinedly crossed.

"I'm not having an abortion," glowered Hazel.

"We'll see about that," replied Gayle.

So, this was the day when her dependable and intelligent youngster switched gears and drove her life full speed into a wall.

Gayle's head was hot from thinking through all the possible outcomes and further actions she could and needed to take to hold her own and her daughters' lives on track.

Doctor Charton agreed to see Hazel in two hours. They left through a back gate, and Guillaume arranged for the streets to be blocked so that none of the journalists could leave and follow them. Nonetheless, they were spotted, and soon they noticed another pod following them again. Luckily, the security at the compound, where the private practice was located, stopped the paparazzi from following them all the way.

Guillaume waited in the pod whilst Gayle led a stoic Hazel along the large front garden and to the villa that housed the gynaecologist's practice.

A preppy receptionist handed a tablet over, where Gayle filled in the most minimal information for Hazel's visit and stated heavy period cramps as a reason.

Doctor Charton knew, of course, the actual reason for their visit, and Gayle watched him examining Hazel and taking an ultrasound.

"Well, you *are* pregnant," the doctor finally confirmed. "There is the heart."

A small pulsating blob was visible on the ultrasound.

Gayle covered her face with her hands. "Why? I don't deserve this."

"There are some things in life we have to accept," said Doctor Charton.

"But not this ... not this."

Gayle walked to the window and looked into the garden, where autumn leaves covered the lawn. When Inga fell pregnant, it was something she had worried about in the back of her mind. Inga was sixteen and had a boyfriend. But Hazel falling pregnant was like a sign from above that maybe she was on the wrong path. Or had her thirteen-year-old, who had started to develop her own mind and oppose her mother, gone and gotten pregnant on purpose, just to make a statement? *She decides about her own body*, Hazel had said on TV.

"I'm not having an abortion," announced Hazel from behind a divan where she got dressed.

"Yes, you will," replied Gayle, pulled back into reality.

Doctor Charton sat down behind his desk. "When was your last period?"

"Twentieth of June," replied Hazel and sat down on the other side of the desk.

Doctor Charton started typing into his computer.

"I would like to make an appointment for her to have an abortion as soon as possible," Gayle said, coming back from the window.

"I would like to cancel that appointment. Have you talked to Inga lately?" shot Hazel across the room.

"Ladies!" interrupted the doctor.

"She just needs some more time to think about it," explained Gayle.

"Did you know that she broke up with Mark?" said Hazel.

"No."

"Ladies, I think I can stop you right here," interrupted Doctor Charton.

"What?" snapped Gayle.

"Hazel is in her fifteenth week, and unless you change the law, she can't have an abortion anymore."

Gayle stared in turns at the doctor and at Hazel.

* * *

Mack had not been clubbing since that Sunday when two of his one-night stands shocked him with being pregnant. He had buried himself in work and had not even thought about a possibility to get in touch with Marsha, who was the first woman who scored under five percent in his genetic risk assessment test. In fact, he was rethinking his actions of the last few years and found that they might not have been the best approach to finding the mother of his children and the person to grow old with. Who knew, maybe he already had a child, and the mother just didn't know that he was the father or worse, she considered him not fit enough to take on the role of a father due to his poor behaviour.

He worked late nights again rather than going to the gym or hitting a trendy bar in Fortitude Valley and stared hypnotized at a running centrifuge in the lab when Tom popped his head through the door.

"I'm going now," said Tom.

"What? Oh, yes."

Tom was a night owl too. Since he started his PhD, he had been late every morning, sometimes as late as turning up at lunchtime, but he was instead working until late in the evening, probably clocking in more hours than he was obliged to in his contract.

When Mack was having a run in his private endeavours, he thought that no one should work more hours than they were being paid for. There was so much more to life than work. But when his social life hibernated, he also worked many more hours, and he found that those were the times when he also climbed up the ladder of success. Everyone had to find the best compromise for their life or decide what was more important to them, but in Mack's experience, no one ever got the best of both worlds.

He wondered whether Tom had decided to climb the ladder of success or whether he just did not have a social life to give him a choice, at least not an adequate choice.

"Hey, Tom. I could show you around Brisbane's nightlife tonight," Mack said, wanting to see what Tom would do if given a chance. Also, work only helped to a limited extent to dissipate his feeling of doom and gloom. He would much rather sacrifice some of his success for a vibrant community network, certainly for a happy family of his own. Why could he not have both?

"Awesome. Can we go to The Hive? I've heard the sheilas there are hot," said Tom.

"Sure. Just give me a minute," said Mack, thinking that even if given the chance at a social life, Tom might not succeed if he used words like 'sheilas' and was probably better off staying in the societal solitude of a science team.

Mack took out the tubes from the centrifuge and put them into a fridge.

"What other clubs do you normally go to?" asked Mack, trying to fill the awkward silence during which Tom was watching him cleaning up the workbenches.

"I usually have drinks with other cosplayers. But a friend of mine told me about The Hive. He was there on the opening night and said it was pretty wild."

"And you haven't been there yet?"

"Nah, we tried a few weeks ago, but they wouldn't let us in because we had no sheilas with us. Why would we bring some if we went there to meet them anyways?"

"Yeah, clubs try to keep a higher women-to-men ratio. It's better for business, and I guess too much testosterone in one place leads to more fights. Maybe you guys looked too manly," suggested Mack.

"Maybe … I mean, we went there in our medieval costumes," pondered Tom.

Mack smiled. He could not believe that Tom took him seriously. Every other person would have realized that he had tried to tease them. This could turn out to be an interesting evening to distract him, and he took a liking to the innocence that Tom unknowingly exuded.

Forty-five minutes later, they had no problems entering the club. It probably helped that they were not wearing tunics or armour and were cleanly shaven.

They squeezed through the hip crowds that bobbed to the funky music the DJ produced from a platform covered in honeycombs.

Tom radiated like a kid in a candy store whilst Mack ducked away from advancing girls to steer them to a quieter end of the bar.

"Whisky, with a dash of water," ordered Mack. "What d'you want?"

"A Long Island Zombie," beamed Tom.

"You sure?"

Not only was Mack surprised by Tom's quick answer, but also that he picked a cocktail that would throw even the hardest drinker off their socks.

Yet, Tom nodded, excited.

They watched the dancing and booty-shaking clubbers, and when their drinks arrived, Mack finished his whisky in one gulp, whilst Tom chewed wide-eyed on his silicon straw.

A second glass of whisky appeared on the bar next to Mack, and as he turned around to reject it, he noticed Amanda.

"Oh, hi. Long time no see," said Mack, trying to decide whether he should strike up an uncommitting conversation or find an excuse to leave.

"Yes, exactly nineteen weeks, one day and," Amanda looked at a clock, "two hours."

Mack was surprised about this precise recollection of their one and only intimate meeting but then caught a glimpse of a small baby bump under Amanda's glitzy shirt.

"Oh no," Mack mumbled.

"I didn't know how to contact you. But I'm frigging glad that we bumped into each other again," said Amanda.

"Tom, I think we should go," said Mack and tapped him on the shoulder.

"What? Why?" asked Tom.

"Come on."

Mack pulled Tom from his chair, making him drop his glass.

"Craig!" shouted Amanda to a bullish doorman who immediately paved his way through the people, eyes fixed on Mack.

Mack tried to weasel his way around the dance floor, but while the crowd parted for Craig like the Red Sea, they seemed to close in front of him like tectonic plates before an earthquake.

There was no escaping, and in no time, a crushing hand came down on Mack's shoulder. As he was involuntarily turned around and made to follow, Tom was already swaying on the other side of the doorman.

They were dragged to the end of a corridor and out the back door into a dimly lit back alley, followed by Amanda.

"How can you be sure it's mine?" cried Mack.

"Get his phone," ordered Amanda, staring Mack down.

Craig searched Mack and pulled his phone out of his inner jacket pocket.

"Hold his hand out," ordered Amanda, and Mack's right hand was almost crushed as Craig held out his index finger for Amanda to activate his phone. She pushed a few buttons to call up his ID and then synced it with her own phone, transferring his full name, address, and phone number to her device.

"Come on, man. You could have just asked nicely," moaned Mack and rubbed his hand.

"I'll talk to you in about four months about child support, but you are free to contact me earlier if you'd like," she snapped. "You've got my number now."

Amanda pushed his phone into Mack's shirt pocket and turned to go.

"Oh, and don't think about moving. My dad's with the police, and he's more pissed than I am."

Amanda and Craig left, and the back door dropped shut.

"What was that?" asked Tom, who stood by like someone caught in a real-life crime show.

Tom suggested that Mack could stay at his place for as long as he needed to, and Mack accepted the offer, at least for the night. He wasn't sure what he was afraid of, but he felt safer staying at a place that none of his amorous encounters knew.

CHAPTER 16

Tom's flat was located on the first floor near a park, and lorikeets fluttered between the eucalyptus trees to reach their nests in hollow trees. As always, the prettier the birds, the more terrible the noises they made, and these birds were awfully loud so early in the morning, as if they were upset about something.

Mack had slept a few restless hours on Tom's sofa and got woken up by what was for him an unusual racket. After he had ensured that there was nothing more going on outside than raucous bird chatter, he sat on one of Tom's brown velvet puffs, shielding his phone from the glare of the early morning sun to read the news. Tom had decorated, or rather filled his flat with a mismatch of furniture that seemed to come either from an old-folks' home or a child's bedroom.

Tom, apparently not used or prepared to have visitors around, woke up not long after Mack and sat on the other velvet puff in a Jedi dressing gown, munching on a bowl of Weetabix.

"Thanks for letting me stay," said Mack, attempting another sip from his cup filled with extra-hot and super-strong coffee. No wonder Tom was able to work half the night.

"No problem. I mean, we bros have to stick together when the sheilas go crazy," answered Tom and nudged Mack on the shoulder.

Mack wondered whether he only put on this 'cool guy' talk to impress him. It seemed so unnatural, certainly for someone like Tom.

"I mean, I've never heard of a guy who got three chicks pregnant at the same time," continued Tom.

Mack had made the mistake of telling Tom last night in a fit of overwhelming panic that he had three women tell him they were pregnant with his child within the course of three months.

"Well, not at the same time," said Mack.

"I know, but I haven't even met a bloke who had three chicks at all."

"Maybe even more." He shouldn't have said that.

"More? Wahoo. How many?" Tom was giddy with excitement.

"More than a hundred?" Instead of keeping quiet about his private life and problems within, Mack had to admit that it felt good to have someone to talk to, and Tom's reactions made him feel a little special.

"Wow." Tom studied Mack like he had just met his idol.

"I'm fairly sure one of them wasn't mine, and who knows about the others. Hey, listen, could I get some milk? This coffee should come with a warning."

"Oh sure," said Tom and bustled off to the fridge to rummage through his jars of pickled vegetables. "I'm not good with keeping on top of my supplies." He sniffed a small bottle of milk. "I once had a bottle of milk explode in my bedroom, and it smelled of vomit for a month. Couldn't let anyone in."

Tom reminisced about the foods that had spoiled whilst in his possession as he handed Mack the milk.

Mack carefully examined it before pouring it into his coffee. Tom kept watching him eagerly.

"Hey, you know what. I need to go to the lab, take some samples out of the thermocycler."

Mack became uncomfortable with Tom's blatant attention.

"Sure, I'll come with you."

"Oh, you don't have to. I don't need help with this. Enjoy your weekend."

"No worries. I need to check on my code, see if any bugs stopped it."

Tom was already up and getting dressed, fishing his T-shirt and trousers from the floor somewhere.

"Don't you have access to the servers from home?" Mack made a final attempt to dissuade Tom from going to the institute with him.

"Sure, but I prefer keeping my work and my private life separate. Plus, I don't have a proper desk yet. Still waiting for my mum to bring my old desk over, but they're in Wagga. Maybe over Christmas they'll come up and visit me."

Mack listened intently, having given up on leaving Tom behind.

Out on the street, Tom automatically crossed the road to walk through the park, and he seemed confused when Mack suggested to call a pod. He usually walked to work for forty-five minutes.

The ten minutes that the pod took to the Institute for Mental Health and Genome Research were surprisingly interesting, as Tom started to tell Mack about his computer code that he was developing, which was a next-generation evolutionary algorithm that predicted the most likely location of mutations in a gene based on its DNA sequence and encoded amino acids and thus forecast changes in the gene function. He began to understand what Professor Lamarck saw in Tom.

Finally at his desk and alone, Mack scanned the internet. He didn't know what he expected to find, but he searched for stories of other men who became fathers with different mothers at the same time. He wanted to get some idea about how they had handled this prospect. After reading multiple articles covering the last fifty years on rich and famous people who had two or three children within a year, he started researching the likelihood of falling pregnant despite being on the pill and using a condom. As he had already known, the probability was extremely small. On their own, birth-control pills were effective in ninety-nine percent of the cases and condoms in ninety-eight, which could be somewhat reduced if mistakes in their application were made. Nonetheless, together, they should be almost completely effective. Pretty unlikely to fall pregnant, yet to be one hundred percent sure, only abstinence from sex could guarantee that.

After the five minutes it took him to process his samples, which could have waited until Monday and pretty much only involved moving them from the thermocycler to the -40°C refrigerator, Mack decided to go home. He passed by Tom's office to say goodbye, as he thought it would be rude to just leave after he had helped him out last night. As he silently watched Tom going through pages and pages of code, every now and then stopping to insert or remove a couple of characters, he became increasingly reluctant to go home.

What if Amanda's father was coming by to check out the father of his presumably first grandchild? Mack felt slightly nauseated. Was this how morning sickness felt? What a stupid idea; he needed to stop this. So far, there was no proof that he was the father of any of these babies. Yet, when he left Tom without saying a word, he walked back to his office.

He avoided home, but the thought of pregnancy didn't leave him alone, and he looked up figures on everything pregnancy related. He found the statistics that showed the increase in teenage pregnancies and abortion rates in recent months and even the short clip of his cousin Hazel announcing her autonomy over her own body. Was she really pregnant? Mack decided to give his aunt a call in the evening.

As he read on and skimmed through one data table after another, he also noticed the pattern that the news reporters had picked up on. Countries where birth control was widely used surprisingly also showed higher pregnancy and therefore abortion rates. This seemed so counterintuitive that Mack looked for data from previous years. He didn't have to go far back, as the data from the previous year showed that birth control used to be quite effective in preventing pregnancies. It seemed odd to have such an increase over the short time of just a year.

The earliest news articles that reported on maternity wards being at capacity stemmed from the East Coast of the United States, more precisely, around the Gulf of Mexico. However, trying to retrieve the underlying data was not possible without access to the US healthcare system. Instead, Mack went down the rabbit hole of conspiracy theories, which naturally had a penchant even for the smallest irregularities. And there were hundreds upon hundreds of blog posts and video clips from people covering the whole array of the human condition. Some started off by chatting about their abortion, only to take a turn, saying that their body had been used for a science experiment; others talked about their virgin conception, and of course, neither had ever had sex before in their lives. Others talked about visits of aliens who were impregnating women to eventually replace humanity, like a silent invasion.

Just as Mack started to relax, Tom popped his head in to let him know that he was going home.

"Hey, how about we go out for another drink? I feel like I should make up for last night," said Mack.

"Really?"

"Yeah, but maybe somewhere a little quieter." Mack wracked his brain about where they could go that guaranteed no unintended run-ins with anyone he knew. "Maybe we try something new."

"Well, I actually meet friends on Saturdays, but you're welcome to join us. It's just some drinks at a pub around the corner from where I live."

Mack was surprised by how startled he was that Tom already had plans. But a change of scenery might be what he needed, and he still didn't have the desire to go home to his lonely apartment where another bad surprise may be waiting for him. He quickly changed his shirt and socks; luckily, he always kept a clean set of clothes in his drawer. He would have changed his underpants too, but Tom kept watching him as he told him about his friends, who all seemed to originate from the cosplay community.

* * *

It had been almost three months since Veronica and Cecilia had been picked up by Doctor Jackson to undergo some more tests at the NASA space centre in Houston.

Veronica's mother and Jeanette Rice were the only two people who knew where they were, but they didn't know the reason for it, which gave rise to speculations and worries. Shortly after they had left, Commander Rice had tried to contact Veronica to see how she was. Because Veronica didn't answer, Commander Rice eventually phoned her emergency contacts, which were Cecilia, who also didn't answer her phone, and Veronica's mother, who did answer. It was during that phone conversation that Mrs. Hernandez began to worry about her daughter, as Commander Rice had no information about another post-mission examination. The commander promised to make inquiries, and even though someone eventually confirmed that Veronica was at the space centre, no more reasons or updates were offered. Commander Rice reassured Mrs. Hernandez that Veronica and her granddaughter were likely to come home soon, despite not having any proof of it, but after another week had passed without any further information, Mrs. Hernandez started to call the space centre on a daily basis. And every day, she was just told that Veronica, Cecilia, and the baby were doing fine. Her requests to speak to her daughter were politely but sternly denied.

The black hole that Veronica seemed to have disappeared into put Mrs. Hernandez on high alert, and she started making threats to go to the press to tell them that NASA had imprisoned her daughter, the world-famous spacewalker from the first manned Mars mission. NASA had tried to defuse her threats by telling her that Veronica and Cecilia were there of their own accord, which was technically not true, and Mrs. Hernandez didn't believe it for a minute. As a last resort, Mrs. Hernandez threatened to tell news agencies about the baby that was conceived during the mission and that she had other insider information about the mission that would get them into trouble. Apparently, she knew or guessed enough that they agreed to let Veronica and Cecilia return home with baby Verity under the precondition that Mrs. Hernandez would also sign a gag order.

As soon as the security guard had left the house, someone knocked on the door. Cecilia checked the camera in the hall but couldn't see anyone. When there was another knocking, she heard Mrs. Hernandez's voice from the stairway and opened.

Flattened against the wall, Mrs. Hernandez shuffled in. With a finger to her lips and then pointing to the camera, she indicated that she was avoiding being recorded.

"I'm not sure I'm allowed to see you," she whispered after Cecilia closed the door behind her.

"I'm sure it's okay," answered Cecilia before being crushed by a hug.

"I'm so glad that you are back. How are you?" asked Mrs. Hernandez.

"We're good," answered Cecilia, and after a probing look, Mrs. Hernandez bustled on to the living room.

"*Menos mal! Gracias a Dios!*" exclaimed Mrs. Hernandez when she saw her daughter.

Veronica laid Verity on the floor to greet her mother, but Mrs. Hernandez only gave her a quick peck on the cheek before turning her full attention to her granddaughter, who was happily flailing her arms and legs.

"Oh, she has grown so big," said Mrs. Hernandez as she picked up Verity. "And she looks so much like you when you were little."

Veronica smiled and threw a secretive glance at Cecilia.

"Can I get you anything?" interrupted Cecilia.

"Yes, I bought some matcha tea. It's in the fridge. Go and get yourself something," said Mrs. Hernandez who had apparently made herself at home during their absence. She sat on the sofa, only having eyes for her granddaughter.

"I'm sorry we couldn't talk to you," said Veronica.

"It's not your fault. Tell me, is she eating and sleeping well?"

"Very well."

"Are you still breastfeeding? You know ..."

"Yes, I am still breastfeeding, Mama," said Veronica.

"And what about the father? Have they finally figured it out?"

This direct question took Veronica by surprise, and Mrs. Hernandez stopped playing with Verity when Veronica did not answer.

"No?" she followed up.

Cecilia came back in with a tray of matcha tea.

"We, we decided ..." Veronica looked to Cecilia, searching for help.

"We decided that we did not need a father to be involved, so we're keeping that information to us," offered Cecilia as she placed the tray on the tea table.

"But they did find out who the father is?" quizzed Mrs. Hernandez.

"Please don't ask. We cannot answer that question," begged Veronica, standing up to take Verity for her nap. Mrs. Hernandez only reluctantly offered up the baby.

"It's not that other spacewalker? She's way to pretty for him."

"Mama, please stop." Veronica walked out, glad that she had a reason to leave the conversation.

Sometimes, her mother's inquisitiveness was a blessing, especially in situations that required getting Veronica out of a sticky situation. Fortunately, such a situation had only occurred once since Veronica left primary school, and that was to get her out of this second involuntary quarantine time.

Verity fell asleep quickly, too quickly. Veronica avoided going back outside and tried to have a nap herself. After half an hour, she heard the front door closing, and Cecilia came into their bedroom.

"She's gone," said Cecilia, and Veronica opened her eyes. "Thought you were sleeping?"

"Sorry. I just didn't want to have to deal with her questions," apologized Veronica.

"We will have to tell her something."

"I know."

"She's invited us to dinner tonight. Said she'd make tacos."

Veronica ruminated on how much they were allowed to tell her mother. "Do you think we could just tell her the truth?"

"I don't know."

Sometimes Cecilia made her furious with her plain answers. Of course, she didn't know, but did she think that they could trust her mother to keep quiet? What could NASA effectively do if the truth came out? How much did her mother already know?

"I wonder who the person is that gave her insider info," asked Veronica out loud.

"If she really had any, but you could ask her tonight and see how much she already knows."

And that was exactly what Veronica was going to do.

The hours until dinnertime stretched and melted away, and every time Veronica thought she had made up her mind, doubts popped up, no matter which way she decided. She wanted to share the secret about her baby. A secret that had alienated her from her own child but brought them so close together ever since it was uncovered. She knew that NASA didn't want any information getting out, as there were still so many open questions that they could not answer. Not having an answer or a reason to an event that had never happened before posed a huge risk to spread misinformation, panic, or even civil unrest in the wider population, something that could endanger their own lives if not treated with caution.

Veronica knew she could trust her mother. Even if her mother couldn't actively help, speaking to her and opening her heart had always given Veronica a sense of relief simply by knowing that she had an ally bound by a shared secret. But she already had this ally in Cecilia. Yet she longed to let her mother in too.

"Did you rest well?" asked Mrs. Hernandez when they sat down at her small table in the kitchen that was bursting with food.

Mrs. Hernandez must have spent the last four hours cooking, as there were bowls with pork steaks in adobo, Veronica's favourite carnitas, lettuce, freshly sliced tomatoes, salsa and guacamole, and plates full of chilies, avocado slices, and a whole pile of still warm tortilla.

"Wow, this looks amazing," said Cecilia.

"Thank you, *mi querida*. Come sit, give me the baby. Sit."

Veronica handed Verity to her mother and sat down near the window. With all of them seated, there was no way Veronica could leave the kitchen, but instead of feeling trapped, she was happy like during family celebrations as a child. She would find a comfortable corner, have some food within reach, and just listen to the chatter and laughter all around her. No need to get up; everything was in order.

But instead of following Cecilia's lead and loading her first tortilla, she had made up her mind.

"Mama, who has contacted you about us while we were gone?" Veronica asked.

"Just your commander and someone I don't know. I just got an anonymous message saying that they're trying to cover something up. A virus that you brought back from Mars," answered Mrs. Hernandez.

"A virus?" asked Veronica, as this was new to her too.

"Yes, or bacteria? I never know the difference."

"And nothing about Verity?" inquired Veronica.

"No. But obviously I used that as well to get them to let you go. It sure wouldn't be a nice story to tell that their spacewalker was raped up there."

"I wasn't," Veronica said.

"No?" Mrs. Hernandez eyed Veronica, obviously avoiding looking at Cecilia.

Cecilia had stopped filling her plate and listened quietly.

"Verity is a true copy of myself," Veronica said.

Mrs. Hernandez kept gazing at Veronica, not comprehending what she just said.

"There was no rape, nor is there a father. I cloned myself. Verity is me."

"A clone? Like Mrs. Gulliver's dog?" asked Mrs. Hernandez finally.

"Yes, sort of," said Veronica with some hesitation.

"Don't pull my leg."

"I'm not."

"Impossible."

"Just like Mrs. Gulliver's dog."

"But why would you do that? Why up there?"

"I didn't do it. That's the mystery. This was not the plan. Something happened during our mission that made my ovaries produce an egg that self-fertilized. At least that is how they explained it."

"*Madre mía.* You're serious?" Mrs. Hernandez took her eyes off Veronica and instead turned to baby Verity on her lap. She studied the baby's face as she tried to grab her necklace. "I said she looked just like you, didn't I?"

"Yes." Veronica smiled at the baffled face of her mother and then shrugged at the stern face of Cecilia.

Mrs. Hernandez started to kiss little Verity. "She is, isn't she? You're not kidding me?"

"No, they checked our entire genomes, and we are a perfect match."

"I still can't believe it. How is this possible? What happened ... wait, you're like the Mother Mary. Immaculate conception!" Mrs. Hernandez glowed. "A saint!"

"But Mama, you cannot tell anyone," implored Veronica, now worried that her mother could, after all, get carried away.

"Of course not. Not a single word should leave my lips. This is our secret," Mrs. Hernandez affirmed.

"I'm not sure we'll be safe here if any of this gets out. There are nutters out there on either side of the spectrum," said Cecilia gloomily.

The three of them quietly acknowledged each other and silently committed to keeping their secret and keeping them safe.

"Eat, before the meat gets cold."

Hungry, Veronica and Cecilia finally tucked in whilst Mrs. Hernandez cradled her granddaughter.

CHAPTER 17

The last evening had been enjoyable, and Mack was surprised how welcoming Tom's friends were towards him. He was sure that Tom wouldn't have been welcomed the same way in his circle of friends, but then he hadn't hung out with anyone in ages. Maybe he had been a little too focussed on his work and finding the woman of his genetic dreams. His mother always said that love would happen when you least expect it; you just have to be open to let it in to your life whenever it showed up. He certainly had many opportunities where love or at least mutual affection had knocked on his door, sometimes repeatedly, but he refused to open up because he was looking for something perfect. Well, he had found a perfect match based on their genomes, but whether he would ever see Marsha again and whether she would want him was something he could not control. In all likelihood, they would never meet again. Where was she from? England? What if he messed up and was now further away from his dream than ever?

At least, Tom had gotten lucky last night, and with a little help from Mack, he had pulled a girl who was surprisingly interested in the board game they had played. Mack doubted that Tom had found his true love yesterday, but he certainly had a fun fifteen minutes by what Mack had heard from the safety of Tom's sofa. He had accepted Tom's offer to stay at his place for one more night, though admittedly that was before Tom and the girl had started eating each other's faces. At that point, Mack had considered going to his apartment, but both Tom and the girl were so drunk that Mack accompanied them to Tom's flat, making sure they didn't end up behind a bush in the park and caused a public nuisance. Both then insisted that it was totally fine if Mack camped out on the sofa; in fact, they insisted that he didn't go all the way home. Luckily, their romantic encounter didn't last too long, and Mack had a rather relaxed night.

Mack got his phone out to check the time. It was only eight in the morning. He considered getting up to pick up a coffee and his Sunday croissant on the way home when his attention was piqued by a news headline. He sat up and read the article. This was huge. He quickly confirmed with other news sites that this was not a hoax, but all reputable outlets ran the same story and linked to the public database with the DNA sequence. Then he called up the statistics he had read yesterday at work. This was unbelievable.

He finally tiptoed to Tom's bedroom and carefully opened the door. Clean and dirty laundry lined the floor, and Mack balanced his way to Tom's bedside.

"Tom. Tom, wake up," he whispered.

"Wa, what?" Tom lifted a heavy head, only to sink right back into his pillow.

"Tom, I have to show you something," urged Mack.

Tom surveyed his room, seemingly to verify where he was. After deducing that he was indeed in his own bedroom, his gaze hung on the naked girl on the other side of the bed. The memory of last night came back to him, and Tom held up his hand.

"Yeah, yeah, well done," said Mack and silently high-fived Tom. He pulled the still-drunk lover boy up and out of bed not caring that he was buck naked.

"Look at this," Mack said when he steadied Tom on a brown velvet puff and held the news article in front of him.

"NASA leak. Alien Baby: Mars Astronaut's baby has no father," mumbled Tom as he read the headline.

"That baby is an identical clone of the mother! I looked up the sequences, and they're exactly the same," whispered Mack excitedly.

"Like a toad?" asked Tom. Obviously, his brain was not fully switched on yet.

"Like parthenogenesis," replied Mack and searched the kitchen for a clean glass to get Tom some water. "I looked up the leaked report online and it seems that this woman, Vargas, has a piece of extra DNA that no one else has.

"Like a new species?"

"I'd bet my doctorate on some sort of virus," mused Mack as he handed Tom a glass of water with a pain-killer that he'd found in a cupboard; or at least he hoped that this medication was a painkiller.

"Uh, uh, what if it's extra-terrestrial?" sputtered Tom after downing the little white pill.

"Quite possible. Look at this." Mack excitedly swiped through window after window of news articles. "I looked up statistics and articles from the last two years yesterday, and it didn't make any sense, but now … look, an abnormal increase in abortions and miscarriages started here in Florida after the return of the Mars mission. From there, it took some weeks until

South America ... Africa ... and Europe showed similar patterns. And since a few months, Australia and Asia report on that too."

Tom and Mack sat in silence. Mack wasn't sure what Tom's brain had managed to absorb, as his eyes were focussed on a spot far behind the tablet, but Mack's brain was hyperventilating. What if Amanda, Brianne, and Michelle also cloned themselves? That would explain why they fell pregnant despite protection, or in Brianne's case even without intercourse at all. He had to get home and check his DNA database.

"I think I should go home," said Mack.

"You sure? What if, what if this girl, you know ..."

Tom clearly had problems sorting his thoughts.

"I'm positive that there is no pregnant lady waiting there to assassinate me. And I do need a clean pair of underpants," answered Mack.

Tom looked down on his naked body and then to his bedroom door. And then without any further word, Tom got up and went back into his room.

"I'll see you tomorrow," called Mack after him and got a silent hand wave in return.

Mack was giddy. He called a pod as he jumped down two steps at once and was glad that it was already waiting out front when he stepped into the Australian spring air. He did not notice that amongst the chatter of the colourful birds in the park, there was one sound missing: the squawking pleas for food of any hatchlings.

He still had a spring in his step when he entered his apartment but hesitated when he saw a notification on his phone for another missed voice message. Knowing what he did now, he listened to the message, just to get it out of the way. It was not another woman to let him know that he was becoming a father. Instead, he heard the well-spoken voice of his mentor and boss, Professor Lamarck.

"Hi, Mack, this is Stephen. Sorry to bother you on the weekend. I just got off an interesting call from the government, and they are pulling together a global task force to work on an issue that has recently come up. Can't tell you more at the moment, but I would like you to be part of the Australian team. There will be a first meeting already tonight in Sydney. Give me a call as soon as you can."

Mack dropped everything and called back. He had a suspicion that he knew what this was about.

"Hi Steve, this is Mack. I just got your message."

"Ah, at the eleventh hour. I'm about to leave for the airport. Are you in?"

"Can you tell me more what this is about?"

"Sorry, chap, not over the phone. I already signed an NDA."

"In that case, I'm in."

"Great, pack some things. I'll send a pod over to pick you up."

Mack packed only for hand luggage to avoid long check-in procedures. If he needed more things, he'd buy them in Sydney. The pod was already waiting for him when he came down, and off he went to the airport. Apparently, Professor Lamarck had prepaid the fare and even forked out for the fastest route as the pod sped into the link tunnel.

He always found it strange entering the tunnel. There were no discernible light sources, but the tunnel was glowing to mimic driving in the sunlight. The walls had been painted in green and blue to resemble nature, something Mack found ridiculous, as most of Australia's nature appeared rather washed out in colour and was dominated by a lot of deserts ripped open and bare from decades boosting the mining industry. Despite the attempt to make a concrete tube appear like a vast open landscape, Mack felt claustrophobic, as if he was trapped in a futuristic alternative reality that only pretended to give you more freedom, when in fact it was highly restrictive.

He inhaled deeply in relief when his pod sped out on the other side and the green and blue was replaced by the grey of the city buildings. Not long after, he arrived at the airport and found Professor Lamarck waiting for him at the check-in.

"Is no one else coming?" Mack asked when they walked through the scanners.

"There will be Doctor Ingram from Melbourne and Professor Lee from Darwin joining us in Sydney," responded the professor and elaborated when they were out of earshot from the security personnel. "This is the first international meeting, and we'll be likely building larger teams when the line of approach is cleared."

"May I ask what this is about?"

"It has something to do with the Mars mission. It seems that quarantine did not cover all escape routes."

"Does it have anything to do with the pregnant astronaut?"

"You read the news?"

"Yes. The baby is an identical clone, and both mother and child are carriers of a unique part of the genome sequence."

"It appears so. Something on the X chromosome."

"Do you think it's a virus?"

"Maybe. Or a transposon, jumping genes activated by the increased radiation in space."

"It seems to be spreading, so anything restricted to the astronaut seems unlikely."

"What do you mean, it's spreading?" asked Professor Lamarck, alarmed.

"It's just a theory, and there might be no statistical significance to it, but there's been an unusual increase in pregnancies and abortions, which started around Florida and is now occurring on all continents."

On their one-hour plane trip, Mack showed the professor the statistics that he had shown Tom in the morning.

"If it really is a virus, it's been highly negligent of the US government to call this meeting so late," said Professor Lamarck gravely when they exited the pod in front of a government building in Sydney where concrete was again made to look like a natural construction.

They were scanned and made to leave their bags behind before being led to an elevator by a uniformed guard.

"Professor Lamarck and Doctor Murdoch have arrived," said the guard into a wristwatch.

Mack checked the time on his phone and noticed that he had no reception.

The elevator door opened, and another guard received them. This one was openly armed, and Mack's innocent excitement about a scientific discovery turned more and more into concern as he realized the significance of the situation.

The guard led them into a neon-lit room underground, which wasn't trying to pretend it was a sun-lit and airy space. They were searched again and had to hand over the last of their possessions. Then, a woman in a grey suit carrying two tablet computers awaited them by a desk.

"Hello, my name is Judith Snell. I work for the National Aeronautics and Space Administration."

"That's a long way to come," commented Professor Lamarck.

"It is," agreed Judith and looked at them expectantly.

"Right. I'm Professor Lamarck, and this is my associate, Doctor Murdoch," introduced the professor. Judith checked the information on her two tablets.

"And you work at the Institute for Mental Health and Genome Research in Brisbane?"

"Yes."

"Good for you." Judith smiled but at the same time gave them an uncomfortable and pervading look for a moment. "I need to ask you to provide fingerprints and a small blood sample to confirm your identities."

Mack and Professor Lamarck exchanged impressed glances and posed their fingers on the device that Judith presented to them. Once their identities were confirmed, she nodded, satisfied, and Mack had the feeling he had passed a difficult exam in front of the headmistress.

"Excellent. If I may ask you now to carefully read and sign with your index and thumbprints this non-disclosure agreement. Take your time and feel free to ask if you don't understand any of the terminology."

"Another one?" asked the professor.

"This one has more specifics, which should also be in your interest."

They sat down at the desk and read through dozens of pages for nearly fifteen minutes. Every detail of what they could and couldn't do during and after the meeting was noted down, and after a short glance at Professor Lamarck, who placed his fingers confidently on the reader, Mack also provided his prints. He felt like he had signed his life away and there was no way back now.

Judith led them to another door, which was solid iron, followed by a short corridor and finally into a large conference room.

"Follow me," said Judith. "Prime Minister, this is Professor Lamarck and Doctor Murdoch from the Institute for Mental Health and Genome Research."

Mack was stunned. Despite all that had happened today, he did not expect to be introduced to Prime Minister Gilbert. They shook hands.

"Professor Lamarck, thank you for coming on such short notice. Your name came out top as a leading expert on human genomics, and we hope you will be a principal member of our task force," said the prime minister with a jovial smile.

Maybe it was Mack's Scottish heritage, but he never warmed to the type of grin that people in power used to cover their incompetence or at least insecurity about what was going to happen.

Judith handed them a thick folder containing a long report with multiple graphs and images, most of which Mack identified as DNA sequence code, lab protocols, and statistics pertaining to the sequencing depth and match rate of the studied genomes.

After having greeted Professor Lee and Doctor Ingram, they sat down at the large round table that occupied most of the room.

Judith prepared the conference call, and a three-dimensional screen appeared in the centre of the table, flickering a few times as the lights dimmed before stabilizing to a shimmering grey with the NASA logo rotating in the middle. Then, a dozen windows opened, and one after the other, their conference partners from across the globe appeared. If Mack was shocked to meet the prime minister of Australia in person, he felt detached from reality when he recognized the presidents of the United States of America, the United Nations of Europe, and The People's Republic of China with their teams. He assumed that the other windows were equally occupied by leaders of countries around the world, but he didn't follow politics closely enough to identify any of them.

Judith spoke quietly into a microphone to check the connection.

"Ladies and gentlemen, thank you for following our call for this global meeting," a man in an army uniform announced from the window of the USA.

"Unfortunately, some news has already leaked last night, which makes this call even more urgent. As you might have already gathered, there have been some ir-regularities in connection with the crewed Mars mission which landed back on Earth in March. One of the female astronauts returned pregnant, and it has since been proven that the child is an identical replica of the mother. We first believed that this was an isolated inci-dent, but the evidence we've accumulated over the last few months suggests that there is a communicable con-dition spreading. Doctor Jackson from the NASA labor-atories will explain further."

As the general switched placed with Doctor Jackson, a quiet beep indicated that someone else wanted to in-terject.

"Yes, President Chen from the People's Republic of China," introduced Judith.

"Why haven't we been informed earlier, if you had evidence for months?" asked President Chen.

"We didn't have enough evidence to call for an emergency meeting. We only knew that there was a novel piece of DNA that was occurring across the coun-try. Please, let Doctor Jackson follow through with his presentation, and we will try to answer any questions later."

The screen switched to a hologram of the human ge-nome, and Doctor Jackson's voice guided them through the facts.

"As we know by now, pieces of foreign DNA se-quences have been found on the X chromosome in all recorded cases. These cases include all five members of the Mars mission, as well as fifty biopsies of aborted foetuses and their mothers." The hologram zoomed in on the double helix of the X chromosome, where a piece of the DNA sequence, about two hundred base pairs long on the q-arm of the chromosome, was highlighted. "The chances of this occurring even by induced mutation are diminishingly small, and our analyses have not revealed any matches in the rest of the genome to suggest a transposition could have occurred."

Mack and Professor Lamarck exchanged a knowing look.

"But how did it get there then?" interrupted an exasperated voice.

"Viruses can easily enter living cells to reproduce. Like a Trojan horse, if you will. Our mitochondria originate from an endosymbiotic bacterium, however, transfecting DNA itself has only been achieved in controlled test series."

"Are you saying that we're facing a man-made pandemic?" interjected the voice of President Chen.

"No, the DNA sequence does not match any known viruses or bacteria on file."

"Again, where is it coming from?" asked the other voice once more.

"This is a question that might be better answered by Ms. Holmes."

The rotating double-helix disappeared, and they could see Doctor Jackson switching places with a woman.

NASA's deputy administrator had to talk over a cacophony of enraged questions. "We are still investigating, but so far, we have found traces of DNA in all of the Mars soil samples. The returned samples were all securely handled in our quarantine labs and have been ruled out as the source of this condition. There was, however, an incident shortly after the departure from Mars which required the engineer, Mr. Schuster, to enter the storage compartment and fix a loose wire that was necessary for the temperature regulation of the samples. We are still reconstructing this incident, but it seems likely that the crew itself got infected while on their way back and served as a live carrier, which matches the timeline of the pregnancy of our spacewalker."

"And you released the crew without identifying this virus?"

"We, there was ... yes," Riley Holmes seemed to look for the right words to minimize outrage. "There was no reason to detain the crew any longer. The pregnancy was believed to have occurred from a normal human interaction between the astronauts."

There was a short pause during which NASA's deputy administrator waited for more questions, but even though Mack could feel the tension in the room, no further comments were made at this stage.

Ms. Holmes changed spots with Doctor Jackson, and the double-helix appeared again.

"Contact tracing based on the crew's movements since being released from quarantine started three months ago. Unfortunately, we know by now that the virus appears to have spread to all continents, based on the increase in abortions. Because we are not dealing with a common disease pattern, unless you count pregnancy as a disease, this silent pandemic had a hundred days in which to remain undetected."

The double-helix dissolved into a map of the world with epicentres in Florida, Germany, and Russia and dots across the globe which were increasing in size over a timeline from March until October.

"So, what does this virus do exactly?" asked another voice from the void.

"Based on our sample, which is admittedly small, every woman showing the novel insertions became pregnant by duplicating her own DNA. They cloned themselves, if you will. However, a specific hormonal level must concur, otherwise, the women did not conceive at all, even if tried under … natural conditions. We have advised the WHO to announce PSI level five and advise every country to identify unaffected individuals."

"But people are not dying. How could we justify strict lockdown measures? People will revolt if we do this without a tangible reason."

"We understand the challenging task ahead, but if we don't establish reliable data as to the true spread of the virus and contain further dissemination as quickly as possible, we might face an irreversible change of mankind." Doctor Jackson's words were aimed at maximum impact to convince the world leaders to take imminent action.

"Is it even logistically possible to take blood samples from every woman?" asked Prime Minister Gilbert.

"Not only from women. Every one of you, ladies and gentlemen, could be infected already."

A buzzing and mumbling filled the room as everybody eyeballed each other. Of course, men also had an

X chromosome, and even if they weren't struck by unwanted pregnancies, they could still act as carriers.

"What, what would be the worst outcome?" The words fell out of Mack's mouth just as the answer formed in his head.

"The male gender could become extinct," confirmed Doctor Jackson.

CHAPTER 18

On their way back to Brisbane the next day, Mack and Professor Lamarck quietly discussed their next steps and what could be done on the global stage.

They had been tasked to form the backbone of the genotyping team that would oversee the sampling and DNA-analyses in Australia to identify unaffected individuals or any new mutations.

"First we need to establish a database with pre-pandemic DNA records to match any new samples against it," whispered the professor.

"I think I might just have what we need," replied Mack, as his heartrate went up. "But it's a dataset that is not publicly available and I need to check whether it is actually usable."

"If it contains samples from last year, it should be perfect. Is it from the Stanford set?"

"No, it's confidential data that I've sourced one by one whenever I had the chance."

The professor hesitated for a split second. "Just make sure that there are no identifiable names."

Mack nodded and was relieved that he didn't have to come up with any further explanation about this private data. "Maybe it would be good to get someone dedicated to data assembly and analysis on board. Tom might be a good fit."

"I think you're right. If everything works out as expected, we should be swamped with big data. We'll also have to update our computing and storage facilities. Do you think Tom can handle this?"

"He seems a clever chap," said Mack. "Do you think Doctor Ingram's suggestion could work?"

"About editing the virus DNA out of the X chromosome? I think it could be done, but then what? If it is a virus with a high transmittance, how would you prevent a reinfection?"

Mack thought about it for a while. It had been difficult enough to get the CRISPR technology approved in agriculture, and there were still high hurdles to apply gene editing in cancer patients. But surely, something that would threaten the survival of mankind would warrant a comprehensive application, even in humans. To prevent a reinfection, people would need to live in isolation, and that would be an even larger problem to enforce. A vaccine could reduce reinfection, but Mack was no immunologist and thus not able to produce an informed thought about this option.

At home, Mack rushed to the computer in his lab to open his database. He had ninety-seven records, and all but the last seven were from before the return of the Mars mission. He opened one from January this year but found that it took too long to scroll through the 155 million base pairs on the X chromosome alone. He opened the command prompt and read in the file to save out the position of the insertion plus an additional two hundred base pairs on either side to make sure that he would cover the entire region where the viral DNA supposedly inserted itself. Instead of doing a digital match, Mack quickly compared the January sample with the printed version of the DNA sample they had been given at their secret meeting in Sydney.

This first sample did not contain the novel insertion. He checked another couple of samples from earlier in the year to confirm that they did not have the insertion. Then he read Amanda's sample in and felt his stomach churn as he waited for the targeted genome region to be saved out. What if she did not have the insertion? He'd be a father soon. But Mack was quickly released from his worries when he found the tell-tale ATG-start of a gene followed by the CATCATCAT sequence encoding a triple histidine. Amanda had cloned herself, and so had Michelle and Brianne. As a last check, he looked at Marsha's DNA sequence and was surprised to find that she did not have the novel insertion.

So, it was possible to still find people who were not infected or maybe even immune to this Martian virus. His thoughts briefly wandered to meeting Marsha in Shanghai and then to a glimpse of a fantasy of her being pregnant with his child. As brief as this wonderful image was, it also stirred an urgency deep inside him. He wasn't sure how many of the people in the meeting understood what was at stake. If this virus couldn't be stopped, there wouldn't be any male babies being born, men would not pass on their DNA and would effectively become unnecessary for reproduction. Maybe he had waited for too long to find a woman to have children with, and this silent pandemic might have erased his last chances for a family of his own.

There was also a high potential that the cloning of women would increase the expression of lethal or at least unfavourable allele variants, which could lead to the total extinction of humankind, but this ultimate threat seemed less daunting to him than never becoming a father.

He resisted the urge to look up Marsha to find a way to reconnect with her and instead focused on his task at hand. He removed all identifying markers from his sample files and transferred them to his work computer. After Tom had signed the NDA, he should be able to write a program to quickly extract the relevant genome areas to establish a template to match all new genome samples against. Mack only hoped that the government would move swiftly towards establishing a national database and put measures in place to contain the spread until a realistic way forward was found.

For his part, he made sure that Tom had all the resources available to implement a fast-working algorithm that could handle thousands of records, each with three billion data points.

It was good that Mack had prepared his records immediately, as Tom's clearance was agreed the next day.

After he had showed Tom the data and explained its structure so that Tom knew what each column and row contained, Mack felt compelled to instil some of his personal urgency of this project into this PhD student.

"My mother died of breast cancer when I was twenty," Mack began.

"I'm so sorry," responded Tom, apparently not finding this personal confession out of the ordinary.

"No worries. She was a *BRCA1* carrier … Look, I don't want anyone to lose their mother like I did … Especially not my own kids."

"I thought you didn't like kids."

"I love kids. That's why I've been trying to find the mother for my children for some time now."

Tom seemed confused, and Mack lost confidence in how much he should share with Tom about his motivations.

"Well, I hope you can pull something together quickly, so that the trust put into us is not disappointed."

"No worries, I think I already have a script that I can tweak."

"Great." Mack turned to leave Tom to his work.

"I think you'd be a great father. And I hope you get a chance," Tom said, and Mack knew that he had understood his predicament.

* * *

Veronica had been at the paediatrician for Verity's four-month check-up and vaccinations. Everything was in good order, and she was happy to truthfully report that she had bonded with her baby. She had been nervous, as it was the first time that she went to a normal general practice and did not see Doctor Jackson or a medical practitioner working for NASA. Moreover, she was sure that by now most people had read her name and the origin of her baby in the news, so she expected to be questioned about it. But the doctor was professional and only did what was customary.

Relieved, she talked to Cecilia on the phone on her way back.

"Please be careful," pleaded Cecilia. "I spent all morning tracing and removing those trolls from social media, but there is only so much I can do without official log-in details. I am balancing on the edge of illegality here."

"We'll be fine. The pod will drop us off right on our doorstep."

Veronica was happy. The last few weeks, she had noticed how her anxiety had fallen off, and she was more confident in her ability to be a mother. Despite being a clone, Verity had not inherited any recessive disorders and was developing perfectly. Cecilia and she had found a good balance between sharing their parenting obligations, and their relationship as a couple had never been better. Having her mother close by turned out to be a blessing, as it meant that Veronica could have some 'me time', even when Cecilia was working, and she had managed to keep Mr. Summer's bees alive on the rooftop and planted several vegetables in their allotment that would soon be ready to give a first harvest.

NASA had treated her pregnancy like an injury that had directly resulted from her employment. Their liability insurance paid out a lump sum to cover any of Veronica's child-related expenses for the next eighteen years, including an estimated top-up for rent, schooling, and even holidays twice a year. Cecilia had suggested that she should talk to their lawyer about making a claim regarding the psychological hardship that she had suffered, but Veronica didn't want to enter a lengthy legal battle.

Verity was asleep in her capsule and clasped Veronica's finger with her tiny hand. Sometimes fate played out in your favour, considering that they would have otherwise taken the donor and IVF route in a few years' time.

The pod pulled up at the curb side, and Veronica paid before unclipping the baby capsule.

"Veronica Vargas?"

Veronica had just put a foot on the first step to the front door, when a woman stepped out of the shadows next to the stairs.

"Yes?" She took another step up and tightened her grip on the handle.

"You devil's whore, God does not permit what you have done!"

The stranger lifted a small spray can, and next thing she knew was a feeling of burning fire in her eyes that spread to her face as if it was melting the skin off her bones. Then, the capsule was snatched violently from her arms, and Veronica fell the two steps back down onto the pavement.

"My baby! My baby!" she screamed, as she pulled herself back up into a standing position.

She couldn't see anything and had to trust blindly when a man grabbed her by the arm to stabilize her.

"What happened?"

"She took my baby!"

"You wait here," said the voice, and Veronica could hear someone running off. Shortly after, she heard cars screeching and people shouting somewhere in the distance.

Desperate, she tried to make out what was happening, but her view was just a haze. She felt her way up the stairs and then counted with her fingers the numbers of doorbells to alert Cecilia.

"Cecie, it's me. I got attacked, Verity is gone."

She could hear the panic in Cecilia's voice, and less than a minute later, the door flung open, and Cecilia grabbed her in a hard embrace.

"What happened?"

"I don't know; there was this woman, and she sprayed something in my face and took the carrier with …" She signalled in the direction that the man had run.

"They've got her," Cecilia interrupted.

"What?"

"A man is bringing back the carrier."

Veronica could hear Verity cry from the top of her lungs.

"There you go, ma'am," the familiar voice of the man said.

"Is she all right?" Veronica felt her way to Verity's face.

"I believe so. I think you should wait until the police arrive. We will make sure that the woman doesn't escape."

Veronica stopped trying to open the harness. "Is she still here?"

"Down at the corner shop. The owner had some handcuffs and took care of her."

"Thank you so much," Veronica sobbed. "I wish I could see your face. I don't know what I would have done without you."

Veronica stretched her hands out, and the man took them into his.

"You should see a doctor for that burn. Make sure it doesn't leave any lasting injuries."

"I'll call your mother to bring some water and take Verity upstairs." Cecilia had unclipped Verity and calmed her in her arms.

A moment later, Mrs. Hernandez rushed out with several bottles of water, and Veronica rinsed her still-burning face. The water did little to remove the spray components, but at least the coolness helped temporarily to relieve some of the blazing sensation, and Veronica found that she was able to recognize faces again.

Fifteen minutes later, the police arrived, followed by an ambulance. There wasn't much that the paramedics could do, and their best recommendation was to blink heavily and remain in the fresh air. Time was the best indicator to predict the dissipation of the effects of pepper spray.

The police took their statements and addresses, and then Veronica's saviour, Devine Jones, was finally able to resume his day. Veronica notified the police that she wanted to press charges and was told to come down to the police station as soon as possible. Then they were left alone as the officers walked up to the corner store to arrest the woman.

"That is crazy. Why would anybody do such a thing?" Mrs. Hernandez asked.

"She knew my name, so I guess Cecilia was right," said Veronica.

For the first time, she wondered what internet posts Cecilia had removed this morning and which ones were still out there accumulating hatred from people they had never heard of. On one side, she wanted to see what she was up against and press charges against every single one of them; on the other side, she knew that she would be fighting windmills and that it was better to not even look for anything.

After Verity was tucked away in her bed, Veronica decided to check on her bees, to stay out in the fresh air. The rooftop was warmer than the street, with the bricks and concrete radiating the stored warmth of the sun. The bees clearly loved this warm but not hot climate of autumn in Florida and were busy swarming in and out of their hives.

First, Veronica watered the flowerpots that were spread out around the roof, where some of the more sensitive blooms were letting their heads already hang down. Then she sat down in the shade of a fragranced jasmine trestle and watched the bees. Their humming resonated inside her, and she relaxed. A fuzzy worker bee landed on her knee, and she watched it as it crawled around on her naked leg, feeling its way over her hair.

A thought hit her as she remembered the beekeeping classes, she had to take to register the hives in her name. A queen bee only used sperm to create female worker bees. The male drones were replicas of the queen which received half of her diploid chromosome set. What if this virus could also infect animals? Would a queen be able to not only produce drones but also workers as an exact copy of herself? And what about other animals?

The worker bee on her leg decided that she was not at the best place to either find food or rest and departed for the nearest hive. Veronica got up and put on her beekeeper hat. She left the gloves off, as they obstructed her sensitivity in her fingers, and she got stung less often if she could feel whether she was squeezing a bee too hard. The hive was thriving, and the queen bee was busy laying more eggs. If bees were impacted by the virus, there was no sign of it. At least for now.

Veronica went back inside to see if Verity was up, but the baby was still sound asleep. Maybe the vaccination was making her a little more tired than usual. Veronica sat down on their bed and picked up her phone. She hesitated, but the curiosity to see what people were writing about her won.

At first, she did a simple search with her name and found dozens of articles regurgitating the same information about the Mars mission, her mysterious pregnancy, and the fact that she had cloned herself. Some added some personal interpretation about Martian radiation or an alien parasite, but most just copied each other. As usual with high-profile topics where only minimal information was public, these online writers were just wasting their own and everybody else's time. But then she noticed that one of the articles had a public comment section, and this was where the juicy stuff could be found, though the beverage turned into poison.

The more harmless comments simply labelled her as a 'bitch' or fantasised about a nine-month-long orgy aboard their spaceship. If only they knew how uncomfortable and unsexy that would have been.

But then there were also the ones who elaborated on their opinion. Someone suggested that she should have been put down like a dog with rabies as soon as she had set foot back on Earth, but another argued that they needed to find out what it was and find a cure first, so instead she should be locked up in a high-security laboratory, or at least consider a dissection after she was dead. Some others were in favour for the lab treatment, but more from a 'science' perspective, as this was a 'once-in-a-lifetime opportunity' to study a leap in evolution. All these comments had in common that they didn't see the person behind it, her and her baby, who were, besides the obvious, perfectly normal people.

She moved on with a few more keywords like 'Mars mission' and 'alien baby' and now got hits on public social media pages where the trolls had found each other. Seemingly uncontrolled, Veronica found death threats against her and her baby, elaborating on how they would do it, to condemnations that Verity either was the devil's spawn sent to test us all, or the opposite that Veronica was like the Virgin Mary and had given birth to their saviour, which was almost equally disturbing. Her baby shouldn't be anything to anyone else apart from her.

Nauseated, she closed her phone and sat in silence for a few moments. Cecilia had been right, and it was a dangerous negligence of NASA to let this information get out. Who was this whistle-blower who thought they had the right to pass on such sensitive information to a pack of wolves? Powerless against these invisible people who hounded her, she also felt emotions arising within herself about how she wished to be able to hurt the snitch.

She didn't want to feel like this and decisively placed her phone face down on the bedside table. Cecilia was in the living room, back on her computer, and judging by her furrowed brows and flushed cheeks, she was concentrating on work.

"Do you want a coffee?" Veronica asked.

"Nah, I'm good." Cecilia nodded towards a bottle of water avoiding eye contact.

Veronica had a strong suspicion that she was hunting online trolls. "Don't obsess about it too much."

"I'm not. I just want us to be safe."

"Maybe we should ask NASA whether we can have police protection."

Cecilia nodded. "Sounds like a plan."

"Verity is still asleep. I'm going to the backyard, see how the carrots are doing, and I'm still feeling a little wheezy. Maybe the fresh air will help."

"Take your phone with you."

"I'm only going into the backyard."

"Still."

Reluctantly, Veronica picked up her phone. No one should be able to enter the yard if they were not living in one of the surrounding flats, but people often left the front doors open to let air in or because they expected a delivery, so it was not a given that no unauthorized person could surprise her. But then, there might be people living wall to wall with them, knowing who they were and where to find them, and who wished her dead.

With a feeling of being watched, Veronica scanned the backyard. The vegetable allotments were right under their window, and when she looked up, she saw Cecilia opening it and giving her a short wave. Reassured, she picked up a small mattock from the community shed and tended to her vegetables. She had found gardening to be an excellent way to relax her senses and release her tensions whilst hacking away at weeds.

She wondered how their lives would be tomorrow or next month. Would they have to watch themselves now every time they left the house? Would the public attention ever go away again? She distracted herself by repeatedly thinking that dreadful things happened to innocent people all the time and nothing would be won if she retreated from the world and locked herself up. No, she wouldn't let other people dictate how she had to live her life. She had done nothing wrong, and if there was a change to society coming, then the people would have to adapt to it. This was her world, just as much as everybody else's.

CHAPTER 19

Amy was sitting in the waiting room of a small law firm; her hair combed a little too straight and her smart outfit not matching her makeup-less face. The bruises on her face had turned to a sickly green, but she just didn't care enough anymore to make any effort to cover them up.

She had lost everything that defined her, as if she had been stripped bare and abandoned in the desert. Every day felt the same since she had been released from hospital, bleak and tasteless.

Her parents had visited her, even paid for additional medical costs. They told her that Gabriel had contacted them to tell her that he was sorry and to try and mediate an amicable solution. Apparently, he had voluntarily sought out psychological help to resolve his anger issues. Yet when her mother asked what she had done that provoked Gabriel into beating her and that she shouldn't rush into a divorce, Amy knew she couldn't count even on her own parents.

On top of that, she was sorry for Miranda and Ozzy, who put up with her. Two days ago, she had started to look for a small flat that she could afford, but all her savings had been used up for the wedding. She was basically destitute and would be living on the street if it were not for Miranda.

In contrast to her parents, Miranda convinced her that she needed to follow through with an official complaint and make Gabriel pay for what he had done.

Without Miranda, Amy would have just stayed in bed and listened to white noise.

"Mrs. Stuart?"

Amy looked at the friendly receptionist, not sure if she meant her.

"Mr. Dawson is ready for you now."

Amy gathered her bag and followed the receptionist into an office.

"Mrs. Stuart, come in." A suited man, well-groomed and in his forties greeted her warmly. "Tea, coffee, water?"

"A tea would be nice. One sugar."

The receptionist nodded and left them alone.

"Please, sit. What can I do for you?" asked the lawyer.

"Um, my friend thinks I should get legal advice for, um, for my divorce. She made the appointment here, Miranda Dutton-Smith."

"It is often advisable to have a lawyer at least as a back-up, even if you don't think you need one."

"Maybe. I just want it to go away."

"I do have a couple of notes here that your friend passed on. You've been physically and mentally abused?"

"He, um, he beat me, yes." Amy waved at the still-visible marks in her face. "But he is not an aggressive person. He took good care of me. He just, he was so stressed, and I, and I …"

Amy couldn't continue. Tears rolled down her cheeks. Mr. Dawson passed her a tissue as the receptionist came in with a cup of tea.

"Are you getting help?" Mr. Dawson asked caringly when they were alone again.

"I'm living with my friend at the moment. I have no means to support myself otherwise."

"I meant professional psychological help."

"Oh, no."

"I think it would help you work through your experiences and get your head clear. Here, this is an incredibly good trauma specialist." He passed her a business card with an address. "And you said that you have no means to support yourself?"

"No, I lost my job, or I should say, I couldn't go back. It was my decision."

"Any savings?"

"No. Gabriel runs our finances."

"You don't have any insight into your accounts?"

"No. I'm not even sure I can afford this meeting."

"This consultation is free," said the lawyer. "Should you decide to hire me, though, I will have to ask for money. But even then, there is a chance to have the other party take on your legal costs if criminal charges are laid, besides just a divorce, and we move to court."

"Criminal charges?"

"From what I gathered, you have suffered domestic battery, which is a criminal offence. Moreover, I believe you have suffered a miscarriage as a direct result from Mr. Stuart's violence towards you."

"But he is not a violent man."

"We have a foetal homicide law in Florida, and I'm afraid a criminal charge is out of your control."

"But I was just … it was not the right time to tell him." Amy's body convulsed uncontrollably as she began crying again. "Sorry," she sobbed.

"It's all right. My wife and I lost two children, and I know the devastation that you feel."

Amy looked at the Mr. Dawson behind the desk and was surprised to recognize him for the man and father he was underneath the uniform of suit and tie.

"Do you have children?" asked Amy.

"One, a daughter. She's eleven now."

This simple fact, this small personal connection to someone who was basically a stranger, seeded a kernel of hope, which felt to Amy so unlikely to happen after months of losing herself and weeks of utter despair, that at first, she didn't recognize it.

"If you decide to hire me, I will work tirelessly for you and be available twenty-four-seven to discuss your case," said Mr. Dawson. "You have a compelling case to proceed with the divorce, as well as making a claim for financial compensations for your suffering. For the battery alone, there might even be a jail sentence on the cards."

"Jail? Oh, I don't want that."

"I suggest that you see the therapist first at this point." Mr. Dawson pointed at the business card that Amy was still holding in her hands. "She is really good and has helped me and my wife through our losses. Once you are more settled and sorted, you can let me know if you want to proceed with me. There are no hard feelings if you decide to go ahead with someone else, but I implore you to get a lawyer, whatever happens."

"Oh, I won't get anyone else. I don't think I could find the strength to get up and do this again. And, I guess, I like you." The seed of hope had grown somewhat, and Amy started to feel like she deserved to be alive, at least for a little while longer.

When she was back at Miranda's, she sat down on the guest bed on the first floor of the small townhouse and turned the business card round and round in her hands. She knew if she didn't make an appointment now, she probably would never do it, and using the little bit of strength that was still with her, she dialled and calmly arranged for a first therapy session next week.

Encouraged from the small steps she managed to do today, she took a shower as a gesture of self-appreciation. The water running down her face and back was soothing, like a mother's stroke, and it must have already been thirty minutes that she had stood there with her arms against the wall and her head leaned against her arms, when a knock on the door pulled her back into reality.

"Is everything all right?" She heard Miranda's voice through the door.

"Yes, I'm good. Be out in a minute," Amy called, and she was surprised that her voice sounded clear and strong.

"You sure you're okay? That was a long shower," asked Miranda when Amy came down into the kitchen.

"Yes. Promise," said Amy and smiled when Miranda studied her face.

"Good, I made us tea. Patrick is sleeping, so we could watch the new episode of *Carnival*."

"I don't think I'm in the mood."

"I miss you, and I don't mean to be pushy. Take as much time as you need," said Miranda.

"I'm going to make you an offer you can't resist," said Amy, and she felt something like joy watching Miranda's eyes light up.

"Refuse."

"What?"

"It's 'I'm going to make him an offer he can't refuse'," said Miranda.

"Really?"

"Yeah, if you quote Don Vito at me, I expect you to do it properly."

"Frankly, my dear, I don't give a damn," said Amy and took her cup to leave to the living room.

"Hey, Rhett, wait for me."

"You talking to me?" giggled Amy as she walked backwards to the sofa.

"Mrs. Robinson, you're trying to seduce me," laughed Miranda and grabbed her own cup of tea. "So, what do you wanna do?"

"Maybe just talk," said Amy, cuddling up on the sofa.

"Um, I'm not sure how good I'll be at that, but I'll give it my best shot. How about you start, though, to ease me in."

Amy smiled wistfully, swirling the tea in her hands and blowing on it to cool. "You don't understand! I coulda had class. I coulda been a contender. I could've been somebody, instead of a bum, which is what I am," she said eventually.

"Oh, so we are still doing that movie quote thing? Gotcha."

"No, I just don't know where to start," said Amy apologetically.

"How about you tell me how it went with the lawyer. Unless there is this whole confidentiality thing, and you need to kill me if you say anything."

"It went well. I think I'm going to move ahead with him. He seemed nice and approachable, although I'm apparently not the best judge when it comes to men."

"I kinda knew that. That's why I vetted him before I made your appointment."

"Thanks," said Amy sarcastically and tickled Miranda with her toes.

Miranda screamed in surprise and spilled some of her tea.

"Oh gosh, I'm so sorry," said Amy and hurried to get a towel from the kitchen.

"Well, now I get why they're called tea towels. Don't worry," said Miranda as Amy fussed over her and dabbed her dry as she had tears running over her cheeks. "All right, Mr. DeMille, I'm ready for my close-up."

Amy smiled and wiped her tears away. "I'm sorry, I don't know what's wrong with me."

"There is nothing wrong with you. I can't even imagine what you are going through, but one thing I know, love means never having to say you're sorry."

Amy nodded and slipped back under their blanket. "Mr. Dawson, the lawyer, said that I suffered domestic battery." Miranda turned quiet. "He says I could get financial compensation and, and that Gabriel might go to jail."

Miranda nodded, and Amy wished she would reveal what she was thinking.

"I don't want him to go to jail," whispered Amy.

Miranda looked up sharply, and Amy knew that she thought Gabriel deserved all the punishment the American justice system had to offer.

"He also suggested that I see a psychologist," continued Amy.

"I think that's good advice."

"I already made an appointment for next week."

"Excellent," said Miranda.

"But I'm afraid you'll have to put up with me a little longer."

"To paraphrase another good friend of mine, keep your enemies close, but your friends closer … Hey, have you heard about the other spacewalker, Veronica Vargas? She cloned herself."

"What?"

"Yeah, she got infected or grilled with radiation during their mission, and somehow her DNA changed, and she got pregnant without having had sex."

"You're kidding, right?"

"No, I'm not. I know it sounds like the plot for a movie and I had to double check the source, but it really is legit. She just popped out a baby."

"Sounds like a dream."

"Well, I don't know. It kinda does help to have a father around."

"But you don't really need a man for that. I mean, as long as you have a partner, a friend, grandparents, anyone really to help. You know what they say, it takes a village, not a man."

Miranda mulled things over. "You really are trying to seduce me, Mrs. Robinson."

Amy laughed. "I'm not saying that the father of your children can't be that partner; all I'm saying is that it would open a lot of other possibilities."

"The stuff dreams are made of. What if you cloned yourself too?"

"What?" Amy was dumbfounded.

"Yes, I mean you tried for ages, and he's apparently impotent ..."

"Infertile."

"Is there a difference?"

"Yes, one is a sharpshooter without a rifle, the other a sharpshooter without bullets."

"Gotcha. Well, whatever, his brain got fried. But isn't it weird that you fell pregnant if he couldn't sharp-shoot for whatever reason?"

Amy let this information or rather speculation sink in for a moment. "That's too weird. I mean, I wasn't on that mission."

"But maybe Gabriel infected you. Oh, I should play the lottery."

"Why?"

"Because I predicted that you'd be like *The Astro-naut's Wife*."

"Not really, at least I hope that I wasn't pregnant with alien twins."

"No, but wouldn't it be kinda cool to raise a clone of yourself?"

"Maybe."

"Although, I was a nightmare as a child. Had that whole princess thing going for years." Miranda rolled her eyes theatrically. "I'm so glad I have boys."

"At least you should know how to handle yourself."

"Yeah, but there is the whole nature versus nurture thing. Even with a clone, you don't know whether you'll get a good egg."

"So, now it's not such a cool thing anymore?" Amy liked the idea of cloning herself, but she had to admit that it also sounded scary.

"Oh, don't listen to me. I guess there is never a guarantee that your kid doesn't turn out to be a psychopath."

"I think children are always a reflection of their parents. The best any parent can do is to love them."

"Speaking of which …" Miranda got up as baby Patrick's wails sounded from the baby monitor.

Miranda breastfed Patrick as they continued discussing the possibility of Amy having been pregnant with an alien. They were still sitting on the sofa when Ozzy came home with Toby, who crawled in with them under the blanket.

Ozzy picked up the baby so that Toby could get his cuddles. "Can I get you two anything?"

"Another tea would be lovely, pudding," said Miranda as she held her cup up.

"And you?" Ozzy asked Amy.

"Tea would be great."

"Two teas coming right up."

"And a juice," demanded Toby, who was sitting like a little bird on his mother's lap.

"Hey," said Amy as Ozzy turned away, laden with the baby in airplane position and their empty teacups in the other hand. "I can take him."

Both Ozzy and Miranda watched as Amy cradled baby Patrick. "What?" she said as she noticed their stares.

"Nothing," said both and laughed.

"It's the first time you're holding him," said Miranda.

"Suits you," said Ozzy, and he bustled off into the kitchen.

* * *

Gayle's head was hammering as she sat in her pod on her way home after a long day of internal meetings and reading lengthy reports on the latest development of pregnancy rates and abortions in Europe and the world. Everything had descended into mayhem since the NASA whistle-blower had released the information about the spacewalker from the Mars mission. Apparently, there were secret government meetings happening, and new regulations were already being prepared that came all the way from the top. All subordinate departments such as her Family and Health Ministry were supposed to be briefed tomorrow.

She heard rumours about what was happening and knew that invisible strings were being pulled, and that people were working until late at night. She only wished she would have been kept in the loop from the beginning, as the threats on her life had become almost too much to bear. Since the news about the cloned baby girl broke, several bombs hidden in deliveries addressed to her had been discovered, colleagues had fallen ill after consuming poisoned food that had been left in the common tearoom, and hacker attacks had tripled.

She now always ordered a bulletproof pod to get to and from work and also pushed through that her daughters were chauffeured to and from school and that the school's security system got an overhaul.

Gayle broke into a silent sob just as the pod pulled up in front of her house, and she sat in silence for a few minutes until she had collected herself. She gathered her bag and folders with more reports she was supposed to study before tomorrow's big general meeting, though all she wished to do was go to bed and fall into a numb sleep as quickly as possible.

Inga sat alone on the big white sofa and was watching a nature documentary when Gayle came in. She was surprised, as her eldest daughter had never shown an interest in anything more than blockbusters and fashion-related shows.

"Hi," said Gayle cautiously.

"Hi," answered Inga without looking at her mother.

Gayle knew that Inga was still not on good speaking terms with her. On one side, an abortion was never an easy procedure, and she should have approached the path with more caution; on the other side, she could not understand why her daughter was still so upset. She didn't really want a baby at sixteen, did she?

The images on the television showed a pride of lions in a reserve in Africa, one of the last where wild animals of the savannah still lived largely without human intervention. Most animal species, or at least mammals, were now under strict conservation control to make sure that future generations could still enjoy these magnificent creatures.

"This is a rare sighting to observe the lion mating with a lioness. Nowadays, artificial insemination and embryo transfers are practiced in zoos as well as nature reserves around the globe to reduce inbreeding and ensure the survival of these endangered species," said a presenter who was lying behind a camouflage shielding and watched the lions mate like a window peeper.

"Where's Hazel?" asked Gayle.

"Don't know."

Gayle hated this answer. Why could her girls not let anyone in the family know where they were? Her pulse was rising, especially considering all the threats that were currently flying around and could easily target her daughter.

She dropped her files off in her home office and logged on to her phone tracker. At least they had all agreed to install an app that allowed them to see where everyone was, so they wouldn't raise a false alarm.

Just as Gayle's phone showed Hazel's location, the front door opened, and her youngster, who was now sixteen weeks pregnant and finally getting over her morning sickness, entered.

"Mum?" Hazel shouted from the hall and stormed into the living room to change the channel.

"Hey, I was watching that," said Inga.

"Did you see this?" asked Hazel when Gayle entered.

"It's another pandemic, just like 2019." Hazel's cheeks were flushed.

"What are you talking about?" asked Gayle.

"This," she said as she finally found what she was looking for.

A news presenter was reading from a teleprompter, interrupted by the breaking news that just came in. "The majority of the forty countries that have instated a travel ban from tomorrow are in the Northern Hemisphere. The ban will start from the first of November to allow travellers to return to their home countries. Australia has already banned citizens and permanent residents from leaving unless a travel exemption has been given. For the full list of countries, visit our website. Tomorrow, the cabinet of the European Nations will come together to debate on further actions that are expected to be implemented soon."

"Did you know about this?" asked Hazel.

"No, well, I know about the meeting tomorrow but not what it is about exactly."

"We are now switching live to Houston, Texas, where Matthew White was arrested today on charges of treason for giving away state secrets. He leaked the DNA sequences of spacewalker Veronica Vargas and her baby, who was conceived in space and born two months ago on Earth. Since then, speculations about a virus or another transmissible disease that causes women to fall pregnant without a male partner have been spread all around the world."

"I told you I didn't have sex," said Hazel defiantly.

Gayle and Hazel joined Inga on the sofa and watched the continuation of the report.

The next images showed a young man being led to an airplane with his arms and legs shackled.

"Arina told me today that she had two abortions in the last three months and that her parents are not allowing her to step outside anymore and that they moved her bedroom into their dressing room so that they can keep an eye on her, even at night. And Tamara is already twenty weeks pregnant. I thought she was, or she had gotten real fat. Anyways, even her winter jumpers can't hide it anymore," announced Hazel, still watching the television, spellbound.

"Did you tell them that you're pregnant?" asked Gayle.

"Yes, it was kinda hard not to say anything. And I think I started showing too," said Hazel, and she lifted her top to show the littlest bit of a belly that could well have been just a large dinner.

A tiny stone fell off Gayle's heart, but a large boulder still remained when she thought about her thirteen-year-old becoming a mother in about five months.

"Think about it. I've cloned myself. I'll be giving birth to myself," gushed Hazel.

"Have you taken your vitamins today?" asked Gayle.

"No, I forgot."

Gayle sighed as she went into the kitchen to fetch Hazel her pregnancy vitamins and a glass of water.

"You know you are iron deficient. Remember to take your pills at least for the next five months," admonished Gayle.

Neither of them took notice that Inga had scooted to one corner of the sofa and watched the live report quietly and withdrawn.

CHAPTER 20

The meeting the next day proved to be even more of a bombshell than Gayle had expected after last night's news update. The European Parliament met at the newly updated Paul-Henry Spaak plenary chamber. Over the years, several of the parliament buildings around the Espace Léopold had been extended and re-modelled according to the developing needs. Most recently, that included new insulation, both for climate and espionage reasons. Although its interior still looked like it did at its conception in 1988 with a post-modern style, its invisible updates could keep up with any secret service centre in the world.

What was different today was the heavy presence of security personnel. There were always guards who staffed the metal detectors and checked IDs, but today, there was also a bomb squad team and armed guards patrolling a fenced perimeter around the entire Espace Léopold. Considering the groups of activists who had already aggregated, Gayle thought that this might have been a wise precaution.

As her pod slowly drove past the demonstrators, she could see and hear that most of them were once again directed at her or at least at causes that were directly related to her ministry. The usual signs demanded the abolition of the conception bill claiming that it violated the right to physical inviolability or variably the message of God to grow and multiply. Gayle wondered how the followers of various religious groups would accept the possibility that women could now clone themselves. She was sure that it wouldn't receive an all-round happy welcome, and her blood ran cold thinking about the possible retaliations that women might sustain on the back of it.

Just as she thought about it, someone broke the barrier and hammered against her pod. The man couldn't have known that she was in the vehicle, as it had blacked-out windows, but the sign he pressed against her window confirmed her fears. It read 'SLUTS beware, you will NEVER rule this world.'

As quickly as the sign appeared, it was ripped off again and with it the angry man, who was tackled to the ground by a guard.

Once Gayle was safely inside the plenary room and had found herself a seat in the hemicycle, her rising anxiety fluctuated between disbelief and anger.

The president of the European Commission gave a rundown of what had been going on behind the world curtains, which confirmed that there was a silent pandemic spreading across all continents, most likely caused by an extra-terrestrial virus, which inserted a piece of DNA into the code of the X chromosome and then allowed infected women to reproduce by cloning themselves.

The one added bit of information that had apparently not yet leaked was that infected women needed a specific hormonal level that was similar to early pregnancy for an egg to initiate duplication of its genetic code and form a diploid zygote which then commenced a real pregnancy.

Whilst she wasn't sure how many members of parliament still had their biology classes in the back of their heads, Gayle understood that this specific hormonal level could be achieved with most hormonal contraceptives, which usually worked by tricking the female body into believing that it was already pregnant.

She closed her eyes and descended into a black hole when she realized that her contraception bill had given this virus fertile soil to express itself.

She got ripped from her bottomless pit when the president of the commission proposed that the contraception bill should be immediately suspended, and the recommendation be given out to remove hormonal implants. An independent committee should be put in place to investigate the current state of the pandemic in Europe and deliberate on the best way forward. The president further suggested that the countries should instate immediate measures to contain any further spread of the virus as well as establish databanks that collected genomic information on the X chromosome until an EU-wide catalogue of counter actions could be agreed upon.

Gayle couldn't believe that she had not been informed earlier about these propositions. Many laws and executive orders in the European Nation were still decided by the individual governments, and she was sure that the health ministers of each country had already been working on their plans for a week or two. She could imagine how pleased they were that her bill, for which she had lobbied for years, was now thrown out, giving them back their sovereignty on family planning. The European Parliament had gained more and more influence over individual countries, however, the further down the hierarchical ladder, the more protest could be heard against 'those up there'.

She sat quietly as a debate raged about data confidentiality and how to avoid panic in the common populace. Eyes kept flitting towards her, despite the serious discussions, and she could only imagine too well that ministers as well as the people outside blamed her for the increased unwanted pregnancies, even though they should know better.

Instead of defending herself, her only way forward was to run an extensive information campaign with hard facts, leaving out the obvious connection to her bill. She needed to state clearly why hormonal implants were now recommended to be removed and with it the use of any hormonal contraception. Her head started to ache just thinking about the monumental task ahead. But then again, the individual health ministers should deal with the actual execution of the plan since they were always so keen on having the ball in their playing field.

Back in her office, she asked Guillaume for a glass of water and a painkiller, and then to make an appointment with Doctor Charton.

She read Guillaume's quizzical frown and explained, "I want to remove Inga's implant. I'll brief you shortly. Just get that water to me."

Guillaume left without further questions. That's what she liked about him. Never asking for unnecessary information and never giving any information away.

She not only informed Guillaume about the unfolding situation and the tasks ahead but her core team as well. She would need all the help she could get.

It was after eleven o'clock when Gayle finally came home and found her girls watching TV in their pyjamas.

"You should be in bed already," she reminded them.

"Just watching the news update," Hazel said. "They are now running a twenty-four-seven commentary on that Mars virus. Apparently, an estimated quarter of pregnancies conceived in the last three months are clones."

Gayle's head swam. "Inga, I've made an appointment for you to get your implant removed tomorrow."

This was one bit of information she had neatly filed away in her head, and she hoped that by including Inga early on, as early as a day's notice could be, her daughter would have time to prepare herself mentally.

"Why?" asked Inga.

"Because the contraception bill has been revoked today, and there is no need to have it anymore," Gayle answered.

"Why?"

"Because I trust you, and I don't want your developing body to get confused by influences that the implant might have." Gayle struggled to find the words.

"Is it because it's the implants that cause pregnancies when you have the virus?" asked Hazel out of the blue.

"What? No. Where did you get that from?"

"That's what they have been reporting for the last two hours."

What was the point of secret meetings if the entire world was kept up to date almost in real time?

"Well, sometimes the reporters only speculate without doing their research," snapped Gayle and walked into the kitchen to get herself another painkiller.

When she came back, Inga and Hazel were on their way up to their bedrooms, and she overheard them on the stairs.

"Do you think Mum is right?" asked Inga.

"I think she knows more than she is letting us know," answered Hazel.

"But why didn't I fall pregnant again?" asked Inga almost inaudibly.

She could ring Mack and see what his thoughts were on this topic. After all, he did something with human DNA. But he was not a virologist or a fertility expert, and even though she trusted him and was sure he would never pass on sensitive information, she needed to be careful what information she gave him. Little did she know what role Mack was already playing.

* * *

Mack was closer than Gayle thought and was currently on a jet to England and had already crossed Belarus. He was one of a small team that had gotten travel exemptions, and the jet was pleasantly quiet, so he had been able to sleep a full seven hours in a business-class seat. With him travelled Professor Lamarck and Tom, as well as Doctor Ingram and Professor Lee. Whilst the professors had several days of meetings ahead, Mack and Gillian Ingram were spearheading the global data collection and were going to visit the laboratories in

London. Tom was supposed to give workshops on his newly developed algorithm to not only identify the alien insertion but also identify any other associations with phenotypes, such as naturally conceived pregnancies or no pregnancy despite hormonal contraception.

Data collection in Australia had picked up speed, and doctors were advised to offer routine blood tests, especially to the currently fertile generations, under the pretext of identifying genetic predispositions such as diabetes, Alzheimer's, certain types of cancer, or simple malnutrition. The list of genetic disorders, of course, also included the detection of this new X-chromosome variant, but most people did not question the official Mars virus insertion *ETMV54* amongst a list of genes like *TP53*, *APOE*, or *HLA-DQA1*.

Australia was, up till now, a trailblazer, building their databank, and the estimates showed that about sixty percent of the population was already infected, which did not give great hope to stopping the spread.

"What about DNA scissors?" asked Tom from the row behind when they had been served their dinner.

"Too slow and won't stop reinfection," answered Mack with a mouth full of chicken curry.

"And a vaccine?"

"Already in development, but not one hundred percent effective."

Tom packed his dinner tray and moved to the seat next to Mack.

"What about artificial wombs?"

"You mean like they use for preterm babies?"

"Yes, apparently, they work pretty well. I just looked it up."

"So far, it's only been applied to foetuses that are twenty weeks or older and only in the Netherlands as far as I know. There is a whole legal debate going on, and I'm sure trying to make babies completely in the lab won't get an easy pass, even if technically possible," explained Mack.

For a few minutes, he got to eat his dinner in silence, but when he used his bread roll to soak up the extra sauce, Tom, who hadn't even started his pasta, had another idea.

"What about accessing the data from all these ancestry sites?"

Mack paused with the sauce dripping from his roll back onto his plate.

"That might be an idea. Can you check how many there are and how many customer samples they have collected?"

Tom put his dinner tray on the next seat and placed his laptop on the foldable table.

"There are six major companies and around two dozen smaller ones. The big ones each have around twenty million samples over the lifetime of the company. But … one second, only around a million each since March this year. Apparently, the demand has been declining over the last decade."

"I wonder whether they have the samples stored somewhere or only keep the electronic records?" mused Mack.

"This one says that they destroy the samples three months after the results are transmitted to the customer."

"I thought so. The next question is whether they store a copy of the genomic code somewhere or transfer that to the customer too, and most importantly, whether they also decoded the X chromosome, as that is not usually considered important for commercial ancestry analyses."

"Do you want me to send an inquiry?" asked Tom.

"Not yet. We should first discuss this with the team and see what legal implications this might have. And I'm sure these companies won't just give up their assets for free."

Mack wondered how valuable these DNA banks were and how much money these private companies would be able to extort from governments.

Shortly after their dinner trays were collected again, Tom's still untouched, they were told that they were going to land in thirty minutes and to take their own seats and buckle up.

Mack was glad that Tom moved back into his seat. He had grown fond of him, but the nearing arrival stirred his nerves, not just about the task ahead but also because he had taken a step he had never done before.

Just before they had left, he had found out Marsha's contact details at the United Banks of Europe and sent a message urging her to see her general practitioner. As he couldn't disclose the true nature of his concern, he threw himself into hot water, telling her that he had contracted hepatitis B and that their encounter in Shanghai was unfortunately within the potential incubation time. He added some courtesy apologies and explained that he 'only wanted to do the right thing', but still expected a scorching response. Instead, though, he received a thank-you note, that she had been vaccinated against hep b, and asked to send messages of this nature to her private email next time and not her monitored work address. At this point, Mack was desperately looking for another reason to get her to see a doctor. He told her that he was also vaccinated, which was true, and yet gotten ill, as vaccinations were not one hundred percent effective. She thanked him again for his concern but didn't say whether she would go and get tested. Fearing that he would come across as a crazy stalker, he left it at that and hoped for the best. If she went to see a doctor to get a test for hepatitis B, they would also test her for the *ETMV54* insertion, as the Isle of Great Britain had adopted the same sneaky approach as Australia, only that they hadn't closed their borders yet. If she still didn't have the insertion, the likelihood was that they would tell her to come in for further tests to determine whether she was simply not yet infected or immune to the virus.

With the time difference between Australia and England, Mack was circling over London in the early hours of the morning. A long way up north in Edinburgh, Marsha was getting ready to see her doctor before going to work. The message the day before yesterday had caught her off guard, but mainly because it came in on her work address. She was not new to getting herself checked for STDs and had gotten tested after she had returned from China but knowing that hepatitis could have an incubation period of several weeks or months, she wanted to be more safe than sorry. Nonetheless, she thought it unlikely that she had gotten anything.

"I see that you are vaccinated against hepatitis B and got tested for chlamydia, gonorrhoea, trichomoniasis, and syphilis only a few months ago, in June," said the general practitioner as he looked through her patient file.

"What can I say, I know how to enjoy myself, and I've gotten notice from someone that I might want to get tested for hep B again," answered Marsha.

"Fair enough. You take care of your health and safety," said the doctor. "Considering your age and that you might be thinking about having children in the future, may I suggest some free genetic testing, since we are already taking a blood sample?"

"I'm not planning to have children."

"Well, you might change your mind, and the screening is also beneficial for you to be able to plan your own health and safety in the future."

"What kind of genetic tests are you talking about?"

"We'd be checking the most common breast cancer genes and some other cancer-causing genes, genetic predispositions for diabetes, which, if you know about it, you can postpone and moderate with your lifestyle choices. There are also some mental disorders, which if identified early, can be treated with much greater success. Here is a list of all the genes that are currently included in our general testing panel."

He passed her a printout from the National Health Service.

"And this is free?" Marsha asked as she scanned the page.

"Yes."

"Why not. How long until I get the results?"

"The gene tests could come back as early as tomorrow, although there has been an increased demand which would delay the results by a couple of days, and the hep b takes up to a week."

"And you'll get in touch if anything is wrong?"

"Only if anything is wrong. Otherwise, you can expect an email with your test results for your own records, but we won't contact you for a follow-up appointment."

Like Marsha, thousands of people unknowingly agreed to get tested for the new insertion of the Mars virus, yet these numbers were still too small to get a reliable picture of the spread of the virus. They needed to make an official call-out without spreading panic. Worryingly, only less than one percent of people returned a test result that showed no insertion, which indicated that all their efforts to stop the virus might already be too late.

Mack was not impressed with the setup of the London testing facility. Whilst all the technology was there, only one overworked lab assistant processed the samples that got sent in for a second confirmation screening. The rest of the huge testing facility was used for other genetic studies, including studies on animals. Whilst this setup might work in the short term with only few samples needing to get retested nationwide, once the full scope of the operation was running, this bottleneck could mean a delay in their reaction response. He urged the laboratory leader to scale up right away and got a promise that this would happen soon, but they had to maintain already approved research projects and obligations to hospitals.

Angry with this mindset, Mack worried that if they did not reveal the worst-case scenario, a pandemic without people dying or even needing intense medical attention would not be taken seriously enough.

Later in the afternoon, he got a shock in the opposite direction when he was shown a secret underground facility in the heart of London, with a biosecurity level four. Mack had never been in a lab that had any biosecurity level, and he was anxious passing through multiple negative air-flow chambers, in each either removing or putting on pieces of clothing, until he was clad in clean white undergarments that would be treated after he left and a hazmat suit with external air supply. He was shown how the security system worked should his air supply get interrupted. His breathing was laboured and chest tight as they walked along the sterile white corridors with hazard warning signs on every door.

Biosecurity level four laboratories were used to study infectious agents or toxins that posed a high risk of aerosol transmission and possibly deadly diseases for which no vaccine or therapy was available. Whilst he was impressed with the measures that were taken for this security level, he was astonished when he was shown a quarantine facility where two women were kept under observation.

"What trial is this? Are you testing substances on humans?" Mack asked incredulously.

"No, this is not a trial. These women are not infected with the Mars virus, and they have agreed to partake in our long-term study on how this virus enters the human body and affects fertility," explained the lab head who was showing him around.

"So, you are infecting these women with the virus?"

"No, we keep them as a control group."

"To what?"

"To other infected women who fall pregnant or not."

"I'm not sure I understand. Correct me if I'm wrong, but I thought most viruses and their impacts can now be modelled on the computer, and even the effects of new mutations can be predicted."

"Correct. It is not a study that is currently active, but we decided that it is essential to have as many healthy specimens as possible for a later stage of the study. We are basically keeping these women safe."

"And later? What is this study? Human incubators? A baby farm? Do they know what is going on?" Mack felt sick.

"I think you do not understand at what abyss humankind is standing," lectured the lab head.

"Oh, I'm fully aware. That's why I'm leading the global data sampling."

"Then you will also be aware that data sampling is only the first step. If we cannot stop this virus, and it is my understanding that the point of no return has long been passed, then we need to plan for the future. A long way into the future."

That night in his hotel room, Mack was staring at the ceiling, digesting what he had learned today. He had done some pretty unethical things himself, but no one was ever harmed by his desire for finding true love and starting a family. At least not more than from any other one-night stand. But this imprisoning of women in a secret high-security lab to make sure that humankind, or more precisely men, could still wander the face of the earth in another hundred years surmounted even his strongest desire for reproduction and leaving a legacy behind.

CHAPTER 21

After London, Mack and the others visited a facility in Spain and then flew to America, where they presented their progress at another global meeting. Mack had strong concerns about the approach taken on the Isle of Great Britain, but it was not his responsibility, nor did he have the authority to reprimand this line of action. Maybe in a few years' time or perhaps next year, that trial would be found to be obsolete or hailed a success that warranted all means.

At the meeting in Washington, DC, Mack realized another component that could quickly become even more threatening to humankind than the slow decline of men in society.

They were again sitting in a secret meeting room and had listened to and watched the first numbers and projections regarding the spread of the virus, which were not good, as well as the different measures that governments had already implemented.

For almost thirty minutes, a preliminary 3-D model of the virus hovered over the table as a group of epidemiologists from Mexico showed their results. Not only was the virus the smallest that had ever been characterized on Earth, which also made it more difficult to study, but it also had a slightly altered protein layer, which protected the short DNA fragment on the inside. This altered protein layer was predicted to be hardier and allow the virus to attach to surfaces easier, which meant that even frequent hand washing was only minimally effective in preventing the spread of the virus. On the other hand, speaking and coughing allowed the small virions to become airborne and remain airborne in a closed room for several hours. Therefore, the recommendation was to impose the wearing of masks and reduce community movement as much as possible. Mack noticed how the older generation of attendees lowered their eyes, probably because they remembered the last pandemic that had made strict limitations of human contact necessary.

A positive note from Mexico was that the virus replicated in host cells very slowly, which meant that infected people were unlikely to experience any health threats and that the development of a vaccine seemed promising. Why the virus also inserted parts of its DNA into the X chromosome was still elusive, as the virus itself did not benefit from it. For now, the scientists speculated that it was just coincidence that the insertion happened and unfortunate that it had such consequences for the host organisms.

Finally, a podgy man on the Swedish connection took the stage. He wore an open tweed jacket over a light-blue shirt and chinos, something that stood in stark contrast to either the white shirts and suit jackets of the politicians or the laid-back and at times flamboyant outfits of the scientists.

"I am Professor Dean Brinkmann, from the Agricultural University of Uppsala," said the man as his presentation flickered in and out whilst a technician on the other end tried to fix the connection. "Thank you very much for letting me present the concerning developments in the food industry. I'll try to keep it short."

The noise in the room only slowly calmed down, but Professor Brinkmann was determined.

"All sectors have failed to successfully inseminate any female livestock. The poultry industry is already collapsing. In two months, we will start to see the effects in the dairy sector as well."

Dean Brinkmann now had the full attention of the room.

"What do you suggest?" asked Professor Lamarck.

"We have been briefed about the potential use of hormones to initiate a pregnancy. I know that the distribution of any hormonal medications has been restricted in most countries, but I urge you to provide livestock producers with hormonal supplements, so that we can keep producing."

"The consumers have to be informed about any medical supplements, and that will lead only to more protests on top of the critical situation," argued the president of the European Commission.

"Within the year, all animal products will run out, and I doubt that food rationing will help to keep riots at bay for the sake of hormone-free livestock production."

After a long day of sleep-inducing meetings, Mack sank onto his bed in his hotel room. He had to be up early again, and his body told him that it didn't want to move anymore, but his mind was racing. He thought about Marsha. If she went to the doctor and they found that she was not infected or even immune, she could end up in that underground laboratory in the middle of a world city. Surely though, they wouldn't hold her against her consent. Still, there was a nagging feeling that the world was heading to a steep cliff, not because of the effect of the virus, but because of human nature.

He turned on the television and was proven right. Now that the cat was more or less out of the bag, the conspiracy theorists also came out of the woodwork, and with them came a first wave of widespread panic, and worse.

* * *

Supermarkets all over the world experienced mass buying, not of animal products, but of flour, bottled water, and toilet paper, of all things. Meat had become more expensive and was not available all day anymore, but when faced with an empty shelf, it was not meat that people went mad about. Maybe if twenty years ago they had consequently restricted meat production in general rather than leaving it to the ten percent of vegetarians to contribute to a reduction in greenhouse gases, it could have resulted in a manageable global temperature.

Subin pushed her way through the Souq market to buy food for her ever-hungry boys. Meat was not on her list, as they couldn't afford it anymore. Subin was glad that she didn't have to go to this section of the market anyway, as she was still struggling with morning sickness, even though she was now halfway through her pregnancy. At least this baby didn't seem to be growing as much as her boys did, and she could still hide her burgeoning middle with clever dressing. Maybe this time it was a girl, she thought, as she passed a stall with brightly coloured fabric. She stopped to feel the material and imagined which patterns she would buy to make dresses for a little girl.

Then she moved on to buy some spices and herbs she needed for cooking and teas to keep her nausea at bay. Sometimes she feared that the baby was small because she couldn't eat properly, but since feeling it move inside her last week, she was reassured that everything was all right. This afternoon, she would visit the doctor to hopefully put even her last fears to rest.

She had always liked the spice market and gazed at the pyramids that some traders constructed from chilies, sesame seeds, and turmeric. The bowls of lentils and peas or fresh coffee beans seemed so inviting that she wanted to submerge her hands into them, though Subin always only stroked the surface, pretending to check the quality. This time, she bought a pack of lentils, some smoked paprika, and red pepper.

On her way back, she stopped at a stall selling children's clothing. Malik needed new shoes and Aarif several trousers. The boy liked to skid around on his buttock and knees, and even the patches she had sewn on were already tattered.

As she stretched to reach for a pair of Nikes, a hand suddenly touched her belly. She pushed it off and saw a man grinning at her.

"Boy or girl?" he asked.

"I don't know," she said, breathless.

"You should be hoping for a boy. There is trouble ahead for girls."

"I already have three boys," she replied, even though she knew she should just keep quiet and give no further reason for the man to stay.

From the depths of the stall, the trader came out to see who was talking, and the man disappeared with another uncomfortable smile.

"Can I help you?" asked the trader, confused.

"How much are the Nikes?" Subin asked, still calming herself.

"Two thousand Sudanese pound."

"Are they genuine?"

"Of course."

"I will think about it and bring my son next time to try them on."

"I can't guarantee that they won't sell. Very sought after."

"That's okay. *Inshallah*."

As she was leaving the market, she noticed the man again who had harassed her earlier. He followed her with his eyes, and Subin decided to walk to a different exit and stay amongst the safety of the busy stalls a little longer. She stopped here and there to inspect some products but kept looking around to see whether she was being followed.

On the opposite corner of the market, she crossed the road to walk around the block and back to a bus stop on her way home.

It took much longer to reach the next crossroad than she had anticipated, and she already wondered whether she had overreacted and should have just taken her normal route, when she became aware of footsteps behind her.

She glanced over her shoulder and recognized the man from the market. In one swift movement, she turned around, dropped her shopping, and was pushed into a house entrance.

The man's spicy breath brushed over her neck as he pushed her head to the side whilst groping her belly.

"No, please," Subin begged.

"You have nothing to fear," he said as he pushed himself harder against her belly.

He had an erection, but otherwise did not attempt to get under her clothes.

"This is just a warning of what will happen to you and all women who allow demons to be born into this world. Our world, the world of men. If you are carrying a girl, you better kill this child of Iblis on the spot. Be warned."

The man released her and disappeared between the cars on the other side of the street.

Subin sank to the ground and caught her breath as she held her belly. She silently prayed for her child to be unharmed and implored it to show a sign of life. This pregnancy was unexpected and hard on her, but she had bonded with her unborn child. As unseemly as her mother made it out to praise a miracle before its time, she spoke to her baby in her thoughts, asked it whether it liked a certain food that she ate or the rocking when she climbed the steps to their flat. She told it about its brothers and how much they would love it, and when she washed herself, she marvelled at her growing belly.

After a long ten minutes, she finally felt a kick in her abdomen and sighed in relief.

"Are you all right?" a male voice asked, and Subin opened her eyes.

A young man in his early twenties was collecting her groceries off the sidewalk and carried them to her.

"Is everything okay?" he asked again.

"Yes, yes. Thank you. Just a little lightheaded," Subin said and got up, only to sink back against the wall.

"Where are you going?" the man asked.

Subin hesitated but finally told him that she wanted to catch the bus down Mohammed Najebi Street. He offered to carry her bags to the bus stop.

When she was alone again, waiting at the bus stop amongst strangers, she wished she had someone with her. Even her smallest son, Aarif, might have deterred that man, and she was upset and frightened that a woman could still not walk alone, minding their own business, without being scrutinized or outright attacked in this world of mankind.

She could already see the bus slowly making its way through the traffic when her phone rang.

"Hello, Mrs. Subin Sulliman?"

"Yes?"

"This is Faiza from the Red Cross practice. How are you, ma'am?"

"I'm good, thank you," said Subin and dreaded that they might postpone her afternoon appointment with the doctor.

"We had some unforeseen emergencies coming in, and Doctor James was wondering whether you could come in earlier?"

"Oh, yes, of course. When should I come?"

"If you can, you could come in now, in the next thirty minutes, or at noon."

"I can come now. I'm already in town."

"That's great, see you soon."

The bus had just opened its doors when Subin picked up her bags to get to the traffic lights and cross to the other side.

Another twenty minutes later and she entered the doctor's practice, sweaty and tired.

"Are you all right, ma'am?" asked the nurse at the entrance.

"Yes, just a little lightheaded," said Subin.

The nurse fetched her a cup of water. "Please sit down. You look a little pale. Doctor James will be with you shortly."

The doctor did the usual routine examinations of checking her blood pressure, which was low, keeping track of her weight, and listening to the baby's heartbeat with a doppler. The galloping sound of the tiny heart reassured Subin, and she felt her colour returning to her cheeks.

"Everything appears to be in perfect order, but I would like to run a blood test to check on your iron levels. They might be a little low."

"Okay."

"Why don't you quickly see the nurse so she can run some tests while we do an ultrasound scan?"

"Does that cost extra?"

"No, one scan is free. Should you wish any more scans, though, we'd charge thirty thousand Sudanese pounds."

Subin audibly released some air.

"And this is still cheaper than the hospital," said the doctor.

Subin was elated about the prospect of seeing her child and didn't even mind the needle this time.

The doctor took ultrasound measurements for a good twenty minutes and reassured Subin that the baby's growth was perfectly on schedule.

"Would you like to know the gender?" asked the doctor.

Subin was tempted and smiled excitedly but declined. No matter if it was a boy or a girl, she knew already that she would love it just as much as her other children, and that was all that mattered.

The bloodwork that came in just a minute later showed that Subin had dangerously low iron levels.

"Did you have any complications in your previous pregnancies?" asked the doctor.

"No, just the usual, morning sickness, swollen ankles towards the end."

"No low blood counts?"

"I had to take some iron supplements with my last son, but I thought that was normal."

"Do you eat meat?"

"Yes, but it's gotten so expensive that we can't afford it."

The doctor nodded, concerned. "I would like you to buy some iron supplements and take them rigorously until at least a month after you have given birth. I will make a note to keep an eye on your blood count. Would you allow me to forward your records to the maternity ward at the hospital?"

"Yes, of course. Is it something that I should worry about?"

Why couldn't there be a day or just a few hours of only good news?

"If you take your iron tablets, your blood count should come up, and you might feel less tired and out of breath. There could be some other factors causing your low blood counts but seeing that you did not have any complications in your previous pregnancies we should be able to get on top of it easily. Here, just in case you won't get to it soon."

The doctor fetched a small white container that contained twenty iron tablets from a glass cabinet. "Take one every day with a meal."

"Thank you so much."

"Not to worry. I'll see you in another eight weeks. Have you contacted the midwives yet?"

"Not yet."

"Get in touch with them soon. I think they are currently quite busy."

Subin liked this doctor, and she wished she didn't have to go to the maternity ward. The midwives there were always overworked and harsh when you asked questions or needed more help than cutting the umbilical cord. Unfortunately, the actual birth was not covered by the Red Cross, and Subin had been lucky to get Doctor James to look after her during this pregnancy.

* * *

James Rice finished the paperwork for his last patient, Subin Suliman, and then packed his bag to go to the hospital. They had requested help from external practitioners, as they had seen a steep increase in not only pregnancies but also botched abortions and injuries from aggressive attacks. He hoped that this was not the beginning of violent unrest.

His wife had told him about the developments at NASA, and he followed the news throughout the day as a learned habit from his work in war zones. His experience told him that the unfolding events about this Mars virus was a burning fuse to a crate of societal injustice that was about to explode, and he feared that the fuse was rather short.

He walked the two kilometres to the hospital and bought a falafel and fresh orange juice on the way. Once at the hospital, he would have very short breaks that were far apart, so he made the most of his walk. Or at least he tried.

James had just finished his food and found a bin to throw away his wrapper. The rock pigeons were cruising around the bin, pecking at anything and everything in the hopes of finding some edible crumbs. They reminded him of the Lovey-Doveys that used to nest on his windowsill and never returned to their nest. He had thrown away the two eggs after three days, worried that they would rot. Now he wondered whether the birds had been unsuccessful in hatching a brood because of this virus. He looked at the bobbing pigeons for a while, trying to determine whether there were any young ones amongst them, but they all looked the same. He couldn't remember ever having seen baby pigeons out and about but perhaps they were just good at hiding their nests and vulnerable chicks until they were fully grown. Maybe there was still hope.

This little pause meant that he had to pick up his pace and he tightened the straps on his backpack. He walked another hundred metres when he got stopped by an apple that rolled out from an obscured lane. He picked up the apple and looked for the owner.

At first, he couldn't see anyone, but he heard muffled noises that made their way out from behind an overflowing dumpster.

"Hello?" James called into the lane and took a few steps into the shadows. "Is there someone? Hello?"

A dark figure jumped out and tackled James, who fell backwards onto the ground. The person was up and gone too quickly for James to have done anything.

He got to his feet and felt like he might have gotten a tailbone contusion, when he saw a ripped bag of apples on the ground next to a pair of legs.

His pain forgotten, he rushed over the rubbish and found a pregnant woman who was profusely bleeding from a stab wound in her abdomen. The blade, a short pocketknife, was lying nearby.

He sprang into action and checked the woman's vitals; she was breathing and conscious.

"Hi, I'm James Rice, a doctor with the Red Cross," he told the woman, to keep her calm. "Can you tell me your name?"

The woman looked at him calmly, which was not a good sign considering her situation. James opened his backpack, pulled on gloves, and carefully inspected the wound. He was relieved to only find this one wound and that it was a clean cut, but by the colour of the blood and intensity of the bleeding, a major vein or organs had been impacted, and the position could pose a threat for the unborn baby.

"Aliyah Bashir," she whispered.

"Hi, Aliyah, I am going to try and stop the bleeding now. How far along are you with your pregnancy?"

James multitasked getting out a compress as well as his phone to call an ambulance.

"Thirty-one weeks."

"Hi, this is Doctor James Rice from the Red Cross," he said into his phone, held between his head and shoulder. "I'm with a young woman, she is thirty-one weeks pregnant and has sustained a stab wound in the abdomen. The woman is conscious but has lost about half a litre of blood and is still bleeding. We are in a lane on Al Ma'arad Street somewhere around street six or seven." James looked around to better describe their location. "There is a discount supermarket on the opposite side of the street."

He was pushing heavily on the wound, trying to stem the blood flow without hurting the child.

"Help is on the way," he reassured the woman, who started to look pale.

"Am I going to see my little girl?" the woman whispered.

"I will do everything I can. We are close to a hospital; an ambulance should be here soon."

"Why did he do it?" asked the woman, delirious.

"Help!" James started to shout out to people on the pavement.

A teenage girl stopped her father to go and have a look.

"There should be an ambulance coming. Flag them down, please," instructed James, and was glad to see the unabashed help they received.

He could see father and daughter peering out in both directions, and after several long minutes, the daughter started to jump and scream, waving down the ambulance.

The woman was drifting in and out of consciousness when she was put in the ambulance. As James was not the next of kin, he was not allowed to travel in the ambulance but was told that they would bring her to the St. Mary's Maternity Hospital.

Now he was definitely late for his shift, and he jogged the last kilometre to the Royal Care International Hospital. He quickly cleaned up and put on his scrubs before being sent to the emergency department.

The last time he worked here was when he was first stationed in Khartoum and made the rounds to get to know the hospitals in the city. Since then, he hadn't been requested for support, which was a testament to the stability in the country.

This return was a shock to his system. Usually, there would be a slight overhead of men who got injured at work or sport, suffered heart attacks, or got into a fight. But what James found now were women, often pregnant, who had been pushed and shoved to the point that a risk for the foetus occurred. None as bad as the young woman he had just found in the lane, but noticeable enough. Their numbers had been steadily increasing over the last week. During the night, James treated two women who had been raped, which was not that rare, but the ferocity of their injuries was stomach churning.

He slept a dead man's sleep that night, and early the next morning, he stopped by the Maternity Hospital to hear how Aliyah was doing. They had delivered the baby via emergency caesarean and had been able to save both their lives. She had required several blood transfusions and surgery to stop the bleeding but was on a good way to recovery. The baby was also doing well considering the circumstances but was at the neo-natal care unit due to her preterm delivery.

The nurse noted that Aliyah had not provided any next of kin information and went to ask her whether she would like to see James before admitting him.

"Hi, I'm James Rice. I found you yesterday. How are you?" he asked when he placed a chair next to her bed.

The nurse pulled some curtains around them.

"I'm good," Aliyah said and broke down in tears. "Thank you for saving my life, our lives."

"I'm glad to hear that you are recovering and that your baby is taken care of. Do you have family around?"

Aliyah moved her head from side to side, neither yes nor no. "My family disowned me when they found out that I was pregnant."

"What about the father?"

She shook her head.

"I'm so sorry. Have you spoken to the police yet?"

"No, they're supposed to come sometime this morning."

And then it just broke out of her. "Why did he do it? He'd already touched me at the market and was creepy. And then he just turned up out of nowhere and pushed me into the alley. It all went so fast."

James' eyes welled up as well, listening to her report and despair. He had no answers for her, nothing could rationally explain any of the man's actions.

"I know it is hard, but I think you should tell the police all of this. Would you like me to come back this afternoon? I am working at another hospital."

"Sorry, yes of course. Please come back if it is not too much trouble."

"No trouble at all."

James felt helpless, and at any other time, he would have spent as much time with her as she needed, but today, and probably for a long time, he would always be in a rush to get to where people needed him most.

CHAPTER 22

DAY 232
HALLOWEEN

James had just come home from another long day at the hospital, though this time he had had the morning shift, which had been quieter.

"I visited her yesterday again, and they were able to save her and the baby," he told Jeanette on their weekly video call. "I'm not quite sure why she was attacked, but it sounded like it was because she was having a girl."

"Maybe they thought it was a clone," suggested Jeanette.

"It can't be. She was thirty-one weeks pregnant, which means the virus would have spread from Houston to Africa in less than a week. That's impossible," said James.

"If you are a fanatic, logic and facts do not count," said Jeanette.

"Or you see logic in everything ... I just hope, I pray that there is not more to come. If the virus does not kill us off, we might do it ourselves."

Jeanette felt for her husband, even though he had seen much worse in his line of work, and whilst she tried to find reasons behind the madness, she was aghast at what humans were capable of. Not that she hadn't heard about wars and crimes, even murders in her own neighbourhood, but to hear the account from her husband about what was happening in Khartoum made her angry and sad, as well as feeling guilty. Since their arrival, she had worked with NASA to improve equipment and work through mistakes that had happened during their mission, one of which was the interruption of the freezer compartment. They had reconstructed how it happened, and Jeanette knew that a potential breach of quarantining their samples had occurred; she just never fathomed that it could destroy the world as they knew it.

By now, the shortage of meat products in the supermarkets was noticeable. A nation that had the largest per capita meat consumption in the world didn't take it lightly to miss out on their daily roast chicken, buffalo wings, steak, or spareribs, and the news stations were running images of empty meat counters all day long. A country like Sudan with only a fifth of the US meat consumption might feel the shortage but wouldn't be that upset about it, as the population was used to eating other foods. Sometimes, Jeanette wasn't even sure whether her fellow countrymen and -women even knew how to cook fresh vegetables or peel an orange.

Today, the government had announced that it had allowed the use of hormones back into livestock production after it had been banned for almost ten years, following the example of the European Nations. The provided reason was a fall in fertility of livestock that had led to the meat shortage. Fertility issues had long been linked to high production levels. The food energy in these animals was diverted towards faster growth and producing dozens of litres of milk a day and did not partition enough towards reproduction. Jeanette wasn't sure whether this was the only reason, as there were believable reports that this Mars virus had something to do with it. She hated that it was impossible to tell which news snippets were true.

After their phone conversation, Jeanette decided to go and stock up on her candy inventory, to make sure she had enough for the trick-or-treaters in the evening. She had already decorated the house a week ago, though she was adding bits and pieces every day. Halloween was her favourite holiday. Some of her most treasured childhood memories were formed on this day, which often had to do with her sister and crappy homemade costumes, but on Halloween, there was something for everyone, and even the crappiest costumes were still appreciated.

Normally, she would have visited her sister and gone out with her niece and nephew, but travel restrictions between states banned her from seeing her relatives this year.

The shop assistants were busy filling the sweets aisle, as the candy sold as soon as it hit the shelves. Jeanette scooped up two extra-large bags of Starbursts, some packs of Hot Tamales and candy corn to complete her assortment of chocolate bars and lollipops at home. On the way to the checkout, she was pleasantly surprised to see that there was some chicken breast and nibbles in the refrigerated shelves, and she picked up several packs that she was going to freeze for harder times.

"You look amazing," said Jeanette when she was on video call to her niece across the border in Mississippi.

"I wish you could be here," Nola said, and her smile looked oddly disturbing behind the full-face makeup of a green-eyed demon.

"What's Louis dressed up as?" Jeanette asked.

"He's going as a chainsaw murderer, but he's already out with his friends."

"Your mum lets him out alone?" said Jeanette overly surprised, as she knew how her sister felt letting the kids out without supervision.

"Only until five, then he'll have to come home to go trick-or-treating together."

"That's sounds more like it. What's your mum dressing up as?"

Nola took her phone to the bathroom, where Jeanette's sister Fabienne, dressed as a sexy-ass witch, put the finishing touches on her husband's neon-coloured skeleton face.

"Looking sharp, sis," whistled Jeanette.

Fabienne did a double take at Jeanette on Nola's phone screen.

"You're not dressed up yet?" Fabienne asked.

"I will in a minute, but it's not the same, all alone."

"Move your sad ass over to Jackson."

"You know I can't do that."

"Come on, who's gonna know? They're not checking the borders."

"I will know."

"Obedient as usual."

"Says who?"

"Me."

"So, Louis is allowed to go trick-or-treating alone this year?"

"Hell no."

"Besides, I've already got stocked up on sweets, even got some chicken for a nice dinner."

"Yeah, our corner store also got a delivery today, but I'm not buying that shit."

"Why not?"

"God knows what they feed these birds, now with all these hormones allowed back in."

"That's only come in today."

"That's what they say."

"Okay, well I'm not coming, but I will have some lovely chicken wings for dinner."

Fabienne stopped touching up her masterpiece to look at Jeanette. "I'm gonna miss you."

"I'm gonna miss you too."

"Well, I sure hope you won't have two heads next time I see you."

"That would sort my costume. I better start cooking."

They both laughed, and Nola took her phone back to her room.

"Aunt J, can I ask you something?" Nola said when she was out of earshot from her mother.

"Sure, anything."

"Is this Mars virus real?"

"I'm afraid so."

"Cause Mum says they're just using it to collect everybody's DNA so they can track everyone, and insurance companies will use it to change their premiums depending on whether you have mutations or not."

"The DNA samples are used to track down whether you have the insertion of the Mars virus. Doctors offer this test in combination with other DNA tests, but none of the results are available to your insurance unless you provide it. It's all voluntary."

"Okay."

"Can I ask you something?" said Jeanette.

"Yeah."

"Are you taking any hormonal contraceptives?"

"No. Mum wanted me to start but we haven't been to a doctor yet."

"Good. Please don't use hormonal contraceptives. There are other ways of protection. Condoms should be on top of your list, and don't listen to any of this bullshit that it doesn't feel good."

"Aunt J!"

"I know you're embarrassed. Just don't have unprotected sex."

"Aunt J!"

"Okay, I'll stop. Have fun tonight, and send me some pictures."

"Will do."

"Love you."

"Love you too."

It was high time for Jeanette to get changed into her trusty pumpkin outfit. She had just finished painting her face orange and drawn some creepy jack-o-lantern eyes on when the doorbell rang, and the first children demanded sweets.

She heard some screams from the porch and knew that her spider decoration had crawled across the door.

With a fast pull, she opened the door for an added scare. She did love Halloween and marvelled at the dressed-up children who had a blast, just like she used to have.

It had just gotten dark, and the visitors were becoming bigger and more grown-up, when her phone rang.

She watched a group of young teenagers showing off their loot, walking down her garden path before finally picking up.

"Where the hell are you?" shouted her sister into the receiver.

"Sorry, a tad busy, you know. Don't want rotten eggs to land on my house."

"Our house is on fire!" interjected Fabienne.

"What?"

"Yes, those dipshits pillaged the corner shop over the chicken meat and then went down the street smashing pods and throwing burning torches in people's front gardens."

"Are you all right?"

"Yes, we just came home when the fire brigade arrived. It's under control now, but they say we can't get in until a safety inspection has been completed."

"Can you stay with some friends?"

"I don't know. The whole street is a mess. I will give Sue a call, but they don't have much space." Fabienne sounded exhausted.

"Come here then."

"Across the border?"

"This is an emergency. Come if you have nowhere else to go."

Between giving out more sweets, Jeanette did the dishes, collected her dirty laundry and put it in the hamper, put fresh bedlinen on the guest bed, and pulled out her camping mats for Nola and Louis. The pumpkin costume got in the way and landed behind the sofa. She turned on the news and listened in the background to the developments in Jackson. The marauders had moved through the neighbourhood, and it had gotten to a mass brawl where several people got hurt and had to be treated in hospital. She didn't hear anything in particular about her sister's house, but apparently the fire brigade had to move out to several arson incidents.

Around ten o'clock, she heard sirens in the distance and feared that the aggression had also seized Baton Rouge, but it remained the only alarm she heard that night. Shortly after, a pod pulled up in front of her house, and Fabienne and her family arrived.

"Hey, how are you?" asked Jeanette as she opened the door, even before anyone had rung the doorbell.

"We are good, just don't know about the house," said Fabienne.

All of them were still wearing their makeup and costumes.

"What do you look like?" asked Fabienne after they hugged.

Jeanette looked down at herself and found that she was only wearing green tights, which allowed a look at her underpants, and an orange sequined top.

"Oh my God, I opened the door like this for the last two hours," she called and rushed inside to pick up the rest of her costume. "I was a pumpkin."

They all had a good laugh.

"I'm sorry, we didn't bring anything but what we have on," said Fabienne after she sank tired onto the sofa.

"No worries, everything will look better in the morning," said Jeanette and went to fetch them a large box of cleaning wipes and clothes to change from hers and James' wardrobe.

* * *

Veronica and Cecilia sat on their sofa and watched the news that unfolded. Police and fire brigades were busy all over the country as Halloween night proceeded. There was no logical explanation for why people erupted in violence other than that the recent developments had simply taken the lid off Pandora's box, and what better night to cause mischief or worse than when half the country was bustling about, masked and unrecognizable.

Veronica was tense and her shoulders were constantly pulled up ever so slightly, even in bed. After the attack, her first reaction had been defiance, but day by day and hour by hour, a subconscious panic had taken hold of her, and she hadn't stepped out onto the street since. Cecilia or her mother had run any errands whilst she spent most of her days on the rooftop.

Even the vegetable garden became too open for her liking, and she felt vulnerable with all the windows around from which people could watch her.

"Are you okay?" asked Cecilia and lifted her hand, which Veronica was squeezing tightly.

"Yes. The news just makes me uncomfortable."

A burglar alarm went off down the street, and Veronica jerked.

"It's okay. I've erased all traces of our address," said Cecilia.

Instead of removing violent comments from trolls, she had moved to the more manageable task to make themselves invisible and untraceable and set up notifications, should their address pop up somewhere online. So far, her trackers had not detected anything.

Veronica got up and checked that their front door was properly locked and even peeked out onto the road through their intercom system. She could see the security guard that NASA had arranged for sitting in his pod on the other side of the road, reading something.

"What is he doing?" she muttered, agitated.

"What are you doing," asked Cecilia when she came back in to look for her phone.

"Nothing," she snapped and then dialled. "Yes, hi, this is Veronica. I just wanted to check whether everything is all right out there. I heard an alarm ... Okay, thank you."

Cecilia looked at her interrogatively.

"Some kids smashed a window at the electronics shop down the road," Veronica explained. "Can you please check that there is no one out there who wants to threaten us?"

This was a ridiculous request. Cecilia couldn't count the thousands of death threats she had seen against Veronica and her family. "You know that there will always be some nutters."

"I know, but is there anyone who knows where we are and actively plans to do something?"

"No one has our address."

"Just do it, please."

Veronica could see Cecilia rolling her eyes when she got her computer.

"Please don't do that," Veronica said.

"What?" Cecilia asked, annoyed, stopping in her tracks.

"Rolling your eyes. Making me feel like I'm crazy."

"Well, you kinda are," Cecilia said, firing up her computer. "You are not going out anymore, you're not working, you're hardly sleeping."

"I *am* working."

"Oh, yeah? Since NASA has switched you to an hourly rate, how big were your pay checks?"

"So what? I've earned so much in the last couple of years, you could only dream about it."

"Fair enough." Cecilia buried her head behind her screen. "I still think you should do something else, simply to keep your head clear."

Veronica knew what she meant, but Cecilia did not know how she felt, how insurmountable this simple suggestion was.

"Anything?" Veronica asked.

"Nothing. No one has our address, no one's declared they are coming tonight or any other day."

"Are you sure your trackers are working?"

"Yes," Cecilia said, "I am sure."

"Are there still people talking about me?"

Cecilia hesitated. "Yes."

Veronica waited for some examples of what they were saying online, and she could see that Cecilia was mulling over what to say.

"I'm going to bed. And so should you," Cecilia finally said. She shut down her computer and left without another word or look.

Veronica stood and listened until Cecilia was in bed, and everything was as quiet as it could get in a large city on Halloween night. She heard people laughing and howling on the streets, but no more sounds of rampage.

Cecilia's computer blinked in sleep mode, and Veronica felt an urge to open it and see for herself what Cecilia was tracking. She knew the password; she knew enough of programming to at least understand any recent output files. She also knew that it was a bad idea.

She had gone down that rabbit hole for a few days after the attack, and it had taken all her strength not to look for it after she had cried herself to sleep for several nights and then slept almost all day.

Verity began to cry in their bedroom and broke the spell.

Veronica went to breastfeed her, but even nursing this innocent baby, Cecilia sleeping peacefully and stretched out on her side of the bed, didn't calm her. If anything, it made her more anxious of losing any of it.

She sat on the edge of the bed for an hour, holding Verity and watching her. She was down the rabbit hole again, though this time it was the entrance to her own fears. Deep down, she saw everything that could happen to them; she saw Verity dead on the side of the road, snatched and dropped by a faceless stranger. She saw Cecilia shot through the heart in some senseless attack, her beautiful face becoming lifeless as she fell backwards in slow motion.

Sobs were building up inside her, and she held her breath to supress them. Her body convulsed as she strained to stay quiet and not wake anyone. She released the air in a slow and constant stream, and with it, the pressure in her head finally dissipated. After a few more deep breaths, she found the strength to get up and put Verity back into her cot.

Veronica was drained from constantly being on edge, but this exhaustion also made her function again. She was too tired to worry anymore.

It was well past midnight when she decided to have a shower to wash off the pain. The soothing warm water had always helped her in tough times, and standing there in the dark, she remembered the shower she had at the quarantine centre after she had found out she was pregnant.

Back then, she had apologized to the foetus inside her for not being able to love it. Now, she was full of love, and the worry of losing any of it was her greatest fear.

She had only just fallen asleep when Verity woke her for another feed. The sun was already up, and she could smell the coffee that Cecilia had made.

Despite having slept for only a few hours, she was more positive. It was true that things always looked better in the morning. Maybe it was just the sunlight that caused a chemical reaction in the brain to lift the mood. Whatever it was, Veronica carried Verity to the living room and sat down on the playmat with her.

"Would you like a coffee?" asked Cecilia when they came in.

"That would be lovely, thanks."

"I didn't expect you to be up for another couple of hours."

"It's okay."

Their conversation was awkward, as if both were walking on eggshells. Veronica knew she owed her an apology but didn't know how to start.

Cecilia quietly handed her a cup, and for a few minutes, no one said anything. Veronica played with Verity, who now managed to roll from her tummy onto her back, which she did with great stamina. Cecilia was back behind her computer, probably working to hide some client's online escapades.

"I'm sorry," Veronica finally said without looking up.

"What?"

"You know what I said." Veronica didn't have the energy to repeat or play games.

"I think you said that you were sorry, but I'm honestly not sure."

Cecilia closed her computer.

"Yes, I'm sorry. I'm sorry that you have to put up with me, that I can't just relax and be happy. I'm just so worried that something could happen to either of you."

Cecilia leaned forward and weighed her words.

"I am worried too, and I fully agree that we need to be careful, but we can't live like we're in a prison. I mean, what are we going to do when Verity goes to school?"

"Home-schooling?" Veronica knew this was a silly answer.

"She needs friends, to go out and learn about the world. Heck, you've been to Mars and back, and your own daughter can't go out of the house?"

"I know, I know you're right. I know I'm being ridiculous. Crazy. It's just so hard. It's so hard to let go."

Veronica began to cry, which she hated, as she didn't want a reaction to her tears but to the emotions that she voiced. Nonetheless, it was comforting when Cecilia came down onto the playmat and embraced her.

"It is okay to feel like that. And I know that it is difficult to come back from where you are. I think it is already a big step that you are out of bed at this hour."

Veronica laughed under her tears. "Please don't leave me," she sobbed.

"Why would I leave you?" Cecilia looked her in the eyes.

"Because I'm a mess. You do everything for us, and I'm lying in bed all the time."

"I'm more worried that you don't want me anymore. That I'm doing something wrong."

"No. No, you are perfect. I wouldn't know what to do without you."

They kissed and held each other for a long time until Verity wailed in frustration because she couldn't turn onto her belly, even though she had tried strenuously.

They laughed, and while Veonica helped Verity with her tummy time, Cecilia sat back on the sofa.

"This might cheer you up a little. The riots in Jackson started over a delivery of chicken meat. Apparently, they'd rather eat no meat than hormone-boosted fillets," said Cecilia.

"Maybe they are worried about falling pregnant," said Veronica.

"Oh. I didn't think about that. I'm sorry, I thought …"

"It's okay. I'm feeling quite good right now. It's just when night falls …"

"Maybe you should see a doctor."

"Maybe."

Later that day, Veronica was sitting on the rooftop again, watching over the city, wondering whether any other babies had already been born that were clones of their mothers. Verity was sleeping in a daybed that they had hung up under an overgrown trellis.

"There you are," said Cecilia behind her.

"Hey, yes."

"I thought you were with your mother."

"No, I like it up here … Kinda removed from the world. Where have you been?" asked Veronica when she noticed a brown paper bag in Cecilia's arms.

"I thought I would get you some sleeping aids."

Cecilia sat down on a bench, and Veronica followed curiously, though she hadn't made up her mind to take any medications yet.

"Here, I got you the latest Jane Quilkey thriller, this book on backyard gardening, and a super old book on the mathematics of architecture. This one made me sleepy just looking at the title."

Veronica thumbed through the pages. "Where did you get these?"

"The library. I thought they would give you something to do at night when you can't sleep, without the temptation of going online."

"I love you." Veronica was close to tears again.

"I love you too. Gotta get back to work now. See you for lunch?"

Veronica nodded, her chest bursting with relief.

The books worked amazingly well to help Veronica to go to sleep, even though she had to read until her eyes closed and Cecilia had to turn off the light and take the book from her hands. After the Jane Quilkey thriller, she went on to read the rest of the author's thriller series. The backyard gardening book inspired her to try new vegetable varieties, sometimes requiring them to look up how to cook them, and the book on architecture was the best sleeping aid she could have hoped for.

Nonetheless, it would take months for Veronica to feel a sense of security again when she went for short strolls around the block.

One sunny Sunday afternoon, she was just harvesting some Romanesco, a neighbour approached her, and her first instinct was to step between Verity in her pram and the potential intruder.

"That is one unusual vegetable you're growing there," said a middle-aged woman. She smiled and stopped at a reasonable distance so that Veronica had time to consider her reaction.

"It's called Romanesco, you can use it like broccoli or cauliflower," answered Veronica.

"Interesting, I must try it myself." The woman smiled. "It is nice to see a young family making good use of these allotments."

"Thank you."

"I've been watching you for a while." Veronica suddenly felt unease again, which must have reflected on her face. "I didn't mean to scare or intrude on you. Just wanted to let you know that we got your back. All of us." The woman waved to the flats that surrounded the backyard.

"Thank you," croaked Veronica. "Would you like to try one of these?" She held out a large Romanesco head with its pointy spiral flowers.

"I'd love to," said the woman.

"Take it, I've got more than we can eat."

Veronica couldn't stop smiling to herself when the woman left. She looked up to their window and saw Ceclia who had watched over her and gave a happy wave before continuing to care for her growing plants. Maybe there was still hope for humanity.

CHAPTER 23

It had been a hectic month, and this day felt like the culmination of her anxiety, which would either send Amy spiralling down again or set her free. She was glad that Miranda was on her side throughout it all. At eight in the morning, they both had an appointment at their local hospital to give blood samples for DNA testing. They were fairly sure that Amy had the virus, and due to their close contact, that also Miranda and her entire family were already infected. Since, however, the virus did not seem to have an impact on health or life, they were not worried about the results.

The waiting area was filled with people of every age and social background, and considering the supposedly easy transmission of the virus, this seemed to be the perfect super-spreader environment.

Just like Amy and Miranda, no one seemed to be worried about being close to the next person, and only here and there, someone had put on a facemask to protect themselves.

Every couple of minutes, a number announced the next patient, and a nurse in normal scrubs would lead the person behind a curtain to quickly take the blood sample and rotate through to the next person.

Every empty chair was quickly taken, and the only unrest happened when more than one person vied for the same seat. Miranda had baby Patrick with her in a pram, and a young man offered his seat, but Miranda declined politely so that they both could stand out of the way. They found a spot near the water cooler and chatted quietly.

"Imagine this on film. They would highlight everything that an infected person touched in neon green and then show how it splattered through the air when someone sneezed, only to land on five more people," whispered Miranda.

"Or maybe the whole room would already be green because everyone is already infected and it's all too late," answered Amy.

"I don't think I have the virus," said a woman audibly who was sitting near them.

"How can you be sure?" asked her friend next to her.

"I've been taking the pill forever, and I am not pregnant."

"Is that what happens?" asked the friend.

"Don't you know? Women who have the virus get pregnant if they take the pill."

Amy was surprised that there were still people who had not heard the news. Granted, the governments still tried to downplay this bit of information, saying that they needed to collect more information.

"Oh. Hubby and I have been trying for ages. Maybe I should take the pill ..."

"Effing feminists," mumbled a man opposite them.

"What did you just say?" asked the first woman.

"I said effing fucking feminists," growled the man out loud.

"That's rude," said the friend, upset.

Amy moved to the side, trying to escape this conflict, and even though Miranda would have probably liked to join in, she unlocked the pram and they walked to the only other empty space, near the ticket machine.

"Oh, yeah? How would you like it if we first took your money, your jobs, and now even your children?" ranted the man, loud enough now that everyone could hear him.

"What's wrong with you, little motherfucker? Does nobody want to blow your dick?" shouted the woman back.

"Good one," Miranda whispered and clenched her fist.

The man jumped out of his seat and pulled the woman to the floor, but before he could hit her, Miranda was on his back holding his arms. Luckily, she didn't have to restrain the man for long, as security guards were quickly there to grab the man and remove him from the waiting room.

"Let me go! Don't you see what they're doing? All of them little slits? We should lock them away until they bear normal children with a father again!" shouted the man as he was dragged to the exit.

"Are you all right?" asked Amy when she gave Miranda a hand to get up.

"Yeah, yeah. I just bumped my elbow."

Miranda, in turn, helped the other woman up.

"What an idiot," the woman mumbled.

"You'd think some of them had time-travelled straight from the Middle Ages," Miranda answered.

The rest of their hour-long waiting period passed quietly, though Amy noticed that they were eyed suspiciously by the other people who had seen the turmoil.

In the afternoon, Amy had Gabriel's sentencing hearing regarding domestic battery in court, and now she was glad that they went to the hospital in the morning, as it had forced her mind off seeing Gabriel in person. But as soon as they stepped outside the hospital to grab some lunch before the court appointment, Amy was a mess again. Her hands were cold and clammy, and even though her heart was beating hard, the blood was slow to circulate. She couldn't decide if she wanted to eat or drink anything, so Miranda ordered for them and ended up eating both their meals.

She tried to remember the breathing exercises that her therapist had shown her, but her brain had unlinked itself from the rest of her body, and so had her heart, legs, and arms. The divorce papers had been delivered and signed weeks ago, and everything could have been handled by their lawyers, but she had agreed to Mr. Dawson's suggestions to demand financial compensations for her injuries and trauma. The case was now in motion, but all Amy wished was to stay where she was until everything had passed.

"We should go," said Miranda.

"What?"

"To the courthouse."

"Oh yes," said Amy without moving.

Miranda had to physically pull her up and manoeuvre her out of the café to get her going.

The courtroom was small, nothing like the big rooms on TV that are open to the public. There were a couple of booths for the plaintiff and the defence and a raised bench for a judge. Some chairs were lined up at the back for any additional attendees, and Miranda had gotten comfortable on one that allowed her a free view of the judge whilst keeping the pram on hand should Patrick wake up.

Gabriel sat in his booth, hands folded on the table as if praying.

Amy greeted Mr. Dawson and avoided looking at Gabriel, as she wasn't sure what she would do if their eyes met.

Even though Mr. Dawson had explained to Amy what would happen today, it still felt strange and unreal, mostly because her expectations were so skewed by fictional legal dramas.

A clerk entered from a back door. "Please rise, the Honourable Judge Turner presiding."

Shortly after, the judge came in, a middle-aged woman in black robes.

"Everyone but the witness may be seated. Mr. Simmons, please swear in the witness," said the judge before sitting down.

"Please raise your right hand. Do you solemnly swear that the evidence you shall give will be the truth, the whole truth, and nothing but the truth?" asked the clerk.

"I do." Amy's legs trembled.

"You may be seated. Your Honour, today's case is Amy Stuart versus Gabriel Stuart."

"Is the prosecution ready?" asked the judge, and Mr. Dawson affirmed the question.

"Is the defence ready?"

"Yes, Your Honour," said Gabriel's attorney.

Mr. Dawson got up and gave his opening statement. "Your Honour, my name is Gentry Dawson, and I am representing Ms. Amy Stuart in this case. We intend to prove that the defendant repeatedly exerted physical and mental cruelty on multiple occasions."

He proceeded to detail everything that Gabriel had said and done during their short marriage and finished with the attack that had led to her miscarriage.

Gabriel's attorney made a persuasive case based on Gabriel's mental health and the stress he had been under to represent America on the world stage as one of the Mars astronauts. In the previous hearings, Gabriel had not denied the attack on Amy, and showed his voluntary participation in anger management and psychological counselling, which was a major point in the defence. When the charges of domestic battery had been brought against him, he had got fired from his job at Praides and currently had no income, which made Amy feel sorry for him, and she wished again she had only filed for divorce.

"Mr. Stuart, there is no excuse for what you have done. However, there are some appeasing circumstances such as your spotless record of character ..." said the judge after both attorneys had brought their cases.

"Bullshit," coughed Miranda in the back.

"... And service to the country. But domestic violence is never a trivial offence, and your battery was of the severest forms I have ever seen in my court. It was established that the accused had knowledge that the victim was with child and that this was the cause for the assault."

The judge looked Gabriel over, as he nodded with remorseful puppy eyes.

"However, I do believe that it was not the intention to kill the foetus."

"What?" spluttered Miranda audibly.

"If the lady in the back can't keep quiet, I will have her removed from my courtroom," said the judge and peered over her glasses. "As this trial was only regarding the domestic battery suffered by Ms. Stuart, this is what my judgement will be based on. Verdict number 4228, I find the accused guilty of first-degree assault with hazarding the consequence of injuring or terminating the pregnancy of the victim. Taking into account the voluntary therapy that the accused has already entered, I sentence the accused to an additional twenty-five hours anger management."

Gabriel exhaled relieved, and his puppy eyes changed to spitefulness.

Amy's fingers cramped on her belly thinking about the child that she had lost.

"The accused is banned from contacting the victim for twelve months. Further, the accused must assume all legal and medical costs for the victim's recovery. There won't be any financial support for the victim beyond that." The judge swung her gavel and left the room without further delay.

Amy felt numb and wasn't sure what just happened.

"I'm sorry," she heard Gabriel's voice say. Something that she had longed for but never thought she deserved.

"I bet you are," snapped Miranda before Amy could say anything. Gabriel jerked toward Miranda but was held back by his lawyer.

"You should shut up, Miranda. You caused this situation as much as she did," Gabriel spat at her.

"Mr. Gabriel Stuart?" Two police officers entered the court room.

"Yes?" answered Gabriel before his lawyer could interfere.

"You are under arrest for the murder of an unborn child."

The second police officer handed a warrant to the lawyer as handcuffs clicked behind Gabriel's back.

"How can it be murder when that thing wasn't even human? Huh?" Gabriel shouted.

Amy looked pleadingly to her lawyer. This was not what she wanted at all.

"This is out of our hands. It's a state crime brought by the district attorney," Mr. Dawson whispered.

The court sentence and the severity of everything that had happened sank painfully into her consciousness.

"You really wanted to carry out that monster?" Gabriel asked her contemptuously, resisting from being led away by the police officers.

Miranda inhaled to reply, but Amy stopped her with a lift of her hand. "I wanted a child so badly, but you made me terrified of it. Now, I don't need you anymore."

For the first time ever, she held Gabriel's stare until he looked away.

"You will regret this," he hissed before being led out the door followed by his attorney.

"We'll put in a bail application," said Gabriel's lawyer before the door shut behind them.

"What happens to him now?" asked Amy.

"He'll be transported straight to prison, but you heard his lawyer. It will be difficult for a murder charge, but they'll try to get him out until trial starts," explained Mr. Dawson.

"Is he, will he ... What's the penalty if he is found guilty?" asked Miranda.

"Depending on the classification of the murder, he could get several years in prison or the death penalty."

Hot tears ran down Amy's cheeks. "Will I have to do anything?" she asked after wiping her tears away with her sleeve.

"It will be a jury trial and you will quite likely be called as a witness."

"I just want it to be over."

"The trial probably won't start for a few months. I'm surprised that it took so long to bring the charges, but maybe the current situation ... We'll talk about it when it comes to it. Go home now and rest, I'll take care of everything else and keep you informed."

For the first time in weeks, Amy went to bed and slept ten hours straight.

* * *

Mack had finally arrived back home after visiting laboratories on every continent. His hands were dry from the constant use of disinfectant, and he had lost two kilos due to the lack of exercise during the long plane travels and even longer meetings.

He had barely slept five hours when he had to get back up for yet another meeting, though by now everyone had agreed that these meetings could be taken from home as long as a secure internet connection was in place.

He showered as the sun came up and moisturized his hands before setting up his camera in his laboratory, facing a blank wall.

This time, there were luckily no topics scheduled that were directly relevant to Mack, so he made sure he had plenty of coffee and alternative reading sources at his fingertips to survive a three-hour meeting that would most likely run for double the time.

First up was Professor Brinkmann again, who gave an update on global livestock production.

"Hormonal treatments started two weeks ago and were successful in most species. Cattle and pig farmers report good fertility rates, though the gestation period is long and there will be an ongoing shortage predicted to peak at the end of the year. The poultry industry, however, is collapsing, as only cockerels have hatched. In some regions of the world, the last chicken meat was already delivered last week, and egg production is expected to taper off within the next six to nine months."

"How can there be eggs but no chicken?" asked a bodyless voice.

"Modern poultry breeds lay eggs even if not fertilized."

"Is it a complete failure or just a heavy reduction in fertility?" asked Professor Lamarck.

"By now it is a complete failure. As I said, we had cockerels hatching, but obviously, they are not equipped to lay any more eggs. We assume this has something to do with the males in poultry or any other birds being the homomorphic sex with two ZZ chromosomes, and the females are heteromorphic ZW. Birds with the WW genotype are not viable, which means that any clones that we can produce at this time are males with the ZZ genotype. I believe this also heavily impacts any wildlife populations where Ms. Nguyen from the FAO will give further details," said Professor Brinkman.

Ms. Nguyen seamlessly took over. "Yes, obviously, the virus does not just impact the agricultural sector, but every animal. Zoos and reserves have started to supplement hormones, though many zoos are still waiting for genome sequences to decide which animals are most likely to produce healthy offspring. As it is, cloning can lead to the expression of recessive genes, which can either be lethal or tremendously impact the health and longevity of the offspring. Unfortunately, genotyping laboratories are working at full capacity on human samples, so the waiting period is long. We have also seen a dramatic decrease in bird populations and expect ninety-five percent of birds to become extinct within the next couple of years if we don't find a solution to eradicate or reverse the impact of this virus."

"What about insects? Are they impacted at all?" asked Professor Lamarck.

"Trials for hormone treatments have begun for insects where the females are homomorphic, such as bugs, grasshoppers, and cockroaches. Unfortunately, there has been very little research in this field, and there is a high risk that we will lose many species before we find an effective way to treat both domestic and wildlife species. Other insects like ants, bees, and wasps have already reproduced by cloning females, and so far, we have not observed any drop in population sizes."

"So, the pollinators remain for crop production?" asked Professor Lamarck. "Or are plants also impacted by the virus?"

"The virus does not seem to affect plants, though many plants also follow sexual reproduction with heterozygous males and homozygous females. And yes, the survival of the most important pollinators is keeping crop production going, though we are still collecting data to make a projection of how the ecosystems will be affected as a whole."

Many more questions were asked by the different leaders of task groups and country heads, but Mack now had serious trouble just staying awake, despite the litre of coffee he had been drinking. At least the frequent trips to the toilet kept him awake. When they paused for a short refreshment break, Mack was considering going to bed, but he was worried about his reputation if he didn't play his part dutifully – as small as it seemed by now, considering the scale of the whole pandemic.

In the end, he heard that most countries had now instated a travel ban, not only to other countries but also within state borders and that the voluntary genetic testing was now to be extended to a mandated testing responsibility. Australia was still at the forefront, and every citizen would get contacted to make an appointment with a testing facility nearest to them from the coming Monday.

There was, however, still no consent over how much of the information circulated at these global meetings should be passed on to the populace. Many countries feared unrest and unnecessary violence, especially toward women, which the latest news proved to have already started.

In the end, there was no common consensus, and each country was going to continue to disseminate as much or as little information to its citizens as it saw necessary, despite the voices that remarked that a fragmented news reporting would only fuel misinformation and conspiracy theories. The topic got postponed until the next meeting in two weeks' time.

At two in the afternoon, Mack finally crashed on his bed, only his trousers off, and fell asleep. He woke up after eight solid hours of sleep. However, this meant it was late in the evening, and he was wide awake.

He tried watching some television, but the shows that usually seemed unrealistic now paled in the face of reality. Instead, he watched news reports about pregnancy rates, riots that targeted supermarkets, and several highly publicised murders of pregnant women from all around the world. A report on demonstrations in Belgium largely targeting and vilifying the Minister for Family and Health reminded Mack that he had wanted to call his aunt.

With the time difference, it should be midday in Europe, so he picked up his phone and dialled.

"Hello?" A young and unfamiliar voice answered the phone.

"Oh, hi, this is Mack from Australia," explained Mack, not sure who he was talking to.

"Cousin Mack?"

"Yeah, yeah, and you are …?"

"Inga. Wait, I'll switch to screen view."

His sixteen-year-old cousin appeared on his screen. She looked so grown up that Mack felt a pang of old age.

"Hi, Inga, so good to see you again," said Mack. "How is everything?"

"It's crazy. We now have twenty-four-hour security, and Mum's driving around with bodyguards."

"I've seen that you have some difficult times. Hope you are keeping your heads up."

"Yeah, we are fine otherwise."

"Who are you talking to?" asked another young voice.

"Is that Hazel?" asked Mack.

"Cousin Mack?" Hazel's face appeared half in one corner.

"Wait," said Inga, and the girls tried to place the camera at a good angle so that they both fit into he screen.

"Are you okay, Hazel? You seem a little ..." Mack struggled to find the right words, just in case Hazel had simply gained some weight.

"Oh, yeah. I'm pregnant," Hazel answered as a matter of fact, showing off her bump.

"I'm sorry to hear."

"It's okay. I sort of made the decision, and I'm happy with it."

Mack was confused. She wanted to get pregnant? She was only thirteen or fourteen years old.

"Really? And how are you, Inga?"

"Not pregnant," said Inga and showed her flat stomach, though she seemed to be less cheerful about it.

"Where is Aunt Gayle?"

"Mum's working. She's got lots to organize with the whole pandemic thing. Her bill got scrapped, and now everyone is blaming her for all the teenage pregnancies. They say that it was her plan all along, though I can't see what she would have wanted to achieve with it."

Hazel had now taken over the conversation, and Inga sat on a chair in the background.

"Well, maybe a heads-up for your mum that data sampling will be made mandatory soon and that they should stock up on freezer space to store the samples, should they run into problems with the delivery of DNA kits."

"Are you, like, a secret agent with insider info?"

"Sort of. I'm coordinating the global database where variants and genome sequences are stored. Just came back from a world tour, visiting labs, and the largest bottleneck I can foresee is storage space."

"You rockstar! World tour, huh? I'll let her know," said Hazel.

"How is the pregnancy going?"

"Good. I'm now halfway through, and I think I can feel the baby move."

Mack noticed that Inga looked up at that information.

"That's wonderful," said Mack. "Well, I better let you go. Enjoy your weekend, and say hi to your mum."

"Will do," said Hazel.

"Bye, Inga."

Inga waved briefly, and Mack wondered whether she was really all right.

It was strange to know that his thirteen-year-old cousin was expecting a baby. He never thought much about his extended family; not that he didn't care about them or liked to stay in touch with them, but he never saw them all as part of a family tree, a pedigree that traced back to their common ancestors, or individuals who would carry it onwards. As it was, it appeared that his teenage relatives would be the only ones to continue their family line.

But Mack wasn't ready yet to give up on the continuation of his direct family. He mulled over donating to a sperm bank and have at least some parts of him preserved so that in future, his offspring might wander this earth as well, but he wasn't satisfied with this solution. As he searched his emotions and desires, it wasn't so much the continuation of his family line but simply the wish to see his children be born and grow up, to teach them how to walk and talk, and the value of kindness and hope. Without him being there, though, he didn't want to put his children into this world.

CHAPTER 24

Since the leak about the virus eighty days ago, surprisingly little had changed in everyday life despite the various official measures that had taken effect. The only strictly controlled regulations were that international travel required a special permit from the departing and the receiving country and that it was mandatory to give a blood sample for DNA testing. Working from home and postponing any non-essential travels within a country were recommended, as were mask wearing and frequent hand washing. However, the still-not-very-visible reason for any of these measures meant that most people went about their lives as usual, and the police had not been given the power to impose fines or arrests.

Even though scientists warned about what the outcome of this pandemic would be, politicians were more worried about the impact on the economy from a population that plunged into fear about their livelihoods. So, their focus was to keep everything running smoothly and not give out too much worrisome information.

The only people who were really impacted were the people who were found to be not infected yet, or at least did not show the insertion on the X chromosome. These people were forced to sign non-disclosure agreements and then incarcerated in laboratories to keep them safe for the sake of mankind.

The disappearance of people was reported on as a side note in the news, if at all, though social media sleuths promoted their own often-correct assumptions, which were quickly condemned by most as conspiracy theorists or just attention-hungry influencers. No one cared about some random woman who had worked for the United Banks of Europe in Scotland and who had fallen from the face of the earth, or girls from a remote tribe in the Amazon who disappeared in the middle of the night.

As long as you stayed away from hormonal medications, life went on as usual, or at least mostly as usual.

Artificial meat companies had finally found a fertile market which craved meat so much that it had dropped their reservations about affordable petri-dish-produced chicken breasts, mince, or fish fillets. The problem for these companies now was to scale up their production to meet the consumer demands, and whilst they had already doubled or tripled their output, the collapse of the livestock industry couldn't have come at a worse time than Christmas, when most of the Christian world wanted a roast dinner.

Despite this superficial normality, people were restless and unnerved, and like-minded people found each other quickly to reinforce their worries and fears to unhealthy levels.

Gayle was working from home, trying to be a good example, but also because the level of threats and actual attempts to harm her had grown so much that she felt safer without the commute to her office near the parliament.

Schools had closed early for Christmas break to stem the spread of the virus, which also meant that both her girls were at home.

Hazel sat on the white sofa, eating a large bowl of Belgian vanilla ice cream watching the news, and Inga was upstairs in her room, listening to music. Both activities happened at an unnecessarily loud volume, at least for Gayle's already-strained mind.

"Mum! Look at this," shouted Hazel from the living room.

"What is it?" shouted Gayle back from her desk.

"You have to see this!"

It had better be something important, thought Gayle, but Hazel always consumed so much news from any channel, she was probably better informed than any secret service, so it might be worth getting up and seeing what she had found.

Gayle came into the living room, already worried that something bad had happened, when Hazel pointed at the ice-cream bowl that was balancing on her protruding belly.

"Did you see that?" asked Hazel, excited when the bowl did a wiggle dance.

"There is a human being in there, and you put a bowl of ice cream on its head," said Gayle sternly, although she was relieved that Hazel's news was so harmless for once. "How would you like that?"

"That'd be fun," said Hazel. She sat up and placed the bowl on her own head. "Look, she takes after me."

"Well, there is no doubt in that," said Gayle with a smirk. "Did you take your vitamins today?"

"No. Not yet."

"I'll get them for you."

Gayle went to the kitchen and saw in passing that Inga was sat on the stairs.

She was just unscrewing the pillbox when the doorbell rang.

"Inga? Can you open the door, please?"

Frustrated upon the silence from the hall, she walked to the door herself. "Inga! Come and help me please."

Inga had disappeared from the steps, and Gayle opened the door to Guillaume, who had brought in their food delivery for the holidays.

"Just right through to the kitchen. Thank you so much. I'll be right there."

Gayle handed Hazel her vitamin pill before picking up another box filled with vegetables from the doorstep.

"Inga!"

She found Inga already in the kitchen, packing the food away, and was sorry for having called out for her.

"Thank you," said Gayle to Inga and Guillaume.

"There was no whole chicken, but I got this fake chicken breast. If you don't like it, I'll take it," explained Guillaume.

Gayle eyed the meat package. It looked real, like it came from a real chicken.

"I think we'll try it," said Gayle. "By the way, what are you doing for Christmas? Can you travel home?"

"No, the border is closed. But I will celebrate with my girlfriend and her family."

"Ah, that's nice. Otherwise, I would have invited you to come here. How about you come on the twenty-sixth? Bring your girlfriend as well."

"Yes, we'd love to."

"Great, come for lunch at twelve, and I'll make a nice … vegetable casserole. I'm afraid it won't be a grand feast by the looks of it."

Gayle sorted away several leeks, carrots, potatoes, and onions.

"Not to worry," reassured Guillaume. "Shall we maybe bring a dessert?"

"That would be lovely. Thank you very much."

Hazel brought her dirty ice-cream bowl into the kitchen, her shirt exposing a bit of her pregnant belly. Gayle watched Guillaume from the side to see his reaction, but he continued unpacking as if nothing unusual had happened. She was pleased at how professional he was.

"Okay, I think that is all. I'll see you in two days?" asked Gayle.

"Yes. Merry Christmas."

"Merry Christmas."

Gayle saw her assistant out and then turned to her girls. "Right, if I could have two hours of silence, please, and then we can get started with the holidays."

"Okay," said Hazel, who had grabbed a pack of crisps before retreating to her seat in front of the TV.

Gayle left for her office, and Inga stood undecided for a while in the quiet kitchen. Then, she followed Hazel into the living room.

A documentary on the development of babies was on TV, and Inga watched from the doorframe.

"In biology, they said that the mother and the father only give half of their chromosomes to the child but that both halves are needed for the baby to be alive," she finally said and sat on the other side of the sofa.

"I know," said Hazel.

Inga's eyes wandered down to Hazel's belly.

"It's alive. It's moving," she said reassuringly.

"Right now?" asked Inga.

Hazel scooted over to her big sister and placed her hands on her belly.

"It's so hard," said Inga.

"What did you expect?" Hazel laughed.

"I don't know. I thought it would be more squishy with all the liquid in there."

Inga watched and waited intently, and suddenly she felt a little nudge. She looked excitedly at Hazel, who nodded smiling, but then she removed her hands and sat quietly again.

The documentary ended, and Hazel switched the channels until she found a live news report from a demonstration on the Place du Luxembourg in the European Quarter of Brussels.

"They should've listened to the Lord. He does not approve of contraceptives," shouted a crazed woman behind the reporter.

"Police have arrived to stop an angry mob from entering the parliament building where Gayle Hamilton has her office. They blame the creator of the contraception bill for destroying their teenagers' lives," said the reporter as a mother dragged her pregnant daughter in front of the camera.

"Look what she's done!" the mother shouted, and the reporter had trouble holding her space.

Behind them, a man held a poster above their heads reading 'Women 1:0 Men'.

"This is so frightening," said Inga.

"I know. I'm so glad Mum's working from home now ... I hope that girl can cope with a mother like that. Wonder whether it was her decision to keep that baby."

Inga only gave an uncommitting noise, but Hazel was already switching through the channels.

"Do you wanna watch something?" Hazel asked after she couldn't find anything worth her while.

"No, thanks."

Hazel left the TV on but picked up a newspaper from the side of the sofa.

Inga eventually left to go back upstairs.

* * *

"Amy! are you ready?" shouted Miranda from downstairs.

"Coming," answered Amy and pushed the letter from Mr. Dawson into her bedside table.

The news that Gabriel had been successful in getting bail until the start of his murder trial couldn't have come at a worse time, but she was grateful that her lawyer had kept her informed. The no-contact order remained intact, which gave her a little peace of mind, especially because she had a secret that she hadn't shared with anyone yet.

Amy came down the stairs where Miranda, Ozzy, and the kids were already waiting for her.

"Right, we have a plan," said Miranda and handed Amy a list of shops. "These are all supermarkets and butchers that advertised that they had real turkeys or chicken. We start at Walmart, Carma Butchers, Meats Galore, and if we then still haven't found a Christmas roast, we'll fashion something from the stuffing and pretend that our turkey is invisible."

"Oh yes," squealed Toby. "A Super Turkey."

"Yes, though I'm sure if there ever was a Super Turkey, it wouldn't get itself slaughtered," said Miranda and gently pushed Toby out the door.

At Walmart, they rushed through the aisles, but the entire meat section was empty. On their way out, they avoided the sweets or toys so that Toby wouldn't remember what else he wanted from Santa.

"Just one second," called Amy when they could already see the exit.

She rushed back in and bought a small package that she hid in her bag before Miranda could see it.

"What did you buy?" asked Miranda.

"Oh, just a little surprise for later, hopefully," said Amy.

"Well, I hope it is that food processor with the automatic cooking and baking function I always wanted," Miranda said.

"Um … no," said Amy, teasing, and she had to smile when Ozzy made big eyes behind his wife to signal Amy to change the topic.

"Well, that's disappointing. Guess I'll keep that vacuum that I got for you," answered Miranda in jest.

They rushed on, but every single shop on their list was sold out on any meat, even the alternative varieties.

On their way home, they noticed a small butcher shop where people were crowding outside, waiting to get in.

"Stop the pod," shouted Miranda. "Ozzy, Amy. If you know what's good for ya, you will run. Spartans! Ready your breakfast and eat hearty … for tonight, we dine in hell!"

Amy and Ozzy jumped out of the pod and hurried to the shop.

"Was that a movie quote?" asked Ozzy as they pushed through the crowed.

"*300*," answered Amy.

They didn't make any friends on their way into the shop, but they weren't here for that.

Inside, they found a frightened butcher behind his empty display cabinet on the phone to the police.

"It's about fifty people, and they won't listen," said the butcher into his phone.

An old man banged the display cabinet with his walking stick. "I swore on my wedding day to provide for my wife. So, don't make me come home without a turkey," he screeched.

"I guess she'll have to take you this Christmas, for better or for worse," said the butcher after he hung up his call.

"That is outrageous," shouted the man and tried to jab the butcher over the counter with his walking stick.

"I am sorry, but everything is sold out until further notice," he called and fended of the prodding stick. "Please leave. The police are already on their way."

The customers complained bitterly, but because people still tried to push in, their exit was more than slow.

Amy and Ozzy had just reached their pod, where Miranda had waited with the kids, when a police car pulled over.

"Nothing?" she asked.

"Not even a minced worm," said Ozzy.

"Ugh," said Toby.

"All righty, invisible Super Turkey it is," said Miranda.

"Yippie!" exclaimed Toby.

Back at home, Miranda and Ozzy started preparing for Christmas dinner. They peeled parsnips, carrots, and onions, half of which they chopped up to mix with breadcrumbs to bulk out the stuffing for their hand-modelled turkey the next day.

"At least we got enough cranberry sauce," sniffled Miranda when she moved some jars in the fridge to make space for a bowl of finely chopped onions. "Seems like no one wants the sauce without the roast."

"You don't need to cry about it," laughed Amy, who prepared multicoloured icing to decorate a last batch of cookies with Toby.

"Happiness is just a teardrop away."

Amy flapped her hands, pretending to have fairy wings. She was very happy at this moment, so happy that she could have burst into tears herself, and she couldn't wait to share her little secret with Miranda.

The cookie decoration took several hours, mainly because either Toby was running around on a sugar high from licking the icing, or Amy trying to make intricate designs with pipe bags, which she had never done before and didn't look at all like she had intended. Toby then gave the finishing touches by burying the cookies in sprinkles and chocolate buttons, but in the end, all that counted was that they were made with love and laughter.

After a light dinner, they each got a plate of cookies and a glass of milk for dessert, and Toby also placed a spare plate and glass on a table next to the Christmas tree.

"We forgot about the carrot for Rudolph," he noticed in horror.

"Help is on the way," said Miranda, and she fetched a carrot that still had the green on it.

Then they all huddled up on the sofa to watch *Little Lord Fauntleroy*, with the promise that Ozzy got to choose the next film when the kids were in bed.

Five minutes before the film ended, all but Amy and Miranda were asleep.

"I don't think either of them have ever seen the end. What shall we watch next?" whispered Miranda.

"It's probably too late for *Titanic*," said Amy.

"Yeah, and I'm more in the mood for something that makes me happy. Those onions have made me cry enough for today."

"How about I give you an early little present now?" asked Amy and her stomach tingled.

"That'd make me happy."

Amy got up and fetched the little box from her bag.

"It's more a present for me, but I think, I hope it makes you happy as well."

Amy passed the box to Miranda, who looked at it confused.

"It's a pregnancy test," she said. "Oh my God, it's a pregnancy test!"

Miranda whispered loud enough that baby Patrick in her arms moved disturbed.

"Oh my God, you didn't. When? How?" asked Miranda.

"After Gabriel's sentencing. I still had a full pack of pills left," explained Amy.

"Are you sure?" asked Miranda.

"I haven't taken a test yet, but I missed my period over a week ago."

"Over a week? Come on, let's use the upstairs loo."

They giggled all the way up, and Amy's hands were getting sweaty as she waited for Miranda to put Patrick in his cot.

"Are you okay?" asked Miranda as she held Amy's clammy hands in the bathroom.

Amy nodded. If she was pregnant, then this would be the happiest Christmas she ever had. She wasn't sure what to do next, as she surely could not live forever with Miranda and Ozzy, but it would be the first step in a new chapter of her life that was hopefully going to be much better than the last.

Amy opened the box and sat on the toilet to pee on the test strip.

Miranda blew in her hands, as she was clearly just as nervous and excited as Amy.

"Miranda? Amy?" They heard Ozzy's voice coming up on the stairs.

"We're in the bathroom. Be right down. Pick a movie."

"Okay," said Ozzy from outside the door. "I just put Toby to bed. Maybe we can watch *Die Hard*."

"The old one or the remake?" asked Miranda and mouthed 'the remake' just as Ozzy said it.

They heard Ozzy trudging back downstairs when the second blue line on the test became visible.

They squealed and hugged in excitement.

"This is so the best revenge ever," said Miranda, then suddenly the light went out.

"What's going on?"

They walked out and found the rest of the house shrouded in darkness.

"Ozzy? What happened?" Miranda shouted.

"I don't know, I think the fuse just went. I'm on it," Ozzy called back up and they could hear him bumping into something.

The light of his phone danced through the hall downstairs.

Then a window shattered, and muffled voices came from the living room.

"Miranda?" Ozzy called out. "Are you okay?"

Two shots exploded downstairs, and the heavy fall of a body permeated the following silence.

"Ozzy," whispered Miranda, and Amy could see her shadow stumbling to the stairs.

"Miranda, no," Amy begged, but she only grabbed thin air.

She heard Miranda quietly walking down the stairs and then another two gunshots rang through the darkness, followed by Miranda falling down the stairs.

Patrick started wailing in his cot, and Toby was calling out to his parents.

Amy's legs were leaden, and she held her breath. What just happened?

Lights from the neighbour's house suddenly poured in from the hallway window, and Amy sank to the floor, crawling along the wall to Toby's bedroom.

"Shh, Toby. Be quiet, please." She pulled Toby in her arms and carried him to his wardrobe, where she crouched with him between his clothes.

She held Toby's head, as he buried his face in her arms, and covered his ears. Patrick was still crying his lungs out in the bedroom next door, but Amy hoped that whoever just entered the house would not harm an infant.

Every breath she took sounded like she was on a life-support machine, and yet she felt like she would suffocate if she breathed any slower.

Through the gap in the wardrobe doors, she could see someone walking along the hallway and heard them opening the door to Patrick's room. The baby's screams rang through even louder, and Amy pressed her hand over her mouth to stop her desperate sobs from escaping.

Sirens in the distance made her ears peak, and she silently prayed that help was coming for them.

"Let's go, let's go," she heard someone whisper nearby, and then footsteps shuffled back downstairs and over some broken glass.

She stayed with Toby in the wardrobe until police arrived. Baby Patrick had cried himself back to sleep, or at least that's what Amy hoped the silence was about.

She heard police requesting ambulances for two homicide victims and was so numb when an officer opened the wardrobe door with a raised weapon that she almost wished he would shoot her as well, were it not for Toby, who was still huddled up in her arms.

She stayed with the children in Miranda and Ozzy's bedroom while the bodies were removed, so that they didn't have to see the crime scene.

A police officer played with Toby as Amy gave a first statement to another officer. Nothing was taken from the house, and it seemed that the intruders had targeted the occupants. Amy could not think of anyone who would have wanted to harm Miranda or Ozzy, though she had a strong and horrific feeling that the attack had been aimed at her.

Amy and the children were brought to a hotel, and Miranda and Ozzy's parents were informed about the tragedy. The next day, Amy was picked up to give another statement at the police station, whilst Toby and Patrick were given into their grandparents' custody.

She told the officers about her suspicion that Gabriel was behind the attack and heard later that day that Gabriel had boarded a plane to Mexico in the morning.

Her own parents arrived to take her home with them, and it would take her years to process the events of this night and get back to a life that was worth living.

CHAPTER 25

The beginning of the new year 2055 seemed to many like the end of the world, and not just to the affluent societies who couldn't buy a proper Christmas roast. Poorer regions of the world felt the entire weight of the sudden breakdown of livestock reproduction. As with so many times in the past, countries on the continents of Africa, South America, and Asia were neglected in the plans to supply hormonal supplements to farmers, and often smallholder farmers still didn't even know why their animals did not reproduce anymore. The interruption of the supply chain to buy any replacement animals meant that the livelihoods of ninety percent of smallholder farmers vanished without any alternatives. Climate change resulted in very little crop production outside of large agricultural estates, and substantial parts of the population had relied on their animal products to sell or trade directly for other foods and goods.

The raids on villages all around the continents started, and it seemed by now that weapons were more abundant than food. Whole communities were burned to the ground and their inhabitants killed to take the few things that were worth anything. The frustration and panic spread all around, and even the large agricultural estates that provided at least some source of food within the countries were paradoxically attacked.

James had been sent to a refugee camp to look after uprooted families who had lost everything. They were handing out a food delivery that had just come in with an airplane from France, and desperate hands grabbed every single parcel that was handed down from the back of the truck.

"*Haleeb*! *Haleeb*! Milk!" begged a woman who had a baby and a toddler strapped to her front and back in a dusty wraparound carrier.

James handed her a small container with milk powder, which she held tightly so that no other hungry hands could snatch it away. Most of the refugees were women and children who had been abandoned by their husbands for having fallen pregnant on the pill or hunted by guerrilla troops simply for being women.

When the refugees had received provisions for their direct needs, James and his comrades unloaded the larger packages from the truck to carry to the storage tent of the camp, which had been opened by the Catholic church.

"D'you know what I don't get? We will all die sooner or later. What difference does it make whether men or women wander the Earth after us?" said James to his comrade.

"I don't know. I kind of understand them. I mean, it boils down to the meaning of life, doesn't it?" said the comrade.

Through the tarp of a nearby tent, James heard a man talking. "Now that God has revoked the purpose of procreation, we should thank him for his kindness. God has sent us a sign."

He hesitated briefly as he thought he heard a scuffle and a female voice whispering something, wondering what was going on in the tent.

"What do you mean? Just because we don't pass anything on anymore, nobody can?" asked James when he was back by the truck to receive another package from his comrade.

"All I'm sayin' is that I can kind of understand—"
A shot out of nowhere hissed by James' ear.
James and his comrade ducked and scanned their lifeless surroundings.

A bloodcurdling scream from the tent that James had passed seconds earlier drew their attention, and a young nun stumbled out, followed by the camp's priest, whose feet awkwardly dragged over the ground. The priest stopped in the open centre of the camp and opened his mouth to say something, but only blood spluttered out before he fell face-first into the sand.

Suddenly, truckloads of armed terrorists stormed towards the camp, and James and his comrade ran to fetch weapons. They were joined by the handful of soldiers who had been stationed to protect the camp.

Women and children ran frightened between the tents, trying to find shelter. Whilst the soldiers were able to keep most of the terrorists at bay, a couple of them managed to enter the camp and opened fire on the women and children huddled together.

James made out the shadow of a man with a machine gun and heard another terrorist saying to spare the boys. Just as the rapid fire of the machine gun began, two distinct shots interrupted the sound of death again. As James ran around to enter the tent, he saw that his comrade had eliminated the terrorist with two clean shots through the tarp. Inside the tent, he was faced with a picture of horror. Women with their children still in their arms lay dead, a few small boys crying over the bodies of their mothers.

James wanted to sink to the ground and give himself up to the despair that usurped him, but his training as a doctor took over, and he methodically checked all the bodies, identifying the living and making mental notes of which injuries to treat first.

He removed the head scarf from a woman who had been shot through the shoulder and ordered the boy who was sitting next to her to press the scarf on the gunshot wound. A little girl lay unconscious but breathing on the ground with her thigh having been hit and smattered by multiple bullets. James took his belt off and tightened it around the leg to stop the bleeding. Then, he rushed out to get dressing material and call for help. Luckily, the terrorists had retreated, and backup was already on the way, so James was able to swiftly provide first aid.

* * *

Jeanette and Fabienne were watching the morning news in horror. A refugee camp just outside Khartoum had been raided, and more than fifty people were killed, amongst them a Catholic priest and several nuns who had led the camp.

Pictures of soldiers carrying dead bodies on stretchers to waiting trucks were shown as the presenter's voice narrated the terrible attack.

"Isn't that where James is?" asked Fabienne.

"Nearby," croaked Jeanette. "I haven't heard from him recently. Last time we spoke, he said he was appointed to deliver food rations. Said he wouldn't be able to get in touch for a while."

Fabienne crawled over to her sister and held her as she cried quietly. Jeanette knew that there was a possibility that James had been at this camp, but the reporter did not mention that any soldiers or doctors were hurt in the attack, so she had hope that her husband was okay.

"Did you hear the news?" asked Nola, who had just gotten out of bed.

Nola saw her aunt crying and also huddled on the sofa to support her.

"Is James okay?" Nola asked quietly.

"I don't know. They didn't say that any soldiers were hurt," said Jeanette, wiping away her tears.

"That's good, though, isn't it?" Nola asked.

"Yes," said Jeanette and got up.

She found her phone and searched through her numbers before dialling. "Yes, hello. This is Jeanette Rice, wife of James Rice. He is stationed in Khartoum, Sudan, and I wanted to check on his status … Yes, one second."

Jeanette went into their bedroom and searched for James' social security and identification number. After a short pause, the receiver confirmed that James had not been reported as a casualty.

"Could you please let him know to get in touch with me as soon as possible?" said Jeanette.

She needed a few seconds to compose herself before she went back to the living room. Fabienne and Nola looked at her expectantly.

"He's all right. He was at the camp during the attack, but he's good. Doing his duty."

A sigh of relief came from her sister and niece.

"Happy New Year," Jeanette said and switched off the television. "I've already had enough. Let's do something nice. How about the beach? Is Louis up yet?"

"He's still sleeping," said Nola, "but I can wake him."

"No, let him sleep," said Fabienne. "I don't know whether the beach is such a good idea, seeing that the situation here is not much better than over there."

"What do you mean? Like in Sudan?"

"Well, yes."

"Are you really comparing an armed terrorist attack on a refugee camp with the gangs of hooligans burning down a butcher shop?" Jeanette was aghast.

"And our house, and all the other violence that is happening around our country. Hospitals and especially maternity wards have called for more security support already, there's no meat anywhere, and we're still not allowed to leave the country."

"Yeah, but it's highly unlikely that a truck of armed terrorists would drive up and shoot us while we're sunbathing."

"Say what you will; my kids and I are staying here."

"Fine, I'll go by myself then," snapped Jeanette and went to pack her beach bag.

After two months of having her sister and her children around, she deserved a break. Their house had been damaged beyond repair in the fire, and besides the removal of the charred remnants, nothing had happened yet, due to the long-winded process of getting money from their insurance. To reduce their housing costs, Fabienne, Nola, and Louis had moved in with Jeanette and were home-schooled by Fabienne whilst her husband stayed with friends in Jackson to continue his work as a senior manager of a large automotive dealership.

Jeanette called a pod to drive to the beach near Port Vincent, got a fresh juice at a café, and then sat on the sand, wrapped in a large shawl, as the wind was quite chilly. She looked over the quiet sea and buried her feet in the sand.

Somehow, she couldn't feel upset about this virus and what it potentially meant for humankind. She had always thought that there were too many people on Earth, despite scientists saying that the Blue Planet could support many millions more if only the resources were tapped and used without waste. She thought this was such an illusion, as for one, all resources were finite, and secondly, there was also a societal aspect to living in large groups and crowded spaces. Whilst humans were herd animals with a complex structure of interdependencies, and living in groups meant more help and protection, they also struggled with groups that became too large and too varied in their hopes and needs. Eventually, there was always a group who suffered to the benefit of another group, or a person who took advantage of another because they wanted or needed something that wasn't offered freely.

Maybe she was an extreme case in her dislike of most people in general. Everybody needed help sooner or later; no one was always self-sufficient as a single person. She made the conscious decision not to have children and bore the burden of having a sister and other extended family with a heroic pride. She contributed to society, but on her terms.

If the population were to shrink dramatically, this could only have a positive effect, in her opinion, and it didn't matter whether the future of humanity was exclusively female. Both men and women had their strengths and flaws, and whilst the existence of both might have had an evolutionary advantage, they had long passed the point where nature was a limiting factor to human survival.

A group of adolescent men trudged along the beach, mafficking and openly drinking. As so often at this age, they didn't care about disturbing others. In fact, they often relished in provoking human reactions from their immediate surroundings, as if their imagination and empathy wasn't enough to predict that they would upset people around them.

They walked so closely around Jeanette that the sand that their feet stirred up hit her face, some daringly slamming their feet down to create even more eruptions, but otherwise laughing and chatting with no care in the world.

If only one gender was to survive, it was a good thing that it wasn't men, thought Jeanette.

She shook the sand from her hair and blew it off her juice cup, which luckily had a lid. Then she packed up her belongings as the beginning of her new year had now well and truly been spoiled. She ordered a pod to take her home as she was walking up the beach and noticed the group of young men hanging around the empty car park.

Some were scanning their phones and watching her. She avoided eye contact as her shoulders tensed up in anticipation of an unwanted interaction, and when one of them pointed at her, she was sure that some altercation was going to happen.

Just go, go away, and mind your own business, thought Jeanette. Why did some people take decades to learn to leave other people be?

She ignored them as she waited for her pod to arrive, but her senses were piqued, and she could hear their footsteps approaching from behind.

"Hey!" she heard one of them call out. "You're the commander, aren't you?"

"Are you talking to me?" said Jeanette, turning around with a smile.

"Yeah, you're the commander from that Mars mission that brought that virus back," said the largest out of their group, who was probably only hanging out with them because he had to do a couple of honour rounds at school.

Jeanette inhaled and renewed her smile. "Look, I just want to have a relaxed start into the new year. And I'm leaving now anyway." Her pod arrived, and she placed her bag inside. "Why can't we all just walk our own way?"

"Because you and your crew have crossed ours, all of ours. We don't have a future because of you."

"Well, that's a bit of an overstatement, isn't it?"

The big guy built himself up in front of her and then tried to grab her by the hair.

He probably hit the gym most days of the week and might have had some training in a fighting sport, but the guy was no match for Jeanette. She quickly deflected the hand that tried to grab her, twisted the arm around on her attacker's back, and slammed him on the hood of the pod.

"Why don't you go home and thank your mother for her gift?"

"Oh, yeah? And what is that?" said the guy, struggling to breathe under her full body weight pressing him down.

"Your life."

She heard someone else approaching and spun around to dodge a king hit aimed at the back of her head, which punched the big guy in the ribs instead. A quick kick in the back of this teenager's knees sent her second attacker to the ground.

"Listen up. I don't want to hurt any of you, but I will, if I am provoked any further. Go home!"

She swiftly disarmed the scrawny teenager on the ground who had pulled out a jack-knife and swivelled the blade in her hand to show that she was not as defenceless as they might have thought.

The gang retreated slowly, and Jeanette jumped in the pod, throwing the knife on the passenger seat.

"Hey, my knife," shouted the scrawny teenager and rapped against the window.

"I'll take care of it," said Jeanette and confirmed her destination on the touch pad.

The teenager was pulled away by his friends, and the pod drove off.

The entire way home, she kept on checking the road behind her and had the pod take a couple of detours when she thought that someone was trailing her.

She didn't tell her sister about the altercation because she didn't want her to gloat. Yet, that night, they got woken up by a brick smashing the living room window.

There was no note or any other evidence as to who had thrown the stone, and it could have been just a random act of vandalism, yet Jeanette couldn't shake the feeling that it was a targeted attack on her and that the deadbeats from the beach were behind it.

She called the police, who couldn't do anything more than take their statements and collect the stone as evidence. Jeanette didn't sleep the rest of the night and instead listened to the noises of the night. In the morning, she called several glaziers. The earliest could some in two weeks, so she bought chipboard to provisionally seal the window, and finally she called NASA to request that her image and any contact details were taken off publicly accessible sites.

She was shocked to hear that Veronica had already had security in place for months due to an attack on her and her baby. No less than twenty-four hours after she had laughed at her sister for being a scaredy-cat, she found herself wondering whether she should also get some security grates along with the new glass.

* * *

Unrest even in Khartoum itself had alarmingly risen, and the government was discussing the use of the army to keep the peace in the city. Most troops, however, were already assigned to various outgroups, and foreign troops had been sent to countries where larger threats loomed due to the number of weapons in circulation and the threat of a famine.

Khartoum was still a prosperous city compared to many other cities in the country or even on the continent, yet no matter what level of prosperity had already been reached, giving anything up and being happy with less was never met with easy acceptance. Crime rates such as theft and burglary had increased so much that the police were unable to process even a third of the complaints, and the harassment and random attacks on women was so rampant that rarely any woman was seen on the streets anymore, even in daylight.

Subin hadn't left the house for weeks, out of fear that something could happen to her, and Rashaad supported her in her decision.

For a while, he had accompanied Subin on her weekly errands, but it had gotten too complicated and interfered with his job to go with her everywhere and then escort her back home. So, he was now doing the weekly grocery trip alone on the weekend, attending parent days at school, or bringing his sons to doctors' appointments or their grandparents' home. At least, because they were boys, Rashaad and Subin were less anxious to let them go to the nearby playground or travel short distances to friends' houses by themselves.

Last night, though, their neighbours across the hall were burgled for their groceries they had brought home during the day. They were an elderly couple who had lived in that apartment their entire married life, brought up their children, and were now probably going to die there as well. Rashaad and Subin had always looked after them and ran errands where they could, so when they heard loud banging and muffled wailing, Rashad had gone outside, thinking that they needed help and that maybe one of them had died.

The door was broken in, and when he walked across the corridor, several masked figures rushed out of the flat carrying bags and electronics. The last one punched him in the stomach so that he doubled over, but this was nothing compared to what this sweet elderly couple had endured.

Mr. Abdallah had suffered a broken nose and several broken ribs, and Mrs. Abdallah had a split lip and sustained a fractured wrist when she fell over after the hit to her face. Police and ambulance arrived the next morning, and Rashaad and Subin did their best to manage the physical and mental pain of their neighbours throughout the night. Both were eventually brought to the hospital.

Despite a sleepless night, Rashaad went out as soon as the shops opened, but he didn't go to just any shop. He went to a shop that he never thought he would visit.

The entrance was in a side alley, and anyone who entered it had only one thing in mind: to buy a weapon.

He felt like the few people that were on the street at such an early hour were watching and judging him. For several minutes, he examined the shop windows to the left and right of the alley despite the shops still being closed.

He told himself that he was doing the right thing for his family, to protect them. He would only use the weapon in self-defence, and considering the current climate, no one could judge him for his fears.

After another five minutes of silently debating with himself, he finally entered the alley and the shop. The hidden location and the dark room didn't make buying a weapon feel any more uplifting and righteous. Rashaad quickly decided on an old model of a Glock handgun and several packs of ammunition. The dealer showed him how to load the rounds into the magazine and pop it in and gave a quick rundown of the three safety mechanisms, which basically only prevented the gun from accidentally releasing a shot if the trigger wasn't pulled correctly. The weapon was light with a thin enough handle that Subin and Mohamad and probably even Malik could use it, if need be.

"I don't want it in the flat," said Subin, when Rashaad showed her his purchase in the bedroom.

"It's for your safety. I need to go to work, and you are alone all day. I want to know that you can defend yourself if I'm not here," implored Rashaad.

"No," said Subin.

"Please, for the love of Allah and our unborn child. Here, I'll put it in the drawer. The magazine is next to it. You just need to insert it here, and you are ready to shoot."

She looked at him with large eyes, and he knew he had chosen the wrong angle, telling her that she would have to shoot someone.

"What if the boys find it? What if they hurt each other?" said Subin.

"Okay, how about we put it in here?" asked Rashaad and placed it in the night table, which had a lock and a little key. "I'll lock it, and you can put the key on your necklace."

Rashaad fumbled with the little key and pulled it out slightly bent. They had never locked the cabinet.

Subin reluctantly took the key.

"Thank you," said Rashaad, relieved. "Boys? Come on, get your shoes on. We must go."

He navigated his three sons out the door as quickly as he could, not just because they were already late, but because he wanted to avoid any further discussions with his wife. With the weapon at home, he was at least a little less anxious to leave her home alone.

CHAPTER 26

Mack had never worked as much in his life as in the last four months, yet his work also had never produced so little tangible output. He had transformed from a scientist into a manager who wrote dozens of emails a day and spent the rest of the time scouring through tables and reports from other people to either write more emails or sit in on more conference calls.

He was also not quite sure how he had gotten into this position, as there was never an official job interview; everything ran under the sheltering hand of Professor Lamarck, who had free rein to engage whom he wanted in his team, and even though it was the professor's name on the reports, it was people like Mack and Tom who did the work. At first, Mack hadn't minded the setup that much, as this work also came with a salary top-up, and he got to be part of something big, something life-changing or even -saving, but now ... not so much anymore.

The money accumulated in his account, but he didn't have the time to enjoy it. Usually around this time of the year, he'd have a sun-kissed and toned body from his outdoor activities, but instead, he thought he resembled Tom with his pasty and scrawny physique more and more. Also, whilst his name was still mentioned somewhere on the global report pages, he was one of hundreds, and there was no discernible way to make out who was a major player and who wasn't. Mack's ego didn't like that his contribution was swamped and absorbed by the greater picture. He always liked to work by himself, to know exactly what was being done in the lab, and to interpret his results in a way that made sense to him.

Yes, he still relied on others to take his findings and translate them into anything that helped people, like pharmaceutical products or therapy approaches. Here though, his work, his interpretation and recommendations were taken, then more names were added, some of which he had never spoken to, and then everything was twisted into some political approach that had nothing to do with his recommendations anymore.

He had suggested to invest in new methods such as external wombs — yes, he knew that he had stolen that idea from Tom — but the idea was shot down anyway, as it would take too long and was too far removed from the principle of reproduction for humankind. As if this pandemic was something that could be resolved quickly and as if sexual intercourse was the only way that people could and should have babies.

He had celebrated Christmas with Tom and his parents, which was strangely wholesome, as Mack had celebrated the last five years alone or gone out to clubs and bars to have a few drinks with strangers.

Tom's parents had turned out to be some lovely middle-class people who had no connection to the geeky world that their son was living in. Yet they loved him simply for who he was — their son — giving Mack something to think about, remembering how he thought of Tom when he first joined the Institute for Mental Health and Genome Research.

A parent's love was truly something unconditional, unshakeable, and everlasting, something that even a child could never quite comprehend, something that you could only experience when you had children of your own.

Now, half of the people on Earth would never be able to experience such a love, as they would never become parents anymore.

Mack was on his way to London for a second inspection of the laboratory works and to discuss any future requirements. The existential crisis he was in didn't help him to focus on his work.

The London lab was just as busy as it was the first time he visited, but all capacities had been shifted to genotyping the entire population for the virus insertion. So far, about half the global population had been analysed, with industrialized countries like the Isle of Great Britain reaching into the ninetieth percentile, whilst other countries had only achieved around fifteen percent.

Of the sixty-eight million genotypes collected on the isle, 0.01 percent had been found without the insertion, and of those, only ten women carried the virus.

Mack passed through the airlock chambers and put the hazmat suit on to inspect the biosecurity lab. He didn't want to be shown what was going on there, as he didn't want to make himself complicit with a crime against humanity. The lab head reminded him about the NDA he had signed, as if he knew that something highly unethical was going on here.

This reminder made him increasingly nervous about what he was going to be shown. The laboratories had been divided into a half-dozen rooms, each containing ten bedsteads with silvery curtains to provide some privacy for the inhabitants. All rooms were fully occupied with women in white tracksuits. They had been provided with all the amenities that a simple hotel room would offer, television, books, a kitchenette to make coffees and teas. Three main meals and additional snacks were provided each day and the rooms and shared bathroom cleaned.

"How long have they been in here?" Mack asked the lab head.

"Between two weeks and four months."

"Four months? Is that even allowed?"

"Every patient signed a written agreement to be treated here, and they are getting a substantial financial compensation."

"What are you treating them for? I assume these are all people who don't have the insertion?"

"We are mainly keeping them safe from infection. The ones that are infected but don't have the insertion are kept separately, and we are trying to determine why the virus failed to insert its DNA."

The lab head walked Mack to the last room. Most curtains here were closed around the beds, and only two women were active, one who made herself a cup of tea, the other coming out of the bathroom.

"Where is the last woman?" asked Mack as he counted three unoccupied beds.

The lab head checked a schedule on a tablet. "Doctor's appointment."

Just then, the last woman entered through an airlock chamber, and Mack's legs stopped working. He recognized the long black hair that was now tied back into a messy bun. Marsha looked strained, almost hopeless compared to the lively and confident woman he had met in Shanghai.

She sat down at the table and stared blankly at the white surface. It pained Mack to see her here, but he also felt a tingle of newfound excitement. He wondered why he felt like this, but then realized that it was the possibility of having children with her. It was twisted, he knew, and yet it seemed like fate to find the only woman who had passed his genetic screening amongst the group who seemed to be immune to the virus.

He could barely take his eyes of her until she went to the bathroom.

"Have there been any results from this group?" he asked the lab head.

"We have identified several single nucleotide poly-morphisms that appear to be unique to this group, but we are still trying to find out their function and exact pathway that stops the virus."

"Any chance of developing a gene-editing treatment from this?"

"Potentially, but we first need to identify the causal mutation."

Mack was uplifted by the news. "And how long will you keep these women here?"

"This particular group for at least another seven months, until the babies are born."

"The babies?" asked Mack incredulously.

"Yes, besides analysing the causes for their re-sistance, we have also inseminated them with sexed sperm to see whether the X chromosome insertion is the only active site that causes this pandemic."

Mack was shocked. Was this a government-approved baby farm?

"And then what? Are you going to keep them indefinitely to produce baby boys?" Mack asked harshly.

"That will be decided after the babies are born and depends on global developments."

Mack felt compelled to flee this lab of horrors, but his legs still wouldn't move.

The woman who had made herself the tea earlier got up to go to the bathroom. Whilst they couldn't hear anything through the soundproof glass window, they saw that the woman was screaming her lungs out after she had opened the bathroom door, and the curtains around all the beds were pulled aside.

The nine women ran to the bathroom and recoiled in horror before beginning to drum against the windows and doors.

The lab head activated the intercom, and they could hear the screams.

"She's dead, she killed herself," a woman shouted.

Mack rushed to the side of the window and saw the legs of Marsha on the floor and a puddle of blood around them.

He later learned that Marsha had smashed the mirror in the bathroom and cut her own throat after stabbing herself multiple times in the abdomen. Nightmares haunted him for the rest of his life, and he regretted that he never had the courage to break his non-disclosure agreement and make the abomination of a human experiment public.

Instead, he called Professor Lamarck as soon as he was in his hotel room and requested to be relieved of all his duties and be able to return to his research on mental health disorders. After a lengthy back and forth that lasted for several weeks and during which he maintained that he was simply suffering from burnout, he was replaced by an associate of Professor Lee's.

During a month-long unpaid leave, which he spent in the solitude of the Tasmanian nature, he decided to leave the Institute for Mental Health and Genome Research altogether. Instead, he chose to focus his mind on cryopreservation, cooperating with a group in India which had recently made large strides in this research area.

* * *

Life-changing events were also happening for Mack's family. Hazel sat cross-legged on the floor, talking to her friend Tamara on the phone.

"The nurse wanted to send me back home, as I'm only like two centimetres dilated, but my mum refused to leave. She said it was difficult enough to get through the protesters, and they couldn't put me through it again when I'm about to have a baby," said Tamara.

"Is your mum allowed to be with you?"

"Yeah, my dad too, but they are both out talking to the nurses or whatever."

"And how much does it hurt?"

"It's pretty bad, but I get about fifteen minutes between each contraction where it doesn't hurt at all, like literally."

"And do you need to push or anything? Is it more on the top or bottom of your belly?"

"Nah, it's like your whole belly gets really hard, like all your muscles do their own thing. I'm not doing anything apart from breathing … ow."

"Is that one?"

"Mh," replied Tamara as she tried to breathe through the pain. "Just a moment."

Tamara got up and walked around the hospital room. "It's kind of worse when I sit or lie, and this funny slide walking that they showed you during prenatal really helps."

"It looked so stupid." Hazel laughed as she could see the swaying movement of her friend on her phone.

"Yeah, but you gotta do what you gotta do."

"Hazel? The pod is here," shouted Gayle from downstairs.

"Coming!" shouted Hazel in reply. "Gotta go to school now. First period got cancelled. Apparently, Ms. Chevelle has also gone into labour. Keep me posted."

"Sure thing."

"I bet she's gonna look like you."

"Ha ha. Imagine if she doesn't. OMG, my parents would be so freaked out. They kinda got over it once they knew that I didn't have sex."

"Hazel! You'll be late," shouted Gayle again.

"Okay, really have to go now. Speedy delivery."

Hazel waddled down the stairs; she was only weeks away from her own delivery, and her belly was now large enough that it had become a noticeable obstacle for everyday movement.

"Tamara is in labour," she told her mother, who was frantically running around trying to find everything she would need at the parliament.

"Oh, how is she?" asked Gayle, absent-minded.

"She's good. It's painful, but she's getting through it."

"Yes, the one disadvantage of giving birth."

"She could get a caesarean."

"She could, but there will still be pain when the narcotics subside, maybe for even longer than with a natural birth."

Gayle paused for a moment in realisation. "How would you like to deliver? We never spoke about that."

"Oh, I want to attempt a natural birth, but every possible drug available should I change my mind."

Gayle raised her eyebrows but found it a reasonable approach.

"Maybe you can write a birth plan this afternoon, and we can go through it together, just so I know what you want to happen."

"Okay. Tamara also said that there were protesters outside the hospital and that her mother didn't want to leave because of them."

Gayle was about to open the door but stopped as she sensed her daughter's worry. "The safety of hospitals and especially maternity wards is one major topic today. I'm sure by the time you give birth, security will be increased. Let's go, or we are both going to be late."

"Are you going to be safe?" asked Hazel.

Gayle opened the door, and an armoured pod waited for them in the driveway.

"Of course, I'll be safe."

Hazel spoke to Tamara late at night for the last time that day. Her friend had been moved to a delivery suit at that point, and their conversation was interrupted every couple of minutes, until the midwife came in to check the baby's heartbeats and how far dilated Tamara was now.

"I'll come and visit you tomorrow after school," Hazel said and went to bed excitedly.

But the next day brought sad and disturbing news. A group of hooligans had entered the maternity ward and wreaked havoc. They had toppled cots and ripped babies from their mothers' arms before enough security personnel had arrived to stop them.

Tamara had still been in the delivery suite, recovering from giving birth to a healthy baby girl when someone in a ski mask burst in and grabbed the towel that her baby was wrapped in. The towel unravelled, and her baby dropped to the floor, but instead of a wail, there was only silence that followed. The baby girl was pronounced dead after doctors had tried to save her for two hours. The brain haemorrhage she sustained had been fatal.

Gayle was horrified by the events of the night. She called an emergency meeting to move the implementation of special security for hospitals forward. Before she left for work, she took a minute in her home office and cried in desperation and exhaustion.

All those innocent lives that died last night, that had died during the centuries because of a man who felt threatened in their superiority by a woman. And even if a man did not concede to physical violence, the degrading comments, scoffs, or simple ignorant silence were just as damning. Did men only do it to women? Of course not. Was hanging out with your mates disdainful? Not in the least. But forming business proposals during private coffee breaks or after-work drinks when other colleagues were not present was a passive-aggressive form of mobbing that still largely affected women. Why was it so difficult even for the most decent type of men to realize how their actions affected the people around them?

On her way to work, Gayle was grabbed by a hatred for men. She watched the people on the streets running errands, the protesters in front of the parliament building, her colleagues in the corridors, and by the time she sat down behind her desk, she blindly hated all people. The bullies, the people who stood by passively watching, the people who just endured the pain.

If it weren't for her daughters, she wouldn't mind if all of humanity got wiped out with one swift wave of God's hand. Surely the world would be better off without such a brutish species.

When Guillaume entered with a cup of tea, she had thought herself into a corner where she couldn't see a way to resolve any of the issues that she found inherently wrong with humanity.

"Is everything all right?" asked Guillaume.

"Yes, thank you."

"I will prepare the conference room now. Espinoza and Novak will join via video call. They have taken leave to care for their daughters and new-born grandchildren at home."

Gayle nodded and felt tears well up. For the first time, she thought that it was her fault that all the teenagers became mothers well before they were ready, well before they had a chance to live.

"Guillaume, can I ask you something?" asked Gayle. "Why are you still with me?"

"Because I think you are a great leader."

"Have you never thought of moving up? Running for office yourself?"

"No." Guillaume smiled. "I like my job, and I think I am good at what I do."

"You are, and I think you would be good at a higher position."

"Maybe I'm just worried of reaching my level of incompetency."

Gayle had to smile at this comment. Guillaume was right. Too many people moved up, but just because they were good at something didn't always mean that they would be good at something else, and unfortunately only few people had the confidence or insight to leave a job because they recognized that they weren't right for it. Instead, they stuck with it, fighting like a wounded animal for survival, whilst at the same time falling into the abyss of incompetency without even realizing it.

On the other hand, many people who would be great and innovative leaders did not reach these positions because they did not manage to shine enough in their early careers.

Maybe she had reached her level of incompetency, Gayle thought. What if she was an utter failure and roadblock as the minister for health and family?

"I do hope though that you will continue with your work. Making a wrong decision once does not make you a failure. As I said, you are a great leader," said Guillaume who had once more miraculously read her mind.

"Thank you. You would have been a great father," said Gayle.

Guillaume stopped on his way out, and Gayle wondered whether she had said something wrong. He came back inside and closed the door.

"I wanted to wait until next month, but since you brought it up, we are expecting a baby," Guillaume said and blushed.

"Oh," said Gayle. "Is it ..." She paused in her curiosity.

"We're expecting a baby girl," he said, smiling. "A clone."

"Did she stop the contraceptives too late?"

"On the contrary. We made the decision together, and I couldn't be happier to have another person like Elodie around."

Gayle couldn't help but get up and hug her assistant. He didn't know that he had just restored Gayle's hope for humanity, and it was a shame that there wouldn't be any more men like Guillaume in future generations, but hopefully there would be women like him.

Uplifted, she went into the meeting, which was surprisingly productive. They agreed to call upon each country of the European Nations to deploy their national armies to sensitive public facilities to secure the safety of the people. Hospitals and doctors who offered any pregnancy- or fertility-related treatments were on highest priority levels, but also schools and childcare facilities would be able to request extra security personnel.

CHAPTER 27

Rashaad was on his way home when Subin called him. He was only two blocks away from home, but the traffic was creeping along Mohammed Najebi Street, so he dared to take the phone call whilst driving.

"Hi," he answered the call.

"Hi, it's me," said Subin.

"I know." He smiled. "I'm almost home. The traffic is terrible."

"Did you remember to buy formula?"

Subin had given birth two weeks ago to a healthy baby girl. Despite the spreading pandemic, Rashaad had been sure that the baby would be a boy again, and when he held his daughter in his arms, he had cried for joy.

Mohamad and Malik had climbed up and down the bed, trying to get a glimpse of their little sister.

"I can't see," Aarif had complained, and Rashaad had lifted the little boy onto the bed. Aarif carefully pulled the blanket aside, so he could see the baby's face.

"This is your sister, Samee," Rashaad had told his boys. "You must protect her from any harm. When she grows up, she will bear children and be a mother herself. That's why we must respect her and your mother, for they bring forth new life. Treat them like precious glass that can easily break."

Mohamad had kissed Samee on the forehead. "I'm your brother Mohamad, and I will take care of you even if it costs my life," his eldest had pledged, and Rashaad had felt proud and terrified at the same time.

Samee was a strong baby girl, just like her mother, and they had left the hospital the same day.

Unfortunately, Subin's own milk production had dwindled even more rapidly than with her boys, and Samee was not gaining as much weight as expected.

"Yes, but I only got one tin. They have rationed the formula, and I only got it because Yusra was at the checkout and confirmed that we just had a baby," said Rashaad as he pulled to a stop again.

"Okay. Maybe I can ask the doctor at the Red Cross centre next time whether we can get any supply through him. Did you get the herbal tea from Madam Zina?"

At this point, people on the sidewalk next to Rashaad's car began screaming, and the last thing he saw and heard was a man covered in explosives, followed by a blast that made his car overturn on the spot.

All sounds were muffled from one second to the next, and instead there was a humming and ringing filling his head that was not received through his ears.

Rashaad hung upside down in his car and looked around in a daze.

He thought he was shouting that everything was all right, that he was all right, to let Subin know not to worry, but after a couple of minutes, he wasn't sure whether he had uttered any sound at all.

Someone opened the car door and unclipped his seatbelt to pull him out of the car. The next thing he remembered was that he was lying on the pavement next to a shop with a burst window. Slowly, his senses came back, he could feel his legs again, heard the screams around him, and remembered the man with the suicide vest.

Where was his phone? He needed to assure Subin that he was all right.

He got up and looked around, but even though he thought he wasn't far from the explosion site, he could not make out his car. As if drawn by an invisible force, he made his way on foot along the two blocks to get home to his family.

Faster and faster, he stumbled as the movement also stimulated his blood flow.

Breathless, he climbed the stairs to his flat and searched his pockets with jittering fingers for his keys, only to remember that they must still be in the car.

"Subin," he hammered against the door. "Open up, it's me. Subin?"

He could hear a chair being moved behind the door and then saw the shadow of an eye in the spyhole.

"It's Papa," he heard Malik's voice whisper, and shortly after, the door opened.

He closed Malik in his arms.

"What happened?" asked Malik, touching his forehead.

"Where is your mother?" asked Rashaad when he saw Mohamad with the Glock in his hands and Aarif and Samee on the floor next to him.

"She went out to find you," said Mohamad.

A second explosion shook their block of flats, and Rashaad looked around like a wild animal.

Quickly, he checked the weapon and found that it was not loaded. He got the magazine and clipped it into the Glock.

"Here, take care of your siblings. I'll go and find your mother. Lock the door behind me, and don't open for anyone apart for me or your mother. Don't go out, whatever you hear. Do you understand?"

Mohamad and Malik nodded silently, and Aarif started crying.

"It'll be all right. I'll be back soon."

Frightened and desperate, he stumbled down the stairway and fell on the last flight of stairs, spraining his ankle. But the pain was nothing compared to the ache that came from his tightening chest.

Which way would Subin have gone? he wondered out on the street. The street was a one-way road, so she would have gone in the direction that cars were coming from, which was the opposite way he had run home.

He could again hear the screams of wounded and scared people, and as soon as he walked around the corner, the images were even more harrowing than the explosion he had experienced. This one seemed to have been a car bomb, and a crater was in the road where the vehicle had been parked.

"Subin!" he shouted as he walked along the destruction, looking into the faces of dead people lying on the ground, afraid to recognize any of them.

And then, he had reached the crater and the empty space around it that had been blasted free by the explosion. His eyes randomly scanned the surroundings, and he almost walked past the blind alley when he saw what he had dreaded the most.

He recognised the bright orange and yellow colours that Subin had been wearing that day, even though they were now stained with blood. Rashaad rushed to her side, but all was too late. Subin stared blankly into a void, and a pool of blood spread around her.

Muted from the pain that flooded him, Rashaad could neither move nor speak. So, he just sat there, his palms turned skywards, waiting for the world to end.

* * *

It had been almost a year since James had been home, and for the last few months, he had barely been able to even call, as he was stationed in remote locations around Sudan. He had planned a trip home for Christmas, but the situation in the country had taken a turn for the worse just at this time, so he had volunteered to stay another three months.

The violence and random attacks had still not abated at this point, as was originally hoped, and they were caught up in a guerrilla war where the killings would not stop until the perceived enemy was eradicated or at least until everything had returned to how it had been for centuries: men fathered children, and women carried and cared for them. It appeared, though, that some radicals would rather destroy all of humankind than accept that an irreversible change to society was coming, just like the husbands who killed their wives if they wanted to divorce, or the fathers who murdered their children to punish their mothers. It didn't make sense and yet, as so often, the few misguided souls terrorised and dictated the narrative of the peaceful majority.

James had arrived back in Khartoum and was on his way to the airport, when one of these misguided souls took his own life and was spiteful enough to try and take as many innocent lives as possible with him.

The bus that James and his comrades were travelling on stopped abruptly when an explosion a hundred metres in front of them ripped a hole into the traffic.

James didn't lose a single minute and jumped off the bus to help the wounded who were strewn about, tossed into the air from the blast.

He pulled a man from a car that had been flipped over, and like a miracle, the man had barely a scratch. James guided him away from the wreckage and made him lie on the pavement as his blood pressure dropped from the shock.

He checked in on a woman who sat between her scattered shopping bags and was screaming incessantly. She didn't react to any of James' questions but instead beseeched the heavens in her despair. Near to her lay a man dead on the ground, a piece of debris sticking out of his chest. James finally understood that this was her husband, but his help came too late, and he could only close the eyes of the man.

Every few metres, James encountered a shocked, wounded, or dead person, and again his training kicked in. He quickly scanned everyone, treated minor wounds by giving the person instructions, or stood up to call for more help.

After about ten minutes, a second explosion shook the ground not far away, and James saw people running screaming from another major road. He quickly assessed the situation here and decided that enough helpers were already in this area.

Around the corner a similar picture awaited him. Burst shop windows, dented and overturned cars, burning paper, and many wounded or dead people amongst the destruction. Several of his comrades had joined him and secured the area.

He settled the people with minor wounds on a clear patch of pavement and provided first aid for others, letting arriving first responders know about the critically injured.

Then, he noticed a man in a blind alley near the explosion site. He recognized the man as the one he had pulled from the car after the first explosion. This time, though, he was kneeling next to a woman, holding her head and rocking quietly back and forth.

James hurried to the couple and immediately knew that the woman was dead, as she stared blankly into the sky. He also recognized her and remembered that he had treated her during her pregnancy. This couple had seen him to request birth control, only for her to fall pregnant due to the virus.

Out of reflex, he felt the woman's pulse, which was quiet, and then closed her eyes, which sent a tremor through her husband, who picked her up and pulled her tight, her lifeless limbs scraping over the ground.

James sat for a couple of minutes with the man in silence. He felt powerless and angry over this nonsensical attack, and for the first time in many years, he found himself praying to God to let humankind find kindness in their hearts.

He missed his flight home but was able to catch another plane to the United States via Spain later in the day. Security had been tightened at the airport, and even if he had been able to sleep as he waited for his flight, every five minutes, guards made sure that no one loitered around the premises. To keep him occupied, he tried calling Jeanette to let her know that he was coming home, which he hadn't been able to do yet. To his dismay, an automated voice told him that the number he was trying to call was currently unavailable, and the whole trip home he had nightmares about finding Jeanette dead in an alleyway.

* * *

The bungalow with the blooming but now overgrown garden in Baton Rouge had boarded-up windows and looked abandoned to any passer-by. Inside, however, Jeanette bunkered with her sister and her children. Several attacks over the last week had forced them to barricade the house, and if it appeared as if no one was home, then this was what they wanted to achieve. They could handle any unsuspecting burglars, but they wanted to avoid the direct attacks on their persons, which had come day or night from shadows that appeared as quickly as they vanished.

Jeanette had been right. That first attack on New Year's Day had been directed towards her as the commander of that fateful Mars mission. By now, NASA had no free capacities anymore for personal protection; the army was deployed to more important parts of the country, and police were equally unavailable to provide twenty-four/seven protection for a single house.

Fabienne's husband was still in Jackson, trying desperately to find a new home where they could hide, and on top of it all, someone had attacked the nearest telephone post last night, and all mobile or internet connections were disrupted.

Louis lay on the bed playing an offline game on his phone, Nola was painting her nails, and Jeanette and Fabienne played a game of double patience in the kitchen.

The sound of a pod door made them all listen up, and as quietly as possible, they resumed their positions that they had mapped out in case of another attack.

Louis picked up a baseball bat and stood behind the front door, Jeanette and Fabienne fetched the largest kitchen knives, Fabienne remaining *en garde* in the kitchen, Jeanette positioning herself in plain sight in the middle of the living room from where she could see both the front and back doors. Nola stood in a dark corner of the living room with Jeanette's bow, ready to shoot.

Jeanette heard steps walking towards the house, hesitating as if checking out potential entry points. Someone touched or tried to move the board that covered the window by the door behind which Louis was standing. He looked panicked, but Jeanette signalled him to stay quiet.

Then a key turned in the lock, and Jeanette's mind raced. There was only one person who had another key to the house. She hoped she was right but stayed alert in case she wasn't. The door opened slowly.

"Hello?" asked James carefully into the darkness of his home.

A loud bang made him jump back, and an arrow vibrated in the back of the door.

"James!" shouted Jeanette.

"I'm sorry, I'm so sorry," yelped Nola. "I didn't mean to shoot."

No one was listening to her; Jeanette had leapt forward and quickly closed the door before holding on to James.

Fabienne came out of the kitchen still with knives in her hands, and Louis looked like a statue with the bat raised ready to beat.

"What is going on here?" asked James, perplexed regarding the defensive welcome.

They explained the situation and what had happened over the last weeks and months. The next day, Fabienne's husband gave the green light that he had secured a flat that was big enough for all of them, and they made their way to Jackson.

Jeanette and James only returned once more to clear out the house before selling it, and she would remember that last summer and forever miss her little paradise garden.

* * *

Gayle sat tired next to Hazel's hospital bed, holding her first grandchild, who had been born in the early hours of the day. It was now late afternoon, and the visitation time was going to end in half an hour.

Inga sat next to her, stroking the little toes that poked out from the blanket.

Hazel sat in bed, devouring potato mash, green beans, and apple compote with vanilla sauce that had been served as dinner.

Sirens and screams blew in from the outside, but the increased security for hospitals, which had been instated a couple of weeks earlier, had given them a relaxed stay, or as relaxed as any mother could be who was about to become a grandmother by her teenage daughter.

"She's perfect," said Inga quietly.

"And she looks just like you," said Gayle, studying the baby's face.

With a heavy heart, she finally got up to put the sleeping baby in her cot. She had made arrangements over the last month to keep her daughters safe as the turmoil began to spiral out of control. So far, she had not mentioned anything to Hazel or Inga, as she feared that they might tell their friends, which could start an even bigger frenzy amongst frightened parents.

Gayle sat on Hazel's bed and kissed her on the forehead.

"Now, before you get a good night's sleep, I need to talk to you both." She indicated for Inga to sit down with her. "I'm sure you're aware of the recent developments. I want you to go and stay with your grandparents until things calm down."

"To Glasgow?" asked Inga in disbelief.

"Nana and Grandpa bought a house in the Highlands a couple of years ago, and they've already set up rooms for you," explained Gayle.

"What about you?" asked Hazel.

"I need to take care of some things, but I promise I'll come as soon as possible."

"When do we have to leave?" asked Inga.

"If Hazel has no complications, tomorrow afternoon."

"But what about school, what about our friends?" asked Hazel.

Gayle smiled briefly; she finally knew something that Hazel didn't. "Schools will close end of the week, and you'll have to see your friends for the next time online."

The girls looked bedevilled.

"We better let you sleep now. Shall I get one of the nurses to get you a sleeping pill? They'll look after Hope if you want."

"No, I'll be fine."

"All right. I'll see you tomorrow."

Gayle and Inga left the room, and they could hear through the closed door that Hazel had turned on the TV to watch the news. Always staying up to date thought Gayle and wondered what this politically engaged teenager would grow up to be, despite having had a baby at thirteen years old.

The way home took longer as the pod had to take a couple of detours and smaller side streets to avoid riots.

Their villa lay dark and quiet in the garden, and Gayle waited for Inga on the steps to the house, where she lingered to look at it.

"Will you stay here?" Inga asked.

"For now."

"Will we ever come back here?"

Gayle paused. "I don't know."

Gayle unlocked the door and let Inga pass before activating the alarm system from inside.

"I want you to pack anything you might need for school and two weeks of clothes," she instructed Inga.

"Two weeks?"

"You can buy anything else up there. Remember that it rains a lot, and the wind can be quite strong, so I'd suggest you leave any short or fancy clothes behind. I already brought a large suitcase into your room."

Inga looked at her sadly but then turned without another word to walk upstairs.

Why was she unable to connect to her eldest daughter, Gayle wondered, distraught about her own disability.

"Hey," she called out, not knowing what she wanted to say.

Inga stopped halfway and looked down at her.

"I love you; I hope you know that."

Inga nodded quietly and proceeded to walk to her room.

The next day was chaos. Gayle had packed Hazel's suitcase and all the baby clothes, but she felt like she had forgotten something. She kept on telling herself that they could buy anything they needed in Scotland, just like she had told Inga, but as usual before any big trip, she couldn't shake the feeling that something was amiss, and she would regret it bitterly when she figured it out later.

Guillaume came to accompany them to the airport. They picked up Hazel from the hospital on the way. Seeing her thirteen-year-old with a baby carrier felt so wrong, and she wished she could have prevented the pregnancy. In ten years or more, she would have been happy to become a grandmother, clone or not. She watched Hazel struggle to put the carrier into the pod and was grateful that Guillaume once more helped without hesitation.

At the airport, they checked in quickly, and as they were already running late, there was not much time to say their goodbyes.

"I'll see you soon," said Gayle and kissed both her daughters before bending down to the carrier.

Baby Hope was stirring but had not opened her eyes yet. She did look just like Hazel, and the sadness in Gayle's heart over her grandchild's early arrival was pushed aside by love and confidence.

"Call you tonight," said Hazel, and she picked up the carrier to walk through security.

Baby Hope started to complain.

"Take care of her," said Gayle to Inga.

"Sure. Talk to you later."

Gayle was restless on the way to Parliament. Today, they would vote on announcing a state of emergency and allowing the national armies to be sent out in their own countries to reinstate order and peace. No one knew how long it would take, and a two-week plan that would get extended as needed was supposed to be set in place. The hope was that once food supply was secure again, the unrest would settle, and people would think more rationally about the virus situation.

"We cannot get to the secure parking lot," announced Guillaume after they had circled the Parliament Square several times.

Thousands of people were out demonstrating against the government's perceived mismanagement, even though a year ago, no one could have predicted what unparalleled events were going to happen that would reshape humankind.

She watched the angry faces outside and read their slogans, which came from a place of fear and uncertainty, yet Gayle thought that it wasn't mankind that was threatened at the moment, but the survival of humanity.

"Can we get in through the main entrance?" asked Gayle.

"I wouldn't recommend it," said Guillaume. "Maybe we should attend the meeting virtually from home."

"We are here now, and I think if the people see politicians actually arriving, it will send a signal that we are working hard to resolve the current problems."

"I will call security and let them know that we are on our way," answered Guillaume.

A few minutes later, their pod slowly cleaved the way to the main entrance across the Espace Léopold. Several burly, heavily armed security guards in black suits blazed their way to their pod to guide them the last ten metres through the crowd.

It was a frenzy, and Gayle felt panic creeping up on her. The shouts around them were full of rage; a bodyguard punched a protester in the face who had tried to block their way. Gayle saw blood spilling out from his broken nose, and then, in that split second that their line of protection was weakened, someone else jumped from the crowd, and a warm sting penetrated her chest.

She looked down and saw a hand pulling a needle-like blade out of her heart.

Gayle collapsed into Guillaume's arms. The world around her turned black, and she could hear a fairground with music coming from a merry-go-round. The wooden horses bobbed up and down, just like in her childhood. Before everything went quiet, she finally remembered the important thing she had forgotten. She should have apologized to Inga and taken the time to listen to her when she still could.

* * *

Hazel and Inga had been picked up by their grandparents from Glasgow Airport only an hour after they had boarded the plane in Brussels.

Now, they were speeding along a street, their grandfather driving himself. Heather-covered mountains rose around them, and a large loch sparkled through trees on their left.

And then they saw snow, which had fallen as a late surprise, covering patches of blooming daffodils and snowdrops with a sparkling white blanket.

Hazel and Inga sat in the back of the car with Hope sleeping peacefully between them.

"Do you think I will ever have a baby?" asked Inga quietly as she watched Hope's tiny hand clasping onto her finger.

"Course you will," said Hazel, confused.

"But why didn't I get pregnant again like you?" asked Inga, the one question that had been on her mind for months.

"I don't know … Maybe it just takes longer after, you know, after an abortion."

Hazel studied her sister's face.

"I watched a documentary, and they said that most women won't get pregnant because their DNA just produces mutants that don't survive." Inga lowered her head, tears rolling over her cheeks.

Hazel grabbed her sister's hand over the baby seat, and they sat in silence as the car drove on further into the snow-covered Highlands.

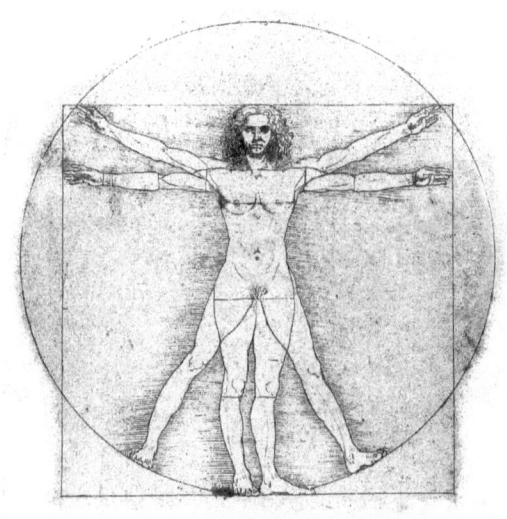

A FINAL NOTE

This book has come a long way from handwriting the first chapter on a rooftop in Edinburgh, to a feature length screenplay that made it into the top 10% of the Blue Cat Screenplay Competition, and back again into a full novel written in the rural town of Armidale, Australia.

The summer during which I started this book in Edinburgh, was also the summer I met my husband – one of the happiest times of my life. May there be many more.

If you liked XX - The History of Mankind, please tell your friends or even pass on your copy and remember to leave a review or a simple star-rating.

Thank you very much for reading!

"Eerily Beautiful"

"Amantos by Eva Laurenson is a remarkable and endearing fantasy novel demonstrating the impermanence of material wealth and the permanence of true love."